WILLIAM MORROW

An Imprint of HarperCollins*Publishers*

July 5, 2006

Dear Reader:

I am delighted to be introducing you to Joe Hill, one of the freshest, smartest, original voices we have ever encountered, and whose debut novel, HEART-SHAPED BOX, has captivated the whole team here at William Morrow.

The premise is deceptively benign: on a whim, Jude buys a "ghost" online. He doesn't really believe he's going to get a ghost delivered to his door, nor does he think that he and his girlfriend are about to embark upon a desperate race for their lives. But, as Jude learns the hard way, sooner or later, the dead catch up...

Early response to HEART-SHAPED BOX has been phenomenal. Film rights have been sold to Warner Brothers; thus far, translation rights have been sold in fourteen countries and counting. We've already had some early response from booksellers, which you'll see on the back cover.

HEART-SHAPED BOX is scary, suspenseful, and a hell of a lot of fun (in a creepy, spine-tingly sort of way), and I hope you will agree that Joe is a natural-born storyteller.

Publication is set for February 2007, and I do hope that we will have your support. I would love to hear what you think, and you can reach me by phone at 212 207 7502 or by email at lisa.gallagher@harpercollins.com

With all best wishes

Yours

Lisa Gallagher
Sr. V. P. & Publisher
William Morrow

Heart-Shaped Box

by JOE HILL

Rock star Judas Coyne is a collector of the bizarre and grotesque. He has a used hangman's noose, a cookbook for cannibals, a snuff movie. So naturally when he learns there's a ghost for sale on the Internet, Jude doesn't think twice. Some impulses require no consideration.

But this ghost is different from the spirits that have haunted Jude most of his life; the abusive father he fled as a boy, the bandmates he betrayed, the lover he abandoned and who killed herself. This ghost isn't just in his head: it's *real*. Delivered to his doorstep in a black heart-shaped box, the latest addition to Jude's collection means to chase him to the limits of sanity—and beyond.

If ever there was a case of caveat emptor, this is it. . . .

Sure to keep readers spellbound, *Heart-Shaped Box* is a terrifying and relentless supernatural thriller from a blazing young talent. Discover the novel that will keep readers sleepless next year.

© Shane Leonard

The author of the critically acclaimed story collection *20th Century Ghosts*, Joe Hill is a two-time winner of the Bram Stoker Award, and a past recipient of the Ray Bradbury Fellowship. His stories have appeared in numerous journals and in a variety of Year's Best collections. He lives in New England with his wife and children.

Fiction • February 2007 • $24.95 ($31.50 Can.) • 384 pages • 6" x 9"
ISBN-13: 978-0-06-114793-7 • ISBN-10: 0-06-114793-1
Available from HarperAudio • 12 hours/10 CDs unabridged
0-06-123587-3 • $39.95 ($49.95 Can.)
HarperLargePrint • 0-06-123324-2 • $24.95 ($31.50 Can.)

BOOKSELLER PRAISE

"In 1973, someone lent me a passed-around copy of a book I'd heard of but had never read—*Jaws*. The world fell away, and I didn't look up until I was done. Reading *Heart-Shaped Box* was like that. By the end of the third chapter I knew I was standing at the edge of something very deep and very scary. Visceral vertigo, a head-spinning reaction that in a wide-screen movie would be represented by changing depth of field and swelling music. **This guy is going to be a star.**"

—Russ Harvey, Cody's, Berkeley, California

"**WOW!** Joe Hill has that rare gift of language that allows him to paint word pictures that are as unique as they are impressive. The only **comparison that comes to mind would be Dean Koontz or John Saul,** but neither of them ever had the counterculture smarts that Joe Hill has. You can't fake that kind of knowledge, and it gave Jude Coyne a credibility that other authors would have had to force. **Bravo!** Encore! I can't wait to make it a Book Sense pick!"

—Sean Curran, Doylestown Bookshop, Doylestown, Pennsylvania

"I am going to be the first person to send in a Book Sense nomination nine months before publication. **I think the book will be huge. Joe Hill will be compared to King and Koontz,** but beyond that he has depth and probes moral questions in addition to providing **a thrilling page-turner.** You have definitely added another thoroughbred to your amazing stable. I look forward to handselling the book."

—Bill Cusumano, Nicola's Books, Ann Arbor, Michigan

"Joe Hill's *Heart-Shaped Box* is **a wonder:** a truly unsettling ghost story peopled with realistically flawed characters that **reads like a runaway train.**"

—Peggy Hailey, Bookpeople, Austin, Texas

ALSO BY JOE HILL

20th Century Ghosts (stories)

HEART-SHAPED BOX

JOE HILL

WILLIAM MORROW
An Imprint of HarperCollinsPublishers

HarperCollins books may be purchased for educational, business, or sales promotional use. For information please write: Special Markets Department, Harper-Collins Publishers, 10 East 53rd Street, New York, NY 10022.

FIRST EDITION

Designed by Susan Yang

Library of Congress Cataloging-in-Publication Data

Hill, Joe.
 Heart-shaped box / Joe Hill. — 1st ed.
   p.   cm.
 ISBN-13: 978-0-06-114793-7
 ISBN-10: 0-06-114793-1
 I. Title.
 PS3608.I4342H43 2007
 813'.6—dc22   2006046548

07 08 09 10 11 [printer ID] 10 9 8 7 6 5 4 3 2 1

HOW MAY THE DEAD HAVE DESTINATIONS?

—Alan Moore, *Voice of the Fire*

BLACK DOG

Jude had a private collection.

He had framed sketches of the Seven Dwarfs on the wall of his studio, in between his platinum records. John Wayne Gacy had drawn them while he was in jail and sent them to him. Gacy liked golden-age Disney almost as much as he liked molesting little kids; almost as much as he liked Jude's albums.

Jude had the skull of a peasant who had been trepanned in the sixteenth century, to let the demons out. He kept a collection of pens jammed into the hole in the center of the cranium.

He had a three-hundred-year-old confession, signed by a witch. "I did spake with a black dogge who sayd hee wouldst poison cows, drive horses mad and sicken children for me if I wouldst let him have my soule, and I sayd aye, and after did give him sucke at my breast." She was burned to death.

He had a stiff and worn noose that had been used to hang a man in England at the turn of the century, Aleister Crowley's childhood chessboard, and a snuff film. Of all the items in Jude's collection, this last was the thing he felt most uncomfortable about possessing. It had come to him by way of a police officer, a man who had worked security at some shows in L.A. The cop had said the video was diseased. He said it with some enthusiasm. Jude had watched it and felt that he was right. It was diseased. It had also, in an indirect way, helped hasten the end of Jude's marriage. Still he held on to it.

Many of the objects in his private collection of the grotesque and the bizarre were gifts sent to him by his fans. It was rare for him to actually buy something for the collection himself. But when Danny Wooten, his personal assistant, told him there was a ghost for sale on the Internet and asked did he want to buy it, Jude didn't even need to think. It was like going out to eat, hearing the special, and deciding you wanted it without even looking at the menu. Some impulses required no consideration.

Danny's office occupied a relatively new addition, extending from the northeastern end of Jude's rambling, 110-year-old farmhouse. With its climate control, OfficeMax furniture, and coffee-and-cream industrial carpet, the office was coolly impersonal, nothing at all like the rest of the house. It might have been a dentist's waiting room, if not for the concert posters in stainless-steel frames. One of them showed a jar crammed with staring eyeballs, bloody knots of nerves dangling from the backs of them. That was for the All Eyes on You tour.

No sooner had the addition been built than Jude had come to regret it. He had not wanted to drive forty-five minutes from Piecliff to a rented office in Poughkeepsie to see to his business, but that would've probably been preferable to having Danny Wooten right here at the house. Here Danny and Danny's work were too close. When Jude was in the kitchen, he could hear the phones ringing in there, both of the office lines going off at once sometimes, and the sound was maddening to him. He had not recorded an album in years, had hardly worked since Jerome and Dizzy had died (and the band with them), but still the phones rang and rang. He felt crowded by the steady parade of petitioners for his time, and by the never-ending accumulation of legal and professional demands, agreements and contracts, promotions and appearances, the work of Judas Coyne Incorporated, which was never done, always ongoing. When he was home, he wanted to be himself, not a trademark.

For the most part, Danny stayed out of the rest of the house. Whatever his flaws, he was protective of Jude's private space. But Danny considered him fair game if Jude strayed into the office—something Jude did, without much pleasure, four or five times a day. Passing through the office was the fastest way to the barn and the dogs. He could've avoided Danny by going out through the front door and walking all the way around the house, but he refused to sneak around his own home just to avoid Danny Wooten.

Besides, it didn't seem possible Danny could always have something to bother him with. But he always did. And if he didn't have anything that demanded immediate attention, he wanted to talk. Danny was from Southern California originally, and there was no end to his talk. He would boast to total strangers about the benefits of wheatgrass, which included making your bowel movements as fragrant as a freshly mowed lawn. He was thirty years old but could talk skateboarding and PlayStation with the pizza-delivery kid like he was fourteen. Danny would get confessional with air-conditioner repairmen, tell them how his sister had OD'd on heroin in her teens and how as a young man he had been the one to find his mother's body after she killed herself. He was impossible to embarrass. He didn't know the meaning of shy.

Jude was coming back inside from feeding Angus and Bon and was halfway across Danny's field of fire—just beginning to think he might make it through the office unscathed—when Danny said, "Hey, boss, check this out." Danny opened almost every demand for attention with just this line, a statement Jude had learned to dread and resent, a prelude to half an hour of wasted time, forms to fill out, faxes to look at. Then Danny told him someone was selling a ghost, and Jude forgot all about begrudging him. He walked around the desk so he could look over Danny's shoulder at his computer screen.

Danny had discovered the ghost at an online auction site, not eBay but one of the wannabes. Jude moved his gaze over the item description while Danny read aloud. Danny would've cut his food for him if Jude gave him the chance. He had a streak of subservience that Jude found, frankly, revolting in a man.

"'Buy my stepfather's ghost,'" Danny read. "'Six weeks ago my elderly stepfather died, very suddenly. He was staying with us at the time. He had no home of his own and traveled from relative to relative, visiting for a month or two before moving on. Everyone was shocked by his passing, especially my daughter, who was very close to him. No one would've thought. He was active to the end of his life. Never sat in front of the TV. Drank a glass of orange juice every day. Had all his own teeth.'"

"This is a fuckin' joke," Jude said.

"I don't think so," Danny said. He went on, "'Two days after his funeral, my little girl saw him sitting in the guest room, which is directly across from her own bedroom. After she saw him, my girl didn't like to be alone in her room anymore, or even to go upstairs. I told her that her grandfather wouldn't ever hurt her, but she said she was scared of his eyes. She said they were all black scribbles and they weren't for seeing anymore. So she has been sleeping with me ever since.

"'At first I thought it was just a scary story she was telling herself, but there is more to it than that. The guest room is cold all the time. I poked around in there and noticed it was worst in the closet, where his Sunday suit was hung up. He wanted to be buried in that suit, but when we tried it on him at the funeral home, it didn't look right. People shrink up a little after they die. The water in them dries up. His best suit was too big for him, so we let the funeral home talk us into buying one of theirs. I don't know why I listened.

"'The other night I woke up and heard my stepfather walking around overhead. The bed in his room won't stay made, and the door opens and slams shut at all hours. The cat won't go upstairs either, and sometimes she sits at the bottom of the steps looking at things I can't see. She stares awhile, then gives a yowl like her tail got stepped on and runs away.

"'My stepfather was a lifelong spiritualist, and I believe he is only here to teach my daughter that death is not the end. But she is eleven and needs a normal life and to sleep in her own room, not in mine. The only thing I can think is to try and find Pop another home, and the world is full of people who want to believe in the afterlife. Well, I have your proof right here.

"'I will "sell" my stepfather's ghost to the highest bidder. Of course a soul cannot really be sold, but I believe he will come to your home and abide with you if you put out the welcome mat. As I said, when he died, he was with us temporarily and had no place to call his own, so I am sure he would go to where he was wanted. Do not think this is a stunt or a practical joke and that I will take your money and send you nothing. The winning bidder will have something solid to show for their investment. I will send you his Sunday suit. I believe if his spirit is attached to anything, it has to be that.

"'It is a very nice old-fashioned suit made by Great Western Tailoring. It has a fine silver pinstripe,' blah, blah, 'satin lining,' blah, blah. . . ." Danny stopped reading and pointed at the screen. "Check out the measurements, Chief. It's just your size. High bid is eighty bucks. If you want to own a ghost, looks like he could be yours for a hundred."

"Let's buy it," Jude said.

"Seriously? Put in a bid for a hundred dollars?"

Jude narrowed his eyes, peering at something on the screen, just below the item description, a button that said YOURS NOW: $1,000. And beneath that: *Click to Buy and End Auction Immediately!* He put his finger on it, tapping the glass.

"Let's just make it a grand and seal the deal," he said.

Danny rotated in his chair. He grinned and raised his eyebrows. Danny had high, arched, Jack Nicholson eyebrows, which he used to great effect. Maybe he expected an explanation, but Jude wasn't sure he could've explained, even to himself, why it seemed reasonable to pay a thousand dollars for an old suit that probably wasn't worth a fifth of that.

Later he thought it might be good publicity: *Judas Coyne buys a polter-geist*. The fans ate up stories like that. But that was later. Right then, in the moment, he just knew he wanted to be the one who bought the ghost.

Jude started on, thinking he would head upstairs to see if Georgia was dressed yet. He had told her to put on her clothes half an hour ago but expected to find her still in bed. He had the sense she planned to stay there until she got the fight she was looking for. She'd be sitting in her underwear, carefully painting her toenails black. Or she'd have her laptop open, surfing Goth accessories, looking for the perfect stud to poke through her tongue, like she needed anymore goddam . . . And then the thought of surfing the Web caused Jude to hold up, wondering something. He glanced back at Danny.

"How'd you come across that anyway?" he asked, nodding at the computer.

"We got an e-mail about it."

"From who?"

"From the auction site. They sent us an e-mail that said, 'We notice you've bought items like this before and thought you'd be interested.'"

"We've bought items like this before?"

"Occult items, I assume."

"I've never bought anything off that site."

"Maybe you did and just don't remember. Maybe I bought something for you."

Jude said, "Fuckin' acid. I had a good memory once. I was in the chess club in junior high."

"You were? That's a hell of a thought."

"What? The idea that I was in the chess club?"

"I guess. It seems so . . . geeky."

"Yeah. But I used severed fingers for pieces."

Danny laughed—a little too hard, convulsing himself and wiping imaginary tears from the corners of his eyes. The sycophantic little suck-ass.

2

The suit came early Saturday morning. Jude was up and outside with the dogs.

Angus lunged as soon as the UPS truck ground to a halt, and the leash was yanked out of Jude's hand. Angus leaped against the side of the parked truck, spit flying, paws scuffling furiously against the driver's-side door. The driver remained behind the wheel, peering down at him with the calm but intent expression of a doctor considering a new strain of Ebola through a microscope. Jude caught the leash and pulled on it, harder than he meant to. Angus sprawled on his side in the dirt, then twisted and sprang back up, snarling. By now Bon was in on the act, straining at the end of her leash, which Jude held in his other hand, and yapping with a shrillness that hurt his head.

Because it was too far to haul them all the way back to the barn and their pen, Jude dragged them across the yard and up to the front porch, both of them fighting him the whole time. He shoveled them in through the front door and slammed it behind them. Immediately they set to flinging themselves against it, barking hysterically. The door shuddered as they slammed into it. Fucking dogs.

Jude shuffled back down into the driveway, and reached the UPS truck just as the rear door slid open with a steely clatter. The deliveryman stood inside. He hopped down, holding a long, flat box under his arm.

"Ozzy Osbourne has Pomeranians," the UPS guy said. "I saw them on TV. Cute little dogs like house cats. You ever think about getting a couple cute little dogs like that?"

Jude took the box without a word and went inside.

He brought the box through the house and into the kitchen. He put it on the counter and poured coffee. Jude was an early riser by instinct and conditioning. When he was on the road, or recording, he had become accustomed to rolling into bed at five in the morning and sleeping through most of the daylight hours, but staying up all night had never come naturally. On the road he would wake at four in the afternoon, bad-tempered and headachy, confused about where the time had gone. Everyone he knew would seem to him clever impostors, unfeeling aliens wearing rubber skin and the faces of friends. It took a liberal quantity of alcohol to make them seem like themselves again.

Only it had been three years since he'd last gone on tour. He didn't have much interest in drinking when he was home and was ready for bed most nights by nine. At the age of fifty-four, he had settled back into the rhythms that had guided him since his name was Justin Cowzynski and he was a boy on his father's hog farm. The illiterate son of a bitch would have dragged him out of bed by the hair if he'd found him in it when the sun came up. It was a childhood of mud, barking dogs, barbed wire, dilapidated farm buildings, squealing pigs with their flaking skin and squashed-in faces, and little human contact, beyond a mother who sat most of the day at the kitchen table wearing the slack, staring aspect of someone who had been lobotomized, and his father, who ruled their acres of pig shit and ruin with his angry laughter and his fists.

So Jude had been up for several hours already but had not eaten breakfast yet, and he was frying bacon when Georgia wandered into the kitchen. She was dressed only in a pair of black panties, her arms folded across her small, white, pierced breasts, her black hair floating around her head in a soft, tangly nest. Her name wasn't really Georgia. It wasn't Morphine either, although she had stripped under that name for two years. Her name was Marybeth Kimball, a handle so simple, so plain, she'd laughed when she first told him, as if it embarrassed her.

Jude had worked his way through a collection of Goth girlfriends who stripped, or told fortunes, or stripped *and* told fortunes, pretty girls who wore ankhs and black fingernail polish, and whom he always called by their state of origin, a habit few of them cared for, because they didn't like to be reminded of the person they were trying to erase with all their living-dead makeup. She was twenty-three.

"Goddam stupid dogs," she said, shoving one of them out of her way with her heel. They were whisking around Jude's legs, excited by the perfume of the bacon. "Woke me the fuck up."

"Maybe it was time to get the fuck up. Ever think?" She never rose before ten if she could help it.

She bent into the fridge for the orange juice. He enjoyed the view, the way the straps of her underwear cut into the almost-too-white cheeks of her ass, but he looked away while she drank from the carton. She left it on the counter, too. It would spoil there if he didn't put it away for her.

He was glad for the adoration of the Goths. He appreciated the sex even more, their limber, athletic, tattooed bodies and eagerness for kink. But he had been married once, to a woman who used a glass and put things away when she was done, who read the paper in the morning, and he missed their talk. It was grown-up talk. She hadn't been a stripper. She didn't believe in fortune-telling. It was grown-up companionship.

Georgia used a steak knife to slice open the UPS box, then left the knife on the counter, with tape stuck to it.

"What's this?" she asked.

A second box was contained within the first. It was a tight fit, and Georgia had to tug for a while to slide the inner box out onto the counter. It was large, and shiny, and black, and it was shaped like a heart. Candies sometimes came in boxes like that, although this was much too big for candies, and candy boxes were pink or sometimes yellow. A lingerie box, then—except he hadn't ordered anything of the kind for her. He frowned. He didn't have any idea what might be in it and at the same time felt somehow he *should* know, that the heart-shaped box contained something he'd been expecting.

"Is this for me?" she asked.

She pried the lid loose and took out what was inside, lifting it for him to see. A suit. Someone had sent him a suit. It was black and old-fashioned, the details blurred by the plastic dry-cleaning bag pulled over it. Georgia held it up by the shoulders, in front of her body, almost as if it were a dress she was thinking of trying on but she wanted his opinion of it first. Her gaze was questioning, a pretty furrow between her eyebrows. For a moment he didn't remember, didn't know why it had come.

He opened his mouth to tell her he had no clue, but then instead heard himself say, "The dead man's suit."

"What?"

"The ghost," he said, remembering as he spoke. "I bought a ghost. Some woman was convinced her stepfather was haunting her. So she put his restless spirit up for sale on the Internet, and I bought it for a grand. That's his suit. She thinks it might be the source of the haunting."

"Oh, cool," Georgia said. "So are you going to wear it?"

His own reaction surprised him. His skin crawled, went rough and strange with gooseflesh. For one unconsidered moment, the idea struck him as obscene.

"No," he said, and she flicked a surprised glance at him, hearing something cold and flat in his voice. Her smirk deepened a little, and he realized he had sounded . . . well, not frightened but momentarily weak. He added, "It wouldn't fit." Although, in truth, it looked as if the poltergeist had been about his height and weight in life.

Georgia said, "Maybe I'll wear it. I'm a little bit of a restless spirit myself. And I look hot in men's clothing."

Again: a sensation of revulsion, a crawling of the skin. She shouldn't put it on. It unsettled him that she would even joke about it, although he couldn't have said why. He wasn't going to let her put it on. In that one instant, he could not imagine anything more repellent.

And that was saying something. There wasn't much that Jude found too distasteful to contemplate. He was unused to feeling disgust. The profane didn't trouble him; it had made him a good living for thirty years.

"I'll stick it upstairs until I figure out what to do with it," he said, trying for a dismissive tone—and not quite making it.

She stared at him, interested at this wavering of his usual self-possession, and then she pulled off the plastic dry-cleaning bag. The coat's silver buttons flashed in the light. The suit was somber, as dark as crow feathers, but those buttons, the size of quarters, gave it something of a rustic character. Add a string tie and it was the sort of thing Johnny Cash might've worn onstage.

Angus began to bark, high, shrill, panicked barking. He shoved himself back on his haunches, tail lowered, rearing away from the suit. Georgia laughed.

"It *is* haunted," she said.

She held the suit in front of her and waved it back and forth, walking it through the air toward Angus, flapping it at him, a bullfighter with cape. She moaned as she closed in on him, the throaty, drawn-out cry of a wandering haunt, while her eyes gleamed with pleasure.

Angus scrambled back, hit a stool at the kitchen counter, and knocked it over with a ringing crash. Bon stared out from beneath the old, blood-stained chopping block, ears flattened against her skull. Georgia laughed again.

"Cut it the fuck out," Jude said.

She shot him a snotty, perversely happy look—the look of a child burning ants with a magnifying glass—and then she made a face of pain and shouted. Swore and grabbed her right hand. She flung the suit aside onto the counter.

A bright drop of blood fattened at the tip of her thumb and fell, *plink*, onto the tiled floor.

"Shit," she said. "Fucking pin."

"You see what you get."

She glared, flipped him the bird, and stalked out. When she was gone, he got up and put the juice back into the fridge. Jude dropped the knife in the sink, got a hand towel to wipe the blood off the floor—and then his gaze caught on the suit, and he forgot whatever it was he'd been about to do.

He smoothed it out, folded the arms over the chest, felt carefully around. Jude couldn't find any pins, couldn't figure out what she'd stuck herself on. He laid it gently back into its box.

An acrid odor caught his attention. He glanced into the pan and cursed. The bacon was burnt.

3

He put the box on the shelf in the back of his closet and decided to stop thinking about it.

4

He was passing back through the kitchen, a little before six, to get
sausages for the grill, when he heard someone whispering in Danny's
office.

The sound jumped him and halted him in his tracks. Danny had gone
home more than an hour ago, and the office was locked, should've been
empty. Jude tilted his head to listen, concentrating intently on the low,
sibilant voice . . . and in another moment he identified what he was
hearing, and his pulse began to slow.

There was no one in there. It was only someone talking on the radio.
Jude could tell. The low tones weren't low enough, the voice itself subtly
flattened out. Sounds could suggest shapes, painted a picture of the
pocket of air in which they'd been given form. A voice in a well had a deep,
round echo, while a voice in a closet sounded condensed, all the fullness
squeezed out of it. Music was also geometry. What Jude was hearing now
was a voice clapped into a box. Danny had forgotten to turn off the radio.

He opened the door to the office, poked his head in. The lights were
off, and with the sun on the other side of the building, the room drowned
in blue shadow. The office stereo was the third-worst in the house, which
was still better than most home stereos, a stack of Onkyo components in

a glass cabinet by the water cooler. The readouts were lit a vivid, unnatural green, the color of objects viewed through a night-vision scope, except for a single, glowing, vertical slash of red, a ruby mark showing the frequency to which the radio was tuned. The mark was a narrow slit, the shape of a cat's pupil, and seemed to stare into the office with an unblinking, alien fascination.

". . . How cold is it going to get tonight?" said the man on the radio in a husky, almost abrasive tone. A fat man, judging by the wheeze when he exhaled. "Do we have to worry about finding bums frozen to the ground?"

"Your concern for the welfare of the homeless is touching," said a second man, this one with a voice that was a little thin, reedy.

It was WFUM, where most of the bands were named after fatal diseases (Anthrax), or conditions of decay (Rancid), and where the DJs tended to be preoccupied with crotch lice, strippers, and the amusing humiliations that attended the poor, the crippled, and the elderly. They were known to play Jude's music, more or less constantly, which was why Danny kept the stereo tuned to them, as an act of both loyalty and flattery. In truth, Jude suspected that Danny had no particular musical preferences, no strong likes or dislikes, and that the radio was just background sound, the auditory equivalent of wallpaper. If he had worked for Enya, Danny would've happily hummed along to Celtic chanting while answering her e-mails and sending faxes.

Jude started across the room to turn off the stereo but had not gone far before his step hitched, a memory snagging at his thoughts. An hour ago he'd been outside with the dogs. He had stood at the end of the dirt turnaround, enjoying the sharpness of the air, the sting on his cheeks. Someone down the road was burning a waste pile of deadfall and autumn leaves, and the faint odor of the spiced smoke had pleased him as well.

Danny had come out of the office, shrugging on his jacket, headed home. They stood talking for a moment—or, to be more accurate, Danny stood jawing at him while Jude watched the dogs and tried to tune him out. You could always count on Danny Wooten to spoil a perfectly good silence.

Silence. The office behind Danny had been silent. Jude could remember the crows going *crawk-crawk* and Danny's steady stream of exuberant chatter, but not the sound of the radio coming from the office behind him. If it had been on, Jude thought he would've heard. His ears were still as sensitive as they'd ever been. They had, against long odds, survived all that he'd inflicted upon them over the last thirty years. By comparison, Jude's drummer, Kenny Morlix, the only other surviving member of his original band, had severe tinnitus, couldn't even hear his wife when she was yelling right in his face.

Jude started forward once more, but he was ill at ease again. It wasn't any one thing. It was all of it. It was the dimness of the office and the glaring red eye staring out from the face of the receiver. It was the idea that the radio hadn't been on an hour ago, when Danny had stood in the open office door zipping his jacket. It was the thought that someone had recently passed through the office and might still be close by, maybe watching from the darkness of the bathroom, where the door was open a crack—a paranoid thing to think and unlike him, but in his head all the same. He reached for the power button on the stereo, not really listening anymore, his gaze on that door. He wondered what he would do if it started to open.

The weatherman said, ". . . cold and dry as the front pushes the warm air south. The dead pull the living down. Down into the cold. Down into the hole. You will di—"

Jude's thumb hit the power button, switching off the stereo, just as he registered what was being said. He twitched, startled, and stabbed the power button again, to get the voice back, figure out what the hell the weatherman had just been going on about.

Except the weatherman was done talking, and it was the DJ instead. ". . . going to freeze our asses off, but Kurt Cobain is warm in hell. Dig it."

A guitar whined, a shrill, wavering sound that went on and on without any discernible melody or purpose except perhaps to drive the listener to madness. The opening of Nirvana's "I Hate Myself and I Want to Die." Was that what the weatherman had been talking about? He'd said something about dying. Jude clicked the power button once more, returning the room to stillness.

It didn't last. The phone went off, right behind him, a startling burst of sound that gave Jude's pulse another unhappy jump. He shot a look at Danny's desk, wondering who would be calling on the office line at this hour. He shifted around behind the desk for a glance at caller ID. It was a 985 number, which he identified immediately as a prefix for eastern Louisiana. The name that came up was COWZYNSKI, M.

Only Jude knew, even without picking up the phone, that it wasn't really Cowzynski, M., on the other end. Not unless a medical miracle had transpired. He almost didn't pick up at all, but then the thought came that maybe Arlene Wade was calling to tell him Martin was dead, in which case he would have to talk to her sooner or later, whether he wanted to or not.

"Hello," he said.

"Hello, Justin," said Arlene. She was an aunt by marriage, his mother's sister-in-law, and a licensed physician's assistant, although for the last thirteen months her only patient had been Jude's father. She was sixty-nine, and her voice was all twang and warble. To her he would always be Justin Cowzynski.

"How are you, Arlene?"

"I'm the same as ever. You know. Me and the dog are gettin' along. Although he can't get up so much now because he's so fat and his knees pain him. But I'm not callin' to tell you about myself or the dog. I'm callin' about your father."

As if there could be anything else she might call about. The line hissed with white noise. Jude had been interviewed over the phone by a radio personality in Beijing and taken calls from Brian Johnson in Australia, and the connections had been as crisp and clear as if they were phoning him from down the street. But for some reason calls from Moore's Corner, Louisiana, came in scratchy and faint, like an AM radio station that's just a little too far away to be received perfectly. Voices from other phone calls would bleed in and out, faintly audible for a few moments and then gone. They might have high-speed Internet connections in Baton Rouge, but in the little towns in the swamps north of Lake Pontchartrain, if you wanted a high-speed connection with the rest of the world, you souped up a car and got the fuck out.

"Last few months I been spoonin' him food. Soft stuff he don't have to chew. He was likin' them little stars. Pastina. And vanilla custard. I never met a dyin' person yet didn't want some custard on their way out the door."

"I'm surprised. He never used to have a sweet tooth. Are you sure?"

"Who's takin' care of him?"

"You are."

"Well, I guess I'm sure, then."

"All right."

"This is the reason I'm callin'. He won't eat custard or little stars or anything else. He just chokes on whatever I put in his mouth. He can't swallow. Dr. Newland was in to see him yesterday. He thinks your dad had another infarction."

"A stroke." It was not quite a question.

"Not a fall-down-and-kill-you kind of stroke. If he had another one of those, there wouldn't be any question of it. He'd be dead. This was one of the little blow-outs. You don't always know when he's had one of the little ones. Especially when he gets like he is now, just starin' at things. He hasn't said a word to anyone in two months. He isn't ever going to say a word to anyone again."

"Is he at the hospital?"

"No. We can care for him just as well or better here. Me livin' with him and Dr. Newland in every day. But we can send him to the hospital. It would be cheaper there, if that matters to you."

"It doesn't. Let 'em save the beds at the hospital for people who might actually get better in them."

"I won't argue you on that one. Too many people die in hospitals, and if you can't be helped, you have to wonder why."

"So what are you going to do about him not eating? What happens now?"

This was met by a moment of silence. He had an idea that the question had taken her by surprise. Her tone, when she spoke again, was both gently reasonable and apologetic, the tone of a woman explaining a harsh truth to a child.

"Well. That's up to you, not me, Justin. Doc Newland can poke a feedin' tube in him and he'll go on a while longer, that's what you want. Till he has another little blowout and he forgets how to breathe. Or we can just let him be. He isn't ever goin' to recover, not at eighty-five years old. It's not like he's bein' robbed of his youth. He's ready to let go. Are you?"

Jude thought, but did not say, that he'd been ready for more than forty years. He had occasionally imagined this moment—maybe it was fair to say he'd even daydreamed of it—but now it had come, and he was surprised to find that his stomach hurt.

When he replied, though, his voice was steady and his own. "Okay, Arlene. No tube. If you say it's time, that's good enough for me. Keep me updated, all right?"

But she wasn't done with him yet. She made an impatient sound, a kind of stiff exhalation of breath, and said, "Are you comin' down?"

He stood at Danny's desk, frowning, confused. The conversation had taken a leap from one thing to another, without warning, like a needle skipping across a record from one track to the next. "Why would I do that?"

"Do you want to see him before he's gone?"

No. He had not seen his father, stood in the same room with him, in three decades. Jude did not want to see the old man before he was gone, and he did not want to look at him after. He had no plans to so much as attend the funeral, although he would be the one to pay for it. Jude was afraid of what he might feel—or what he wouldn't. He would pay whatever he had to pay not to have to share his father's company again. It was the best thing the money could buy: distance.

But he could no more say this to Arlene Wade than he could tell her he'd been waiting on the old man to die since he was fourteen. Instead he replied, "Would he even know if I was there?"

"It's hard to say what he knows and what he doesn't. He's aware of people in the room with him. He turns his eyes to watch folks come and watch folks go. He's been less responsive lately, though. People get that way, once enough lights have burned out."

"I can't make it down. This week isn't good," Jude said, reaching for the easiest lie. He thought maybe the conversation was over and was prepared to say good-bye. Then he surprised himself by asking a question, one he hadn't known was even on his mind until he heard himself speaking it aloud. "Will it be hard?"

"For him to die? Naw. When an old fella gets to this stage, they waste away pretty quick without bein' hooked to the feed bag. They don't suffer none."

"You sure on that?"

"Why?" she asked. "Disappointed?"

5

Forty minutes later Jude drifted into the bathroom to soak his feet—size fourteen, flat arches, and a constant source of pain to him—and found Georgia leaning over the sink sucking her thumb. She had on a T-shirt and pajama bottoms with a cute pattern of tiny red figures that might've been hearts printed on them. It was only when you got close that you could see that all those tiny red figures were actually images of shriveled dead rats.

He leaned into her and pulled her hand out of her mouth to inspect her thumb. The tip was swollen and had a white, soft-looking sore on it. He let go of her hand and turned away, disinterested, pulling a towel off the heated rack and throwing it over his shoulder.

"Ought to put something on that," he said. "Before it festers and rots. There's less work for pole dancers with visible disfigurements."

"You're a sympathetic son of a bitch, you know that?"

"You want sympathy, go fuck James Taylor."

He glanced over his shoulder at her as she stalked out. As soon as he said it, a part of him wished he could take it back. But he didn't take it back. In their metal-studded bracelets and glossy black, dead-girl lipstick, they wanted harshness, the girls like Georgia. They wanted to prove something to themselves about how much they could take, to prove they were hard. That was why they came to him, not in spite of the things he said to them or the way he treated them but because of those things. He didn't want anyone to go away disappointed. And it was just understood that sooner or later they *would* go away.

Or at least *he* understood it, and if they didn't at first, then they always figured it out eventually.

6

One of the dogs was in the house.

Jude woke just after three in the morning at the sound of it, pacing in the hallway, a rustle and a light swish of restless movement, a soft bump against the wall.

He had put them in their pens just before dark, remembered doing this very clearly, but didn't worry about that fact in the first few moments after coming awake. One of them had got into the house somehow, that was all.

Jude sat for a moment, still drunk and stuporous from sleep. A blue splash of moonlight fell across Georgia, sleeping on her belly to his left. Dreaming, her face relaxed and scrubbed of all its makeup, she looked almost girlish, and he felt a sudden tenderness for her—that, and also an odd embarrassment to find himself in bed with her.

"Angus?" he murmured. "Bon?"

Georgia didn't stir. Now he heard nothing in the hallway. He slid out of bed. The damp and the cold took him by surprise. The day had been the coolest in months, the first real day of fall, and now there was a raw, clinging chill in the air, which meant it had to be even colder outside. Maybe that was why the dogs were in the house. Maybe they had burrowed under the wall of the pen and somehow forced their way in, desperate to be warm. But that didn't make sense. They had an indoor-outdoor pen, could go into the heated barn if they were cold. He started toward the door, to peek into the hall, then hesitated at the window and twitched aside the curtain to look outside.

The dogs were in the outdoor half of the pen, both of them, up against the wall of the barn. Angus roamed back and forth over the straw, his body long and sleek, his sliding, sideways movements agitated. Bon sat primly in one corner. Her head was raised, and her gaze was fixed on Jude's window—on him. Her eyes flashed a bright, unnatural green in the darkness. She was too still, too unblinking, like a statue of a dog instead of the real thing.

It was a shock to look out the window and see her staring directly back at him, as if she'd been watching the glass for who knew how long, waiting for him to appear. But that was not as bad as knowing that something else was in the house, moving around, bumping into things in the hallway.

Jude glanced at the security panel next to the bedroom door. The house was monitored, inside and out, by a collection of motion detectors. The dogs weren't big enough to set them off, but a grown man would trip them, and the panel would note movement in one part of the house or another.

The readout, however, showed a steady green light and read only SYS-TEM READY. Jude wondered if the chip was smart enough to tell the difference between a dog and a naked psychotic scrambling around on all fours with a knife in his teeth.

Jude had a gun, but it was in his private recording studio, in the safe. He reached for the Dobro guitar leaning against the wall. Jude had never been one to smash a guitar for effect. His father had smashed his very first guitar for him, in an early attempt to rid Jude of his musical ambitions. Jude hadn't been able to repeat the act himself, not even onstage, for show, when he could afford all the guitars he wanted. He was, however, perfectly willing to use one as a weapon to defend himself. In a sense he supposed he had always used them as weapons.

He heard one floorboard creak in the hall, then another, then a sigh, as of someone settling. His blood quickened. He opened the door.

But the hallway was empty. Jude plashed through long rectangles of icy light, cast by the skylights. He stopped at each closed door, listened, then glanced within. A blanket tossed across a chair looked, for a moment, like a deformed dwarf glaring at him. In another room he found a tall, gaunt figure standing behind the door, and his heart reared in his chest, and he almost swung the guitar, then realized it was a coatrack, and all the breath came rushing unsteadily out of him.

In his studio, at the end of the hall, he considered collecting the gun, then didn't. He didn't want it on him—not because he was afraid to use it but because he wasn't afraid enough. He was so keyed up he might react to a sudden movement in the dark by pulling the trigger and wind up blowing a hole in Danny Wooten or the housekeeper, although why they would be creeping about the house at this hour he couldn't imagine. He returned to the corridor and went downstairs.

He searched the ground floor and found only shadow and stillness, which should've reassured him but didn't. It was the wrong kind of stillness, the shocked stillness that follows the bang of a cherry bomb. His eardrums throbbed from the pressure of all that quiet, a dreadful silence.

He couldn't relax, but at the bottom of the stairs he pretended to, a charade he carried on for himself alone. He leaned the guitar against the wall and exhaled noisily.

"What the fuck are you doing?" he said. By then he was so ill at ease the sound of his own voice unnerved him, sent a cool, prickling rush up his forearms. He had never been one to talk to himself.

He climbed the stairs and started back down the hall to the bedroom. His gaze drifted to an old man, sitting in an antique Shaker chair against the wall. As soon as Jude saw him, his pulse lunged in alarm, and he looked away, fixed his gaze on his bedroom door, so he could only see the old man from the edge of his vision. In the moments that followed, Jude felt it was a matter of life and death not to make eye contact with the old man, to give no sign that he saw him. He did not see him, Jude told himself. There was no one there.

The old man's head was bowed. His hat was off, resting on his knee. His hair was a close bristle, with the brilliance of new frost. The buttons down the front of his coat flashed in the gloom, chromed by moonlight. Jude recognized the suit in a glance. He had last seen it folded in the black, heart-shaped box that had gone into the rear of his closet. The old man's eyes were closed.

Jude's heart pounded, and it was a struggle to breathe, and he continued on toward the bedroom door, which was at the very end of the hallway. As he went past the Shaker chair, against the wall to his left, his leg brushed the old man's knee, and the ghost lifted his head. But by then Jude was beyond him, almost to the door. He was careful not to run. It didn't matter to him if the old man stared at his back, as long as they didn't make eye contact with one another, and besides, there was no old man.

He let himself into the bedroom and clicked the door shut behind him. He went straight to his bed and got into it and immediately began to shake. A part of him wanted to roll against Georgia and cling to her, let her body warm him and drive away the chills, but he stayed on his side of the bed so as not to wake her. He stared at the ceiling.

Georgia was restless and moaned unhappily in her sleep.

He didn't expect to sleep but dozed off at first light and then woke uncharacteristically late, after nine. Georgia was on her side, her small hand resting lightly on his chest and her breath soft on his shoulder. He slipped out of bed and away from her, let himself into the hall and walked downstairs.

The Dobro leaned against the wall where he had left it. The sight of it gave his heart a bad turn. He'd been trying to pretend had not seen what he'd seen in the night. He had set himself a goal of not thinking about it. But there was the Dobro.

When Jude looked out the window, he spotted Danny's car parked by the barn. He had nothing to say to Danny and no reason to bother him, but in another moment he was at the door of the office. He couldn't help himself. The compulsion to be in the company of another human, someone awake and sensible and with a head full of everyday nonsense, was irresistible.

Danny was on the phone, craned back in his office chair, laughing about something. He was still in his suede jacket. Jude didn't need to ask why. He himself had a robe over his shoulders and was hugging himself under it. The office was filled with a damp cold.

Danny saw Jude looking around the door and winked at him, another favorite ass-kissing Hollywood habit of his, although on this particular morning Jude didn't mind it. Then Danny saw something on Jude's face and frowned. He mouthed the words, *You okay?* Jude didn't answer. Jude didn't know.

Danny got rid of whoever he was talking to, then rotated in his chair to turn a solicitous look upon him. "What's going on, Chief? You look like fucking hell."

Jude said, "The ghost came."

"Oh, did it?" Danny asked, brightening. Then he hugged himself, mock-shivered. Tipped his head toward the phone. "That was the heating people. This place is a fucking tomb. They'll have a guy out here to check on the boiler in a little while."

"I want to call her."

"Who?"

"The woman who sold us the ghost."

Danny lowered one of his eyebrows and raised the other, making a face that said he had lost Jude somewhere. "What do you mean, the ghost came?"

"What we ordered. It came. I want to call her. I want to find some things out."

Danny seemed to need a moment to process this. He swiveled partway back to his computer and got the phone, but his gaze remained fixed on Jude. He said, "You sure you're all right?"

"No," he said. "I'm going to see to the dogs. Find her number, will you?"

He went outside in his bathrobe and his underwear, to set Bon and Angus loose from their pens. The temperature was in the low fifties, and the air was white with a fine-grained mist. Still, it was more comfortable than the damp, clinging cold of the house. Angus licked at his hand, his tongue rough and hot and so real that for a moment Jude felt an almost painful throb of gratitude. He was glad to be among the dogs, with their stink of wet fur and their eagerness for play. They ran past him, chasing one another, then ran back, Angus snapping at Bon's tail.

His own father had treated the family dogs better than he ever treated Jude, or Jude's mother. In time it had rubbed off on Jude, and he'd learned to treat dogs better than himself as well. He had spent most of his childhood sharing his bed with dogs, sleeping with one on either side of him and sometimes a third at his feet, had been inseparable from his father's unwashed, primitive, tick-infested pack. Nothing reminded him of who he was, and where he had come from, faster than the rank smell of dog, and by the time he reentered the house, he felt steadier, more himself.

As he stepped through the office door, Danny was saying into the phone, "Thanks so much. Can you hold a moment for Mr. Coyne?" He pressed a button, held out the receiver. "Name's Jessica Price. Down in Florida."

As Jude took the receiver, he realized that this was the first time he'd ever heard the woman's full name. When he had put down his money on the ghost, he'd simply not been curious, although it seemed to him now that it was the kind of thing he should've made a point to know.

He frowned. She had a perfectly ordinary sort of name, but for some reason it caught his attention. He didn't think he had ever heard it before, but it was so inherently forgettable it was hard to be sure.

Jude put the receiver to his ear and nodded. Danny pressed the button again to take it off hold.

"Jessica. Hello. Judas Coyne."

"How'd you like your suit, Mr. Coyne?" she asked. Her voice carried a delicate southern lilt, and her tone was easy and pleasant . . . and something else. There was a hint in it, a sweet, teasing hint of something like mockery.

"What did he look like?" Judas asked. He had never been one to take his time getting to the point. "Your stepfather."

"Reese, honey," the woman said, talking to someone else, not Jude. "Reese, will you turn off that TV and go outside?" A girl, away in the background, registered a sullen complaint. "Because I'm on the phone." The girl said something else. "Because it's private. Go on, now. Go on." A screen door slapped shut. The woman sighed, a bemused, "you know kids" sound, and then said to Jude, "Did you see him? Why don't you tell me what *you* think he looks like, and I'll say if you're right."

She was fucking with him. *Fucking* with him.

"I'm sending it back," Jude told her.

"The suit? Go ahead. You can send the suit back to me. That doesn't mean he'll come with it. No refunds, Mr. Coyne. No exchanges."

Danny stared at Jude, smiling a puzzled smile, his brow furrowed in thought. Jude noticed then the sound of his own breath, harsh and deep. He struggled for words, to know what to say.

She spoke first. "Is it cold there? I bet it's cold. It's going to get a lot colder before he's through."

"What are you out for? More money? You won't get it."

"She came back home to kill herself, you asshole," she said, Jessica Price of Florida, whose name was unfamiliar to him, but maybe not quite as unfamiliar as he would've liked. Her voice had suddenly, without warning, lost the veneer of easy humor. "After you were done with her, she slashed her wrists in the bathtub. Our stepdaddy is the one who found her. She would've done anything for you, and you threw her away like she was garbage."

Florida.

Florida. He felt a sudden ache in the pit of his stomach, a sensation of cold, sick weight. In the same moment, his head seemed to come clear, to shake off the cobwebs of exhaustion and superstitious fear. She had always been Florida to him, but her name was really Anna May McDermott. She told fortunes, knew tarot and palmistry. She and her older sister both had learned how from their stepfather. He was a hypnotist by trade, the last resort of smokers and self-loathing fat ladies who wanted to be done with their cigarettes and their Twinkies. But on the weekends Anna's stepfather hired himself out as a dowser and used his hypnotist's pendulum, a silver razor on a gold chain, to find lost objects and to tell people where to drill their wells. He hung it over the bodies of the ill to heal their auras and slow their hungry cancers, spoke to the dead with it by dangling it over a Ouija board. But hypnotism was the meal ticket: *You can relax now. You can close your eyes. Just listen to my voice.*

Jessica Price was talking again. "Before my stepfather died, he told me what to do, how I should get in touch with you and how to send you his suit and what would happen after. He said he'd see to you, you ugly, no-talent motherfucker."

She was Jessica Price, not McDermott, because she had married and was a widow now. Jude had the impression her husband had been a re-servist who bought it in Tikrit, thought he recalled Anna telling him that. He wasn't sure Anna had ever mentioned her older sister's married name, although she'd told him once that Jessica had followed their step-father into the hypnotism trade. Anna had said her sister made almost seventy thousand dollars a year at it.

Jude said, "Why did I have to buy the suit? Why didn't you just send it to me?" The calm of his own voice was a source of satisfaction to him. He sounded calmer than she did.

"If you didn't pay, the ghost wouldn't really belong to you. You had to pay. And, boy, are you goin' to."

"How'd you know I'd buy it?"

"I sent you an e-mail, didn't I? Anna told me all about your sick little collection . . . your dirty little oh-cult pervert shit. I figured you couldn't help yourself."

"Someone else could've bought it. The other bids—"

"There weren't any other bids. Just you. I put all those other bids up there, and the biddin' wasn't goin' to be done until you made an offer. How do you like your purchase? Is it what you were hopin' for? Oh, you have got some fun ahead of you. I'm goin' to spend that thousand dollars

you paid me for my stepdad's ghost on a bouquet for your funeral. Goin'
to be one hell of a nice spread."

You can just get out, Jude thought. *Just get out of the house. Leave the
dead man's suit and the dead man behind. Take Georgia for a trip to L.A.
Pack a couple suitcases, be on a flight in three hours. Danny can set it up,
Danny can . . .*

As if he had said it aloud, Jessica Price said, "Go ahead and check in
to a hotel. See what happens. Wherever you go, he'll be right there.
When you wake up, he'll be settin' at the foot of your bed." She was starting to laugh. "You're goin' to die, and it's goin' to be his cold hand over
your mouth."

"So Anna was living with you when she killed herself?" he said. Still
in possession of himself. Still perfectly calm.

A pause. The angry sister was out of breath, needed a moment before
she could reply. Jude could hear a sprinkler running in the background,
children shouting in the street.

Jessica said, "It was the only place she had. She was depressed. She'd
always been bad depressed, but you made it worst. She was too miserable to go out, get help, see anyone. You made her hate herself. You
made it so she wanted to die."

"What makes you think she killed herself because of me? You ever
think it was the pleasure of your company drove her over the edge? If
I had to listen to you all day, I'd probably want to slash my wrists, too."

"You're going to die—" she spat.

He cut her off. "Think up a new line. And while you're working on that,
here's something else to think about: I know a few angry souls myself.
They drive Harleys, live in trailers, cook crystal meth, abuse their children,
and shoot their wives. You call 'em scumbags. I call 'em fans. Want to see
if I can find a few who live in your area to drop in and say hello?"

"No one will help you," she said, voice strangled and trembling with
fury. "The black mark on you will infect anyone who joins your cause.
You will not live, and no one who gives you aid or comfort will live."

Reciting it through her anger, as if it were a speech she had rehearsed, which perhaps she had. "Everyone will flee from you or be undone like you will be undone. You're goin' to die alone, you hear me? *Alone.*"

"Don't be so sure. If I'm going down, I might like some company," he said. "And if I can't get help, maybe I'll come see you myself." And banged the phone down.

8

Jude glared at the black phone, still gripped in his white-knuckled hand, and listened to the slow, martial drumbeat of his heart.

"Boss," Danny breathed. "Ho. Lee. Shit. *Boss*." He laughed: thin, wheezing, humorless laughter. "What the hell was all that?"

Jude mentally commanded his hand to open, to let go of the phone. It didn't want to. He knew that Danny had asked a question, but it was like a voice overheard through a closed door, part of a conversation taking place in another room, nothing to do with him.

It was beginning to settle in that Florida was dead. When he had first heard she'd killed herself—when Jessica Price threw it in his face—it had not meant anything, because he couldn't let it mean anything. Now, though, there was no running from it. He felt the knowledge of her death in his blood, which went heavy and thick and strange on him.

It did not seem possible to Jude she could be gone, that someone with whom he'd shared his bed could be in a bed of dirt now. She was twenty-six—no, twenty-seven; she'd been twenty-six when she left. When he sent her away. She'd been twenty-six, but she asked questions like a four-year-old. *You go fishin' much on Lake Pontchartrain? What's the best dog you ever owned? What do you think happens to us when we die?* Enough questions to drive a man mad.

She'd been afraid she was going mad. She was depressed. Not fashionably depressed, in the way of some Goth chicks, but clinically. She had been overcome with it in their last couple of months together, didn't sleep, wept for no reason, forgot to put on her clothes, stared at the TV for hours without bothering to turn it on, answered the phone when it rang but then wouldn't say anything, just stood there holding it, as if she'd been switched off.

But before that there'd been summer days in the barn while he rebuilt the Mustang. There'd been John Prine on the radio, the sweet smell of hay baking in the heat, and afternoons filled with her lazy, pointless questions—a never-ending interrogation that was, at turns, tiresome, amusing, and erotic. There'd been her body, tattooed and icy white, with the bony knees and skinny thighs of a long-distance runner. There'd been her breath on his neck.

"Hey," Danny said. He reached out, and his fingers grazed Jude's wrist. At his touch, Jude's hand sprang open, releasing the phone. "Are you going to be all right?"

"I don't know."

"Want to tell me what's going on?"

Slowly Jude lifted his gaze. Danny half stood behind his desk. He had lost some of his color, his ginger freckles standing out in high relief against the white of his cheeks.

Danny had been her friend, in the unthreatening, easygoing, slightly impersonal way he made himself a friend to all of Jude's girls. He played the role of the urbane, understanding gay pal, someone they could trust to keep their secrets, someone they could vent to and gossip with, someone who provided intimacy without involvement. Someone who would tell them things about Jude that Jude wouldn't tell them himself.

Danny's sister had OD'd on heroin when Danny was just a freshman in college. His mother hanged herself six months later, and Danny had been the one who discovered her. Her body dangled from the single rafter in the pantry, her toes pointed downward, turning in small circles above a kicked-over footstool. You didn't need to be a psychologist to see that the double-barreled blast of the sister and the mother, dying at almost the same time, had wiped out some part of Danny as well, had frozen him at nineteen. Although he didn't wear black fingernail polish or rings in his lips, in a way Danny's attraction to Jude wasn't so different from Georgia's, or Florida's, or any of the other girls'. Jude collected them in almost exactly the same way the Pied Piper had collected rats, and children. He made melodies out of hate and perversion and pain, and they came to him, skipping to the music, hoping he would let them sing along.

Jude didn't want to tell Danny about what Florida had done to herself, wanted to spare him. It would be better not to tell him. He wasn't sure how Danny would take it.

He told him anyway. "Anna. Anna McDermott. She cut her wrists. The woman I was just talking to is her sister."

"Florida?" Danny said. He settled back into his chair. It creaked beneath him. He looked winded. He pressed his hands to his abdomen, then leaned forward slightly, as if his stomach were cramping up. "Oh, shit. Oh, fucking shit," Danny said sweetly. No words had ever sounded less obscene.

A silence followed. Jude noticed, for the first time, that the radio was on, murmuring softly. Trent Reznor sang that he was ready to give up his empire of dirt. It was funny hearing Nine Inch Nails on the radio just then. Jude had met Florida at a Trent Reznor show, backstage. The fact of her death hit him fresh, all over again, as if he were just realizing it for the first time. *You go fishin' much on Lake Pontchartrain?* And then the shock began to coalesce into a sickened resentment. It was so pointless and stupid and self-involved that it was impossible not to hate her a little, not to want to get her on the phone and curse her out, except he couldn't get her on the phone, because she was dead.

"Did she leave a note?" Danny asked.

"I don't know. I didn't get much information from her sister. It wasn't the world's most helpful phone call. Maybe you noticed."

But Danny wasn't listening. He said, "We used to go out for margaritas sometimes. She was one hell of a sweet kid. Her and her questions. She asked me once if I had a favorite place to watch the rain when I was a kid. What the hell kind of question is that? She made me shut my eyes and describe what it looked like outside my bedroom window when it was raining. For ten minutes. You never knew what she was going to ask next. We were big-time compadres. I don't understand this. I mean, I know she was depressed. She told me about it. But she really didn't want to be. Wouldn't she have called one of us if she was going to do something like . . . ? Wouldn't she have given one of us a chance to talk her out of it?"

"I guess not."

Danny had dwindled somehow in the last few minutes, shrunk into himself. He said, "And her sister . . . her sister thinks it's your fault? Well, that's . . . that's just crazy." But his voice was weak, and Jude thought he didn't sound entirely sure of himself.

"I guess."

"She had emotional problems going back before she met you," Danny said, with a little more confidence.

"I think it runs in her family," Jude said.

Danny leaned forward again. "Yeah. *Yeah*. I mean—what the Christ? Anna's sister is the person who sold you the ghost? The dead man's suit? What the fuck is going on here? What happened that made you want to call her in the first place?"

Jude didn't want to tell Danny about what he'd seen last night. In that moment—pushed up against the stony truth of Florida's death—he wasn't entirely sure *what* he'd seen last night anymore. The old man sitting in the hallway, outside his bedroom door at 3:00 A.M., just didn't seem as real now.

"The suit she sent me is a kind of symbolic death threat. She tricked us into buying it. For some reason she couldn't just send it to me, I had to pay for it first. I guess you could say sanity isn't her strong suit. Anyway. I could tell there was something wrong about it as soon as it came. It was in this fucked-up black heart-shaped box and—this will maybe sound a little paranoid—but it had a pin hidden inside to stick someone."

"There was a needle hidden in it? Did it stick you?"

"No. It poked Georgia good, though."

"Is she all right? Do you think there was something on it?"

"You mean like arsenic? No. I don't get the sense Jessica Price of Psychoville, Florida, is actually that stupid. Deeply and intensely crazy, but not stupid. She wants to scare me, not go to jail. She told me her stepdaddy's ghost came with the suit and he's going to get me for what I did to Anna. The pin was probably, I don't know, part of the voodoo. I grew up not far from the Panhandle. Place is crawling with toothless, possum-eating trailer trash full of weird ideas. You can wear a crown of thorns to your job at the Krispy Kreme and no one will bat an eye."

"Do you want me to call the police?" Danny asked. He was finding his footing now. His voice wasn't so winded, had regained some of its self-assurance.

"No."

"She's making threats on your life."

"Who says?"

"You do. Me, too. I sat right here and heard the whole thing."

"What did you hear?"

Danny stared for a moment, then lowered his eyelids and smiled in a drowsy kind of way. "Whatever you say I heard."

Jude grinned back, in spite of himself. Danny was shameless. Jude could not, at the moment, recall why it was he sometimes didn't like him.

"Naw," Jude said. "That's not how I'm going to deal with this. But you can do one thing for me. Anna sent a couple letters after she went home. I don't know what I did with them. You want to poke around?"

"Sure, I'll see if I can lay a hand on them." Danny was eyeing him uneasily again, and even if he had recovered his humor, he had not got back his color. "Jude . . . when you say that's not how you're going to deal with this . . . what's *that* mean?" He pinched his lower lip, brow screwed up in thought again. "That stuff you said when you hung up. Talking about sending people after her. Going down there yourself. You were pretty pissed. Like I've never heard you. Do I need to be worried?"

"You? No," Jude said. "Her? Maybe."

His mind leaped from one bad thing to another, Anna nude and hollow-eyed and floating dead in scarlet bathwater, Jessica Price on the phone—*You're goin' to die, and it's goin' to be his cold hand over your mouth*—the old man sitting in the hall in his black Johnny Cash suit, slowly lifting his head to look at Jude as Jude walked by.

He needed to quiet the noise in his head, a thing usually best accomplished by making some noise with his hands. He carried the Dobro to his studio, strummed at it experimentally, and didn't like the tuning. Jude went into the closet to look for a capo to choke the strings and found a box of bullets instead.

They were in a heart-shaped box—one of the yellow heart-shaped boxes his father used to give to his mother, every Valentine's Day and every Mother's Day, on Christmas and on her birthday. Martin never gave her anything else—no roses or rings or bottles of champagne—but always the same big box of chocolates from the same department store.

Her reaction was as unvarying as his gift. Always, she smiled, a thin, uncomfortable smile, keeping her lips together. She was shy about her teeth. The uppers were false. The real ones had been punched in. Always, she offered the box first to her husband, who, smiling proudly, as if

his gift were a diamond necklace and not a three-dollar box of chocolates, would shake his head. Then she presented them to Jude.

And always Jude picked the same one, the one in the center, a
chocolate-covered cherry. He liked the *gloosh* of it when he bit into it,
the faintly corrupt, sticky-sweet sap, the rotten-soft texture of the cherry
itself. He imagined he was helping himself to a chocolate-covered eyeball.
Even in those days, Jude took pleasure in dreaming up the worst, reveled
in gruesome possibilities.

Jude found the box nestled in a rat's nest of cables and pedals and
adapters, in a guitar case leaned against the back of his studio closet. It
wasn't just any guitar case, but the one he'd left Louisiana with thirty years
before, although the used, forty-dollar Yamaha that had once occupied it
was long gone. The Yamaha he had left behind, onstage in San Francisco,
where he'd opened for Zeppelin one night in 1975. He'd been leaving a lot
of things behind in those days: his family, Louisiana, swine, poverty, the
name he'd been born with. He did not waste a lot of time looking back.

No sooner had he picked the candy box out of the guitar case than
his hands went nerveless, and he dropped it. Jude knew what was in it
without even opening it, knew at first sight. If there was any doubt at all,
though, it fled when the box hit the ground and he heard the brass shells
jingle-jangle inside. The sight of it caused him to recoil in an almost
atavistic terror, as if he'd gone digging through the cables and a fat, furry-
legged spider had crawled out across the back of his hand. He had not
seen the box of ammo in more than three decades and knew he'd left it
stuck between the mattress and the box spring of his childhood bed,
back in Moore's Corner. It had not left Louisiana with him, and there
was no way it could be lying there in his old guitar case, only it was.

He stared at the yellow heart-shaped box for a moment, then forced
himself to pick it up. He pulled off the lid and tipped the box over. Bullets spilled onto the floor.

He had collected them himself, as avid for them as some children
were for baseball cards: his first collection. It had started when he was

eight, when he was still Justin Cowzynski, years and years before he'd ever imagined that someday he would be someone else. One day he was tramping across the east field and heard something snap underfoot. He bent to see what he'd stepped on and picked an empty shotgun shell out of the mud. One of his father's, probably. It was fall, when the old man shot at turkeys. Justin sniffed the splintered, flattened case. The whiff of gunpowder itched his nostrils—a sensation that should've been unpleasant but which was strangely fascinating. It came home with him in his dungaree pocket and went into one of his mother's empty candy boxes.

It was soon joined by two live shells for a .38, swiped from the garage of a friend, some curious silver empties he had discovered at the rifle range, and a bullet from a British assault rifle, as long as his middle finger. He had traded for this last, and it had cost him dear—an issue of *Creepy* with a Frazetta cover—but he felt he had got value for value. He would lie in bed at night looking his bullets over, studying the way the starlight shone on the polished casings, smelling the lead, the way a man might sniff at a ribbon scented with a lover's perfume; thoughtfully, with a head full of sweet fantasy.

In high school he strung the British bullet on a leather thong and wore it around his throat until the principal confiscated it. Jude wondered that he had not found a way to kill someone in those days. He'd possessed all the key elements of a school shooter: hormones, misery, ammunition. People wondered how something like Columbine could happen. Jude wondered why it didn't happen more often.

They were all there—the crushed shotgun shell, the silver empties, the two-inch bullet from the AR-15, which couldn't be there, because the principal had never given it back. It was a warning. Jude had seen a dead man in the night, Anna's stepfather, and this was his way of telling Jude that their business was not done.

It was a crazy thing to think. There had to be a dozen more reasonable explanations for the box, for the bullets. But Jude didn't care what was reasonable. He wasn't a reasonable man. He only cared what was true. He had seen a dead man in the night. Maybe, for a few minutes, in Danny's sun-splashed studio, he'd been able to block it out, pretend it hadn't happened, but it had.

He was steadier now, found himself considering the bullets coolly. It came to him that maybe it was more than a warning. Perhaps it was also a message. The dead man, the ghost, was telling him to arm himself.

Jude considered the Super Blackhawk, in the safe, under his desk. But what would he shoot at? He understood that the ghost existed first and foremost within his own head. That maybe ghosts always haunted minds, not places. If he wanted to take a shot at it, he'd have to turn the barrel against his own temple.

He brushed the bullets back into his mother's candy box, pushed the lid back on. Bullets wouldn't do him any good. But there were other kinds of ammunition.

He had a collection of books on the shelf at one end of the studio, books about the occult and the supernatural. Around the time Jude was just beginning his recording career, Black Sabbath came out big, and Jude's manager advised him that it couldn't hurt to at least imply that he and Lucifer were on a first-name basis with each other. Jude had already taken up the study of group psychology and mass hypnosis, on the theory that if fans were good, cultists were even better. He added volumes by Aleister Crowley and Charles Dexter Ward to the reading list, and he worked his way through them with a careful, joyless concentration, underlining concepts and key facts.

Later, after he was a celebrity, Satanists and Wiccans and spiritualists, who from listening to his music mistakenly thought he shared their enthusiasms—he really didn't give a fuck; it was like wearing leather pants, just part of the costume—sent him even more (admittedly fascinating) reading: an obscure manual, printed by the Catholic Church in the thirties, for performing exorcisms; a translation of a five-hundred-year-old book of perverted, unholy psalms written by a mad Templar; a cookbook for cannibals.

Jude placed the box of bullets up on the shelf among his books, all thought of finding a capo and playing some Skynyrd gone. He ran his thumbnail along the spines of the hardcovers. It was cold enough in his studio to make his fingers stiff and clumsy, and it was hard to turn pages, and he didn't know what he was looking for.

For a while he struggled to make his way through a strangled discourse on animal familiars, creatures of intense feeling who were bound by love and blood to their masters, and who could deal with the dead directly. But it was written in dense eighteenth-century English, without any punctuation. Jude would labor over a single paragraph for ten minutes, then wouldn't know what he'd read. He set it aside.

In another book he lingered on a chapter about possession, by way of demon or hateful spirit. One grotesque illustration showed an old man sprawled on his bed, among tangled sheets, his eyes bulging in horror and his mouth gaping open, while a leering, naked homunculus climbed out from between his lips. Or, a worse thought: Maybe the thing was climbing in.

Jude read that anyone who held open the golden door of mortality, for a peek at the other side, risked letting something through, and that the ill, the old, and those who loved death were especially in danger. The tone was assertive and knowledgeable, and Jude was encouraged until he read that the best method of protection was to wash yourself in urine. Jude had an open mind when it came to depravity, but he drew the line at water sports, and when the book slipped from his cold hands, he didn't bother to pick it up. Instead he kicked it away.

He read about the Borley rectory, about contacting spirit companions by way of the Ouija board, and about the alchemical uses of menstrual blood, his eyes going in and out of focus, and then he was flinging books, lashing them about the studio. Every word was crap. Demons and familiars and enchanted circles and the magical benefits of piss. One volume swept a lamp off his desk with a crash. Another hit a framed platinum record. A spiderweb of gleaming shatter lines leaped through the glass over the silver disk. The frame dropped from the wall, hit the floor, tilted onto its face with a crunch. Jude's hand found the candy box full of bullets. It struck the wall, and ammo sprayed across the floor in a ringing clatter.

He grabbed another book, breathing hard, his blood up, just looking to do some damage now and never mind to what, then caught himself, because the feel of the thing in his hand was all wrong. He looked and saw a black, unlabeled videotape instead. He didn't know right what way it was, had to think awhile before it came to him. It was his snuff film. It had been sitting up on the shelf with the books, apart from the other videos for . . . what? Four years? It had been there so long he'd stopped seeing it among the hardcovers. It had become just a part of the general clutter on the shelves.

Jude had walked into the studio one morning and found his wife, Shannon, watching it. He was packing for a trip to New York and had come looking for a guitar to take with him. He stopped in the doorway at the sight of her. Shannon stood in front of the television, watching a man suffocate a naked teenage girl with a clear plastic bag, while other men watched.

Shannon frowned, her brow wrinkled in concentration, watching the girl in the movie die. He didn't worry about her temper—anger didn't impress him—but he'd learned to be wary of her when she was like this, calm and silent and drawn into herself.

At last she said, "Is this real?"

"Yes."

"She's really dying?"

He looked at the TV. The naked girl had gone slack and boneless on the floor. "She's really dead. They killed her boyfriend, too, didn't they?"

"He begged."

"A cop gave it to me. He told me the two kids were Texas junkies who shot up a liquor store and killed someone, then ran for Tijuana to hide out. Cops keep some sick shit lying around."

"He begged for her."

Jude said, "It's gruesome. I don't know why I still have it."

"I don't either," she said. She rose and ejected the movie, then stood looking at it, as if she had never seen a videotape before and was trying to imagine what purpose one might serve.

"Are you all right?" Jude asked.

"I don't know," she said. She turned the glassy, confused look upon him. "Are you?"

When he didn't reply, she crossed the room and slipped past him. At the door Shannon caught herself and realized she was still holding the tape. She set it gently on the shelf before she walked out. Later the housekeeper shoved the video in with the books. It was a mistake Jude never bothered to correct, and soon enough he forgot it was even there.

He had other things to think about. After he returned from New York, he found the house empty, Shannon's side of the closet cleaned out. She didn't bother with a note, no Dear John saying their love had been a mistake or that she'd loved some version of him that didn't really exist, that they'd been growing apart. She was forty-six and had been married and divorced once before. She didn't do junior-high theatrics. When she had something to say to him, she called. When she needed something from him, her lawyer called.

Looking at the tape now, he really didn't know why he had held on to it—or why it had held on to him. It seemed to him he should've sought it out and got rid of it when he came home and found her gone. He was not even sure why he had accepted it in the first place, when the tape had been offered to him. Jude teetered then on the edge of an uncomfortable thought, that he had, over time, become a little too willing to take what he was offered, without wondering at the possible consequences. And look at the trouble it had led to. Anna had offered herself to him, and he had taken, and now she was dead. Jessica McDermott Price had offered him the dead man's suit, and now it was his. Now it was his.

He had not gone out of his way to own a dead man's suit, or a videotape of Mexican death-porn, or any of the rest of it. It seemed to him instead that all these things had been drawn to him like iron filings to a magnet, and he could no more help drawing them and holding on to them than a magnet could. But this suggested helplessness, and he had never been helpless. If he was going to throw something into the wall, it ought to be this tape.

But he'd stood too long thinking. The cold in the studio sapped him, so that he felt tired, felt his age. He was surprised he couldn't see his own breath; that was how cold it felt. He couldn't imagine anything more foolish—or weak—than a fifty-four-year-old man pitching his books in a fit of rage, and if there was one thing he despised, it was weakness. He wanted to drop the tape and crunch it underfoot, but instead he turned to put it back on the shelf, feeling that it was more important to recover his composure, to act, at least for a moment, like an adult.

"Get rid of it," Georgia said from the door.

10

His shoulders twitched in reflexive surprise. He turned and looked. She was naturally pale to begin with, but now her face was bloodless, like polished bone, so she resembled a vampire even more than usual. He wondered if it was a trick of makeup before he saw that her cheeks were damp, the fine black hairs at her temples pasted down with sweat. She stood in pajamas, clutching herself and shivering in the cold.

"You sick?" he asked.

"I'm fine," she said. "Picture of health. Get rid of it."

He gently set the snuff film back on the shelf. "Get rid of what?"

"The dead man's suit. It smells bad. Didn't you notice the way it smelled when you took it out of the closet?"

"It isn't in the closet?"

"No, it isn't in the closet. It was laying on the bed when I woke up. It was spread out right next to me. Did you forget to put it back? Or forget you took it out in the first place? I swear to God, it's a surprise sometimes you remember to put your dick back in your pants after you take a piss. I hope all the pot you smoked in the seventies was worth it. What the hell were you doing with it anyway?"

If the suit was out of the closet, then it had walked out on its own.

There was no percentage in telling Georgia that, though, so he said nothing, pretended an interest in cleaning up.

Jude went around the desk, bent, and turned over the framed record that had dropped to the floor. The record itself was as busted as the plate of glass on top of it. He popped the frame apart and tipped it on its side. Broken glass slid with a musical clash into the wastebasket by his desk. He plucked out the pieces of his smashed platinum album—*Happy Little Lynch Mob*—and stuck them in the trash, six gleaming scimitar blades of grooved steel. What to do now? He supposed a thinking man would go and have another look at the suit. He rose and turned to her.

"Come on. You should lie down. You look like hell. I'll put the suit away, and then I'll tuck you in."

He put his hand on her upper arm, but she pulled free. "No. The bed smells like it, too. It's all over the sheets."

"So we'll get new sheets," he said, taking her arm again.

Jude turned her and guided her into the hallway. The dead man was sitting two-thirds of the way down the corridor, in the Shaker chair on the left, his head lowered in thought. A drape of morning sunshine fell across where his legs should have been. They disappeared where they passed into the light. It gave him the look of a war veteran, his trousers ending in stumps, midway down his thighs. Below this splash of sunshine were his polished black loafers, with his black-stockinged feet stuck in them. Between his thighs and his shoes, the only legs that were visible were the legs of the chair, the wood a lustrous blond in the light.

No sooner had Jude noticed him than he looked away, did not want to see him, did not want to think about him being there. He glanced at Georgia, to see if she had spotted the ghost. She was staring at her feet as she shuffled along with Jude's hand on her arm, her bangs in her eyes. He wanted to tell her to look, wanted to know if she could see him as well, but he was too in dread of the dead man to speak, afraid the ghost would hear him and glance up.

It was crazy to think somehow the dead man wasn't going to notice them walking past, but for no reason he could explain, Jude felt that if they were both very quiet, they could slip by unseen. The dead man's eyes were closed, his chin almost touching his chest, an old man who had nodded off in the late-morning sun. More than anything Jude wanted him to stay just as he was. Not to stir. Not to wake. Not to open his eyes; please, not to open his eyes.

They drew closer, but still Georgia didn't glance his way. Instead she laid a sleepy head on Jude's shoulder and closed her eyes. "So you want to tell me why you had to trash the studio? And were you shouting in there? I thought I heard you shouting, too."

He didn't want to look again but couldn't help himself. The ghost remained as he was, head tipped to the side, smiling just slightly, as if musing on a pleasant thought or a dream. The dead man didn't seem to hear *her*. Jude had an idea then, unformed, difficult to articulate. With his closed eyes and his head tilted just so, the ghost seemed not so much to be asleep as to be *listening* for something. Listening for him, Jude thought. Waiting, perhaps, to be acknowledged, before he would (or could) acknowledge Jude in return. They were almost on top of him now, about to walk past him, and Jude shrank against Georgia to avoid touching him.

"That's what woke me up, the noise, and then the smell—" She made a soft coughing sound and lifted her head to squint blearily at the bedroom door. She still didn't notice the ghost, although they were crossing directly in front of him now. She came up short, stopped moving. "I'm not going in there until you do something about that suit."

He slipped his hand down her arm to her wrist and squeezed it, shoving her forward. She made a thin sound of pain and protest and tried to pull away from him. "What the fuck?"

"Keep walking," he said, and then realized a moment later, with a pitiful throb in the heart, that he had spoken.

He glanced down at the ghost, and at the same time the dead man lifted his head and his eyes rolled open. But where his eyes belonged was only a black scribble. It was as if a child had taken a Magic Marker—a truly magic marker, one that could draw right on the air—and had desperately tried to ink over them. The black lines squirmed and tangled among one another, worms tied into a knot.

Then Jude was past him, shoving Georgia down the hallway while she struggled and whined. When he was at the door to the bedroom, he looked back.

The ghost came to his feet, and as he rose, his legs moved out of the sunlight and painted themselves back into being, the long black trouser legs, the sharp crease in his pants. The dead man held his right arm out to the side, the palm turned toward the floor, and something fell from the hand, a flat silver pendant, polished to a mirror brightness, attached to a foot of delicate gold chain. No, not a pendant but a curved blade of some kind. It was like a dollhouse version of the pendulum in that story by Edgar Allan Poe. The gold chain was connected to a ring around one of his fingers, a wedding ring, and the razor was what he had married. He allowed Jude to look at it for a moment and then twitched his wrist, a child doing a trick with a yo-yo, and the little curved razor leaped into his hand.

Jude felt a moan struggling to force its way up from his chest. He shoved Georgia through the door, into the bedroom, and slammed it.

"What are you doing, Jude?" she cried, pulling free at last, stumbling away from him.

"Shut up."

She hit him in the shoulder with her left hand, then slugged him in the back with her right, the hand with the infected thumb. This hurt her more than it hurt him. She made a sick gasping sound and let him be.

He still held the doorknob. He listened to the corridor. It was quiet.

Jude eased the door back and looked through a three-inch opening, ready to slam it again, expecting the dead man to be there with his razor on a chain.

No one was in the hallway.

He shut his eyes. He shut the door. He put his forehead against it, pulled a deep breath down into his lungs and held it, let it go slowly. His face was clammy with sweat, and he lifted a hand to wipe it away. Something icy and sharp and hard lightly grazed his cheek, and he opened his eyes and saw the dead man's curved razor in his hand, the blue-steel blade reflecting an image of his own wide, staring eyeball.

Jude shouted and flung it down, then looked at the floor, but already it wasn't there.

11

He backed away from the door. The room was filled with the sound of strained breathing, his own and Marybeth's. In that moment she was Marybeth. He couldn't recall what it was he usually called her.

"What kind of shit are you on?" she asked, in a voice that hinted at a hillbilly drawl, faint but distinctly southern.

"Georgia," he said, remembering then. "Nothing. I couldn't be more sober."

"Oh, the hell. What are you taking?" And that subtle, barely-there drawl was gone, receding as quickly as it had come. Georgia had lived a couple years in New York City, where she'd made a studied effort to lose her accent, didn't like being taken for a cornpone hick.

"I got off all my shit years ago. I told you."

"What was that in the hall? You saw something. What'd you see?"

He glared a warning at her, which she ignored. She stood huddled before him in her pajamas, her arms crossed under her breasts, hands tucked out of sight against her sides. Her feet were spread slightly apart, as if, should he try to move past her into the rest of the bedroom, she would block his way—an absurd prospect for a girl a hundred pounds lighter than he was.

"There was an old man sitting out in the hall. In the chair," he said at last. He had to tell her something and didn't see any reason to lie. Her opinion of his sanity didn't trouble him. "We walked right by him, but you didn't see him. I don't know if you *can* see him."

"That's lunatic bullshit." She said it with no special conviction.

He started toward the bed, and she got out of his way, pressed herself to the wall.

The dead man's suit was spread neatly across his side of the mattress. The deep, heart-shaped box lay on the floor, the black lid resting next to it, white tissue paper hanging out. He caught a whiff of the suit when he was still four paces away from it and flinched. It hadn't smelled that way when it first came out of the box, he would've noticed. Now it was impossible not to notice it. It had the ripe odor of corruption, something dead and spoiling.

"Christ," Jude said.

Georgia stood at a distance, a hand cupped over her mouth and nose. "I know. I was wondering if there was something in one of the pockets. Something going bad. Old food."

Breathing through his mouth, Jude patted down the jacket. He thought it very likely he was about to discover something in an advanced state of decomposition. It would not have surprised him to find that Jessica McDermott Price had stuffed a dead rat into the suit, a little something extra to go with his purchase, at no additional charge. Instead, though, he felt only a stiff square of what was maybe plastic in one pocket. He slipped it out for a look.

It was a photograph, one he knew well, Anna's favorite picture of them. She had taken it with her when she left. Danny snapped it one afternoon in late August, the sunlight reddish and warm on the front porch, the day swarming with dragonflies and glittering motes of dust. Jude perched on the steps in a worn denim jacket, his Dobro over one knee. Anna sat beside him, watching him play, her hands squeezed between her thighs. The dogs were sprawled in the dirt at their feet, staring quizzically up at the camera.

It had been a good afternoon, maybe one of the last good afternoons before things started to go bad, but looking at the photograph now brought him no pleasure. Someone had taken a Sharpie to it. Jude's eyes had been marked out in black ink, covered over by a furious hand.

Georgia was saying something from where she stood a few feet away, her voice shy, uncertain. "What did he look like? The ghost in the hall?"

Jude's body was turned so she couldn't see the photograph, a lucky thing. He didn't want her to see it.

He struggled to find his voice. It was hard to get past the unhappy shock of those black scribbles blotting out his eyes in the picture. "An old man," he managed at last. "He was wearing this suit."

And there were these awful fucking black scribbles floating in front of his eyes and they looked just like this, Jude imagined telling her, turning to show her the snapshot at the same time. He didn't do it, though.

"He just sat there?" Georgia asked. "Nothing else happened?"

"He stood up and showed me a razor on a chain. A funny little razor."

On the day Danny took the picture, Anna was still herself, and Jude thought she'd been happy. Jude had spent most of that late-summer afternoon beneath the Mustang, and Anna had stayed close by, crawling under herself to pass him tools and necessary parts. In the photo there was a smear of motor oil on her chin, dirt on her hands and knees—an appealing, well-earned grime, the kind of filth you could take pride in. Her eyebrows were bunched up, a pretty dimple between them, and her mouth was open, as if she were laughing—or, more likely, about to ask him a question. *You go fishin' much on Lake Pontchartrain? What's the best dog you ever owned?* Her with her questions.

Anna had not asked him why he was sending her away, however, when it was over. Not after the night he found her wandering the side of the highway in a T-shirt and nothing else, people honking at her as they went past. He hauled her into the car and pulled back his fist to hit her, then slugged the steering wheel instead, punching it until his knuckles bled. He said enough was enough, that he was going to pack her shit for her, send her on her way. Anna said she'd die without him. He said he'd send flowers to the funeral.

So: She at least had kept her word. It was too late to keep his.

"Are you messing with me, Jude?" Georgia asked. Her voice was close. She was creeping toward him, in spite of her aversion to the smell. He slid the picture back into the pocket of the dead man's suit before she could see. "Because if this is a joke, it sucks."

"It isn't a joke. I guess it's possible I'm losing my mind, but I don't think that's it either. The person who sold me the . . . suit . . . knew what she was doing. Her little sister was a fan who committed suicide. This woman blames me for her death. I talked to her on the phone just an hour ago, and she told me so herself. That's one part of this thing I'm sure I didn't imagine. Danny was there. He heard me talking to her. She wants to get even with me. So she sent me a ghost. I saw him just now in the hall. And I saw him last night, too."

He began to fold the suit, intending to return it to its box.

"Burn it," Georgia said, with a sudden vehemence that surprised him. "Take the fucking suit and burn it."

Jude felt, for an instant, an almost overpowering impulse to do just that, find some lighter fluid, douse it, cook it in the driveway. It was an impulse he immediately mistrusted. He was wary of any irrevocable action. Who knew what bridges might be burned along with it? He felt the slightest flicker of an idea, something about the awful-smelling suit and how it might be of use, but the thought drifted away before he could fix on it. He was tired. It was hard to pin a solid thought in place.

His reasons for wanting to hold on to the suit were illogical, superstitious, unclear even to himself, but when he spoke, he had a perfectly reasonable explanation for keeping it. "We can't burn it. It's evidence. My lawyer is going to want it later, if we decide to build a case against her."

Georgia laughed, weakly, unhappily. "What? Assault with a deadly spirit?"

"No. Harassment, maybe. Stalking. It's a death threat anyway, even if it's a crazy one. There's laws on that."

He finished folding the suit and set it back in its nest of tissue paper, inside the box. He breathed through his mouth as he did it, head turned from the stink.

"The whole room smells. I know this is pussy, but I feel like I might yak," she said.

He slipped a sideways look at her. She was absentmindedly clutching her right hand to her chest, staring blankly at the glossy black heart-shaped box. She had, until just a few moments before, been hiding the hand against her side. The thumb was swollen, and the place where the pin had gone in was now a white sore, the size of a pencil eraser, glistening with pus. She saw him looking at it, glanced down at herself, then up again, smiling miserably.

"You got a hell of an infection there."

"I know. I been putting Bactine on it."

"Maybe you ought to see someone about it. If it's tetanus, Bactine won't take care of it."

She closed her fingers around the injured thumb, squeezed it gently. "I pricked it on that pin hidden in the suit. What if it was poisoned?"

"I guess if it had cyanide on it, we'd know by now."

"Anthrax."

"I spoke to the woman. She's country-fried stupid, not to mention in need of some superior fucking psychiatric drugs, but I don't think she would've sent me anything with poison on it. She knows she'd go to jail for that." He touched Georgia's wrist, pulled her hand toward him, and studied the thumb. The skin around the area of infection was soft and rotten and pruned up, as if it had been soaking in water for a long time. "Why don't you go and set in front of the TV. I'll have Danny book an appointment with the doctor."

He let go of her wrist and nodded toward the door, but she didn't move.

"Will you look and see if he's in the hall?" she asked.

He stared for a moment, then nodded and went to the door. He opened it half a foot and peeked out. The sun had shifted or moved behind a cloud, and the hallway was in cool shadow. No one sat in the Shaker chair against the wall. No one stood in the corner with a razor on a chain.

"All clear."

She touched his shoulder with her good hand. "I saw a ghost once. When I was a kid."

He wasn't surprised. He hadn't met a Goth girl yet who hadn't had some kind of brush with the supernatural, who didn't believe, with utter, embarrassing sincerity, in astral forms or angels or Wiccan spellcraft.

"I was living with Bammy. My grandmother. This was just after the first time my daddy threw me out. One afternoon I went in the kitchen to pour myself a glass of her lemonade—she makes real nice lemonade—and I looked out the back window, and there was this girl in the yard. She was picking dandelions and blowing on them to make them fly apart, you know, like kids do, and she was singing to herself while she was doing it. This girl a few years younger than myself, in a real cheap dress. I pushed up the window to yell out to her, find out what she was doing in our yard. When she heard the window squeak, she looked up at me, and that's when I knew she was dead. She had these messed-up eyes."

"How do you mean messed-up?" Jude asked. The skin on his forearms prickled and tightened, going rough with gooseflesh.

"They were black eyes. No, they weren't even like eyes at all. It was more like . . . like they were covered over."

"Covered over," Jude repeated.

"Yes. Marked out. Black. Then she turned her head and seemed to look over at the fence. In another moment she hopped up and walked across the yard. She was moving her mouth, like she was talking to someone, only no one was there, and I couldn't hear any words coming out of her. I could hear her when she was picking dandelions and singing to herself, but not when she got up and seemed to be talking to someone. I always thought was a strange thing—that I could only hear her when she sang. And then she reached up, like there was an invisible person standing in front of her, just on the other side of Bammy's fence, and she was taking his hand.

"And I got scared all of a sudden, like got chills, because I felt something bad was going to happen to her. I wanted to tell her to let go of his hand. Whoever was taking her hand, I wanted her to get away from him. Only I was too scared. I couldn't get my breath. And the little girl looked back at me one more time, kind of sad, with her marked-over eyes, and then she came up off the ground—I swear to God—and floated over the fence. Not like she was flying. Like she was being picked up by invisible hands. The way her feet dangled in the air. They bumped into the pickets. She went over, and then she was gone. I got the flop sweats and had to sit down on the kitchen floor."

Georgia darted a look at Jude's face, maybe to see if he thought she was being foolish. But he only nodded that she should go on.

"Bammy came in and cried out and said, 'Girl, what's the matter?' But when I told her what I saw, that was when she got really upset and started crying. She sat down on the floor with me and said she believed me. She said I had seen her twin sister, Ruth.

"I knew about Ruth, who died when Bammy was little, but it wasn't until then that Bammy told me what really happened to her. I always thought she got run over by a car or something, but it wasn't like that. One day, when they were both about seven or eight—this was 1950-something—their mother called them in for lunch. Bammy went, but Ruthie stayed out, because she didn't feel like eating and because she was just naturally disobedient. While Bammy and her folks were inside, someone snatched her out of the backyard. She wasn't ever seen again. Except now and then, people at Bammy's house spot her blowing on dandelions and singing to herself, and then someone who isn't there takes her away. My mother saw Ruth's ghost, and Bammy's husband seen her once, and some of Bammy's friends, and Bammy, too.

"Everyone who saw Ruth was just like me. They wanted to tell her not to go, to stay away from whoever was on the other side of the fence. But everyone who sees her is too scared by the sight of her to speak. And Bammy said she thought it wouldn't ever be over until someone found their voice and spoke up. That it was like Ruth's ghost was in a kind of dream, stuck repeating her last minutes, and she'll be that way until someone calls out to her and wakes her up."

Georgia swallowed, fell silent. She bowed her head, so her dark hair hid her eyes.

"I can't believe the dead want to hurt us," she said finally. "Don't they need our help? Don't they always need our help? If you see him again, you should try and talk to him. You should find out what he wants."

Jude didn't believe that it was a matter of if, only when. And he already knew what the dead man wanted.

"He didn't come for talk," Jude said.

12

Jude wasn't sure what to do next, so he made tea. The simple, automatic gestures of filling the kettle, spooning loose tea into the strainer, and finding a mug had a way of clearing his head and slowing time, opening a useful silence. He stood at the range listening to the kettle tick.

He did not feel panicked, a realization that brought him some satisfaction. He was not ready to run, had doubts there was anything to gain from running anyway. Where could he go that would be better than here? Jessica Price had said the dead man belonged to him now and would follow him wherever he went. Jude flashed to an image of himself sliding into a first-class seat on a flight to California, then turning his head to see the dead man sitting next to him, with those black scribbles floating in front of his eyes. He shuddered, shook off the thought. The house was as good a place as any to make a stand—at least until he figured out some spot that made more sense. Besides, he hated to board the dogs. In the old days, when he went on tour, they always came on the bus with him.

And no matter what he'd said to Georgia, he had even less interest in calling the police or his lawyer. He had an idea that dragging the law into it might be the worst thing he could do. They could bring a case against

Jessica McDermott Price, and there just might be some pleasure in that, but getting even with her wouldn't make the dead man go away. He knew that. He'd seen lots of horror movies.

Besides, calling in the police to rescue him rubbed against his natural grain, no small matter. His own identity was his first and single most forceful creation, the machine that had manufactured all his other successes, which had produced everything in his life that was worth having and that he cared about. He would protect that to the end.

Jude could believe in a ghost but not a boogeyman, a pure incarnation of evil. There had to be more to the dead man than black marks over his eyes and a curved razor on a golden chain. He wondered, abruptly, what Anna had cut her wrists with, became conscious all over again of how cold it was in the kitchen, that he was leaning toward the kettle to absorb some of its ambient heat. Jude was suddenly certain she had slashed her wrists with the razor on the end of her father's pendulum, the one he'd used to mesmerize desperate suckers and to search for well water. He wondered what else there was to know about how Anna had died and about the man who'd been a father to her and who had discovered her body in a cold bath, the water darkened with her blood.

Maybe Danny had turned up Anna's letters. Jude dreaded reading them again and at the same time knew that he had to. He remembered them well enough to know now that she'd been trying to tell him what she was going to do to herself and he'd missed it. No—it was more terrible than that. He had not wanted to see, had willfully ignored what was right in front of him.

Her first letters from home had conveyed a breezy optimism, and their subtext was that she was getting her life together, making sound, grown-up decisions about her future. They arrived on rich white card stock and were composed in delicate cursive. As with her conversation, these letters were filled with questions, although, in her correspondence at least, she didn't seem to expect any answers. She would write that she had spent the month sending out job applications, then rhetorically ask if it was a mistake to wear black lipstick and motorcycle boots to an interview at a day-care center. She would describe two colleges and wonder at length about which would be better for her. But it was all a con, and Jude knew it. She never got the job at the day care, never mentioned it again after that one letter. And when the spring semester rolled around, she had moved on to applying for a spot at a beauticians' academy, college forgotten.

Her last few letters were a truer picture of the place she'd been in mentally. They came on plain, ruled paper, torn out of a notebook, and her cursive was cramped, hard to read. Anna wrote that she couldn't get any rest. Her sister lived in a new development, and there was a house going up right next door. She wrote she heard them hammering nails all day long and that it was like living next to a coffin maker after a plague. When she tried to sleep at night, the hammers would start up again, just as she was drifting off, and never mind that there was no one over there. She was desperate to sleep. Her sister was trying to get her on a treatment plan for her insomnia. There were things Anna wanted to talk about, but she didn't have anyone to talk to, and she was tired of talking to herself. She wrote that she couldn't stand to be so tired all the time.

Anna had begged him to call, but he had not called. Her unhappiness wore on him. It was too much work to help her through her depressions. He'd tried, when they were together, and his best hadn't been good enough. He'd given it his best, it hadn't panned out, and still she wouldn't leave him alone. He didn't know why he even read her letters, let alone sometimes responded to them. He'd wished they would just stop coming. Finally they had.

Danny could dig them out and then make a doctor's appointment for Georgia. As plans went, it wasn't much, but it was better than what he had ten minutes before, which was nothing. Jude poured the tea, and time started up again.

He drifted with his mug into the office. Danny wasn't at his desk. Jude stood in the doorway, staring at the empty room, listening intently to the stillness for some sign of him. Nothing. He was in the bathroom, maybe—but no. The door was slightly ajar, as it had been the day before, and the crack revealed only darkness. Maybe he had taken off for lunch.

Jude started over toward the window, to see if Danny's car was in the driveway, then held up before he got there, took a detour to Danny's desk. He flipped through some stacks of paper, looking for Anna's letters. If Danny had found them, however, he'd tucked them somewhere out of sight. When Jude didn't turn them up, he settled into Danny's chair and launched the Web browser on his computer, intending to do a search on Anna's stepdaddy. It seemed like there was something about everyone online. Maybe the dead man had his own MySpace account. Jude laughed—choked, ugly laughter—down in his throat.

He couldn't remember the dead man's first name, so he ran a search for "McDermott hypnosis dead." At the top of Jude's search results was a link to an obituary, which had appeared in last summer's *Pensacola News Journal,* for a Craddock James McDermott. That was it: Craddock.

Jude clicked on it—and there he was.

The man in the black-and-white photograph was a younger version of the man Jude had seen twice now in the upstairs hallway. In the picture he looked a vigorous sixty, his hair cut in that same close-to-the-scalp military bristle. With his long, almost horsey face, and wide thin lips, he bore more than a passing resemblance to Charlton Heston. The most startling thing about the photograph was discovering that Craddock, in life, had eyes like any man's eyes. They were clear and direct and stared into Forever with the challenging self-assurance of motivational speakers and evangelical preachers everywhere.

Jude read. It said that a life of learning and teaching, exploring and adventuring, had ended when Craddock James McDermott had died of cerebral embolism at his stepdaughter's home in Testament, Florida, on Tuesday, August 10. A true son of the South, he had grown up the only child of a Pentecostal minister and had lived in Savannah and Atlanta, Georgia, and later Galveston, Texas.

He was a wide receiver for the Longhorns in 1965 and enlisted in the service upon graduation, where he served as a member of the army's psychological operations division. It was there that he discovered his calling, when he was introduced to the possibilities of hypnosis. In Vietnam he earned a Purple Heart and a Bronze Star. He was discharged with honors and settled in Florida. In 1980 he was wed to Paula Joy Williams, a librarian, and became stepfather to her two children, Jessica and Anna, whom he later adopted. Paula and Craddock shared a love built upon quiet faith, deep trust, and a mutual fascination with the unexplored possibilities of the human spirit.

At this, Jude frowned. It was a curious sentence—"a mutual fascination with the unexplored possibilities of the human spirit." He didn't even know what it meant.

Their relationship endured until Paula passed away in 1986. In his life Craddock had attended to almost ten thousand "patients"—Jude snorted at the word—using deep hypnotic technique to alleviate the suffering of the ill and to help those in need to overcome their weaknesses, work that his oldest stepdaughter, Jessica McDermott Price, carried on still, as a private consultant. Jude snorted again. She had probably written the obituary herself. He was surprised she hadn't included the phone number for her service. *Mention that you heard about us in my father's obit and receive 10 percent off your first session!!!*

Craddock's interest in spiritualism and the untapped potential of the mind led him to experiment with "dowsing," the old country technique of discovering underground water sources with the use of a rod or pendulum. But it was the way in which he led so many of his fellow life travelers to discover their own hidden reservoirs of strength and self-worth for which he will be best remembered by his surviving adopted daughter and his loved ones. "His voice may have fallen silent, but it will never be forgotten."

Nothing about Anna's suicide.

Jude passed his gaze over the obit again, pausing on certain combinations of words that he didn't much care for: "psychological operations," "unexplored possibilities," "the untapped potential of the mind." He looked again at Craddock's face, taking in the chilly confidence of his pale black-and-white eyes and the almost angry smile set on his thin, colorless lips. He was a cruel-looking son of a bitch.

Danny's computer pinged to let Jude know that an e-mail had come through. Where the hell was Danny anyway? Jude glanced at the computer's clock, saw he'd been sitting there for twenty minutes already. He clicked over to Danny's e-mail program, which picked up messages for both of them. The new e-mail was addressed to Jude.

Jude flicked a glance at the address of the sender, then shifted in the chair, sitting up straight, muscles tightening across his chest and abdomen, as if he were readying himself for a blow. In a way he was. The e-mail was from craddockm@box.closet.net.

Jude opened the e-mail and began to read.

dear jude

we will ride at nightfall we will ride to the hole i am dead you will die anyone who gets too close will be infected with the death on you us we are infected together we will be in the death hole together and the grave dirt will fall in on top of us lalala the dead pull the living down if anyone tries to help you i us we will pull them down and step on them and no one climbs out because the hole is too deep and the dirt falls too fast and everyone who hears your voice will know it is true jude is dead and i am dead and you will die you will hear my our voice and we will ride together on the night road to the place the final place where the wind cries for you for us we will walk to the edge of the hole we will fall in holding each other we will fall sing for us sing at our at your grave sing

lalala

Jude's chest was an airless place, stuck full of icy-hot pins and needles. *Psychological operations,* he thought almost randomly, and then he was angry, the worst kind of angry, the kind that had to stay bottled up, because there was no one around to curse at, and he wouldn't allow himself to break anything. He had already spent a chunk of the morning throwing books, and it hadn't made him feel better. Or not much better any-way. Now, though, he meant to keep himself under control.

He clicked back to the browser, thinking he might have another glance at his search results, see what else he could learn. He looked blankly at the *Pensacola News* obituary one more time, and then his gaze fixed on the photograph. It was a different picture now, and in it Craddock was grin-ning and old, face lined and gaunt, almost starved, and his eyes were scrib-bled over with furious black marks. The first lines of the obituary said that a life of learning and teaching, exploring and adventuring, had ended when Craddock James McDermott died of cerebral embolism at his step-daughter's home and now he was coming lalala and it was cold he was cold Jude would be cold too when he cut himself he was going to cut himself and cut the girl and they would be in the deathhole and Jude could sing for them, sing for all of them—

Jude stood up so quickly, and with such sudden force, that Danny's chair was flung back and toppled over. Then his hands were on the com-puter, under the monitor, and he lifted, heaving it off the desk and onto the floor. It hit with a short, high-pitched kind of chirp and a crunch of breaking glass, followed by a sudden pop of surging electricity. Then quiet. The fan that cooled the motherboard hushed slowly to a stop. He had hurled it instinctively, moving too quickly to think. Fuck it. Self-control was overrated.

His pulse was jacked. He felt shaky and weak in the legs. Where the fuck was Danny? He looked at the wall clock, saw it was almost two, too late in the day for lunch. Maybe he'd gone out on an errand. Usu-ally, though, he paged Jude on the intercom to let him know he was headed out.

Jude came around the desk and finally made it to the window with the view of the drive. Danny's little green Honda hybrid was parked in the dirt turnaround, and Danny was in it. Danny sat perfectly still in the driver's seat, one hand on the steering wheel, his face ashy, rigid, blank.

The sight of him, just sitting there, going nowhere, looking at nothing, had the effect of cooling Jude off. He watched Danny through the window, but Danny didn't do anything. Never put the car in drive to leave. Never so much as glanced around. Danny looked—Jude felt an uneasy throb in his joints at the thought—like a man in a trance. A full minute passed, and then another, and the longer he watched, the more ill at ease Jude felt, the more sick in his bones. Then his hand was on the door and he was letting himself out, to find out what was wrong with Danny.

13

The air was a cold shock that made his eyes water. By the time he got to the side of the car, Jude's cheeks were burning, and the tip of his nose was numb. Although it was going on early afternoon, Jude was still in his worn robe, a muscle shirt, and striped boxers. When the breeze rose, the freezing air burned his bare skin, raw and lacerating.

Danny didn't turn to look at him but went on peering blankly through the windshield. He looked even worse close up. He was shivering, lightly and steadily. A drop of sweat trickled across his cheekbone.

Jude rapped his knuckles on the window. Danny started, as if springing awake from a light doze, blinked rapidly, fumbled for the button to roll down the glass. He still didn't look directly up at Jude.

"What are you doing in your car, Danny?" Jude asked.

"I think I should go home."

"Did you see him?"

Danny said, "I think I should go home now."

"Did you see the dead man? What did he do?" Jude was patient. When he had to be, Jude could be the most patient man on earth.

"I think I have a stomach flu. That's all."

Danny lifted his right hand from his lap to wipe his face, and Jude saw it was clutching a letter opener.

"Don't you lie, Danny," Jude said. "I just want to know what you saw."

"His eyes were black marks. He looked right at me. I wish he didn't look right at me."

"He can't hurt you, Danny."

"You don't know that. You don't know."

Jude reached through the open window to squeeze his shoulder. Danny shrank from his touch. At the same time, he made a whisking gesture at Jude with the letter opener. It didn't come anywhere close to cutting him, but Jude withdrew his hand anyway.

"Danny?"

"Your eyes are just like his," Danny said, and clunked the car into reverse.

Jude jumped back from the car before Danny could back out over his foot. But Danny hesitated, his own foot on the brake.

"I'm not coming back," he said to the steering wheel.

"Okay."

"I'd help you if I could, but I can't. I just can't."

"I understand."

Danny eased the car back down the driveway, tires grinding on the gravel, then turned it ninety degrees and rolled down the hill, toward the road. He watched until Danny passed through the gates, turned left, and disappeared from sight. Jude never saw him again.

14

He set out for the barn and the dogs.

Jude was grateful for the sting of the air on his face and the way each inhalation sent a stunned tingle through his lungs. It was real. Ever since he had seen the dead man that morning, he felt increasingly crowded by unnatural, bad-dream ideas leaking into everyday life where they didn't belong. He needed a few hard actualities to hold on to, clamps to stop the bleeding.

The dogs watched him mournfully as he undid the latch to their pen. He slipped in before they could clamber out past him, and hunkered down, let them climb on him, smell his face. The dogs: They were real, too. He stared back at them, into their chocolate eyes and long, worried faces.

"If there was something wrong with me, you'd see it, wouldn't you?" he asked them. "If there were black marks over my eyes?"

Angus lapped his face, once, twice, and Jude kissed his wet nose. He stroked Bon's back, while she sniffed anxiously at his crotch.

He let himself out. He wasn't ready to go back inside and found his way into the barn instead. He wandered over to the car and had a look at himself in the mirror on the driver's-side door. No black marks. His eyes were the same as always: pale gray under bushy black brows and intense, like he meant murder.

Jude had bought the car in sorry shape from a roadie, a '65 Mustang, the GT fastback. He'd been on tour, almost without rest, for ten months, had gone out on the road almost as soon as his wife left him, and when he came back, he found himself with an empty house and nothing to do. He spent all of July and most of August in the barn, gutting the Mustang, pulling out parts that were rusted, burnt out, shot, dented, corroded, caked in oils and acids, and replacing them: HiPo block, authentic cranks and heads, transmission, clutch, springs, white pony seats— everything original except for the speakers and the stereo. He installed a bazooka bass in the trunk, affixed an XM radio antenna to the roof, and laid in a state-of-the-art digital sound system. He drenched himself in oil, banged knuckles, and bled into the transmission. It was a rough kind of courtship, and it suited him well.

Around that time Anna had come to live with him. Not that he ever called her by that name. She was Florida then, although somehow, since he'd learned of her suicide, he'd come to think of her as Anna again. Maybe you could not have nicknames for the dead.

She sat in the backseat with the dogs while he worked, her boots sticking out a missing window. She sang along with the songs she knew and talked baby talk to Bon and kept at Jude with her questions. She asked him if he was ever going to go bald ("I don't know"), because she'd leave him if he did ("Can't blame you"), and if he'd still think she was sexy if she shaved off all her hair ("No"), and if he'd let her drive the Mustang when it was done ("Yes"), and if he'd ever been in a fistfight ("Try to avoid them—hard to play guitar with a broken hand"), and why he never talked about his parents (to which he said nothing), and if he believed in fate ("No," he said, but he was lying).

Before Anna and the Mustang, he had recorded a new CD, a solo disc, and had traveled to some twenty-four nations, played more than a hundred shows. But working on the car was the first time since Shannon had left him that he felt gainfully employed, doing work that mattered, in the truest sense—although why rebuilding a car should feel like honest work instead of a rich man's hobby, while recording albums and playing arenas had come to seem like a rich man's hobby instead of a job, he couldn't have said.

The idea crossed his mind again that he ought to go. Put the farm in the rearview mirror and take off, it didn't matter for where.

The thought was so urgent, so demanding—*get in the car and get out of here*—that it set his teeth on edge. He resented being made to run. Throwing himself into the car and taking off wasn't a choice, it was panic. This was followed by another thought, disconcerting and unfounded, yet curiously convincing: the thought that he was being herded, that the dead man *wanted* him to run. That the dead man was trying to force him away from . . . from what? Jude couldn't imagine. Outside, the dogs barked in concert at a passing semi.

Anyway, he wasn't going anywhere without talking to Georgia about it. And if he did eventually decide to light out, he would probably want to get dressed beforehand. Yet in another moment he found himself inside the Mustang, behind the wheel. It was a place to think. He'd always done some of his best thinking in the car, with the radio on.

He sat with the window halfway down, in the dark, earth-floored garage, and it seemed to him if there was a ghost nearby, it was Anna, not the angry spirit of her stepfather. She was as close as the backseat. They had made love there, of course. He had gone into the house to get beer and had come back, and she was waiting in the rear of the Mustang in her boots and no more. He dropped the open beers and left them foaming in the dirt. In that moment nothing in the world seemed more important than her firm, twenty-six-year-old flesh, and her twenty-six-year-old sweat, and her laughter, and her teeth on his neck.

He sat in the cold shadow, leaned back against the white leather, feeling his exhaustion for the first time all day. His arms were heavy, and his bare feet were half numb from the cold. The keys were in it, so he clicked the engine over to the battery to run the heat.

Jude was no longer sure why he had climbed into the car, but now that he was sitting, it was hard to imagine moving. From what seemed a long way off, he could hear the dogs barking again, their voices strident and alarmed. He found he could drown them out by switching on the radio.

John Lennon sang "I Am the Walrus." Heat roared from the vents, over Jude's bare legs, and he shivered briefly, then relaxed, let his head rest on the back of the seat. Paul McCartney's slinky bass kept drifting away, getting lost under the low mutter of the Mustang's engine, which was funny, since Jude hadn't turned the engine on, only the battery. The Beatles were followed by a parade of commercials. Lew at Imperial Autos said, "You won't find offers like ours anywhere in the tristate area. We're pulling deals our competition can't come close to matching. The dead pull the living down. Come on in and get behind the wheel of your next ride and take it for a spin on the nightroad. We'll go together. We'll sing together. You won't ever want the trip to end. It won't."

Ads bored Jude, and he found the strength to flip to another channel. On FUM they were playing one of his songs, his very first single, a thunderous AC/DC ripoff titled "Souls for Sale." In the gloom it seemed as if ghostly shapes, unformed wisps of menacing fog, had begun to swirl around the car. He shut his eyes again and listened to the faraway sound of his own voice.

> *More than silver and more than gold,*
> *You say my soul is worth,*
> *Well, I'd like to make it right with God,*
> *But I need beer money first.*

He snorted softly to himself. It wasn't selling souls that got you into trouble, it was buying them. Next time he would have to make sure there was a return policy. He laughed, opened his eyes a little. The dead man, Craddock, sat in the passenger seat next to him. He smiled at Jude, to show crooked and stained teeth and his black tongue. He smelled of death, also of car exhaust. His eyes were hidden behind those odd, continuously moving black brushstrokes.

"No returns, no exchanges," Jude said to him. The dead man nodded sympathetically, and Jude shut his eyes again. Somewhere, miles away, he could hear someone shouting his name.

. . . ude! Jude! Answer me Ju . . .

He didn't want to be bothered, though, was dozy, wanted to be left alone. He cranked the seat back. He folded his hands across his stomach. He breathed deeply.

He had just nodded off when Georgia got him by the arm and hauled him out of the car, dumped him in the dirt. Her voice came in pulses, drifting in and out of audibility.

"*. . . get out of there Jude get the fuck . . .*

. . . on't be dead don't be . . .

. . . leeeeeese, please . . .

. . . eyes open your fucking . . ."

He opened his eyes and sat up in one sudden movement, hacking furiously. The barn door was rolled back, and the sunshine poured through it in brilliant, crystalline beams, solid-looking and sharp-edged. The light stabbed at his eyes, and he flinched from it. He inhaled a deep, cold breath, opened his mouth to say something, to let her know he was all right, and his throat was filled with bile. He rolled onto all fours and retched in the dirt. Georgia had him by the arm and bent over him while he horked up.

Jude was dizzy. The ground tilted underneath him. When he tried to look outside, the world spun, as if it were a picture painted on the side of a vase, turning on a lathe. The house, the yard, the drive, the sky, streamed by him, and a withering sensation of motion sickness rolled through him, and he upchucked again.

He clutched the ground and waited for the world to stop moving. Not that it ever would. That was one thing you found out when you were stoned, or wasted, or feverish: that the world was always turning and that only a healthy mind could block out the sickening whirl of it. He spat, wiped at his mouth. His stomach muscles were sore and cramped, as if he'd just done a few dozen abdominal crunches, which was, when you thought about it, very close to the truth. He sat up, turned himself to look at the Mustang. It was still running. No one was in it.

The dogs danced around him. Angus leaped into his lap and thrust his cold, damp nose into his face, lapped at Jude's sour mouth. Jude was too weak to push him away. Bon, always the shy one, gave Jude an anxious, sidelong look, then lowered her head to the thin gruel of his vomit and covertly began to gobble it up.

He tried to stand, grabbing Georgia's wrist, but didn't have the strength in his legs and instead pulled her down with him, onto her knees. He had a dizzying thought—*the dead pull the living down*—that spun in his head for a moment and was gone. Georgia trembled. Her face was wet against his neck.

"Jude," she said. "Jude, I don't know what's happening to you."

He couldn't find his voice for a minute, didn't have the air yet. He stared at the black Mustang, shuddering on its suspension, the restrained idling force of the engine shaking the entire chassis.

Georgia continued, "I thought you were dead. When I grabbed your arm, I thought you were dead. Why are you out here with the car running and the barn door shut?"

"No reason."

"Did I do something? Did I fuck it up?"

"What are you talking about?"

"I don't know," she said, beginning to cry. "There must be some reason you're out here to kill yourself."

He turned on his knees. He found he was still holding one of her thin wrists, and now he took the other. Her nest of black hair floated around her head, bangs in her eyes.

"Something's wrong, but I wasn't out here trying to kill myself. I sat in the car to warm up, but I didn't turn it on. It turned itself on."

She wrenched her wrists away. "Stop it."

"It was the dead man."

"Stop it. Stop it."

"The ghost from the hall. I saw him again. He was in the car with me. Either he started the Mustang or I started it without knowing what I was doing, because he wanted me to."

"Do you know how crazy that sounds? How crazy all of this sounds?"

"If I'm crazy, then Danny is, too. Danny saw him. That's why he's gone. Danny couldn't hack it. He had to go."

Georgia stared at him, her eyes lucid and bright and fearful behind the soft curl of her bangs. She shook her head in an automatic gesture of denial.

"Let's get out of here," he said. "Help me stand."

She hooked an arm under his armpits and pushed off the floor. His knees were weak springs, all loose bounce and no support. No sooner had he come to his heels than he started to roll forward. He put his hands out to stop his fall and caught himself on the warming hood of the car.

He said, "Shut it off. Get the keys."

Georgia climbed, coughing, waving her hands at the fog of exhaust, into the car, and shut it off. The silence was sudden and alarming.

Bon pressed herself against Jude's leg, looking for reassurance. His knees threatened to fold. He drove her aside with his knee, then put his heel to her ass. She yelped and leaped away.

"Fuck off me," he said.

"Whyn't you leave her be?" Georgia asked. "The both of them saved your life."

"How do you figure?"

"Didn't you hear them? I was coming out to shut them up. They were hysterical."

He regretted kicking Bon then and looked around to see if she was close enough to put a hand on. She had retreated into the barn, though, and was pacing in the dark, watching him with morose and accusing eyes. He wondered about Angus and glanced around for him. Angus stood in the barn door, his back to them, his tail raised. He was staring steadily down the driveway.

"What does he see?" Georgia asked, an absurd thing to ask. Jude had no idea. He stood bracing himself against the car, too far from the sliding barn door to see out into the yard.

Georgia pushed the keys into the pocket of her black jeans. She had dressed somewhere along the line and wrapped her right thumb in bandages. She slipped past Jude and went to stand next to Angus. She ran her hand over the dog's spine, glanced down the drive, then back at Jude.

"What is it?" Jude asked.

"Nothing," she said. She held the right hand against her breastbone and grimaced a little, as if it were paining her. "Do you need help?"

"I'm managing," he said, and shoved off the Mustang. He was conscious of a building black pressure behind his eyeballs, a deep, slow, booming pain that threatened to become one of the all-time great headaches.

At the big sliding barn doors, he paused, with Angus between himself and Georgia. He peered down the drive of frozen mud, to the open gates of his farm. The skies were clearing. The thick, curdled gray cloud cover was coming apart, and the sun blinked irregularly through the rents.

The dead man, in his black fedora, stared back at him from the side of the state highway. He was there for a moment, when the sun was behind a cloud, so that the road was in shadow. He grinned, showing stained teeth. As sunshine fluttered around the edges of a cloud, Craddock flickered away. His head and hands disappeared first, so that only a hollow black suit remained, standing empty. Then the suit disappeared, too. He stammered back into being a moment later, when the sun retreated under cover once more.

He lifted his hat to Jude and bowed, a mocking, oddly southern gesture.

The sun came and went and came again, and the dead man flashed like Morse code.

"Jude?" Georgia asked. He realized he and Angus were standing there staring down the drive in just the same way. "There isn't anything there, is there, Jude?" She didn't see Craddock.

"No," he said. "Nothing there."

The dead man faded back into existence long enough to wink. Then the breeze rose in a soft rush and, high above, the sun broke through for good, at a place where the clouds had been pulled into strings of dirty wool. The light shone strongly on the road, and the dead man was gone.

15

Georgia led him into the music library on the first floor. He did not notice her arm around his waist, supporting and guiding him, until she let go. He sank onto the moss-colored couch, asleep almost as soon as he was off his feet.

He dozed, then woke, briefly, his vision swimmy and unclear, when she bent to lay a throw blanket across him. Her face was a pale circle, featureless, except for the dark line of her mouth and the dark holes where her eyes belonged.

His eyelids sank shut. He could not remember the last time he'd been so tired. Sleep had him, was pulling him steadily under, drowning reason, drowning sense, but as he went down again, that image of Georgia's face swam before him, and he had an alarming thought, that her eyes had been missing, hidden behind black scribbles. She was dead, and she was with the ghosts.

He struggled back toward wakefulness and for a few moments almost made it. He opened his eyes fractionally. Georgia stood in the door to the library, watching him, her little white hands balled into little white fists, and her eyes were her own. He felt a moment of sweet relief at the sight of her.

Then he saw the dead man in the hallway behind her. His skin was pulled tight across the knobs of his cheekbones, and he was grinning to show his nicotine-stained teeth.

Craddock McDermott moved in stop motion, a series of life-size still photographs. In one moment his arms were at his sides. In the next, one of his gaunt hands was on Georgia's shoulder. His fingernails were yellowed and long and curled at the end. The black marks jumped and quivered in front of his eyes.

Time leaped forward again. Abruptly Craddock's right hand was in the air, held high above Georgia's head. The gold chain dropped from it. The pendulum at the end of it, a curved three-inch blade, a slash of silvery brightness, fell before Georgia's eyes. The blade swung in slight arcs before her, and she stared straight at it with eyes that were suddenly wide and fascinated.

Another stop-motion twitch ahead in time and Craddock was bent forward in a frozen pose, his lips at her ear. His mouth wasn't moving, but Jude could just hear the sound of him whispering, a noise like someone sharpening the blade of a knife on a leather strop.

Jude wanted to call to her. He wanted to tell her to watch out, the dead man was right next to her, and she needed to run, to get away, not to listen to him. But his mouth felt wired shut, and he couldn't produce any sound except for a fitful moan. The effort it took even to keep his eyelids open was more than he could sustain, and they rolled shut. He flailed against sleep, but he was weak—an unfamiliar sensation. He went down once more, and this time he stayed down.

Craddock was waiting for him with his razor, even in sleep. The blade dangled at the end of its gold chain before the broad face of a Vietnamese man, who was naked save for a white rag belted around his waist, and seated in a stiff-backed chair in a dank concrete room. The Vietnamese's head had been shaved, and there were shiny pink circles on his scalp, where he'd been burnt by electrodes.

A window looked out on Jude's rainy front yard. The dogs were right up against the glass, close enough so their breath stained it white with condensation. They were yapping furiously, but they were like dogs on TV, with the volume turned all the way down; Jude heard no sound of them at all.

Jude stood quietly in the corner, hoping he would not be seen. The razor moved back and forth in front of the Vietnamese's amazed, sweat-beaded face.

"The soup was poisoned," Craddock said. He was speaking in Vietnamese, but in the way of dreams, Jude understood just what he was saying. "This is the antidote." Gesturing with his free hand at a massive syringe resting inside a black heart-shaped box. In the box with it was a wide-bladed bowie knife with a Teflon handle. "Save yourself."

The VC took the syringe and stuck it, without hesitation, into his own neck. The needle was perhaps five inches long. Jude flinched, looked away.

His gaze leaped naturally to the window. The dogs remained just on the other side of the glass, jumping against it, no sound coming from them. Beyond them Georgia sat on one end of a seesaw. A little tow-headed girl in bare feet and a pretty flowered dress sat on the other end. Georgia and the girl wore blindfolds, diaphanous black scarves made of some sort of crepelike material. The girl's pale yellow hair was tied into a loose ponytail. Her expression was an unreadable blank. Although she looked vaguely familiar to Jude, it was still a long-drawn-out moment before it came to him, with a jolt of recognition, that he was looking at Anna, as she had been at nine or ten. Anna and Georgia went up and down.

"I'm going to try to help you," Craddock was saying, speaking to the prisoner in English now. "You're in trouble, you hear? But I can help you, and all you need to do is listen close. Don't think. Just listen to the sound of my voice. It's almost nightfall. It's almost time. Nightfall is when we turn on the radio and listen to the radio voice. We do what the radio man says to do. Your head is a radio, and my voice is the only broadcast."

Jude looked back, and Craddock wasn't there anymore. In his place, where he had sat, was an old-fashioned radio, the face lit up all in green, and his voice came out of it. "Your only chance to live is to do just as I say. My voice is the only voice you hear."

Jude felt a chill in his chest, didn't like where this was going. He came unstuck and in three steps was at the side of the table. He wanted to rid them of Craddock's voice. Jude grabbed the radio's power cord, where it was plugged in to the wall, and yanked. There was a pop of blue electricity, which stung his hand. He recoiled, throwing the line to the floor. And still the radio chattered on, just as before.

"It's nightfall. It's nightfall at last. Now is the time. Do you see the knife in the box? You can pick it up. It's yours. Take it. Happy birthday to you."

The VC looked with some curiosity into the heart-shaped box and picked out the bowie knife. He turned it this way and that, so the blade flashed in the light.

Jude moved to look down at the face of the radio. His right hand still throbbed from the jolt it had taken, was clumsy, hard to manipulate. He didn't see a power button, so he spun the dial, trying to get away from Craddock's voice. There was a sound Jude at first took for a burst of static, but which in another moment resolved into the steady, atonal hum of a large crowd, a thousand voices chattering all together.

A man with the knowing, streetwise tone of a fifties radio personality said, "Stottlemyre is hypnotizing them today with that twelve-to-six curve-ball of his, and down goes Tony Conigliaro. You've probably heard that you can't make people do things they don't want to do when they've been hypnotized. But you can see here it just isn't true, because you can tell that Tony C. sure didn't want to swing at that last pitch. You can make anyone do any awful thing. You just have to soften them up right. Let me demonstrate what I mean with Johnny Yellowman here. Johnny, the fingers of your right hand are poisonous snakes. Don't let them bite you!"

The VC slammed himself back into his chair, recoiling in shock.

His nostrils flared, and his eyes narrowed, with a sudden look of fierce determination. Jude turned, heel squeaking on the floor, to cry out, to tell him to stop, but before he could speak the Vietnamese prisoner whacked the knife down.

His fingers fell from his hand, only they were the heads of snakes, black, glistening. The VC did not scream. His damp, almond-brown face was lit with something like triumph. He lifted the right hand to show the stumps of his fingers, almost proudly, the blood bubbling out of them, down the inside of his arm.

"This grotesque act of self-mutilation has been brought to you courtesy of orange Moxie. If you haven't tried a Moxie, it's time to step up to the plate and find out why Mickey Mantle says it's the bee's knees. Side retired in order. . . ."

Jude turned, reeled toward the door, tasting vomit in the back of his throat, smelling vomit when he exhaled. At the very periphery of his vision, he could see the window, and the seesaw. It was still going up and down. No one was on it. The dogs lay on their sides, asleep in the grass.

He shoved through the door and banged down two warped steps and into the dusty dooryard behind his father's farm. His father sat with his back to him, on a rock, sharpening his straight razor with a black strop. The sound of it was like the dead man's voice, or maybe it was the other way around, Jude no longer knew for sure. A steel tub of water sat in the grass next to Martin Cowzynski, and a black fedora floated in it. That hat in the water was awful. Jude wanted to scream at the sight of it.

The sunshine was intense and direct on his face, a steady glare. He staggered in the heat, swayed back on his heels, and brought a hand up to shield his eyes from the light. Martin drew the blade across the strop, and blood fell from the black leather in fat drops. When Martin scraped the blade forward, the strop whispered "death." When he jerked the razor back, it made a choked sound like the word "love." Jude did not slow to speak with his father but kept going on around the back of the house.

"Jude," Martin called to him, and Jude flicked a sidelong look at him, couldn't help himself. His father wore a pair of blind man's sunglasses, round black lenses with silver frames. They gleamed when they caught the sunlight. "You need to get back in bed, boy. You're burning up. Where do you think you're going all dressed up like that?"

Jude glanced down and saw he was wearing the dead man's suit. Without breaking stride he began to pull at the buttons of the coat, undoing them as he reeled forward. But his right hand was numb and clumsy—it felt as if he were the one who had just chopped off his fingers—and the buttons wouldn't come free. In a few more steps, he gave up. He felt sick, cooking in the Louisiana sun, boiling in his black suit.

"You look like you're headed to someone's funeral," his father said. "You want to watch out. Could be your'n."

A crow was in the tub of water where the hat had been, and it took off, fanning its wings furiously, throwing spray, as Jude went past it in his stumbling, drunkard's gait. In another step he was at the side of the Mustang. He fell into it, slammed the door behind him.

Through the windshield the hardpack wavered like an image reflected in water, shimmering through the heat. He was sodden with sweat and gasping for breath in the dead man's suit, which was too hot, and too black, and too restricting. Something stank, faintly, of char. The heat was worst of all in his right hand. The feeling in the hand couldn't be described as pain, not anymore. It was, instead, a poisonous weight, swollen not with blood but liquefied ore.

His digital XM radio was gone. In its place was the Mustang's original, factory-installed AM. When he thumbed it on, his right hand was so hot it melted a blurred thumbprint in the dial.

"If there is one word that can change your life, my friends," came the voice on the radio, urgent, melodious, unmistakably southern. "If there is just one word, let me tell you, that word is 'holyeverlastinJesus'!"

Jude rested his hand on the steering wheel. The black plastic immediately began to soften, melting to conform to the shape of his fingers. He watched, dazed, curious. The wheel began to deform, sinking in on itself.

"Yes, if you keep that word in your heart, hold that word to your heart, clasp it to you like you clasp your children, it can save your life, it really can. I believe that. Will you listen to my voice, now? Will you listen only to my voice? Here's another word that can turn your world upside down and open your eyes to the endless possibilities of the living soul. That word is 'nightfall.' Let me say it again. Nightfall. Nightfall at last. The dead pull the living down. We'll ride the glory road together, hallelujah."

Jude took his hand off the wheel and put it on the seat next to him, which began to smoke. He picked the hand up and shook it, but now the smoke was coming out of his sleeve, from the inside of the dead man's jacket. The car was on the road, a long, straight stretch of blacktop, punching through southern jungle, trees strangled in creepers, brush choking the spaces in between. The asphalt was warped and distorted in the distance, through the shimmering, climbing waves of heat.

The reception on the radio fizzed in and out, and sometimes he could hear a snatch of something else, music overlapping the radio preacher, who wasn't really a preacher at all but Craddock using someone else's voice. The song sounded plaintive and archaic, like something off a Folkways record, mournful and sweet at the same time, a single ringing guitar played in a minor key. Jude thought, without sense, *He can talk, but he can't sing*.

The smell in the car was worse now, the smell of wool beginning to sizzle and burn. Jude was beginning to burn. The smoke was coming out both his sleeves now and from under his collar. He clenched his teeth and began to scream. He had always known he would go out this way: on fire. He had always known that rage was flammable, dangerous to store under pressure, where he had kept it his whole life. The Mustang rushed along the unending back roads, black smoke boiling from under the hood, out the windows, so he could hardly see through the fog of it. His eyes stung, blurred, ran with tears. It didn't matter. He didn't need to see where he was going. He put the pedal down.

———

Jude lurched awake, a feeling of unwholesome warmth in his face. He was turned on his side, lying on his right arm, and when he sat up, he couldn't feel the hand. Even awake he could still smell the reek of something burning, an odor like singed hair. He looked down, half expecting to find himself dressed in the dead man's suit, as in his dream. But no; he was still in his tatty old bathrobe.

The suit. The key was the suit. All he had to do was sell it again, the suit and the ghost both. It was so obvious he didn't know why it had taken so long for the idea to occur to him. Someone would want it; maybe lots of people would want it. He'd seen fans kick, spit, bite, and claw over drumsticks that had been thrown into the crowd. He thought they would want a ghost, straight from the home of Judas Coyne, even more. Some hapless asshole would take it off his hands, and the ghost would have to leave. What happened to the buyer after that didn't much trouble Jude's conscience. His own survival, and Georgia's, was a matter that concerned him above all others.

He stood, swaying, flexed his right hand. The circulation was coming back into it, accompanied by a sensation of icy prickling. It was going to hurt like a bitch.

The light was different, had shifted to the other side of the room, pale and weak as it came through the lace curtains. It was hard to say how long he'd been asleep.

The smell, that stink of something burning, lured him down the darkened front hall, through the kitchen, and into the pantry. The door to the backyard patio was open. Georgia was out there, looking miserably cold, in a black denim jacket and a Ramones T-shirt that left the smooth, white curve of her midriff exposed. She had a pair of tongs in her left hand. Her breath steamed in the cold air.

"Whatever you're cooking, you're fuckin' it up," he said, waving his hand at all the smoke.

"No I'm not," she said, and flashed him a proud and challenging smile. She was, in that instant, so beautiful it was a little heartbreaking—the white of her throat, the hollow in it, the delicate line of her just-visible collarbones. "I figured out what to do. I figured out how to make the ghost go away."

"How's that?" Jude asked.

She picked at something with the tongs and then held it up. It was a burning flap of black fabric.

"The suit," she said. "I burned it."

16

An hour later it was dusk. Jude sat in the study to watch the last of the light drain out of the sky. He had a guitar in his lap. He needed to think. The two things went together.

He was in a chair, turned to face a window that looked over the barn, the dog pen, and the trees beyond. Jude had it open on a crack. The air that came in had a crisp bite to it. He didn't mind. It wasn't much warmer in the house, and he needed the fresh air, was grateful for the mid-October perfume of rotten apples and fallen leaves. It was a relief from the reek of exhaust. Even after a shower and a change of clothes, he could still smell it on him.

Jude had his back to the door, and when Georgia came into the room, he saw her in reflection. She had a glass of red wine in each hand. The swaddling of bandages around her thumb forced her to grip one of the glasses awkwardly, and she spilled a little on herself when she sank to her knees beside his chair. She kissed the wine off her skin, then set a glass in front of him, on the amp near his feet.

"He isn't coming back," she said. "The dead man. I bet you. Burning the suit got rid of him. Stroke of genius. Besides, that fucking thing had to go. *Whoo-ee.* I wrapped it in two garbage bags before I brought it downstairs, and I still thought I was going to gag from the stink."

It was in his mind to say, *He wanted you to do it,* but he didn't. It wouldn't do her any good to hear it, and it was over and done with now.

Georgia narrowed her eyes at him, studying his expression. His doubts must've been there in his face, because she said, "You think he'll be back?" When Jude didn't reply, she leaned toward him and spoke again, her voice low, urgent. "Then why don't we go? Get a room in the city and get the hell out of here?"

He considered this, forming his reply slowly, and only with effort. At last he said, "I don't think it would do any good, just to up and run. He isn't haunting the house. He's haunting me."

That was part of it—but only part. The rest was too hard to put into words. The idea persisted that everything to happen so far had happened for reasons—the dead man's reasons. That phrase, "psychological operations," rose to Jude's mind with a feeling of chill. He wondered again if the ghost wasn't trying to make him run, and why that would be. Maybe the house, or something in the house, offered Jude an advantage, although, try as he might, he couldn't figure what.

"You ever think *you* ought to take off?" Jude asked her.

"You almost died today," Georgia said. "I don't know what's happening to you, but I'm not going anywhere. I don't think I'm going to let you out of my sight ever again. Besides, your ghost hasn't done anything to me. I bet he can't touch me."

But Jude had watched Craddock whispering in her ear. He had seen the stricken look on Georgia's face as the dead man held his razor on a chain before her eyes. And he had not forgotten Jessica Price's voice on the telephone, her lazy, poisonous, redneck drawl: *You will not live, and no one who gives you aid or comfort will live.*

Craddock could get to Georgia. She needed to go. Jude saw this clearly now—and yet the thought of sending her away, of waking alone in the night and finding the dead man there, standing over him in the dark, made

him weak with dread. If she left him, Jude felt she might take what remained of his nerve with her. He did not know if he could bear the night
and the quiet without her close—an admission of need that was so stark
and unexpected it gave him a brief, bad moment of vertigo. He was a man
afraid of heights, watching the ground lunge away beneath him, while the
Ferris wheel yanked him helplessly into the sky.

"What about Danny?" Jude said. He thought his own voice sounded
strained and unlike him, and he cleared his throat. "Danny thought he
was dangerous."

"What did this ghost do to Danny? Danny saw something, got scared,
and ran for his life. Wasn't like anything got done to him."

"Just because the ghost *didn't* do anything doesn't mean he *can't*.
Look at what happened to me this afternoon."

Georgia nodded at this. She drank the rest of her wine in one swallow, then met his gaze, her eyes bright and searching. "And you swear
you didn't go into that barn to kill yourself? You swear, Jude? Don't be
mad at me for asking. I need to know."

"Think I'm the type?" he asked.

"Everyone's the type."

"Not me."

"Everyone. I tried to do it. Pills. Bammy found me passed out on the
bathroom floor. My lips were blue. I was hardly breathing. Three days
after my last day of high school. Afterward my mother and father came
to the hospital, and my father said, 'You couldn't even do that right.'"

"Cocksucker."

"Yup. Pretty much."

"Why'd you want to kill yourself? I hope you had a good reason."

"Because I'd been having sex with my daddy's best friend. Since I was
thirteen. This forty-year-old guy with a daughter of his own. People
found out. His daughter found out. She was my friend. She said I ruined
her life. She said I was a whore." Georgia rolled her glass this way and
that in her left hand, watching the glimmer of light move around and

around the rim. "Pretty hard to argue with her. He'd give me things, and I'd always take them. Like, he gave me a brand-new sweater once with fifty dollars in the pocket. He said the money was so I could buy shoes to go with it. I let him fuck me for shoe money."

"Hell. That wasn't any good reason to kill yourself," Jude told her. "It was a good reason to kill him."

She laughed.

"What was his name?"

"George Ruger. He's a used-car salesman now, in my old hometown. Head of the county Republican steering committee."

"Next time I get down Georgia way, I'll stop in and kill the son of a bitch."

She laughed again.

"Or at least thoroughly stomp his ass into the Georgia clay," Jude said, and played the opening bars of "Dirty Deeds."

She lifted his glass of wine off the amp, raised it in a toast to him, and had a sip.

"Do you know what the best thing about you is?" she asked.

"No idea."

"Nothing grosses you out. I mean, I just told you all that, and you don't think I'm . . . I don't know. Ruined. Hopelessly fucked up."

"Maybe I do and I just don't care."

"You care," she said. She put a hand on his ankle. "And nothing shocks you."

He let that pass, did not say he could've guessed the suicide attempt, the father who didn't care, the family friend who molested her, almost from the first moment he saw her, wearing a dog collar, her hair hacked into uneven spikes and her mouth painted in a white lipstick like cake frosting.

She said, "So what happened to you? Your turn."

He twitched his ankle out of her grasp.

"I'm not into feelbad competitions."

He glanced at the window. Nothing remained of the light except for a faint, reddish bronze flush behind the leafless trees. Jude considered his own semitransparent reflection in the glass, his face long, seamed, gaunt, with a flowing black beard that came almost to his chest. A haggard, grim-visaged ghost.

Georgia said, "Tell me about this woman who sent you the ghost."

"Jessica Price. She didn't just send him to me either. Remember, she tricked me into paying for him."

"Right. On eBay or something?"

"No. A different site, a third-rate clone. And it only looked like a regular internet auction. She was orchestrating things from behind the scenes to make sure I'd win." Jude saw the question forming in Georgia's eyes and answered it before she could speak. "Why she went to all that trouble I can't tell you. I get the feeling, though, that she couldn't just mail him to me. I had to agree to take possession of him. I'm sure there's some profound moral message in that."

"Yeah," Georgia said. "Stick with eBay. Accept no substitutes." She tasted some wine, licked her lips, then went on. "And this is all because her sister killed herself? Why does she think that's your fault? Is it because of something you wrote in one of your songs? Is this like when that kid killed himself after listening to Ozzy Osbourne? Have you written anything that says suicide is okay or something?"

"No. Neither did Ozzy."

"Then I don't see why she's so pissed off at you. Did you know each other in some way? Did you know the girl who killed herself? Did she write you crazy fan letters or something?"

He said, "She lived with me awhile. Like you."

"Like me? Oh."

"Got news for you, Georgia. I wasn't a virgin when I met you." His voice sounded wooden and strange to him.

"How long did she live here?"

"I don't know. Eight, nine months. Long enough to overstay her welcome."

She thought about that. "I've been living with you for about nine months."

"So?"

"So have I overstayed mine? Is nine months the limit? Then it's time for some fresh pussy? What, was she a natural blonde, and you decided it was time for a brunette?"

He took his hands off his guitar. "She was a natural psycho, so I threw her ass out. I guess she didn't take it well."

"What do you mean, she was a psycho?"

"I mean manic-depressive. When she was manic, she was a hell of a lay. When she was depressive, it was a little too much work."

"She had mental problems, and you just chucked her out?"

"I didn't sign on to hold her hand the rest of her life. I didn't sign on to hold yours either. I'll tell you something else, Georgia. If you think our story ends 'and they lived happily ever after,' then you've got the wrong fuckin' fairy tale." As he spoke, he became aware that he'd found his chance to hurt her and get rid of her. He had, he understood now, been steering the conversation toward this very moment. The idea recurred that if he could sting her badly enough to make her leave—even if it was just for a while, a night, a few hours—it might be the last good thing he ever did for her.

"What was her name? The girl who killed herself?"

He started to say "Anna" then said "Florida" instead.

Georgia stood quickly, so quickly she tottered, looked as if she might fall over. He could've reached out to steady her but didn't. Better to let her hurt. Her face whitened, and she took an unsteady half step back. She stared at him, bewildered and wounded—and then her eyes sharpened, as if she were suddenly bringing his face into focus.

"No," she breathed softly. "You're not going to drive me away like that. You say any shitty thing you want. I'm sticking, Jude."

She carefully set the glass she was holding on the edge of his desk.

She started away from him, then paused at the door. She turned her head but didn't quite seem able to look into his face.

"I'm going to get some sleep. You come on to bed, too." Telling him, not asking.

Jude opened his mouth to reply and found he had nothing to say. When she left the room, he gently leaned his guitar against the wall and stood up. His pulse was jacked, and his legs were unsteady, the physical manifestations of an emotion it took him some time to place—he was that unused to the sensation of relief.

17

Georgia was gone. That was the first thing he knew. She was gone, and it was still night. He exhaled, and his breath made a cloud of white smoke in the room. He shoved off the one thin sheet and got out of bed, then hugged himself through a brief shivering fit.

The idea that she was up and wandering the house alarmed him. His head was still muddy with sleep, and it had to be close to freezing in the room. It would've been reasonable to think Georgia had gone to figure out what was wrong with the heat, but Jude knew that wasn't it. She'd been sleeping badly as well, tossing and muttering. She might have come awake and gone to watch TV—but he didn't believe that either.

He almost shouted her name, then thought better of it. He quailed at the idea that she might not reply, that his voice might be met with a ringing silence. No. No yelling. No rushing around. He felt if he went slamming out of the bedroom and rushing through the unlit house, calling for her, it would tip him irrevocably toward panic. Also, the darkness and quiet of the bedroom appalled him, and he understood that he was afraid to go looking for her, afraid of what might be waiting beyond the door.

As he stood there, he became aware of a guttural rumble, the sound of an idling engine. He rolled his eyes back, looked at the ceiling. It was lit an icy white, someone's headlights, pointing in from the driveway below. He could hear the dogs barking.

Jude crossed to the window and shifted aside the curtain.

The pickup parked out front had been blue once, but it was at least twenty years old and had not seen another coat in all that time, had faded to the color of smoke. It was a Chevy, a working truck. Jude had whiled away two years of his life twisting a wrench in an auto garage for $1.75 an hour, and he knew from the deep, ferocious mutter of the idling engine that it had a big block under the hood. The front end was all aggression and menace, with a wide silver bumper like a boxer's mouthpiece and an iron brush guard bolted over the grill. What he had taken at first for headlights were a pair of floods attached to the brush guard, two round spots pouring their glare into the night. The pickup sat almost a full foot off the ground on four 35s, a truck built for running on washed-out swamp roads, banging through the ruts and choking brush of the Deep South, the bottoms. The engine was running. No one was in it.

The dogs flung themselves against the chain link wall of the pen, a steady crash and clang, yapping at the empty pickup. Jude peered down the driveway, in the direction of the road. The gates were closed. You had to know a six-digit security code to get them open.

It was the dead man's truck. Jude knew the moment he saw it, knew with a calm, utter certainty. His next thought was, *Where we going, old man?*

The phone by the bed chirped, and Jude half jumped in surprise, letting go of the curtain. He turned and stared. The clock beside the phone read 3:12. The phone rang again.

Jude moved toward it, tiptoeing quickly across cold floorboards. Stared down at it. It rang a third time. He didn't want to answer. He had an idea it would be the dead man, and Jude didn't want to talk to him. Jude didn't want to hear Craddock's voice.

"Fuck it," he said, and he answered. "Who is it?"

"Hey, Chief. It's Dan."

"Danny? It's three in the morning."

"Oh. I didn't know it was so late. Were you asleep?"

"No." Jude fell silent, waited.

"I'm sorry I left like I did."

"Are you drunk?" Jude asked. He looked at the window again, the blue-tinted glare of the floodlights shining around the edges of the curtains. "Are you calling drunk because you want your job back? Because if you are, this is the wrong fuckin' time—"

"No. I can't . . . I can't come back, Jude. I was just calling to say I'm sorry about everything. I'm sorry I said anything about the ghost for sale. I should've kept my mouth shut."

"Go to bed."

"I can't."

"What the fuck is wrong with you?"

"I'm out walking in the dark. I don't even know where I am."

Jude felt the back of his arms prickling with goose bumps. The thought of Danny out on the streets somewhere, shuffling around in the dark, disturbed him more than it should've, more than made sense.

"How'd you get there?"

"I just went walking. I don't even know why."

"Jesus, you're drunk. Take a look around for a street sign and call a fuckin' cab," Jude said, and hung up.

He was glad to let go of the phone. He hadn't liked Danny's tone of spaced-out, unhappy confusion.

It wasn't that Danny had said anything so incredible or unlikely. It was just that they'd never had a conversation like it before. Danny had never called in the night, and he'd never called drunk. It was difficult to imagine him going for a walk at 3:00 A.M., or walking so far from his home as to get lost. And whatever his other flaws, Danny was a problem solver. That was why Jude had kept him on the payroll for eight years. Even shitfaced, Danny probably wouldn't call Jude first if he didn't know where he was. He'd walk to a 7-Eleven and get directions. He'd flag down a cop car.

No. It was all wrong. The phone call and the dead man's truck in the driveway were two parts of the same thing. Jude knew. His nerves told him so. The empty bed told him so.

He glanced again at the curtain, lit from behind by those floods. The dogs were going crazy out there.

Georgia. What mattered now was finding Georgia. Then they could figure out about that truck. Together they could get a handle on the situation.

Jude looked at the door to the hallway. He flexed his fingers, his hands numb from the cold. He didn't want to go out there, didn't want to open the door and see Craddock sitting in that chair with his hat on his knee and that razor on a chain dangling from one hand.

But the thought of seeing the dead man again—of facing whatever was next—held him for only a moment more. Then he came unstuck, went to the door, and opened it.

"Let's do it," he said to the hallway before he had even seen if anyone was there.

No one was.

Jude paused, listening past his own just slightly haggard breathing to the quiet of the house. The long hall was draped in shadows, the Shaker chair against the wall empty. No. Not empty. A black fedora rested in the seat.

Noises—muffled and distant—caught his attention: the murmur of voices on a television, the distant crash of surf. He pulled his gaze away from the fedora and looked to the end of the hallway. Blue light flickered and raced at the edges of the door to the studio. Georgia was in there, then, watching TV after all.

Jude hesitated at the door, listening. He heard a voice shouting in Spanish, a TV voice. The sound of surf was louder. Jude meant to call her name then, Marybeth—not Georgia, Marybeth—but something bad happened when he tried: His breath gave out on him. He was able to produce only a wheeze in the faint sound of her name.

He opened the door.

Georgia was across the room in the recliner, in front of his flat-screen TV. From where he stood, he couldn't see anything of her but the back of her head, the fluffy swirl of her black hair surrounded by a nimbus of unnatural blue light. Her head also largely blocked the view of whatever was on the TV, although he could see palm trees and tropical blue sky. It was dark, the lights in the room switched off.

She didn't respond when he said, "Georgia," and his next thought was that she was dead. When he got to her, her eyes would be rolled up in their sockets.

He started toward her, but had gone only a couple of steps when the phone rang on the desk.

Jude could view enough of the TV now to see a chubby Mex in sunglasses and a beige jogging suit, standing at the side of a dirt track in jungly hill country somewhere. Jude knew what she was watching then, although he hadn't looked at it in several years. It was the snuff film.

At the sound of the phone, Georgia's head seemed to move just slightly, and he thought he heard her exhale, a strained, effortful breath. Not dead, then. But she didn't otherwise react, didn't look around, didn't get up to answer.

He took a step to the desk, caught the phone on the second ring.

"That you, Danny? Are you still lost?" Jude asked.

"Yeah," Danny said with a weak laugh. "Still lost. I'm on this pay phone in the middle of nowhere. It's funny, you almost never see pay phones anymore."

Georgia did not glance around at the sound of Jude's voice, did not shift her gaze from the TV.

"I hope you aren't calling because you want me to come looking for you," Jude said. "I've got my hands full at the moment. If I have to come looking for you, you better hope you stay lost."

"I figured it out, Chief. How I got here. Out on this road in the dark."

"How's that?"

"I killed myself. I hung myself a few hours ago. This road in the dark . . . this is dead."

Jude's scalp crawled, a trickling, icy sensation, almost painful.

Danny said, "My mother hung herself just the same way. She did a better job, though. She broke her neck. Died instantly. I lost my nerve at the last second. I didn't fall hard enough. I strangled to death."

From the television across the room came gagging sounds, as if someone were strangling to death.

"It took a long time, Jude," Danny went on. "I remember swinging for a long time. Looking at my feet. I'm remembering lots of things now."

"Why'd you do it?"

"He made me. The dead man. He came to see me. I was going to come back to the office and find those letters for you. I was thinking I could at least do that much. I was thinking I shouldn't have bailed out on you like I did. But when I went in my bedroom to get my coat, he was waiting there. I didn't even know how to knot a noose until he showed me," Danny said. "That's how he's going to get you. He's going to make you kill yourself."

"No he's not."

"It's hard not to listen to his voice. I couldn't fight it. He knew too much. He knew I gave my sister the heroin she OD'd on. He said that was why my mother killed herself, because she couldn't live knowing what I had done. He said I should've been the one to hang, not my mom. He said if I had any decency, I would've killed myself a long time ago. He was right."

"No, Danny," Jude said. "No. He wasn't right. You shouldn't—"

Danny sounded short of breath. "I did. I *had* to. There was no arguing with him. You can't argue with a voice like that."

"We'll see," Jude said.

Danny had no reply for that. In the snuff film, two men were bickering in Spanish. The choking sounds went on and on. Georgia still did not look away. She was moving just slightly, shoulders hitching now and then in a series of random, almost spastic shrugs.

"I have to go, Danny." Still Danny said nothing. Jude listened to the faint crackle on the line for a moment, sensing that Danny was waiting for something, some final word, and at last he added, "You keep walking, boy. That road must go somewhere."

Danny laughed. "You aren't as bad as you think, Jude. You know that?"

"Yeah. Don't tell."

"Your secret is safe," Danny said. "Good-bye."

"Good-bye, Danny."

Jude leaned forward, gently set the phone back in its cradle. As he was bent across the desk, he glanced down and behind it and saw that the floor safe was open. His initial thought was the ghost had opened it, an idea he discarded almost immediately. Georgia, more likely. She knew the combination.

He pivoted, looked at the back of her head, at the halo of flickering blue light, at the television beyond.

"Georgia? What are you doin', darlin'?"

She didn't reply.

He came forward, moving silently across the thick carpet. The picture on the flat-screen came into view first. The killers were finishing off the skinny white kid. Later they would get his girlfriend in a cinder-block hut close to a beach. Now, though, they were on an overgrown track somewhere in the bush, in the hills above the Gulf of California. The kid was on his stomach, his wrists bound together by a pair of white plastic flexi-cuffs. His skin was fish-belly pale in the equatorial sunlight. A diminutive, wall-eyed Anglo, with a clownish Afro of crinkly red hair, stood with one cowboy boot on the kid's neck. Parked down the road was a black van, the back doors thrown open. Next to the rear fender was the chubby Mex in the warm-up suit, an affronted expression hung on his face.

"Nos estamos yendo," said the man in the sunglasses. "Ahora."

The wall-eyed redhead made a face and shook his head, as if in disagreement, but then pointed the little revolver at the skinny kid's head and pulled the trigger. The muzzle flashed. The kid's head snapped forward, hit the ground, bounced back. The air around his head was suddenly clouded with a fine spray of blood.

The Anglo took his boot off the boy's neck and stepped daintily away, careful to get no blood on his cowboy boots.

Georgia's face was a pale, rigid blank, her eyes wide and unblinking, gaze fixed on the television. She wore the Ramones T-shirt she'd had on earlier, but no underwear, and her legs were open. In one hand—the bad hand—she had clumsy hold of Jude's pistol, and the barrel was pushed deep into her mouth. Her other hand was between her legs, thumb moving up and down.

"Georgia," he said, and for an instant she shot a sidelong glance at him—a helpless, pleading glance—then immediately looked back to the TV. Her bad hand rotated the gun, turning it upside down, to point the barrel against the roof of her mouth. She made a weak choking sound on it.

The remote control was on the armrest. Jude hit the power button. The television blinked off. Her shoulders leaped, a nervous, reflexive shrug. The left hand kept working between her legs. She shivered, made a strained, unhappy sound in her throat.

"Stop it," Jude said.

She pulled the hammer back with her thumb. It made a loud snap in the silence of the studio.

Jude reached past her and gently pried the gun out of her grip. Her whole body went abruptly, perfectly still. Her breath whistled, short and fast. Her mouth was wet, glistening faintly, and it came to him then that he was semihard. His cock had begun to stiffen at the smell of her in the air and the sight of her fingers teasing her clit, and she was at just the right height. If he moved in front of the chair, she could suck his dick while he held the gun to her head, he could stick the barrel in her ear while he shoved his cock—

He saw a flicker of motion, reflected in the partly open window beyond his desk, and his gaze jumped to the image in the glass. He could see himself there and the dead man standing beside him, hunched and whispering in his ear. In the reflection Jude could see that his own arm had come up, and he was holding the pistol to Georgia's head.

His heart lurched, all the blood rushing to it in a sudden, adrenalized burst. He looked down, saw it was true, he was holding the gun to her head, saw his finger squeezing the trigger. He tried to stop himself, but it was already too late—he pulled it, waited in horror for the hammer to fall.

It didn't fall. The trigger wouldn't depress the last quarter inch. The safety was on.

"Fuck," Jude hissed, and lowered the gun, trembling furiously now. He used his thumb to ease the hammer back down. When he had settled it into place, he flung the pistol away from himself.

It banged heavily against the desk, and Georgia flinched at the sound, cried out softly. Her stare, however, remained fixed on some abstract point off in the darkness before her.

Jude turned, looking for Craddock's ghost. No one stood beside him. The room was empty, except for himself and Georgia. He turned back to her and tugged on her slender white wrist.

"Get up," he said. "Come on. We're going. Right now. I don't know where we're going, but we're getting out of here. We're going someplace where there are lots of people and bright lights, and we're going to try to figure this out. You hear me?" He could no longer recall his logic for staying. Logic was out the window.

"He isn't done with us," she said, her voice a shuddering whisper.

He pulled, but she didn't rise, her body rigid in the chair, uncooperative. She still wouldn't look at him, wouldn't look anywhere except straight ahead.

"Come on," he said. "While there's time."

"There is no more time," she said.

The television blinked on again.

♥ 18

It was the evening news. Bill Beutel, who had started his journalism career when the assassination of Archduke Ferdinand was the breaking story of the day, sat stiffly behind the news desk. His face was a network of spiderweb wrinkles, radiating out from around his eyes and the corners of his mouth. His features were set in their grief expression, the look that said there was more bad news in the Middle East or that a school bus had gone off the interstate and rolled, killing all passengers, or a tornado in the South had inhaled a trailer park and coughed out a mess of ironing boards, splintered shutters, and human bodies.

". . . there will be no survivors. We'll bring you more as the situation continues to unfold," Beutel said. He turned his head slightly, and the reflected blue screen of the teleprompter floated in the lenses of his bifocals for a moment. "Late this afternoon the Dutchess County sheriff's department confirmed that Judas Coyne, the popular lead singer of Jude's Hammer, apparently shot and killed his girlfriend, Marybeth Stacy Kimball, before turning the weapon on himself to take his own life."

The program cut to video of Jude's farmhouse, framed against a sky of dingy, featureless white. Police cruisers had parked haphazardly in the turnaround, and an ambulance stood backed up almost to the door of Danny's office.

Beutel continued to speak in voice-over: "Police are only beginning to piece together the picture of Coyne's last days. But statements from those who knew him suggest he had been distraught and was worried about his own mental health."

The footage jumped to a shot of the dogs in their pen. They were stretched out on their sides in the short, stubbly grass, neither of them moving, legs stretched stiffly away from their bodies. They were dead. Jude tightened up at the sight of them. It was a bad thing to see. He wanted to look away but couldn't seem to pry his gaze free.

"Detectives also believe that Coyne played a role in the death of his personal assistant, Daniel Wooten, thirty, who was found in his Woodstock home earlier this morning, also an apparent suicide."

Cut to two paramedics, one at either end of a sagging blue plastic body bag. Georgia made a soft, unhappy sound in her throat, watching one of the paramedics climb backward into the ambulance, hefting his end.

Beutel began to talk about Jude's career, and they cut away to file footage of Jude onstage in Houston, a clip six years old. Jude was in black jeans and black steel-toed boots, but bare-chested, his torso glowing with sweat, the bearish fur on it plastered to his breast, stomach heaving. A sea of a hundred thousand half-naked people surged below him, a rioting flood of raised fists, crowd surfers tumbling this way and that along the flow of humanity beneath.

Dizzy was already dying by then, although at the time almost no one except Jude knew. Dizzy with his heroin addiction and his AIDS. They played back-to-back, Dizzy's mane of blond hair in his face, the wind blowing it across his mouth. It was the last year the band had been together. Dizzy died, and Jerome, and then it was over.

In the file footage, they were playing the title song off their last album as a group, "Put You in Yer Place", their last hit, the last really good song Jude had written, and at the sound of those drums—a furious cannonade—he was jolted free from whatever hold the television seemed to have over him. That had been real. Houston had happened, that day had happened. The engulfing, mad rush of the crowd below and the engulfing, mad rush of the music around him. It was real, it had happened, and all the rest was—

"Bullshit," Jude said, and his thumb hit the power button. The television popped off.

"It isn't true," Georgia said, her voice hardly more than a whisper. "It isn't true, is it? Are we . . . are you . . . Is that going to happen to us?"

"No," Jude said.

And the television popped back on. Bill Beutel sat behind the news desk again, a sheaf of papers clasped in his hands, his shoulders squared to the camera.

"Yes," Bill said. "You will both be dead. The dead pull the living down. You will get the gun, and she will try to get away, but you will catch her, and you will—"

Jude hit the power button again, then threw the remote control at the screen of the television. He went after it, put his foot on the screen and then straightened his leg, shoved the television straight through the open back of the cabinet. It hit the wall, and something flared, a white light going off like a flashbulb. The flat-screeen dropped out of sight into the space between cabinet and TV, hit with a crunch of plastic and a short, electrical, fizzing sound that lasted for only a moment before ending. Another day of this and there would be nothing left to the house.

He turned, and the dead man stood behind Georgia's chair. Craddock's ghost reached around the back, to cup her head between his hands. Black lines danced and shimmered before the old man's eye sockets.

Georgia did not try to move or look around, was as still as a person faced with a poisonous snake, afraid to do anything—even to breathe—for fear of being struck.

"You didn't come for her," Jude said. As he spoke, he was stepping to the left, circling along one side of the room and toward the doorway to the hall. "You don't want her."

In one instant Craddock's hands were gently cradling Georgia's head. In the next his right arm had come up to point out and away from his body: *Seig heil.* Around the dead man, time had a way of skipping, a scratched DVD, the picture stuttering erratically from moment to moment, without any transitions in between. The golden chain fell from his raised right hand. The razor, shaped like a crescent moon, gleamed brilliantly at the end. The edge of the blade was faintly iridescent, the way a rainbow slick of oil is on water.

Time to ride Jude.

"Go away," Jude said.

If you want me to go, you just have to listen to my voice. You have to listen hard. You have to be like a radio, and my voice is the broadcast. After nightfall it's nice to have some radio. If you want this to end, you have to listen hard as you can. You have to want it to end with all your heart. Don't you want it to end?

Jude tightened his jaw, clamped his teeth together. He wasn't going to answer, sensed somehow it would be a mistake to give any reply, then was startled to find himself nodding slowly.

Don't you want to listen hard? I know you do. I know. Listen. You can tune out the whole world and hear nothing but my voice. Because you are listening so hard.

And Jude went on nodding, bobbing his head slowly up and down, while around him all the other sounds of the room fell away. Jude had not even been aware of these other noises until they were gone: the low rumble of the truck idling outside, the thin whine of Georgia's breath in her throat, matched by Jude's own harsh gasping. His ears rang at the sudden utter absence of sound, as if his eardrums had been numbed by a shattering explosion.

The naked razor swayed in little arcs, back and forth, back and forth. Jude dreaded the sight of it, forced himself to look away.

You don't need to look at it, Craddock told him. *I'm dead. I don't need a pendulum to get inside your mind. I'm there already.*

And Jude found his gaze sliding back to it anyway, couldn't help himself.

"Georgia," Jude said, or tried to say. He felt the word on his lips, in his mouth, in the shape of his breath, but did not hear his own voice, did not hear anything in that awful, enveloping silence. He had never heard any noise as loud as that particular silence.

I am not going to kill her. No, sir, said the dead man. His voice never varied in tone, was patient, understanding, a low, resonant hum that brought to mind the sound of bees in the hive. *You are. You will. You want to.*

Jude opened his mouth to tell him how wrong he was, said, "Yes," instead. Or assumed he said it. It was more like a loud thought.

Craddock said, *Good boy.*

Georgia was beginning to cry, although she was making a visible effort to hold herself still, not to tremble. Jude couldn't hear her. Craddock's blade slashed back and forth, whisking through the air.

I don't want to hurt her, don't make me hurt her, Jude thought.

It ain't going to be the way you want it. Get the gun, you hear? Do it now.

Jude began to move. He felt subtly disconnected from his body, a witness, not a participant in the scene playing itself out. He was too empty-headed to dread what he was about to do. He knew only that he had to do it if he wanted to wake up.

But before he reached the gun, Georgia was out of the chair and bolting for the door. He didn't have any idea she could move, thought that Craddock had been holding her there somehow, but it had just been fear holding her, and she was already almost by him.

Stop her, said the only voice left in the world, and as she lunged past him, Jude saw himself catch her hair in one fist and snap her head back. She was wrenched off her feet. Jude pivoted and threw her down. The furniture jumped when she hit the floor. A stack of CDs on an end table slid off and crashed to the floor without a sound. Jude's foot found her stomach, a good hard kick, and she jerked herself into a fetal position. The moment after he'd done it, he didn't know why he'd done it.

There you go, said the dead man.

It disoriented Jude, the way the dead man's voice came at him out of the silence, words that had an almost physical presence, bees whirring and chasing one another around the inside of his head. His head was the hive that they flew into and out of, and without them there was a waxy, honeycombed emptiness. His head was too light and too hollow, and he would go mad if he didn't get his own thoughts back, his own voice. The dead man was saying now, *You need to show that cunt. If you don't mind me sayin' so. Now get the gun. Hurry.*

Jude turned to get the gun, moving quickly now. Across the floor, to the desk, the gun at his feet, down on one knee to pick it up.

Jude did not hear the dogs until he was reaching for the revolver. One high-strung yap, then another. His attention snagged on that sound like a loose sleeve catching on a protruding nail. It shocked him, to hear anything else in that bottomless silence besides Craddock's voice. The window behind the desk was still parted slightly, as he had left it. Another bark, shrill, furious, and another. Angus. Then Bon.

Come on now, boy. Come on and do it.

Jude's gaze flitted to the little wastebasket next to the desk and to the pieces of the platinum record shoved into it. A nest of chrome knife blades sticking straight up into the air. The dogs were both barking in unison now, a tear in the fabric of the quiet, and the sound of them called to mind, unbidden, their smell, the stink of damp dog fur, the hot animal reek of their breath. Jude could see his face reflected in one of those silver record shards, and it jolted him: his own rigid, staring look of desperation, of horror. And in the next moment, mingled with the relentless yawping of the dogs, he had a thought that was his own, in his own voice. *The only power he has, over either one of you, is the power you give him.*

In the next instant, Jude reached past the gun and put his hand over the wastebasket. He set the ball of his left palm on the sharpest, longest-looking spear of silver and lunged, driving all his weight down onto it. The blade sank into meat, and he felt a tearing pain lance through his hand and into the wrist. Jude cried out, and his eyes blurred, stung with tears. He instantly yanked his palm free from the blade, then clapped his right hand and the left together. Blood spurted between them.

What the fuck are you doin' to yourself, boy? Craddock's ghost asked him, but Jude wasn't listening anymore. Couldn't pay attention through the feeling in his hand, a sensation of having been deeply pierced, almost to the bone.

I'm not through with you, Craddock said, but he was, he just didn't know it. Jude's mind reached for the sound of the barking dogs like a drowning man grasping at a life preserver, found it and clasped it to him. He was on his feet, and he began to move.

Get to the dogs. His life—and Georgia's—depended on it. It was an idea that made no rational sense, but Jude did not care what was rational. Only what was true.

The pain was a red ribbon he held between his hands, following it away from the dead man's voice and back to his own thoughts. He had a great tolerance for pain, always had, and at other times in his life had even willfully sought it out. There was an ache way down in his wrist, in the joint, a sign of how deep his wound was, and some part of him appreciated that ache, wondered at it. He caught sight of his reflection in the window as he rose. He was grinning in the straggles of his beard, a vision even worse than the expression of terror he'd glimpsed in his own face a moment before.

Get back here, said Craddock, and Jude slowed for an instant, then found his step and kept on.

He shot a look at Georgia on his way by—couldn't risk a glance back to see what Craddock was doing—and she was still curled on the floor, her arms around her stomach and her hair in her face. She glanced back at him from under her bangs. Her cheeks were damp with sweat. Her eyelids fluttered. The eyes beneath pleaded, questioned, fogged over with pain.

He wished there were time to say he hadn't meant to hurt her. He wanted to tell her that he wasn't running, wasn't leaving her, that he was leading the dead man away, but the pain in his hand was too intense. He couldn't think past it to line words up into clear sentences. And besides, he didn't know how long he'd be able to think for himself, before Craddock would get a hold of him again. He had to control the pace of what happened next, and it had to happen fast. That was fine. It was better that way. He had always been at his best operating in 5/4 time.

He heaved himself down the hall, made the stairs and took them fast, too fast almost, four at a time, so it was like falling. He crashed down the last few steps to the red clay tiles of the kitchen. One ankle turned under him. He stumbled into the chopping block, with its slender legs and scarred surface stained with old blood. A cleaver was buried in the soft wood at one edge, and the wide, flat blade glinted like liquid mercury in the dark. He saw the stairs behind him reflected in it and Craddock standing on them, his features blurred, his hands raised over his head, palms out, a tent revival preacher testifying to the flock.

Stay, Craddock said. *Get the knife.* But Jude concentrated on the throbbing in the palm of his hand. It was the deep hurt of pierced muscle and had the effect of clearing his head and centering him. The dead man couldn't make Jude do what he wanted if Jude was in too much pain to hear him. He shoved himself back from the chopping block, and his momentum carried him away from it and down the length of the kitchen.

He hit the door into Danny's office, pushed through it, and rushed on into darkness.

19

Three steps through the door, he pulled up, hesitated for a moment to get his bearings. The shades were drawn. There was no light anywhere. He could not see his way in all that darkness and had to move forward more slowly, shuffling his feet, hands stretched before him, feeling for objects that might be in his path. The door wasn't far, and then he would be outside.

As he went forward, though, he felt an anxious constriction in his chest. It was a little more work to breathe than he liked. He felt at any moment his hands would settle on Craddock's cold, dead face in the dark. At the thought he found himself fighting not to panic. His elbow struck a standing lamp, and it crashed over. His heart throbbed. He kept moving his feet forward in halting baby steps, but he had no sense of getting any closer to where he was going.

A red eye, the eye of a cat, opened slowly in the darkness. The speakers that flanked the stereo cabinet came on with a thump of bass and a low, empty hum. The constriction was around Jude's heart, a sickening tightness. *Keep breathing,* he told himself. *Keep moving. He's going to try to stop you from getting outside.* The dogs barked and barked, voices rough, strained, not far away now.

The stereo was on, and there should've been radio, but there was no radio. There was no sound at all. Jude's fingers brushed the wall, the doorframe, and then he grasped the doorknob with his punctured left hand. An imaginary sewing needle turned slowly in the wound, producing a cold flare of pain.

Jude twisted the doorknob, pulled the door back. A slash opened in the darkness, looking out into the glare of the floodlights on the front of the dead man's truck.

"You think you're something special because you learnt how to play a fuckin' guitar?" said Jude's father from the far end of the office. He was on the stereo, his voice loud and hollow.

In the next moment, Jude became aware of other sounds coming from the speakers—heavy breathing, scuffling shoes, the thud of someone bumping a table—noises that suggested a quiet, desperate wrestling match, two men struggling with each other. There was a little radio play going. It was a play Jude knew well. He had been one of the actors in the original.

Jude stopped with the door half open, unable to plunge out into the night, pinned in place by the sounds coming from the office stereo.

"You think knowin' how to do that makes you better than me?" Martin Cowzynski, his tone amused and hating all at the same time. "Get over here."

Then came Jude's own voice. No, not Jude's voice—he hadn't been Jude then. It was Justin's, a voice in a slightly higher octave, one that cracked sometimes and lacked the resonance that had come with the development of his adult pipes. "Momma! Momma, help!"

Momma did not say anything, did not make a sound, but Jude remembered what she'd done. She had stood up from the kitchen table and walked to the room where she did her sewing and gently closed the door behind her, without daring to look at either of them. Jude and his mother had never helped each other. When they needed it most, they had never dared.

"I said get the fuck over here," Martin told him.

The sound of someone knocking into a chair. The sound of the chair banging against the floor. When Justin cried out again, his voice wavered with alarm.

"Not my hand! No, Dad, not my hand!"

"Show you," his father said.

And there came a great booming sound, like a door slamming, and Justin-the-boy-on-the-radio screamed and screamed again, and at the sound of it Jude pitched himself out into the night air.

He missed a step, stumbled, dropped to his knees in the frozen mud of the driveway. Picked himself up, took two running steps, and stumbled again. Jude fell onto all fours in front of the dead man's pickup. He stared over the front fender at the brutal framework of the brush guard and the floodlights attached to it.

The front of a house or a car or a truck could sometimes look like a face, and so it was with Craddock's Chevy. The floodlights were the bright, blind, staring eyes of the deranged. The chrome bar of the fender was a leering silver mouth. Jude expected it to lunge at him, tires spinning on the gravel, but it didn't.

Bon and Angus leaped against the chain link walls of their pen, barking relentlessly—deep, throaty roars of terror and rage, the eternal, primitive language of dogs: *See my teeth, stay back or you will feel them, stay back, I am worse than you.* He thought for an instant they were barking at the truck, but Angus was looking past him. Jude glanced back to see at what. The dead man stood in the door to Danny's office. Craddock's ghost lifted his black fedora, set it carefully on his head.

Son. You come on back here, son, the dead man said, but Jude was trying not to listen to him, was concentrating intently on the sound of the dogs. Since their barking had first disrupted the spell he'd been under, up in the studio, it had seemed like the most important thing in the world to get to them, although he could not have explained to anyone, including himself, why it mattered so. Only that when he heard their voices, he remembered his own.

Jude hauled himself up off the gravel, ran, fell, got up, ran again, tripped at the edge of the driveway, came crashing down on his knees once more. He crawled through the grass, didn't have the strength in his legs to launch himself onto his feet again. The cold air stung in the pit of his wounded hand.

He glanced back. Craddock was coming. The golden chain dropped from his right hand. The blade at the end of it began to swing, a silver slash, a streak of brilliance tearing at the night. The gleam and flash fascinated Jude. He felt his gaze sticking to it, felt the thought draining out of him—and in the next instant he crawled straight into the chain-link fence with a crash and dropped to his side. Rolled onto his back.

He was up against the swinging door that held the pen shut. Angus banged into the other side, eyes turned up in his head. Bon stood rigidly behind him, barking with a steady, shrill insistency. The dead man walked toward them.

Let's ride, Jude, said the ghost. *Let's go for a ride on the nightroad.*

Jude felt himself going empty, felt himself surrendering to that voice again, to the sight of that silver blade cutting back and forth through the dark.

Angus hit the chain-link fence so hard he bounced off it and fell on his side. The impact brought Jude out of his trance again.

Angus.

Angus wanted out. He was already back on his feet, barking at the dead man, scrabbling his paws against the chain link.

And Jude had a thought then, wild, half formed, remembered something he had read yesterday morning, in one of his books of occultism. Something about animal familiars. Something about how they could deal with the dead directly.

The dead man stood at Jude's feet. Craddock's gaunt, white face was rigid, fixed in an expression of contempt. The black marks shivered before his eyes.

You listen, now. You listen to the sound of my voice.

"I've heard enough," Jude said.

He reached up and behind him found the latch to the pen, released it.

Angus hit the gate an instant later. It crashed open, and Angus leaped at the dead man, making a sound Jude had never heard from his dog before, a choked and gravelly snarl that came from the deep barrel of his chest. Bon shot past a moment later, her black lips drawn back to show her teeth and her tongue lolling.

The dead man took a reeling step backward, his face confused. In the seconds that followed, Jude found it difficult to make sense of what he was actually seeing. Angus leaped at the old man—only it seemed in that instant that Angus was not one dog but two. The first was the lean, powerfully built German shepherd he'd always been. But attached to this shepherd was an inky darkness in the shape of a dog, flat and featureless but somehow solid, a living shadow.

Angus's material body overlapped this shadow form, but not perfectly. The shadow dog showed around the edges, especially in the area of Angus's snout—and gaping mouth. This second, shadowy Angus struck the dead man a fraction of an instant ahead of the real Angus, coming at him from his left-hand side, away from the hand with the gold chain and the swinging silver blade. The dead man cried out—a choked, furious cry—and was *spun*, staggered backward. He shoved Angus off him, clipped him across the snout with an elbow. Only no; it wasn't Angus he was shoving, it was that other, black dog that dipped and leaned like a shadow thrown by candle flame.

Bon launched herself at Craddock's other side. Bon was two dogs as well, had a wavering shadow twin of her own. As she leaped, the old man snapped the gold chain at her, and the crescent-shaped silver blade whined in the air. It passed through Bon's front right leg, up around the shoulder, without leaving a mark. But then it sank into the black dog attached to her, snagged its leg. The shadow Bon was caught and, for one moment, pulled a little out of shape, deformed into something not quite dog, not quite . . . anything. The blade came loose, snapped back to the dead man's hand. Bon yelped, a horrid, piercing shout of pain. Jude did not know which version of Bon did the yelping, the shepherd or the shadow.

Angus threw himself at the dead man once more, jaws agape, reaching for his throat, his face. Craddock couldn't spin fast enough to get him with his swinging knife. The shadow Angus put his front paws on his chest and heaved, and the dead man stumbled down into the driveway. When the black dog lunged, it could stretch itself almost a full yard away from the German shepherd it was attached to, lengthening and going slim like a shadow at the end of day. Its black fangs snapped shut a few inches from the dead man's face. Craddock's hat flew. Angus—both the German shepherd and the midnight-colored dog attached to him—scrambled on top of him, gouging at him with his claws.

Time skipped.

The dead man was on his feet again, backed against the truck. Angus had skipped through time with him, was ducking and tearing. Dark teeth ripped through the dead man's pant leg. Liquid shadow drizzled from scratches in the dead man's face. When the drops hit the ground, they hissed and smoked, like fat falling in a hot frying pan. Craddock kicked, connected, and Angus rolled, came up on his feet.

Angus crouched, that deep snarl boiling up from inside him, his gaze fixed on Craddock and Craddock's swinging gold chain with its crescent-shaped blade on the end of it. Looking for an opening. The muscles in the big dog's back bunched under the glossy short fur, coiled for the spring. The black dog attached to Angus leaped first, by just a fraction of an instant, mouth yawning open, teeth snapping at the dead man's crotch, going for his balls. Craddock shrieked.

Skip.

The air reverberated with the sound of a slamming door. The old man was inside his Chevy. His hat was in the road, mashed in on itself.

Angus hit the side of the truck, and it rocked on its springs. Then Bon hit the other side, paws scrabbling frantically on steel. Her breath steamed the window, her slobber smeared the glass, just as if it were a real truck. Jude didn't know how she had got all the way over there. A moment ago she'd been cowering next to him.

Bon slipped, turned in a circle, threw herself at the pickup truck once more. On the other side of the truck, Angus jumped at the same time. In the next instant, though, the Chevy was gone, and the two dogs bounded into one another. Their heads audibly knocked, and they crashed down onto the frozen mud where the truck had been only an instant before.

Except it wasn't gone. Not entirely. The floodlights remained, two circles of light floating in midair. The dogs sprang back up, wheeled toward the lights, then began barking furiously at them. Bon's spine was humped up, her fur bristling, and she backed away from the floating, disembodied lights as she yapped. Angus had no throat left for barking, each roaring yawp hoarser than the one before. Jude noted that their shadow twins had vanished, fled with the truck, or had gone back inside their corporeal bodies, where they'd always been hiding, perhaps. Jude supposed—the thought seemed quite reasonable—that those black dogs attached to Bon and Angus had been their souls.

The round circles of the floodlights began to fade, going cool and blue, shrinking in on themselves. Then they winked out, leaving nothing behind except faint afterimages printed on the backs of Jude's retinas, wan, moon-colored disks that floated in front of him for a few moments before fading away.

20

Jude wasn't ready until the sky in the east was beginning to lighten with the first show of false dawn. Then he left Bon in the car and brought Angus inside with him. He trotted up the stairs and into the studio. Georgia was where he'd left her, asleep on the couch, under a white cotton sheet he'd pulled off the bed in the guest room.

"Wake up, darlin'," he said, putting a hand on her shoulder.

Georgia rolled toward him at his touch. A long strand of black hair was pasted to her sweaty cheek, and her color was bad—cheeks flushed an almost ugly red, while the rest of her skin was bone white. He put the back of his hand against her forehead. Her brow was feverish and damp.

She licked her lips. "Whafuck time is it?"

"Four-thirty."

She glanced around, sat up on her elbows. "What am I doing here?"

"Don't you know?"

She looked up at him from the bottoms of her eyes. Her chin began to tremble, and then she had to look away. She covered her eyes with one hand.

"Oh, God," she said.

Angus leaned past Jude and stuck his snout against her throat, under her jaw, nudging at it, as if telling her to keep her chin up. His great staring eyes were moist with concern.

She jumped when his wet nose kissed her skin, sat the rest of the way up. She gave Angus a startled, disoriented look and laid a gentle hand on his head, between his ears.

"What's he doing inside?" She glanced at Jude, saw he was dressed, black Doc Martens, ankle-length duster. At almost the same time, she seemed to register the throaty rumble of the Mustang idling in the driveway. It was already packed. "Where are you going?"

"Us," he said. "South."

RIDE ON

21

The daylight began to fail when they were just north of Fredericksburg, and that was when Jude saw the dead man's pickup behind them, following at a distance of perhaps a quarter mile.

Craddock McDermott was at the wheel, although it was hard to make him out clearly in the weak light, beneath the yellow shine of the sky, where the clouds glowed like banked embers. Jude could see he was wearing his fedora again, though, and drove hunched over the wheel, shoulders raised to the level of his ears. He had also put on a pair of round spectacles. The lenses flashed with a weird orange light, beneath the sodium-vapor lamps over I-95, circles of gleaming flame—a visual match for the floods on the brush guard.

Jude got off at the next exit. Georgia asked him why, and he said he was tired. She hadn't seen the ghost.

"I could drive," she said.

She had slept most of the afternoon and now sat in the passenger seat with her feet hitched under her and her head resting on her shoulder.

When he didn't reply, she took an appraising look at his face and said, "Is everything all right?"

"I just want to get off the road before dark."

Bon stuck her head into the space between the front seats to listen to them talk. She liked to be included in their conversations. Georgia stroked her head, while Bon stared up at Jude with a look of nervous misgiving visible in her chocolate eyes.

They found a Days Inn less than half a mile from the turnpike. Jude sent Georgia to get the room, while he sat in the Mustang with the dogs. He didn't want to take a chance on being recognized, wasn't in the mood. He hadn't been in the mood for about fifteen years.

As soon as Georgia was out of the car, Bon scrambled into her empty seat, curled up in the warm assprint Georgia had left in the leather. As Bon settled her chin on her front paws, she gave Jude a guilty look, waiting for him to yell, to tell her to get in the back with Angus. He didn't yell. The dogs could do what they wanted.

Not long after they first got on the road, Jude had told Georgia about how the dogs had gone after Craddock. "I'm not sure even the dead man knew that Angus and Bonnie could go at him like that. But I do think Craddock sensed they were some kind of threat, and I think he would've been glad to scare us out of the house and away from them, before we figured out how to use the dogs against him."

At this, Georgia had twisted around in her seat, to reach into the back and dig behind Angus's ears, leaning far enough into the rear to rub her nose against Bon's snout. "Who are my little hero dogs? Who is it? Yeah, you are, that's right," and so forth, until Jude had started to feel half mad with hearing it.

Georgia came out of the office, a key hooked over one finger, which she wiggled at him before turning and walking around the corner of the building. He followed in the car and parked at an empty spot, in front of a beige door among other beige doors, at the rear of the motel.

She went inside with Angus while he walked with Bon along a tangle of scrub woods at the edge of the parking lot. Then he came back and left Bon with Georgia and took Angus for the walk. It was important for neither of them to stray far from the dogs.

These woods, behind the Days Inn, were different from the forest around his farmhouse in Piecliff, New York. They were unmistakably southern woods, smelled of sweet rot and wet moss and red clay, of sulfur and sewage, orchids and motor oil. The atmosphere itself was different, the air denser, warmer, sticky with dampness. Like an armpit. Like Moore's Corner, where Jude had grown up. Angus snapped at the fireflies, blowing here and there in the ferns, beads of ethereal green light.

Jude returned to the room. In the ten minutes it took to pass through Delaware, he had stopped at a Sunoco for gas and thought to buy a half dozen cans of Alpo in the convenience store. It had not occurred to him, however, to buy paper plates. While Georgia used the bathroom, Jude pulled one of the drawers out of the dresser, opened two cans, and slopped them in. He set the drawer on the floor for the dogs. They fell upon it, and the sound of wet slobbering and swallowing, harsh grunts and gasps for air, filled the room.

Georgia came out of the bathroom, stood in the door in faded white panties and a strappy halter that left her midriff bare, all evidence of her Goth self scrubbed away, except for her shiny, black-lacquered toenails. Her right hand was wrapped in a fresh knot of bandage. She looked at the dogs, nose wrinkled in an expression of amused disgust.

"Boy, are we livin' foul. If housekeepin' finds out we been feedin' our dogs from the dresser drawers, we will *not* be invited back to the Fredericksburg Days Inn." She spoke in cornpone, putting on for his bemusement. She had been dropping g's and drawing out her vowels off and on throughout the afternoon—doing it sometimes for laughs and sometimes, Jude believed, without knowing she was doing it. As if in leaving New York she was also traveling away from the person she'd been there, unconsciously slipping back into the voice and attitudes of who she'd been before: a scrawny Georgia kid who thought it was a laugh to go skinny-dipping with the boys.

"I seen people treat a hotel room worst," he said. "Worst" instead of "worse." His own accent, which had become very slight over the years, was thickening up as well. If he wasn't careful, he would be talking like an extra from *Hee Haw* by the time they got to South Carolina. It was hard to venture back near the place you'd been bred without settling into the characteristics of the person you'd been there. "My bassist, Dizzy, took a shit in a dresser drawer once, when I wouldn't get out of the bathroom fast enough."

Georgia laughed, although he saw her watching him with something close to concern—wondering, maybe, what he was thinking. Dizzy was dead. AIDS. Jerome, who'd played rhythm guitar and keyboards and pretty much everything else, was dead, too, had run his car off the road, ninety miles an hour, rolled his Porsche six times before it exploded into flames. Only a handful of people knew that it wasn't a drunk-driving accident, but that he had done it cold sober, on purpose.

Not long after Jerome cashed out, Kenny said it was time to call it a day, that he wanted to spend some time with his kids. Kenny was tired of nipple rings and black leather pants and pyrotechnics and hotel rooms, had been faking it for a while anyway. That was it for the band. Jude had been a solo act ever since.

Maybe he wasn't even that anymore. There was his box of demos in the studio at home, almost thirty new songs. But it was a private collection. He had not bothered to play them for anyone. It was just more of the same. What had Kurt Cobain said? Verse chorus verse. Over and over. Jude didn't care anymore. AIDS got Dizzy, the road got Jerome. Jude didn't care if there was any more music.

It didn't make sense to him, the way things had worked out. He had always been the star. The band had been called Jude's Hammer. He was the one who was supposed to die tragically young. Jerome and Dizzy were meant to live on, so they could tell PG-13 stories about him years later, on a VH1 retrospective—the both of them balding, fat, manicured, at peace with their wealth and their rude, noisy pasts. But then Jude had never been good at sticking to the script.

Jude and Georgia ate sandwiches they'd picked up in the same Delaware gas station where Jude had bought the Alpo. They tasted like the Saran Wrap they'd come wrapped in.

My Chemical Romance was on Conan. They had rings in their lips and eyebrows, their hair done up in spikes, but beneath the white pancake makeup and black lipstick they looked like a collection of chubby kids who had probably been in their high-school marching band a few years earlier. They leaped around, falling into each other, as if the stage beneath them were an electrified plate. They played frantically, pissing themselves with fear. Jude liked them. He wondered which of them would die first.

After, Georgia switched off the lamp by the bed and they lay together in the dark, the dogs curled up on the floor.

"I guess it didn't get rid of him," she said. "Burning his suit." No Daisy Duke accent now.

"It was a good idea, though."

"No it wasn't." Then: "He made me do it, didn't he?"

Jude didn't reply.

"What if we can't figure out how to make him go away?" she asked.

"Get used to smellin' dog food."

She laughed, her breath tickling his throat.

She said, "What are we going to do when we get where we're going?"

"We're going to talk to the woman who sent me the suit. We're going to find out if she knows how to get rid of him."

Cars droned on I-95. Crickets thrummed.

"Are you going to hurt her?"

"I don't know. I might. How's your hand?"

"Better," she said. "How's yours?"

"Better," he said.

He was lying, and he was pretty sure she was, too. She had gone into the bathroom to re-dress the hand when they first got into the room. He had gone in after, to re-dress his, and found her old wraps in the trash. He pulled the loops of gauze out of the wastebasket to inspect them. They stank of infection and antiseptic cream, and they were stained with dried blood and something else, a yellow crust that had to be pus.

As for his own hand, the gouge he'd put in it probably needed stitches. Before leaving the house that morning, he had tugged a first-aid kit out of an upper cabinet in the kitchen and used some Steri-Strips to pull the gash closed, then wound it in white bandages. But the gouge continued to seep, and by the time he took the wraps off, blood was beginning to soak them through. The hole in his left hand bulged open between the Steri-Strips, a red, liquid eye.

"The girl who killed herself," Georgia began. "The girl this is all about . . ."

"Anna McDermott." Her real name now.

"Anna," Georgia repeated. "Do you know why she killed herself? Was it because you told her to scram?"

"Her sister obviously thinks so. Her stepdaddy, too, I guess, since he's haunting us."

"The ghost . . . can make people do things. Like getting me to burn the suit. Like making Danny hang himself."

He'd told her about Danny in the car. Georgia had turned her face to the window, and he'd heard her crying softly for a while, making little damp, choked sounds, which evened out after a time into the slow, regular inhalations of sleep. This was the first either of them had mentioned Danny since.

Jude continued, "The dead man, Anna's stepdaddy, learned hypnotism torturing Charlie in the army and stayed with it after he got out. Liked to call himself a mentalist. In his life he used that chain of his, with the silver razor on the end of it, to put people into trances, but now he's dead, he don't need it anymore. Something about when he says things, you just have to do it. All of a sudden, you're just sitting back, watching him run you here and there. You don't even feel anything. Your body is a suit of clothes, and he's the one wearing it, not you." *A dead man's suit,* Jude thought, and his arms roughened with gooseflesh. Then he said, "I don't know much about him. Anna didn't like to talk on him. But I know she worked for a while as a palm reader, and she said her stepdaddy was the one who taught her how. He had an interest in the less-understood aspects of the human mind. Like, for example, on the weekends he'd hire himself out as a dowser."

"Those are people who find water by waving sticks in the air? My grandma hired an old hillbilly with a mouthful of gold teeth to find her a fresh spring after her well went dry. He had a hickory stick."

"Anna's stepdaddy, Craddock, didn't bother with a stick. He just used that pretty razor on a chain he's got. Pendulums work about as well, I guess. Anyway, the psycho bitch who sent me the suit, Jessica McDermott Price, wanted me to know that her pop had said he'd get even with me after he was dead. So I think the old man had some ideas about how to come back. In other words, he's not an accidental ghost, if that makes sense. He got the way he is now on purpose."

A dog yapped somewhere in the distance. Bon lifted her head, gazed thoughtfully in the direction of the door, then lowered her chin back to her forepaws.

"Was she pretty?" Georgia asked.

"Anna? Yeah. Sure. You want to know if she was good in the sack?"

"I'm just asking. You don't got to be a son of a bitch about it."

"Well, then. Don't ask questions you don't really want to know the answers to. Notice I never inquire about your past lays."

"Past lays. Goddamn it. Is that the way you think of me? The present lay, soon to be the past lay?"

"Christ. Here we go."

"And I'm not being a snoop. I'm trying to figure this out."

"How is knowing whether she was pretty going to help you figure anything out about our ghost problem?"

She held the sheet to her chin and stared at him in the dark.

"So she was Florida and I'm Georgia. How many other states has your dick visited?"

"I couldn't tell you. I don't have a map somewhere with pins in it. You really want me to make an estimate? While we're on the subject, why stop with states? I've had thirteen world tours, and I always took my cock along with me."

"You fuckin' asshole."

He grinned in his beard. "I know that's probably shocking, to a virgin such as yourself. Here's some news for you: I got a past. Fifty-four years of it."

"Did you love her?"

"You can't leave it alone, can you?"

"This is important, goddamn it."

"How's it important?"

She wouldn't say.

He sat up against the headboard. "For about three weeks."

"Did she love you?"

He nodded.

"She wrote you letters? After you sent her home?"

"Yeah."

"Angry letters?"

He didn't reply at first, considering the question.

"Did you even fuckin' read 'em, you insensitive shitbird?" There it was again, an unmistakably rural and southern cadence in her voice. Her temper was up, and she'd forgotten herself for a moment. Or maybe it was not a case of forgetting herself, Jude thought, so much as the opposite.

"Yeah, I read 'em," he said. "I was hunting around for them when the shit blew up in our faces back in New York."

He was sorry Danny had not found them. He had loved Anna and lived with her and talked with her every day but now understood he had not learned nearly enough about her. He knew so little of the life she'd lived before him—and after.

"You deserve whatever happens to you," she said. Georgia rolled away from him. "We both deserve it."

He said, "They weren't angry. Sometimes they were emotional. And sometimes they were scary, because there was so little emotion in them. In the last one, I remember she said something about how she had things she wanted to talk about, things she was tired of keeping secret. She said she couldn't stand to be so tired all the time. Which should've been a warning sign to me right there. Except she said stuff like that other times, and she never . . . anyway. I been trying to tell you she wasn't right. She wasn't happy."

"But do you think she still loved you? Even after you put your boot in her ass?"

"I didn't—" he started, then let out a thin, seething breath. Wouldn't let himself be baited. "I suppose probably she did."

Georgia didn't speak for a long time, her back to him. He studied the curve of her shoulder. At last she said, "I feel bad for her. It's not a lot of fun, you know."

"What?"

"Being in love with you. I've been with a lot of bad guys who made me feel lousy about myself, Jude, but you're something special. Because I knew none of them really cared about me, but you do, and you make me feel like your shitty hooker anyway." She spoke plainly, calmly, without looking at him.

It made him catch his breath a little, what she said, and for an instant he wanted to tell her he was sorry, but he shied from the word. He was out of practice at apologies and loathed explanations. She waited for him to reply, and when he didn't, she pulled the blanket up to cover her shoulder.

He slid down against the pillow, put his hands behind his head.

"We'll be passing through Georgia tomorrow," she said, still not turning toward him. "I want to stop and see my grandma."

"Your grandma," Jude repeated, as if he weren't sure he'd heard her right.

"Bammy is my favorite person in the world. She bowled a perfect three hundred once." Georgia said it as if the two things followed one another naturally. Maybe they did.

"You know the trouble we're in?"

"Yeah. I was vaguely aware."

"Do you think it's a good idea to start making detours?"

"I want to see her."

"How about we stop in on our way back? You two can catch up on old times then. Hell, maybe the two of you could go bowl a couple strings."

Georgia was a little while in answering. At last she said, "I was feelin' like I ought to see her now. It's been on my mind. I don't think it's any sure thing we'll be making the trip back. Do you?"

He pulled his beard, staring at the shape of her under the sheet. He didn't like the idea of slowing for any reason but felt the need to offer her something, some concession, to make her loathe him a little less. Also, if Georgia had things she wanted to say to someone who loved her, he supposed it made sense not to wait around. Putting off anything that mattered no longer seemed like sensible planning.

"She keep lemonade in the fridge?"

"Fresh made."

"Okay," Jude said. "We'll stop. Not too long, though, okay? We can be in Florida this time tomorrow if we don't mess around."

One of the dogs sighed. Georgia had opened a window to air out the odor of Alpo, the window that looked into the courtyard at the center of the motel. Jude could smell the rust of the chain link fence and a dash of chlorine, although there was no water in the pool.

Georgia said, "Also, I used to have a Ouija board, once upon a time. When we get to my grandma's, I want to poke around for it."

"I already told you. I don't need to talk to Craddock. I already know what he wants."

"No," Georgia said, her voice short with impatience. "I don't mean so we can talk to *him*."

"Then what do you mean?"

"We need it if we're going to talk to Anna," Georgia said. "You said she loved you. Maybe she can tell us how to get out of this mess. Maybe she can call him off."

22

Lake Pontchartrain, huh? I didn't grow up too far from there. My parents took us campin' there once. My stepdaddy fished. I can't remember how he did. You go fishin' much on Lake Pontchartrain?"

She was always after him with her questions. He could never decide if she listened to the answers or just used the time when he was talking to think of something else to pester him about.

"Do you like to fish? Do you like raw fish? Sushi? I think sushi is disgusting, except when I'm drinkin', and then I'm in the mood. Repulsion masks attraction. How many times have you been to Tokyo? I hear the food is really nasty—raw squid, raw jellyfish. Everything is raw there. Did they not invent fire in Japan? Have you ever had bad food poisonin'? Sure you have. On tour all the time.

"What's the hardest you ever puked? You ever puked through your nostrils? You have? That's the worst.

"But did you fish Lake Pontchartrain much? Did your daddy take you? Isn't that the prettiest name? Lake Pontchartrain, Lake Pontchartrain, I want to see the rain on Lake Pontchartrain. You know what the most romantic sound in the world is? Rain on a quiet lake. A nice spring rain. When I was a kid, I could put myself into a trance just sittin' at my window watchin' the rain. My stepdad used to say he never met anyone as easy to put into a trance as me. What were you like growin' up? When'd you decide to change your name?

"Do you think I should change my name? You should pick out a new name for me. I want you to call me whatever you want to call me."

"I already do," *he said.*

"That's right. You do. From now on, my name is Florida. Anna Mc-Dermott is dead to me. She's a dead girl. All gone. I never liked her anyway. I'd rather be Florida. Do you miss Louisiana? Isn't it funny we only lived four hours apart from each other? We coulda crossed paths. Do you think you and I were ever in the same room, at the same time, and didn't know it? Probably not, though, right? Because you blew out of Louisiana before I was even born."

It was either her most endearing habit or her most infuriating. Jude was never sure. Maybe it was both at the same time.

"You ever shut up with the questions?" *he asked her the first night they slept together. It was two in the morning, and she'd been interrogating him for an hour.* "Were you one of those kids who would drive their momma crazy going, 'Why is the sky blue? Why doesn't the earth fall into the sun? What happens to us when we die?'"

"What do you think happens to us when we die?" *Anna asked.* "You ever seen a ghost? My stepdaddy has. My stepdaddy's talked to them. He was in Vietnam. He says the whole country is haunted."

By then he already knew that her stepfather was a dowser as well as a mesmerist, and in business with her older sister, also a hypnotist by trade, the both of them back in Testament, Florida. That was almost the full extent of what he knew about her family. Jude didn't push for more—not then, not later—was content to know about her what she wanted him to know.

He had met Anna three days before, in New York City. He'd come down to do a guest vocal with Trent Reznor for a movie soundtrack—easy money—then stuck around to see a show Trent was doing at Roseland. Anna was backstage, a petite girl, violet lipstick, leather pants that creaked when she walked, the rare Goth blonde. She asked if he wanted an egg roll and got it for him and then said, "Is it hard to eat with a beard like that? Do you get food in it?" *At him with the questions almost from hello.* "Why do you think so many guys, bikers and stuff, grow beards to look threatening? Don't you think they'd actually work against you in a fight?"

"How would a beard work against you in a fight?" *he asked.*

She grabbed his beard in one fist and yanked at it. He bent forward, felt a tearing pain in the lower half of his face, ground his teeth, choked on an angry cry. She let go, continued, "Like if I was ever in a fight with a bearded man, that's the first thing I'd do. ZZ Top would be pushovers. I could take all three of them myself, little itty-bitty me. Course, those guys are stuck, they *can't* shave. If they ever shaved, no one would know who they were. I kind of guess you're in the same boat, now I think about it. It's who you are. That beard gave me bad dreams as a little girl, when I used to watch you in videos. Hey! You know, you could be completely anonymous without your beard. You ever think of that? Instant vacation from the pressures of celebrity. Plus, it's a liability in combat. Reasons to shave."

"My face was a liability to getting laid," *he said.* "If my beard gave you bad dreams, you should see me without it. You'd probably never sleep again."

"So it's a disguise. An act of concealment. Like your name."

"What about my name?"

"That isn't your real name. Judas Coyne. It's a pun." *She leaned toward him.* "Name like that, are you from a nutty Christian family? I bet. My stepdaddy says the Bible is all bunk. He was raised Pentecostal, but he wound up a spiritualist, which is how he raised us. He's got a pendulum— he can hang it over you and ask you questions and tell if you're lying by the way it swings back and forth. He can read your aura with it, too. My aura is black as sin. How about yours? Want me to read your palm? Palm reading is nothing. Easiest trick in the book."

She told his fortune three times. The first time she was kneeling naked in bed beside him, a gleaming line of sweat showing in the crease between her breasts. She was flushed, still breathing hard from their exertions. She took his palm, moved her fingertips across it, inspecting it closely.

"Look at this lifeline," *Anna said.* "This thing goes on for miles. I guess you live forever. I wouldn't want to live forever myself. How old is too old? Maybe it's metaphorical. Like your music is forever, some malarkey along those lines. Palm reading ain't no exact science."

And then once, not long after he finished rebuilding the Mustang, they had gone for a drive into the hills overlooking the Hudson. They wound up parked at a boat ramp, staring out at the river, the water flecked with diamond scales beneath a high, faded-blue sky. Fluffy white clouds, thousands of feet high, crowded the horizon. Jude had meant to drive Anna to an appointment with a psychiatrist—Danny had set it up—but she'd dissuaded him, said it was too nice a day to spend it in a doctor's office.

They sat there, windows down, music low, and she picked up his hand, lying on the seat between them. She was having one of her good days. They'd been coming less and less often.

"You love again after me," *she said.* "You get another chance to be happy. I don't know if you'll let yourself take it. I kind of think not. Why don't you want to be happy?"

"What do you mean, after you?" *he asked. Then he said,* "I'm happy now."

"No you aren't. You're still angry."

"With who?"

"Yourself," *she said, as if it were the most obvious thing.* "Like it's your fault Jerome and Dizzy died. Like anyone could've saved them from themselves. You're still real pissed with your daddy, too. For what he did to your mother. For what he did to your hand."

This last statement stole his breath. "What are you talking about? How do you know about what he did to my hand?"

She flicked her gaze toward him: an amused, cunning look. "I'm starin' at it right now, aren't I?" *She turned his hand over, moved her thumb across his scarred knuckles.* "You don't have to be psychic or anything. You just have to have sensitive fingers. I can feel where the bones healed. What'd he hit this hand with to smash it? A sledgehammer? They healed real bad."

"The basement door. I took off one weekend to play a show in New Orleans. A battle-of-the-bands thing. I was fifteen. Helped myself to a hundred bucks bus fare out of the family cash box. I figured it wouldn't be like stealing, 'cause we'd win the contest. Five-hundred-dollar cash prize. Pay it all back with interest."

"How'd you do?"

"Took third. We all got T-shirts," *Jude said.* "When I came back, he dragged me over to the basement door and smashed my left hand in it. My chord-making hand."

She paused, frowning, then glanced at him in confusion. "I thought you made chords with the other hand."

"I do now."

She stared.

"I kinda taught myself how to make them with my right hand while my left was healing, and I just never went back."

"Was that hard?"

"Well. I wasn't sure my left would ever be good for making chords again, so it was either that or stop playing. And it would've been a lot harder to stop."

"Where was your mom when this happened?"

"Can't remember." *A lie. The truth was, he couldn't forget. His mother had been at the table when his father started to pull him across the kitchen, toward the basement door, and he had screamed for her to help, but she only got up and put her hands over her ears and left for the sewing room. He could not, in truth, blame her for refusing to intervene. Supposed he had it coming, and not for taking a hundred dollars out of the cash box either.* "S'okay. I wound up playing better guitar after I had to switch hands anyway. It just took about a month of making the most horrible fuckin' noises you ever heard. Eventually someone explained I had to restring my guitar backwards if I was going to play with my hands reversed. After that I picked it up pretty easy."

"Plus, you showed your daddy, didn't you?"

He didn't answer. She examined his palm once more, and rolled her thumb across his wrist. "He isn't through with you yet. Your daddy. You'll see him again."

"No I won't. I haven't looked at him for thirty years. He doesn't figure in my life anymore."

"Sure he does. He figures into it every single day."

"Funny, I thought we decided to skip visiting the psychiatrist this afternoon."

She said, "You have five luck lines. You're luckier than a cat, Jude Coyne. The world must still be payin' you back for all your daddy did to you. Five luck lines. The world is never going to be done payin' you back." *She laid his hand aside.* "Your beard and your big leather jacket and your big black car and your big black boots. No one puts on all that armor unless they been hurt by someone who didn't have no right to hurt them."

"Look who's talking," *he said.* "Is there any part of you, you won't stick a pin in?" *She had them in her ears, her tongue, one nipple, her labia.* "Who are you trying to scare away?"

Anna gave him his final palm reading just a few days before Jude packed her stuff. He looked out the kitchen window early one evening and saw her trudging through a cold February rain to the barn, wearing only a black halter and black panties, her naked flesh shocking in its paleness.

By the time he caught up to her, she had crawled into the dog pen, the part of it that was inside the barn, where Angus and Bon went to get out of the rain. She sat in the dirt, mud smeared on the backs of her thighs. The dogs whisked here and there, shooting worried looks her way and giving her space.

Jude climbed into the pen on all fours, angry with her, sick to death of the way it had been the last two months. He was sick of talking to her and getting dull, three-word answers, sick of laughter and tears for no reason. They didn't make love anymore. The thought repelled him. She didn't wash, didn't dress, didn't brush her teeth. Her honey-yellow hair was a rat's nest. The last few times they had attempted to have sex, she'd turned him off with the things she wanted, had embarrassed and sickened him. He didn't mind a certain amount of kink, would tie her up if she wanted, pinch her nipples, roll her over and put it in her ass. But she wasn't happy with that. She wanted him to hold a plastic bag over her head. To cut her.

She was hunched forward, with a needle in one hand. She pushed it into the thumb of the other, working intently and deliberately—pricking herself once, then again, producing fat, gem-bright drops of blood.

"The hell you doing?" *he asked her, struggling to keep the anger out of his voice and failing. He took her by the wrist, to stop her sticking herself.*

She let the pin drop into the mud, then reversed his grip, squeezed his hand in hers and stared down at it. Her eyes glowed with fever in their dark, bruised-looking hollows. She was down to sleeping three hours a night at best.

"You're running out of time almost as fast as I am. I'll be more useful when I'm gone. I'm gone. We have no future. Someone is going to try and hurt you. Someone who wants to take everything away from you." *She rolled her eyes up to look into his face.* "Someone you can't fight. You'll fight anyway, but you can't win. You won't win. All the good things in your life will soon be gone."

Angus whined anxiously and slipped in between them, burrowing his snout in her crotch. She smiled—first smile he'd seen in a month—and dug behind his ears.

"Well," *she said.* "You'll always have the dogs."

He twisted free of her grip, took her by the arms, lifted her to her feet. "I don't listen to nothing you say. You've told my fortune three times at least, and it comes out a different way every time."

"I know," *she said.* "But they're all true anyway."

"Why were you sticking yourself with a needle? Why you want to do that?"

"I done it since I was a girl. Sometimes if I stick myself a couple times, I can make the bad thoughts go away. It's a trick I taught myself to clear my head. Like pinchin' yourself in a dream. You know. Pain has a way of wakin' you up. Of remindin' you who you are."

Jude knew.

Almost as an afterthought, she added, "I guess it isn't workin' too good anymore." *He led her out of the pen and back across the barn. She spoke again, said,* "I don't know what I'm out here for. In my underwear."

"I don't either."

"You ever dated anyone as crazy as me, Jude? Do you hate me? You've had a lot of girls. Tell me honest, am I the worst? Who was your worst?"

"Why do you got to ask so many damn questions?" *He wanted to know.*

As they went back out into the rain, he opened his black duster and closed it over her thin, shivering body, clasped her against him.

"I'd rather ask 'em," *she said,* "than answer them."

23

He woke a little after nine with a melody in his head, something with the feel of an Appalachian hymn. He nudged Bon off the bed—she had climbed up with them in the night—and pushed aside the covers. Jude sat on the edge of the mattress, mentally running over the melody again, trying to identify it, to remember the lyrics. Only it couldn't be identified, and the lyrics couldn't be recalled, because it hadn't existed until he thought it up. It wouldn't have a name until he gave it one.

Jude rose, slipped across the room and outside, onto the concrete breezeway, still in his boxers. He unlocked the trunk of the Mustang and pulled out a battered guitar case with a '68 Les Paul in it. He carried it back into the room.

Georgia hadn't moved. She lay with her face in the pillow, one bone-white arm above the sheets and curled tight against her body. It had been years since he dated anyone with a tan. When you were a Goth, it was important to at least imply the possibility you might burst into flames in direct sunlight.

He let himself into the john. By now Angus and Bon were both trailing him, and he whispered at them to stay. They sank to their bellies outside the door, staring forlornly in at him, accusing him with their eyes of failing to love them enough.

He wasn't sure how well he could play with the puncture wound in his left hand. The left did the picking and the right found the chords. He lifted the Les Paul from its case and began to fiddle, bringing it into tune. When he strummed a pick across the strings, it set off a low flare of pain—not bad, almost just an uncomfortable warmth—in the center of his palm. It felt as if a steel wire were sunk deep into the flesh and beginning to heat up. He could play through that, he thought.

When the guitar was in tune, he searched for the proper chords and began to play, reproducing the tune that had been in his head when he woke. Without the amp the guitar was all flat, soft twang, and each chord made a raspy, chiming sound. The song itself might have been a traditional hill-country melody, sounded like something that belonged on a Folkways record or a Library of Congress retrospective of traditional music. Something with a name like "Fixin' to Dig My Grave." "Jesus Brung His Chariot." "Drink to the Devil."

"'Drink to the Dead,'" he said.

He put the guitar down and went back into the bedroom. There was a small notepad on the nighttable, and a ballpoint pen. He brought them into the bathroom and wrote down "Drink to the Dead." Now it had a title. He picked up the guitar and played it again.

The sound of it—the sound of the Ozarks, of a gospel—gave him a little prickle of pleasure, which he felt along his forearms and across the back of his neck. A lot of his songs, when they started out, sounded like old music. They arrived on his doorstep, wandering orphans, the lost children of large and venerable musical families. They came to him in the form of Tin Pan Alley sing-alongs, honky-tonk blues, Dust Bowl plaints, lost Chuck Berry riffs. Jude dressed them in black and taught them to scream.

He wished he had his DAT recorder, wanted to get what he had down on tape. Instead he put the guitar aside once more, and scribbled the chords on the notepad, beneath his title. Then he took up the Les Paul and played the lick again, and again, curious to see where it would take him. Twenty minutes later there were spots of blood showing through the bandage around his left hand, and he had worked out the chorus, which built naturally from the initial hook, a steady, rising, thunderous chorus, a whisper to a shout: an act of violence against the beauty and sweetness of the melody that had come before.

"Who's that by?" Georgia asked, leaning in through the bathroom door, knuckling the sleep out of her eyes.

"Me."

"I like that one."

"It's okay. Sound even better if this thing was plugged in."

Her soft black hair floated around her head, had a swirled, airy look to it, and the shadows under her eyes drew his attention to how large they were. She smiled drowsily down at him. He smiled back.

"Jude," she said, in a tone of almost unbearable, erotic tenderness.

"Yeah?"

"You think you could get your ass out of the bathroom, so I could pee?"

When she shut the door, he dropped his guitar case on the bed and stood in the dimness of the room, listening to the muffled sound of the world beyond the drawn shades: the drone of traffic on the highway, a car door slamming, a vacuum cleaner humming in the room directly above. It came to him then that the ghost was gone.

Ever since the suit had arrived at his house in its black heart-shaped box, he had sensed the dead man lingering close to him. Even when Jude couldn't see him, he was conscious of his presence, felt it almost as a barometric weight, a kind of pressure and electricity in the air, such as precedes a thunderstorm. He had existed in that atmosphere of dreadful waiting for days, a continuous crackle of tension that made it difficult to taste his food or find his way into sleep. Now, though, it had lifted. He had somehow forgotten the ghost while he'd been writing the new song—and the ghost had somehow forgotten him, or at least not been able to intrude into Jude's thoughts, into Jude's surroundings.

He walked Angus, took his time. Jude was in short sleeves and jeans, and the sun felt good on the back of his neck. The smell of the morning—the pall of exhaust over I-95, the swamp lilies in the brush, the hot tarmac—got his blood going, made him want to be on the road, to be driving somewhere, anywhere. *He* felt good: an unfamiliar sensation. Maybe he was randy, thought about the pleasant tousle of Georgia's hair and her sleep-puffy eyes and lithe white legs. He was hungry, wanted eggs, a chicken-fried steak. Angus chased a groundhog into waist-high grass, then stood at the edge of the trees, yapping happily at it. Jude went back to give Bon a turn to stretch her legs and heard the shower.

He let himself in the bathroom. The room was steamy, the air hot and close. He undressed, slipped in around the curtain, and climbed into the tub.

Georgia jumped when his knuckles brushed her back, twisted her head to look at him over her shoulder. She had a black butterfly tattooed on her left shoulder and a black heart on her hip. She turned toward him, and he put his hand over the heart.

She pressed her damp, springy body against his, and they kissed. He leaned into her, over her, and to balance herself, Georgia put her right hand against the wall—then inhaled, a sharp, thin sound of pain, and pulled the hand back as if she had burned it.

Georgia tried to lower her hand to her side, but he caught her wrist and lifted it. The thumb was inflamed and red, and when he touched it lightly, he could feel the sick heat trapped inside it. The palm, around the ball of the thumb, was also reddened and swollen. On the inside of the thumb was the white sore, glittering with fresh pus.

"What are we going to do about this thing?" he asked.

"It's fine. I'm putting antiseptic cream on it."

"This isn't fine. We ought to run you to the emergency room."

"I'm not going to sit in some emergency room for three hours to have someone look at the place I poked myself with a pin."

"You don't know what stuck you. Don't forget what you were handling when this happened to you."

"I haven't forgotten. I just don't believe that any doctor is going make it better. Not really."

"You think it's going to get better on its own?"

"I think it'll be all right—if we make the dead man go away. If we get him off our backs, I think we'll *both* be all right," she said. "Whatever's wrong with my hand, it's part of this whole thing. But you know that, don't you?"

He didn't know anything, but he had notions, and he was not happy to hear they matched her own. He bowed his head, considering, wiped at the spray on his face. At last he said, "When Anna was at her worst, she'd poke herself in the thumb with a pin. To clear her head, she told me. I don't know. Maybe it's nothing. It just makes me uneasy, you getting stuck like she used to stick herself."

"Well. It doesn't worry me. Actually, that almost makes me feel better about it." Her good hand moved across his chest as she spoke, her fingers exploring a landscape of muscle beginning to lose definition and skin going slack with age, and all of it overgrown with a mat of curling silver hairs.

"It does?"

"Sure. It's something else her and I got in common. Besides you. I never met her, and I don't hardly know anything about her, but I feel connected to her somehow. I'm not afraid of that, you know."

"I'm glad it's not bothering you. I wish I could say the same. Speaking for myself, I don't much like thinking about it."

"So don't," she said, leaning into him and pushing her tongue into his mouth to shut him up.

24

Jude took Bon for her overdue walk while Georgia busied herself in the bathroom, dressing and rebandaging her hand and putting in her studs. He knew she might be occupied for twenty minutes, so he stopped by the car and pulled her laptop out of the trunk. Georgia didn't even know they had it with them. He'd packed it automatically, without thinking, because Georgia took it with her wherever she went and used it to stay in touch with a gaggle of geographically far-flung friends by way of e-mail and instant message. And she dribbled away countless hours browsing, message boards, blogs, concert info, and vampire porn (which would've been hilarious if it weren't so depressing). But once they were on the road, Jude had forgotten they had the laptop with them, and Georgia had never asked about it, so it had spent the night in the trunk.

Jude didn't bring his own computer—he didn't have one. Danny had handled his e-mail and all the rest of his online obligations. Jude was aware that he belonged to an increasingly small segment of the society, those who could not quite fathom the allure of the digital age. Jude did not want to be wired. He had spent four years wired on coke, a period of time in which everything seemed hyperaccelerated, as in one of those time-lapse movies, where a whole day and night pass in just a few seconds, traffic reduced to lurid streaks of light, people transformed into blurred mannequins rushing jerkily here and there. Those four years now felt more like four bad, crazy, sleepless days to him—days that had begun with a New Year's Eve hangover and ended at crowded, smoky Christmas parties where he found himself surrounded by strangers trying to touch him and shrieking with inhuman laughter. He did not ever want to be wired again.

He had tried to explain the way he felt to Danny once, about compulsive behavior and time rushing too fast and the Internet and drugs. Danny had only lifted one of his slender, mobile eyebrows and stared at him in smirking confusion. Danny did not think coke and computers were anything alike. But Jude had seen the way people hunched over their screens, clicking the refresh button again and again, waiting for some crucial if meaningless hit of information, and he thought it was almost exactly the same.

Now, though, he was in the mood to score. He lugged her laptop back to the room, plugged in, and went online. He didn't make any attempt to access his e-mail account. In truth, he wasn't sure *how* to access his e-mail. Danny had a program all set up to reel in Jude's messages from the Net, but Jude couldn't have said how to get at that information from someone else's computer. He knew how to Google a name, however, and he Googled Anna's.

Her obituary was short, half the length her father's had been. Jude was able to read it in a glance, which was all it merited. It was her photograph that caught his attention and gave him a brief hollow sensation in the pit of his stomach. He guessed it had been taken close to the end of her life. She was glancing blankly into the camera, some strands of pale hair blown across a face that was gaunt, her cheeks sunken hollows beneath her cheekbones.

When he had known her, she'd sported rings in her eyebrows and four apiece in each of her ears, but in the photo they were gone, which made her too-pale face that much more vulnerable. When he looked closely, he could see the marks left by her piercings. She'd given them up, the silver hoops and crosses and ankhs and glittering gems, the studs and fishhooks and rings she had stuck into her skin to make herself look dirty and tough and dangerous and crazy and beautiful. Some of it was true, too. She really had been crazy and beautiful; dangerous, too. Dangerous to herself.

The obituary said nothing about a suicide note. It said nothing about suicide. She had died not three months before her stepfather.

He ran another search. He tapped in "Craddock McDermott, dowsing," and half a dozen links popped up. He clicked on the topmost result, which brought him to a nine-year-old article in the *Tampa Tribune*, from their living/arts section. Jude looked at the pictures first—there were two—and stiffened in his chair. It was a while before he could unlock his gaze from those photographs and shift his attention to the text beside it.

The story was titled "Dowsing for the dead." The slug line read: *20 years after Vietnam, Capt. Craddock McDermott is ready to lay some ghosts to rest . . . and raise some others.*

The article opened with the story of Roy Hayes, a retired biology professor, who at the age of sixty-nine had learned to fly light planes and who had, one fall morning in 1991, taken an ultralight up over the Everglades to count egrets for an environmental group. At 7:13 A.M. a private strip south of Naples had received a transmission from him.

> "I think I'm having a stroke," Hayes said. "I'm dizzy. I can't tell how low I am. I need help."

That was the last anyone had heard from him. A search party, involving more than thirty boats and a hundred men, had not been able to find a trace of either Hayes or his plane. Now, three years after his disappearance and presumed death, his family had taken the extraordinary step of hiring Craddock McDermott, Captain U.S. Army (ret.), to lead a new search for his remains.

"He didn't go down in the 'Glades. McDermott states with a confident grin. "The search parties were always looking in the wrong place. The winds that morning carried his plane farther north, over Big Cypress. I put his position less than a mile south of I-94."

McDermott believes he can pinpoint the site of the crash to an area the size of a square half mile. But he didn't work out his estimate by consulting meteorological data from the morning of the disappearance, or by examining Dr. Hayes's final radio transmissions, or by reading eyewitness reports. Instead he dangled a silver pendulum above an outsize map of the region. When the pendulum began to swing rapidly back and forth, over a spot in south Big Cypress, McDermott announced he had found the impact zone.

And when he takes a private search team into the Big Cypress swamp later this week, to look for the downed ultralight, he will not be bringing with him sonar, metal detectors, or hound dogs. His plan for locating the vanished professor is much more simple—and unnerving. He means to appeal to Roy Hayes directly—to call upon the deceased doctor himself to lead the party to his final resting place.

The article shifted to backstory, exploring Craddock's earliest encounters with the occult. A few lines were spent detailing the more gothic details of his early family life. It touched briefly on his father, the Pentecostal minister with a penchant for snake handling, who had disappeared when Craddock was just a boy. It lingered for a paragraph on his mother, who had twice moved them across the country, after seeing a phantom she called "the walking-backwards man," a vision that foretold of ill luck. After one such visit from the walking-backwards man, little Craddock and his mother departed an Atlanta apartment complex, not three weeks before the building burned to the ground in an electrical fire.

Then it was 1967, and McDermott was an officer stationed in Vietnam, where he was placed in charge of interrogating the captured elite of the People's Liberation Army. He found himself assigned to the case of one Nguyen Trung, a chiromancer, who had reportedly learned his fortune-telling arts from Ho Chi Minh's own brother and who had offered his services to a variety of higher-ups among the Vietcong. To put his prisoner at ease, McDermott asked Trung to help him understand his spiritual beliefs. What followed was a series of extraordinary conversations on the subjects of prophecy, the human soul, and the dead, discussions McDermott said had opened his eyes to the supernatural all around him.

"In Vietnam the ghosts are busy," McDermott avers. "Nguyen Trung taught me to see them. Once you know how to look for them, you can spot them on every street corner, their eyes marked out and their feet not touching the ground. The living are often known to employ the dead over there. A spirit that believes it has work to do won't leave our world. It'll stay until the job is done.

"That was when I first began to believe we were going to lose the war. I saw it happen on the battlefield. When our boys died, their souls would come out of their mouths, like steam from a teakettle, and run for the sky. When the Vietcong died, their spirits remained. Their dead went right on fighting."

After their sessions had concluded, McDermott lost track of Trung, who disappeared around the time of Tet. As for Professor Hayes, McDermott believed that his final fate would be known soon enough.

"We'll find him," McDermott said. "His spirit is unemployed at the moment, but I'll give him some work. We're going to ride together—Hayes and I. He's going to lead me right to his body."

At this last—*We're going to ride together*—Jude felt a chill crawling on the flesh of his arms. But that was not as bad as the peculiar feeling of dread that came over him when he looked at the photographs.

The first was a picture of Craddock leaning against the grill of his smoke-blue pickup. His barefoot stepdaughters—Anna was maybe twelve, Jessica about fifteen—sat on the hood, one to either side of him. It was the first time Jude had ever seen Anna's older sister, but not the first time he'd ever looked upon Anna as a child—she was just the same as she'd been in his dream, only without the scarf over her eyes.

In the photograph Jessica had her arms around the neck of her smiling, angular stepfather. She was almost as rangy as he was, tall and fit, her skin honey-colored and healthy with tan. But there was something off about her grin—toothy and wide, maybe too wide, too enthusiastic, the sell-sell-sell grin of a frantic real estate salesperson. And there was something off about her eyes, too, which were as bright and black as wet ink, and disconcertingly avid.

Anna sat a little apart from the other two. She was bony, all elbows and knees, and her hair came almost to her waist—a long, golden, spill of light. She was also the only one not putting on a smile for the camera. She wasn't putting on any kind of expression at all. Her face was dazed and expressionless, her eyes unfocused, the eyes of a sleepwalker. Jude recognized it as the expression she wore when she was off in the monochromatic, upside-down world of her depression. He was struck with the troubling idea that she had wandered that world for most of her childhood.

Worst of all, though, was a second, smaller photograph, this one of Captain Craddock McDermott, in fatigues and a sweat-stained fishing hat, M16 slung over one shoulder. He posed with other GIs on hard-packed yellow mud. At his back were palms and standing water; it might've been a snapshot of the Everglades, if not for all the soldiers, and their Vietnamese prisoner.

The prisoner stood a little behind Craddock, a solidly built man in a black tunic, with shaved head, broad, handsome features, and calm eyes of a monk. Jude knew him at first glance as the Vietnamese prisoner he had encountered in his dream. The fingers missing from Trung's right hand were a dead giveaway. In the grainy, poorly colored photo, the stumps of those fingers had been freshly stitched with black thread.

The same caption that identified this man as Nguyen Trung described the setting as a field hospital in Dong Tam, where Trung had received care for combat-related injuries. That was almost right. Trung had lopped off his own fingers only because he thought they were about to attack—so it had been combat of a sort. As for what had happened to him, Jude thought he knew. Jude thought it was likely that after Trung had no more to tell Craddock McDermott—about ghosts and the work ghosts did—he'd gone for a ride on the nightroad.

The article did not say if McDermott had ever found Roy Hayes, retired professor and ultralight pilot, but Jude believed he had, although there was no rational reason to think such a thing. To satisfy himself he did another search. Roy Hayes's remains had been laid to rest five weeks later, and in fact Craddock had not found him—not personally. The water was too deep. A state police scuba team had gone in and pulled him out, in the place where Craddock told them to dive.

Georgia threw open the bathroom door, and Jude quit her browser.

"Whatchu doin'?" she asked.

"Trying to figure out how to check my mail," he lied. "You want a turn?"

She looked at her computer for a moment, then shook her head and wrinkled her nose. "No. I don't have the least interest in going online. Isn't that funny? Usually you can't peel me off."

"Well, see? Running for your life ain't all bad. Just look at how it's building character."

He pulled out the dresser drawer again and slopped another can of Alpo into it.

"Last night the smell of that shit was making me want to gag," Georgia said. "Strangely, this morning it's getting me hungry."

"Come on. There's a Denny's up the street. Let's go for a walk."

He opened the door, then held out his hand to her. She was sitting on the edge of the bed, in her stone-washed black jeans, heavy black boots, and sleeveless black shirt, which hung loose on her slight frame. In the golden beam of sunlight that fell through the door, her skin was so pale and fine it was almost translucent, looked as if it would bruise at the slightest touch.

Jude saw her glance at the dogs. Angus and Bon bent over the drawer, heads together as they went snorkeling in their food. He saw Georgia frown, and he knew what she was thinking, that they'd been safe as long as they kept the dogs close. But then she squinted back at Jude, standing in the light, took his hand, and let him pull her to her feet. The day was bright. Beyond the door the morning waited for them.

He was, for himself, not scared. He still felt under the protection of the new song, felt that in writing it he had drawn a magic circle around the both of them that the dead man could not penetrate. He had driven the ghost away—for a time anyhow.

But as they crossed the parking lot—thoughtlessly holding hands, a thing they never did—he happened to glance back at their hotel room. Angus and Bon stared out through the picture window at them, standing side by side on their hind legs, with their front paws on the glass and their faces wearing identical looks of apprehension.

25

The Denny's was loud and overcrowded, thick with the smell of bacon fat and burnt coffee and cigarette smoke. The bar, just to the right of the doors, was a designated smoking area. That meant that after five minutes of waiting up front to be seated, you could plan on smelling like an ashtray by the time you were led to your table.

Jude didn't smoke himself and never had. It was the one self-destructive habit he'd managed to avoid. His father smoked. On errands into town, Jude had always willingly bought him the cheap, long boxes of generics, had done it even without being asked, and they both knew why. Jude would glare at Martin across the kitchen table, while his father lit a cigarette and took his first drag, the tip flaring orange.

"If looks could kill, I'd have cancer already," Martin said to him one night, without any preamble. He waved a hand, drew a circle in the air with the cigarette, squinting at Jude through the smoke. "I got a tough constitution. You want to kill me off with these, you're gonna have to wait a while. You really want me dead, there's easier ways to do it."

Jude's mother said nothing, concentrated on shelling peas, face screwed up in an expression of intent study. She might have been a deaf-mute.

Jude—Justin then—did not speak either, simply went on glaring at him. He was not too angry to speak but too shocked, because it was as if his father had read his mind. He'd been staring at the loose, chicken-flesh folds of Martin Cowzynski's neck with a kind of fury, wanting to will a cancer into it, a lump of black-blossoming cells that would devour his father's voice, choke his father's breath. Wanting that with all his heart: a cancer that would make the doctors scoop out his throat, shut him up forever.

The man at the next table had had his throat scooped out and used an electrolarynx to talk, a loud, crackling joy buzzer that he held under his chin to tell the waitress (and everyone else in the room): "YOU GOT AIR-CONDITIONIN'? WELL, TURN IT ON. YOU DON'T BOTHER TO COOK THE FOOD, WHY YOU WANNA TO FRAH YOUR PAYIN' CUSTOMERS? JESUS CHRIST. I'M EIGHTY-SEVEN." This was a fact he felt to be of such overwhelming importance that he said it again after the waitress walked away, repeating himself to his wife, a fantastically obese woman who didn't look up from her newspaper as he spoke. "I'M EIGHTY-SEVEN YEARS OLD. CHRIST. FRAH US LIKE AIGS." He looked like the old man from that painting, *American Gothic,* down to the gray strands of hair combed over his balding dome.

"Wonder what sort of old couple we'd make," Georgia said.

"Well. I'd still be hairy. It would just be white hair. And it would probably be growing in tufts out of all the wrong places. My ears. My nose. Big, crazy hairs sticking out my eyebrows. Basically like Santa, gone horribly fuckin' wrong."

She scooped a hand under her breasts. "The fat in these is going to drain steadily into my ass. I got a sweet tooth, so probably my teeth will fall out on me. On the bright side, I'll be able to pop out my dentures for toothless, old-lady blow jobs."

He touched her chin, lifted her face toward his. He studied her high cheekbones and the eyes in deep, bruised hollows, eyes that watched with a wry amusement that did not quite mask her desire to meet with his approval.

"You got a good face," he said. "You got good eyes. You'll be all right. With old ladies it's all about the eyes. You want to be an old lady with lively eyes, so it looks like you're always thinking of something funny. Like you're looking for trouble."

He drew his hand away. She peered down into her coffee, smiling, flattered into an uncharacteristic shyness.

"Sounds like you're talking about my grandma Bammy," she said. "You'll love her. We could be there by lunch."

"Sure."

"My grandma looks like the friendliest, most harmless old thing. Oh, but she likes tormenting people. I was living with her by the time I was in the eighth grade. I'd have my boyfriend Jimmy Elliott over—to play Yahtzee, I said, but really we were sneaking wine. Bammy would leave a half-full bottle of red in her fridge most days, leftover from dinner the night before. And she knew what we were doing, and one day she switched purple ink for the booze and left it for us. Jimmy let me take the first slug. I got a mouthful and went and coughed it all down myself. When she came home, I still had a big purple ring on my mouth, purple stains all down my jaw, purple tongue. It didn't come out for a week either. I expected Bammy to paddle me good, but she just thought it was funny."

The waitress came for their order. When she was gone, Georgia said, "What was it like being married, Jude?"

"Peaceful."

"Why did you divorce her?"

"I didn't. She divorced me."

"She catch you in bed with the state of Alaska or something?"

"No. I didn't cheat—well, not too often. And she didn't take it personal."

"She didn't? Are you for real? If we were married and you helped yourself to a piece, I'd throw the first thing came to hand at you. And the second. I wouldn't drive you to the hospital either. Let you bleed." She paused, bent over her mug, then said, "So what did it?"

"It would be hard to explain."

"Because I'm too stupid?"

"No," he said. "More like I'm not smart enough to explain it to myself, let alone anyone else. For a long time, I wanted to work at being a husband. Then I didn't. And when I didn't anymore—she just knew it. Maybe I made sure she knew it." And as he said it, Jude was thinking how he'd started staying up late, waiting for her to get tired and go to bed without him. He'd slip in later, after she was asleep, so there was no chance of making love. Or how he would sometimes start playing guitar, picking at a tune, in the middle of her telling him something—playing right over her talk. Remembering how he'd held on to the snuff movie instead of throwing it away. How he'd left it out where she could find it—where he supposed he knew she *would* find it.

"That doesn't make sense. Just all of a sudden, you didn't feel like making the effort? That doesn't seem like you. You aren't the type to give up on things for no reason."

It wasn't for no reason, but what reason there was defied articulation, could not be put into words in a way that made sense. He had bought his wife the farmhouse, bought it for both of them. He bought Shannon one Mercedes, then another, a big sedan and a convertible. They took weekends, sometimes, in Cannes, and flew there on a private jet where they were served jumbo shrimp and lobster tail on ice. And then Dizzy died— died as badly and painfully as a person could die—and Jerome killed himself, and still Shannon would come into Jude's studio and say, "I'm worried about you. Let's go to Hawaii" or "I bought you a leather jacket—try it on," and he would begin to strum at his guitar, hating the chirp of her voice and playing over it, hating the thought of spending more money, of owning another jacket, of going on another trip. But mostly just hating the contented, milk-fed look of her face, her fat fingers with all their rings, the cool look of concern in her eyes.

At the very end, when Dizzy was blind and raging with fever and soiling himself almost hourly, he got the idea in his head that Jude was his father. Dizzy wept and said he didn't want to be gay. He said, "Don't hate me anymore, Dad, don't hate me." And Jude said, "I don't. I never." And then Dizzy was gone, and Shannon went right on ordering Jude clothes and thinking about where they should eat lunch.

"Why didn't you have children with her?" Georgia asked.

"I was worried I'd have too much of my father in me."

"I doubt you're anything like him," she said.

He considered this over a forkful of food. "No. He and I have pretty much exactly the same disposition."

"What scares me is the idea of having kids and then them finding out the truth about me. Kids always find out. I found out about my folks."

"What would your kids find out about you?"

"That I dropped out of high school. That when I was thirteen I let a guy turn me into a prostitute. The only job I was ever good at involved taking my clothes off to Mötley Crüe for a roomful of drunks. I tried to kill myself. I been arrested three times. I stole money from my grandma and made her cry. I didn't brush my teeth for about two years. Am I missing anything?"

"So this is what your kid would find out: No matter what bad thing happens to me, I can talk to my mother, because she's been through it all. No matter what shitty thing happens to me, I can survive it, because my mom was through worse, and she made it."

Georgia lifted her head, smiling again, her eyes glittering bright with pleasure and mischief—the kind of eyes Jude had been talking about only a few minutes before.

"You know, Jude," she said, reaching for her coffee with the fingers of her bandaged hand. The waitress was behind her, leaning forward with the coffeepot to refill Georgia's mug and not looking at what she was doing, staring instead down at her check pad. Jude saw what was going to happen but couldn't force the warning out of his throat in time. Georgia went on talking, "Sometimes you're such a decent guy, I can almost forget what an assh—"

"The waitress poured just as Georgia moved her cup and dumped coffee over the bandaged hand. Georgia wailed and yanked the hand back, drawing it tight against her chest, her face twisting in a hurt, sickened grimace. For a moment there was glassy shock in her eyes, a flat and empty shine that made Jude think she might be about to pass out.

Then she was up, clutching the bad hand in her good one. "Want to watch where the fuck you're pourin' that, you dumb bitch?" she shouted at the waitress, that accent coming over her again, her voice going country on her.

"Georgia," Jude said, starting to rise.

She made a face and waved him back to his chair. She thudded the waitress with her shoulder, on her way by her, stalking toward the hall to the bathrooms.

Jude nudged his plate aside. "Guess I'll take the check when you get a chance."

"I am so sorry," the waitress said.

"Accidents happen."

"I am so sorry," the waitress repeated. "But that is no reason for her to talk to me that way."

"She got burnt. I'm surprised you didn't hear worse."

The waitress said, "The two of you. I knew what I was serving the moment I laid eyes on you. And I served you just as nice as I'd serve anyone else."

"Oh? You knew what you were serving? What was that?"

"Pair of lowlifes. You look like a drug peddler."

He laughed.

"And you only got to take one glance at her to know what she is. You payin' her by the hour?"

He stopped laughing.

"Get me the check," he said. "And get your fat ass out of my sight."

She stared at him a moment longer, her mouth screwed up as if she were getting ready to spit, then hurried away without another word.

The people at the tables immediately around him had stopped their conversations to gawk and listen. Jude swept his gaze here and there, staring back at anyone who dared stare at him, and one by one they returned to their food. He was fearless when it came to making eye contact, had looked into too many crowds for too many years to lose a staring contest now.

Finally the only people left watching him were the old man out of *American Gothic* and his wife, who might've been a circus fat lady on her day off. She at least made an effort to be discreet, peeping at Jude from the corners of her eyes while pretending to be interested in the paper spread before her. But the old man just stared, his tea-colored eyes judging and also somehow amused. In one hand he held the electrolarynx to his throat—it hummed faintly—as if he were about to comment. Yet he said nothing.

"Got something on your mind?" Jude asked when staring right into the old man's eyes didn't embarrass him into minding his own business.

The old man raised his eyebrows, then wagged his head back and forth: *No, nothing to say.* He lowered his gaze back to his plate with a comic little sniff. He set the electrolarynx down beside the salt and pepper.

Jude was about to look away, when the electrolarynx came to life, vibrating on the table. A loud, toneless, electric voice buzzed forth: "YOU WILL DIE."

The old man stiffened, sat back in his wheelchair. He stared down at his electrolarynx, bewildered, maybe not really sure it had said anything. The fat lady curled her paper and peered over the top of it at the device, a wondering frown set on a face as smooth and round as the Pillsbury Doughboy's.

"I AM DEAD," the electrolarynx buzzed, chattering across the surface of the table like a cheap windup toy. The old man plucked it up between his fingers. It made joy-buzzer sounds from between them. "YOU WILL DIE. WE WILL BE IN THE DEATH HOLE TOGETHER."

"What's it doin'?" said the fat woman. "Is it pickin' up a radio station again?"

The old man shook his head: *Don't know.* His gaze rose from the electrolarynx, which now rested in the cup of his palm, to Jude. He peered at Jude through glasses that magnified his astonished eyes. The old man held his hand out, as if offering the device to Jude. It hummed and jittered about.

"YOU WILL KILL HER KILL YOURSELF KILL THE DOGS THE DOGS WON'T SAVE YOU WE'LL RIDE TOGETHER LISTEN NOW LISTEN TO MY VOICE WE WILL RIDE AT NIGHTFALL. YOU DON'T OWN ME. I OWN YOU. I OWN YOU NOW."

"Peter," the fat woman said. She was trying to whisper, but her voice choked, and when she forced her next breath up, it came out shrill and wavering. "Make it stop, Peter."

Peter just sat there holding it out to Jude, as if it were a phone and the call was for him.

Everyone was looking, the room filled with crosscurrents of worried murmuring. Some of the other customers had come up out of their chairs to watch, didn't want to miss what might happen next.

Jude was up, too, thinking, *Georgia.* As he rose and started to turn toward the hallway to the restrooms, his gaze swept the picture windows that looked out front. He stopped in midmovement, his gaze catching and holding on what he saw in the parking lot. The dead man's pickup idled there, waiting close to the front doors, the floodlights on, globes of cold white light. No one sitting in it.

A few of the onlookers were standing around, at tables just behind his, and he had to shove through them to reach the corridor to the bathrooms. Jude found a door that said WOMEN, slammed it in.

Georgia stood at one of the two sinks. She didn't glance up at the sound of the door banging against the wall. She stared at herself in the mirror, but her eyes were unfocused, not really fixed on anything, and her face wore the wistful, grave expression of a child almost asleep in front of the television.

She cocked her bandaged fist back and drove it into the mirror, hard as she could, no holding back. She pulverized the glass in a fist-size circle, with shatter lines jagging out away from the hole in all directions. An instant later silver spears of mirror fell with a ringing crash, broke musically against the sinks.

A slender, yellow-haired woman with a newborn in her arms stood a yard away, beside a changing table that folded out from the wall. She grabbed the baby to her chest and began to scream, "Oh, my God! Oh, my *God!*"

Georgia grabbed an eight-inch scythe blade of silver, a gleaming crescent moon, raised it to her throat, and tipped her chin back to gouge into the flesh beneath. Jude broke out of the shock that had held him in the doorway and caught her wrist, twisted it down to her side, then bent it back, until she made a pitiful cry and let go. The mirrored scythe fell to the white tiles and shattered with a pretty clashing sound.

Jude spun her, twisting her arm again, hurting her. She gasped and shut her eyes against tears but let him force her forward, march her to the door. He wasn't sure why he hurt her, if it was panic or on purpose, because he was angry at her for going off or angry at himself for letting her.

The dead man was in the hall outside the bathroom. Jude didn't register him until he'd already walked past him, and then a shudder rolled through him, left him on legs that wouldn't stop trembling. Craddock had tipped his black hat at them on their way by.

Georgia could barely hold herself up. Jude shifted his grip to her upper arm, supporting her, as he rammed her across the dining room. The fat lady and the old man had their heads together.

". . . WASN'T NO RADIO STATION . . ."

"Weirdos. Weirdos playing a prank."

"SHADDAP, HERE THEY COME."

Others stared, jumped to get out of the way. The waitress who only a minute before had accused Jude of being a drug peddler and Georgia of being his whore stood up at the front counter talking to the manager, a little man with pens in his shirt pocket and the sad eyes of a basset hound. She pointed at them as they crossed the room.

Jude slowed at his table long enough to throw down a pair of twenties. As they went by the manager, the little man lifted his head to regard them with his tragic gaze but did not say anything. The waitress went on sputtering in his ear.

"Jude," Georgia said when they went through the first set of doors. "You're hurting me."

He relaxed his grip on her upper arm, saw that his fingers had left waxy white marks in her already pale flesh. They thumped through the second set of doors and were outside.

"Are we safe?" she asked.

"No," he said. "But we will be soon. The ghost has a healthy fear of them dogs."

They walked quickly past Craddock's empty and idling pickup truck. The passenger-side window was rolled down about a third of the way. The radio was on inside. One of the AM right-wingers was talking, in a smooth, confident, almost arrogant voice.

". . . it feels good to embrace those core American values, and it feels good to see the right people win an election, even if the other side is going to say it wasn't fair, and it feels good to see more and more people returning to the politics of common Christian good sense," said the deep, dulcet voice. "But you know what would feel even better? To choke that bitch standing next to you, choke that bitch, then step into the road in front of a semi, lay down for it, lay down and . . ."

Then they were past, the voice out of earshot.

"We're going to lose this thing," Georgia said.

"No we aren't. Come on. It isn't a hundred yards back to the hotel."

"If he doesn't get us now, he's going to get us later. He told me. He said I might as well kill myself and get it over, and I was going to. I couldn't help myself."

"I know. That's what he does."

They started along the highway, right at the edge of the gravel breakdown lane, with the long stalks of sawgrass whipping at Jude's jeans.

Georgia said, "My hand feels sick."

He stopped, lifted it for a look. It wasn't bleeding, either from punching the mirror or from lifting up the curved blade of glass. The thick, muffling pads of the bandage had protected her skin. Still, even through the wraps he could feel an unwholesome heat pouring off it, and he wondered if she had broken a bone.

"I bet. You hit the mirror pretty hard. You're lucky you aren't all hacked up." Nudging her forward, getting them moving again.

"It's beating like a heart. Going *whump-whump-whump*." She spat, spat again.

Between them and the motel was an overpass, a stone train trestle, the tunnel beneath narrow and dark. There was no sidewalk, no room even for the breakdown lane at the sides of the road. Water dripped from the stone ceiling.

"Come on," he said.

The overpass was a black frame, boxed around a picture of the Days Inn. Jude's eyes were fixed on the motel. He could see the Mustang. He could see their room.

They did not slow as they passed into the tunnel, which stank of stagnant water, weeds, urine.

"Wait," Georgia said.

She turned, doubled over, and gagged, bringing up her eggs, lumps of half-digested toast, and orange juice.

He held her left arm with one hand, pulled her hair back from her face with the other. It made him edgy, standing there in the bad-smelling dark, waiting for her to finish.

"Jude," she said.

"Come on," he said, tugging at her arm.

"Wait—"

"Come on."

She wiped her mouth, with the bottom of her shirt. She remained bent over. "I think—"

He heard the truck before he saw it, heard the engine revving behind him, a furious growl of sound, rising to a roar. Headlights dashed up the wall of rough stone blocks. Jude had time to glance back and saw the dead man's pickup rushing at them, Craddock grinning behind the wheel and the floodlights two circles of blinding light, holes burned right into the world. Smoke boiled off the tires.

Jude got an arm under Georgia and pitched himself forward, carrying her with him and out the far end of the tunnel.

The smoke-blue Chevy slammed into the wall behind him with a shattering crash of steel smashing against stone. It was a great clap of noise that stunned Jude's eardrums, set them ringing. He and Georgia fell onto wet gravel, clear of the tunnel now. They rolled away from the side of the road, tumbled down the brush, and landed in dew-damp ferns. Georgia cried out, clipped him in the left eye with a bony elbow. He put a hand down into something squishy, the cool unpleasantness of swamp muck.

He lifted himself up, breathing raggedly. Jude looked back. It wasn't the dead man's old Chevy that had hit the wall but an olive Jeep, the kind that was open to the sky, with a roll bar in the back. A black man with close-cropped, steel-wool hair sat behind the steering wheel, holding his forehead. The windshield was fractured in a network of connected rings where his skull had hit it. The whole front driver's side of the Jeep had been gouged down to the frame, steel twisted up and back in smoking, torn pieces.

"What happened?" Georgia asked, her voice faint and tinny, hard to make out over the droning in his ears.

"The ghost. He missed."

"Are you sure?"

"That it was the ghost?"

"That he missed."

He came to his feet, his legs unsteady, knees threatening to give. He took her wrist, helped her up. The whining in his eardrums was already beginning to clear. From a long way off, he could hear his dogs, barking hysterically, barking mad.

26

Heaping their bags into the back of the Mustang, Jude became aware of a slow, deep throb in his left hand, different from the dull ache that had persisted since stabbing himself there yesterday. When he looked down, he saw that his bandage was coming unraveled and was soaked through with fresh blood.

Georgia drove while he sat in the passenger seat, with the first-aid kit that had accompanied them from New York open in his lap. He undid the wet, tacky dressings and dropped them on the floor at his feet. The Steri-Strips he'd applied to the wound the day before had peeled away, and the puncture gaped again, glistening, obscene. He had torn it open getting out of the way of Craddock's truck.

"What are you going to do about that hand?" Georgia asked, shooting him an anxious look before turning her gaze back to the road.

"Same thing you're doing about yours," he said. "Nothing."

He began to clumsily apply fresh Steri-Strips to the wound. It felt as if he were putting a cigarette out on his palm. When he'd closed the tear as best he could, he wrapped the hand with clean gauze.

"You're bleeding from the head, too," she said. "Did you know that?"

"Little scrape. Don't worry about it."

"What happens next time? Next time we wind up somewhere without the dogs to look out for us?"

"I don't know."

"It was a public place. We should've been safe in a public place. People all around, and it was bright daylight, and he went and come at us anyway. How are we supposed to fight somethin' like him?"

He said, "I don't know. If I knew what to do, I'd be doing it already, Florida. You and your questions. Lay off a minute, why don't you?"

They drove on. It was only when he heard the choked sound of her weeping—she was struggling to do it in silence—that he realized he'd called her Florida, when he had meant to say Georgia. It was her questions that had done it, one after another, that and her accent, those Daughter of the Confederacy inflections that had steadily been creeping into her voice the last couple days.

The sound of Georgia trying not to cry was somehow worse than if she wept openly. If she would just go ahead and cry, he could say something to her, but as it was, he felt it necessary to let her be miserable in private and pretend he hadn't noticed. Jude sank low in the passenger seat and turned his face toward the window.

The sun was a steady glare through the windshield, and a little south of Richmond he fell into a disgusted, heat-stunned trance. He tried to think what he knew about the dead man who pursued them, what Anna had told him about her stepfather when they were together. But it was hard to think, too much effort—he was sore, and there was all that sun in his face and Georgia making quiet, wretched noises behind the steering wheel—and anyway he was sure Anna hadn't said much.

"I'd rather ask questions," *she told him*, "than answer them."

She had kept him at bay with those foolish, pointless questions for almost half a year: *Were you ever in the Boy Scouts? Do you shampoo your beard? What do you like better, my ass or my tits?*

What little he knew should have invited curiosity: the family business in hypnotism, the dowser father who taught his girls to read palms and talk to spirits, a childhood shadowed by the hallucinations of preadolescent schizophrenia. But Anna—Florida—didn't want to talk about who she'd been before meeting him, and for himself, he was happy to let her past be past.

Whatever she wasn't telling him, he knew it was bad, a certain kind of bad. The specifics didn't matter—that's what he believed then. He had thought, at the time, that this was one of his strengths, his willingness to accept her as she was, without questions, without judgments. She was safe with him, safe from whatever ghosts were chasing her.

Except he hadn't kept her safe, he knew that now. The ghosts always caught up eventually, and there was no way to lock the door on them. They would walk right through. What he'd thought of as a personal strength—he was happy to know about her only what she wanted him to know—was something more like selfishness. A childish willingness to remain in the dark, to avoid distressing conversations, upsetting truths. He had feared her secrets—or, more specifically, the emotional entanglements that might come with knowing them.

Just once had she risked something like confession, something close to self-revelation. It was at the end, shortly before he sent her home.

She'd been depressed for months. First the sex went bad, and then there was no sex at all. He'd find her in the bath, soaking in ice water, shivering helplessly, too confused and unhappy to get out. Thinking on it now, it was as if she were rehearsing for her first day as a corpse, for the evening she would spend cooling and wrinkling in a tub full of cold water and blood. She prattled to herself in a little girl's crooning voice but went mute if he tried to talk to her, stared at him in bewilderment and shock, as if she'd just heard the furniture speak.

Then one night he went out. He no longer remembered for what. To rent a movie maybe, or get a burger. It was just after dark as he drove home. Half a mile from the house, he heard people honking their horns, the oncoming cars blinking their headlights.

Then he passed her. Anna was on the other side of the road, running in

the breakdown lane, wearing nothing but one of his oversize T-shirts. Her
yellow hair was windblown and tangled. She saw him as he passed, going
the other way, and lunged into the road after him, waving her hand frantically and stepping into the path of an oncoming eighteen-wheeler.

The truck's tires locked and shrieked. The trailer's rear end fishtailed to
the left while the cab swung right. It banged to a stop, two feet from rolling
over her. She didn't appear to notice. Jude had stopped himself by then, and
she flung open the driver's-side door, fell against him.

"Where did you go?" she screamed. "I looked for you everywhere. I
ran, I ran, and I thought you were gone, so I ran, I ran lookin'."

The driver of the semi had his door open, one foot out on the step-down.
"What the fuck is up with that bitch?"

"I got it," Jude said to him.

The trucker opened his mouth to speak again, then fell silent as Jude
hauled Anna in across his legs, an act that hiked up her shirt and raised her
bare bottom to the air.

Jude threw her into the passenger seat, and immediately she was up
again, falling into him, shoving her hot, wet face against his chest.

"I was scared I was so scared and I ran—"

He shoved her off him with his elbow, hard enough to slam her into the
passenger-side door. She fell into a shocked silence.

"Enough. You're a mess. I've had it. You hear? You aren't the only one
who can tell fortunes. You want me to tell you about your future? I see
you holding your fuckin' bags, waitin' for a bus," he said.

His chest was tight, tight enough to remind him he wasn't thirty-three
but fifty-three, almost thirty years older than she. Anna stared. Her eyes
round and wide and uncomprehending.

He put the car into drive and began to roll for home. As he turned in to
the driveway, she bent over and tried to unzip his pants, to give him a blow
job, but the thought turned his stomach, was an unimaginable act, a thing
he could not let her do, so he hit her with the elbow again, driving her back
once more.

He avoided her most of the next day, but the following night, when he came in from walking the dogs, she called from the top of the back stairs. She asked if he would make her some soup, just a can of something. He said all right.

When he brought it to her, a bowl of chicken noodle on a small tray, he could see she was herself again. Washed out and exhausted, but clear in her head. She tried to smile for him, something he didn't want to see. What he had to do was going to be hard enough.

She sat up, took the tray across her knees. He sat on the side of the bed and watched her take little swallows. She didn't really want it. It had only been an excuse to get him up to the bedroom. He could tell from the way her jaw tightened before each tiny, fretful sip. She had lost twelve pounds in the last three months.

She set it aside after finishing less than a quarter of the broth, then smiled, in the way of a child who has been promised ice cream if she'll choke down her asparagus. She said thank you, it was nice. She said she felt better.

"I have to go to New York next Monday. I'm doing Howard Stern," Jude said.

An anxious light flickered in her pale eyes. "I . . . I don't think I ought to go."

"I wouldn't ask you to. The city would be the worst thing for you."

She looked at him so gratefully he had to glance away.

"I can't leave you here either," *he said.* "Not by yourself. I was thinking maybe you ought to stay with family for a while. Down in Florida." *When she didn't reply, he went on,* "Is there someone in your family I can call?"

She slid down into her pillows. She drew the sheet up to her chin. He was worried she would start crying, but when he looked, she was staring calmly at the ceiling, her hands folded one atop the other on her breastbone.

"Sure," *she said finally.* "You were good to put up with me for as long as you did."

"What I said the other night . . ."

"I don't remember."

"That's good. What I said is better forgotten. I didn't mean any of it anyhow." *Although in fact what he'd said was exactly what he meant, had only been the harshest possible version of what he was telling her now.*

The silence drew out between them until it was uncomfortable, and he felt he should prod her again, but as he was opening his mouth, she spoke first.

"You can call my daddy," *she said.* "My stepdaddy, I mean. You can't call my real daddy. He's dead, of course. You want to talk to my stepdaddy, he'll drive all the way up here to pick me up in person if you want. Just give him the word. My stepdaddy likes to say I'm his little onion. I bring tears to his eyes. Isn't that a cute thing to say?"

"I wouldn't make him come get you. I'll fly you private."

"No plane. Planes are too fast. You can't go south on a plane. You need to drive. Or take a train. You need to watch the dirt turn to clay. You need to look at all the junkyards full of rustin' cars. You need to go over a few bridges. They say that evil spirits can't follow you over running water, but that's just humbug. You ever notice rivers in the North aren't like rivers in the South? Rivers in the South are the color of chocolate, and they smell like marsh and moss. Up here they're black, and they smell sweet, like pines. Like Christmas."

"I could take you to Penn Station and put you on the Amtrak. Would that take you south slow enough?"

"Sure."

"So I'll call your da— your stepfather?"

"Maybe I better call him," *she said. It crossed his mind then how rarely she spoke to anyone in her family. They'd been together more than a year. Had she ever called her stepfather, to wish him happy birthday, to tell him how she was doing? Once or twice Jude had come into his record library and found Anna on the phone with her sister, frowning with concentration, her voice low and terse. She seemed unlike herself then, someone engaged in a disagreeable sport, a game she had no taste for but felt obliged to play out anyway.* "You don't have to talk to him."

"Why don't you want me to talk to him? 'Fraid we won't get along?"

"It's not that I'm worried he'll be rude to you or nothin'. He isn't like that. My daddy is easy to talk to. Everybody's friend."

"Well then, what?"

"I never talked to him about it yet, but I just know what he thinks about us taking up with each other. He won't like it. You the age you are and the kind of music you play. He hates that kind of music."

"There's more people don't like it than do. That's the whole point."

"He doesn't think much of musicians at all. You never met a man with less music in him. When we were little, he'd take us on these long drives, to someplace where he'd been hired to dowse for a well, and he'd make us listen to talk radio the whole way. It didn't matter what to him. He'd make us listen to a continuous weather broadcast for four hours." *She pulled two fingers slowly through her hair, lifting a long, golden strand away from her head, then letting it slip through her fingers and fall. She went on,* "He had this one creepy trick he could do. He'd find someone talkin', like one of those Holy Rollers that are always kickin' it up for Jesus on the AM. And we'd listen and listen, until Jessie and me were beggin' him for anything else. And he wouldn't say anything, and he wouldn't say anything, and then, just when we couldn't stand it anymore, he'd start to talk to himself. And he'd be sayin' exactly what the preacher on the radio was sayin', at exactly the same time, only in his own voice. Recitin' it. Deadpan, like. 'Christ the Redeemer bled and died for you. What will you do for Him? He carried His own cross while they spat on Him. What burden will you carry?' Like he was readin' from the same script. And he'd keep going until my momma told him to stop it. That she didn't like it. And he'd laugh and turn the radio off. But he'd keep talkin' to himself. Kind of mutterin'. Sayin' all the preacher's lines, even with the radio off. Like he was hearin' it in his head, gettin' the broadcast on his fillings. He could scare me so bad doing that."

Jude didn't reply, didn't think a reply was called for, and anyway was not sure whether the story was true or the latest in a succession of self-delusions that had haunted her.

She sighed, let another strand of her hair flop. "I was sayin', though, that he wouldn't like you, and he has ways of gettin' rid of my friends when he doesn't like them. A lot of daddies are overprotective of their little girls, and if someone comes around they don't care for, they might try and scare 'em off. Lean on 'em a little. Course that never works, because the girl always takes the boy's side, and the boy keeps after her, either because he can't be scared or doesn't want her to *think* he can be scared. My stepdaddy's smarter than that. He's as friendly as can be, even with people he'd like to see burnt alive. If he ever wants to get rid of someone he doesn't want around me, he drives them off by tellin' 'em the truth. The truth is usually enough.

"Give you an example. When I was sixteen, I started running around with this boy I just knew my old man wouldn't like, on account of this kid was Jewish, and also we'd listen to rap together. Pop hates rap worst of all. So one day my stepdaddy told me it was going to stop, and I said I could see who I wanted, and he said sure, but that didn't mean the kid would keep wantin' to see me. I didn't like the sound of that, but he didn't explain himself.

"Well, you've seen how I get low sometimes and start thinkin' crazy things. That all started when I was twelve, maybe, same time as puberty. I didn't see a doctor or anything. My stepdaddy treated me himself, with hypnotherapy. He could hold things in check pretty good, too, as long as we sat down once or twice a week. I wouldn't get up to any of my crazy business. I wouldn't think there was a dark truck circling the house. I wouldn't see little girls with coals for eyes watchin' me from under the trees at night.

"But he had to go away. He had to go to Austin for some conference on hypnoglogic drugs. Usually he took me along when he went on one of his trips, but this time he left me at home with Jessie. My mom was dead by then, and Jessie was eighteen and in charge. And while he was gone I started havin' trouble sleepin'. That's always the first sign I'm gettin' low, when I start havin' insomnia.

"After a couple nights, I started seein' the girls with the burning eyes. I couldn't go to school on Monday, because they were waitin' outside under the oak tree. I was too scared to go out. I told Jessie. I said she had to make Pop come home, that I was gettin' bad ideas about things again. She told me she was tired of my crazy shit and that he was busy and I would be all right till he got back. She tried to make me go to school, but I wouldn't. I stayed in my room and watched television. But pretty soon they started talkin' to me through the TV. The dead girls. Tellin' me I was dead like they was. That I belonged in the dirt with them.

"Usually Jessie got back from school at two or three. But she didn't come home that afternoon. It got later and later, and every time I looked out the window, I saw the girls starin' back in at me. They'd be right on the other side of the glass. My stepdad called, and I told him I was in trouble and please come home, and he said he'd come quick as he could, but he wouldn't be back until late. He said he was worried I might hurt myself and he'd call someone to come be with me. After he hung up, he phoned Philip's parents, who lived up the street from us."

"Philip? Was this your boyfriend? The Jewish kid?"

"Uh-huh. Phil came right over. I didn't know him. I hid under the bed from him, and I screamed when he tried to touch me. I asked him if he was with the dead girls. I told him all about them. Jessie showed up pretty soon afterward, and Philip ran off quick as he could. After that he was so freaked out he didn't want to have anything to do with me. And my stepdaddy just said what a shame. He thought Philip was my friend. He thought Philip, more than anyone else, could be trusted to look out for me when I was havin' a rough time."

"So is that what's worrying you? Your old man is going let me know you're a lunatic and I'll be so shocked I won't ever want to see you again? 'Cause I got to tell you, Florida, hearing you get kind of crazy now and then wouldn't exactly be a newsflash."

She snorted, soft breathy laughter. Then she said, "He wouldn't say that. I don't know what he'd say. He'd just find something to make you like me a little less. If you *can* like me any less."

"Let's not start with that."

"No. No, on second thought maybe you best call my sister instead. She's an unkind bitch—we don't get along a lick. She never forgave me for being cuter than her and gettin' better Christmas presents. After Momma died, she had to be Susie Homemaker, but I still got to be a kid. Jessie was doin' our laundry and cookin' our meals by the time she was twelve, and no one has ever been able to appreciate how hard she had to work or how little fun she got to have. But she'll arrange to get me home without any nonsense. She'll like havin' me back, so she can boss me around and make rules for me."

But when Jude called her sister's house, he got the old man anyway, who answered on the third ring.

"What'n I do for you? Go ahead and talk. I'll help you if I can."

Jude introduced himself. He said Anna wanted to come home for a while, making it out to be more her idea than his. Jude wrestled mentally with how to describe her condition, but Craddock came to his rescue.

"How's she sleepin'?" *Craddock asked.*

"Not too well," *Jude said, relieved, understanding somehow that this said it all.*

Jude offered to have a chauffer drive Anna from the train station in Jacksonville to Jessica's house in Testament, but Craddock said no, he would meet her at the Amtrak himself.

"A drive to Jacksonville will suit me fine. Any excuse to get out in my truck for a few hours. Put the windows down. Make faces at the cows."

"I hear that," *Jude said, forgetting himself and warming to the old man.*

"I appreciate you takin' care of my little girl like you done. You know, when she was just a pup, she had posters of you all over her walls. She always did want to meet you. You and that fella from . . . what was their name? That Mötley Crüe? Now, she *really* loved them. She followed them for half a year. She was at all their shows. She got to know some of them, too. Not the band, I guess, but their road team. Them were her wild years. Not that she's real settled now, is she? Yeah, she loved all your albums. She loved all kinds of that heavy metal music. I always knew she'd find herself a rock star."

Jude felt a dry, ticklish sensation of cold spreading behind his chest. He knew what Craddock was telling him—that she had fucked roadies to hang with Mötley Crüe, that star fucking was a thing with her, and if she wasn't sleeping with him, she'd be in the sack with Vince Neil or Slash—and he also knew why Craddock was telling him. For the same reason he had let Anna's Jewish friend see her when she was out of her head, to put a wedge between them.

What Jude had not foreseen was that he could know what Craddock was doing and it could work anyway. No sooner had Craddock said it than Jude started thinking where he and Anna had met, backstage at a Trent Reznor show. How had she got there? Who did she know, and what did she have to do for a backstage pass? If Trent had walked into the room right then, would she have sat at his feet instead and asked the same sweet, pointless questions?

"I'll take care of her, Mr. Coyne. You just send her back to me. I'll be waitin'," *Craddock told him.*

Jude took her to Penn Station himself. She'd been at her best all morning—was trying very hard, he knew, to be the person he'd met, not the unhappy person she really was—but whenever he looked at her, he felt that dry sensation of chill in his chest again. Her elfish grins, the way she tucked her hair behind her ears to show her studded little pink earlobes, her latest round of goofy questions, seemed like cold-blooded manipulations and only made him want to get away from her even more.

If she sensed, however, that he was holding her at a distance, she gave no sign, and at Penn Station she stood on her tiptoes and put her arms around his neck in a fierce hug—an embrace without any sexual connotations at all. When she kissed him, it was a sisterly touch of the lips on his cheek.

"We had us some fun, didn't we?" she asked. Always with her questions.

"Sure," he said. He could've said more—that he'd call her soon, that he wanted her to take better care of herself—but he didn't have it in him, couldn't wish her well. When the urge came over him, to be tender, to be compassionate, he heard her stepdaddy's voice in his head, warm, friendly, persuasive: "I always knew she'd find herself a rock star."

Anna grinned, as if he had replied with something quite clever, and squeezed his hand. He stayed long enough to watch her board but didn't remain to see the train depart. It was crowded and loud on the platform, noisy with echoing voices. He felt harried and jostled, and the stink of the place— a smell of hot iron, stale piss, and warm, sweating bodies—oppressed him.

But it wasn't any better outside, in the rainy fall cool of Manhattan. The sense of being jostled, hemmed in from all sides, remained with him all the way back to the Pierre Hotel, all the way back even to the quiet and emptiness of his suite. He was belligerent, needed to do something with himself, needed to make some ugly noises of his own.

Four hours later he was in just the right place, in Howard Stern's broadcasting studio, where he insulted and hectored, humiliated Stern's entourage of slow-witted ass kissers when they were foolish enough to interrupt him, and delivered his fire sermon of perversion and hate, chaos and ridicule. Stern loved him. His people wanted to know when Jude could come back.

He was still in New York City that weekend, and in the same mood, when he agreed to meet some of the guys from Stern's crew at a Broadway strip club. They were all the same people he had mocked in front of an audience of millions earlier in the week. They didn't take it personally. Being mocked was their job. They were crazy for him. They thought he had killed.

His mood, though, hadn't improved. He ordered a beer he didn't drink and sat at the end of a runway that appeared to be one long, frosted pane of glass, lit from beneath with soft blue gels. The faces gathered in the shadows around the runway all looked wrong to him, unnatural, unwholesome: the faces of the drowned. His head hurt. When he shut his eyes, he saw the lurid, flashing fireworks show that was prelude to a migraine.

When he opened his eyes, a girl with a knife in one hand sank to her knees in front of him. Her eyes were closed. She folded slowly backward, so the back of her head touched the glass floor, her soft, feathery black hair spread across the runway. She was still on her knees.

She moved the knife down her body, a big-bladed hunting bowie with a wide, serrated edge. She wore a dog collar with silver rings on it, a teddy with laces across the bosom that squeezed her breasts together, black stockings.

When the handle of the knife was between her legs, blade pointing at the ceiling—parody of a penis—she flung it into the air, and her eyes sprang open, and she caught it when it came down and arched her back at the same time, raising her chest to the ceiling like an offering, and sliced the knife downward.

She hacked the black lace down the middle, opening a dark red slash, as if slitting herself from throat to crotch. She rolled and threw off the costume, and beneath she was naked except for the silver rings through her nipples, which swung from her breasts, and a G-string pulled up past her hard hip bones. Her supple, sealskin-smooth torso was crimson with body paint.

AC/DC was playing "If You Want Blood You Got It," and what turned him on wasn't her young, athletic body or the way her breasts swung with the hoops of silver through them or how, when she looked right at him, her stare was direct and unafraid.

It was that her lips were moving, just barely. He doubted if anyone else in the whole room besides him even noticed. She was singing to herself, singing along to AC/DC. She knew all the words. It was the sexiest thing he'd seen in months.

He raised his beer to her, only to find that it was empty. He had no *memory of drinking it. The waitress brought him another a few minutes later. From her he learned that the dancer with the knife was named Morphine and was one of their most popular girls. It cost him a hundred to get her phone number and to find out she'd been dancing for around two years, almost to the day she stepped off the bus from Georgia. It cost him another hundred to get that when she wasn't stripping, she answered to Marybeth.*

27

Jude took the wheel just before they crossed into Georgia. His head hurt, an uncomfortable feeling of pressure on his eyeballs more than anything else. The sensation was aggravated by the southern sunshine glinting off just about everything—fenders, windshields, road signs. If not for his aching head, the sky would've been a pleasure, a deep, dark, cloudless blue.

As the Florida state line approached, he was conscious of a mounting anticipation, a nervous tickle in the stomach. Testament was by then perhaps only four hours away. He would be at her house tonight, Jessie Price, née McDermott, sister to Anna, elder stepdaughter to Craddock, and he did not know what he might do when he reached the place.

It had crossed his mind that when he found her, it might end in death for someone. He had thought already that he could kill her for what she'd done, that she was *asking* for it, but for the first time, now that he was close to facing her, the idea became more than angry speculation.

He'd killed pigs as a boy, had picked up the fall-behinds by the legs and smashed their brains out on the concrete floor of his father's cutting room. You swung them into the air and then hit the floor with them, silencing them in midsqueal with a sickening and somehow hollow splitting sound, the same noise a watermelon would make if dropped from a great height. He'd shot other hogs with the bolt gun and imagined he was killing his father as he did it.

Jude had made up his mind to do whatever he had to. He just didn't know what that was yet. And when he thought about it closely, he dreaded learning, was almost as afraid of his own possibilities as he was of the thing coming after him, the thing that had once been Craddock McDermott.

He thought Georgia was dozing, did not know she was awake until she spoke.

"It's the next exit," she said in a sand-grain voice.

Her grandmother. Jude had forgotten about her, had forgotten he'd promised to stop.

He followed her instructions, hung a left at the bottom of the off-ramp and took a two-lane state highway through the shabby outskirts of Crickets, Georgia. They rolled by used-car lots, with their thousands of red, white, and blue plastic pennants flapping in the wind, let the flow of traffic carry them into the town itself. They cruised along one edge of the grassy town square, past the courthouse, the town hall, and the eroded brick edifice of the Eagle Theater.

The route to Bammy's house led them through the green grounds of a small Baptist college. Young men, with ties tucked into their V-neck sweaters, walked beside girls in pleated skirts, with combed, shining hairdos straight out of the old Breck shampoo commercials. Some of the students stared at Jude and Georgia, in the Mustang, the shepherds standing up in the backseat, Bon and Angus breathing steam on the rear windows. A girl, walking beside a taller boy who sported a yellow bow tie, shrank back against her companion as they went past. Bow Tie put a comforting arm around her shoulders. Jude did not flip them off and then drove for a few blocks feeling good about himself, proud of his restraint. His self-control, it was like iron.

Beyond the college they found themselves on a street lined with well-kept Victorians and Colonials, shingles out front advertising the practices of lawyers and dentists. Farther down the avenue, the houses were smaller, and people lived in them. At a lemon Cape with yellow roses growing on a flower trellis to one side, Georgia said, "Turn in."

The woman who answered the door was not fat but stocky, built like a defensive tackle, with a broad, dark face, a silky mustache and clever, girlish eyes, a brown shot through with jade. Her flip-flops smacked against the floor. She stared at Jude and Georgia for a beat, while Georgia grinned a shy, awkward grin. Then something in her grandmother's eyes (Grandmother? How old was she? Sixty? Fifty-five? The disorienting thought crossed Jude's mind that she might even be younger than himself) sharpened, as if a lens had been brought into focus, and she screamed and threw open her arms. Georgia fell into them.

"M.B.!" Bammy cried. Then she leaned away from her, and, still holding her by the hips, stared into her face. "What is wrong with you?"

She put a palm to Georgia's forehead. Georgia twisted from her touch. Bammy saw her bandaged hand next, caught her by the wrist, gave it a speculative look. Then she let go of the hand—almost flung it away.

"You strung out? Christ. You smell like a dog."

"No, Bammy. I swear to God, I am not on no drugs right now. I smell like a dog because I've had dogs climbin' all over me for most of two days. Why do you always got to think the worst damn thing?" The process that had begun almost a thousand miles before, when they started traveling south, seemed to have completed itself, so that everything Georgia said sounded country now.

Only had her accent really started reasserting itself once they were on the road? Or had she started slipping into it even earlier? Jude thought maybe he'd been hearing the redneck in her voice going all the way back to the day she stuck herself with the nonexistent pin in the dead man's suit. Her verbal transformation disconcerted and unsettled him. When she talked that way—*Why do you always got to think the worst damn thing?*—she sounded like Anna.

Bon squeezed into the gap between Jude and Georgia and looked hopefully up at Bammy. The long pink ribbon of Bon's tongue hung out, spit plopping from it. In the green rectangle of the yard, Angus tracked this way and that, whuffing his nose at the flowers growing around the picket fence.

Bammy looked first at Jude's Doc Martens, then up to his scraggly black beard, taking in scrapes, the dirt, the bandage wrapped around his left hand.

"You the rock star?"

"Yes, ma'am."

"You both look like you been in a fight. Was it with each other?"

"No, Bammy," Georgia said.

"That's cute, with the matchin' bandages on your hands. Is that some kind of romantic thing? Did you two brand each other as a sign of your affection? In my day we used to trade class rings."

"No, Bammy. We're fine. We were drivin' through on our way to Florida, and I said we should stop. I wanted you to meet Jude."

"You should've called. I would've started dinner."

"We can't stay. We got to get to Florida tonight."

"You don't got to get anywhere except bed. Or maybe the hospital."

"I'm fine."

"The hell. You're the furthest thing from fine I've ever laid eyes on." She plucked at a strand of black hair stuck to Georgia's damp cheek. "You're covered in sweat. I know sick when I see it."

"I'm just boiled, is all. I spent the last eight hours trapped inside that car with those ugly dogs and bad air-conditionin'. Are you going to move your wide ass out of the way, or are you going to make me climb back into that car and drive some more?"

"I haven't decided yet."

"What's the holdup?"

"I'm tryin' to figure what the chances are you two are here to slaughter me for the money in my purse and take it to buy OxyContin. Everyone is on it these days. There's kids in junior high prostitutin' themselves for it. I learned about it on the news this morning."

"Lucky for you we aren't in junior high."

Bammy seemed about to reply, but then her gaze flicked past Jude's elbow, fixed on something in the yard.

He glanced back to see what. Angus was in a squat, body contracted as if his torso contained an accordion, the shiny black fur of his back humped up into folds, and he was dropping shit after shit into the grass.

"I'll clean up. Sorry about that," Jude said.

"I'm not," Georgia said. "You take a good look, Bammy. If I don't see a toilet in the next minute or two, that's gonna be me."

Bammy lowered her heavily mascaraed eyelids and stepped out of the way. "Come on in, then. I don't want the neighbors seein' you standin' around out here anyway. They'll think I'm startin' my own chapter of the Hells Angels."

28

When they had been introduced, formally, Jude found out her name was Mrs. Fordham, which is what he called her from then on. He could not call her Bammy; paradoxically, he could not really think of her as Mrs. Fordham. Bammy she was, whatever he called her.

Bammy said, "Let's put the dogs out back where they can run."

Georgia and Jude traded a look. They were all of them in the kitchen then. Bon was under the kitchen table. Angus had lifted his head to sniff at the counter, where there were brownies on a plate under green Saran Wrap.

The space was too small to contain the dogs. The front hallway had been too small for them, too. When Angus and Bon came running down it, they had struck a side table, rattling the china on top of it, and reeled into walls, thudding them hard enough to knock pictures askew.

When Jude looked at Bammy again, she was frowning. She'd seen the glance that had passed between Jude and Georgia and knew it meant something, but not what.

Georgia spoke first. "Aw, Bammy, we can't put them out in a strange place. They'll get into your garden."

Bon clouted aside a few chairs to squirm out from under the table.

One fell over with a sharp bang. Georgia leaped toward her, caught her by the collar.

"I'll take her," Georgia said. "Is it all right if I run through the shower? I need to wash and maybe lie down. She can stay with me, where she won't get into trouble."

Angus put his paws up on the counter to get his snout closer to the brownies.

"Angus," Jude said. "Get your ass over here."

Bammy had cold chicken and slaw in the fridge. Also homemade lemonade, as promised, in a sweating glass pitcher. When Georgia went up the back stairs, Bammy fixed Jude a plate. He sat with it. Angus flopped at his feet.

From his place at the kitchen table, Jude had a view of the backyard. A mossy rope hung from the branch of a tall old walnut. The tire that had been attached to it once was long gone. Beyond the back fence was an alley, unevenly floored in old bricks.

Bammy poured herself a lemonade and leaned with her bottom against the kitchen counter. The windowsill behind her was crowded with bowling trophies. Her sleeves were rolled up to show forearms as hairy as his.

"I never heard the romantic story of how you two met."

"We were both in Central Park," he said. "Picking daisies. We got to talking and decided to have a picnic together."

"It was either that or you met in some perverted fetish club."

"Come to think of it, it might've been a perverted fetish club."

"You're eating like you never seen food before."

"We overlooked lunch."

"What's your hurry? What's happenin' in Florida you're in such a rush to get to? Some friends of yours havin' an orgy you don't want to miss?"

"You make this slaw yourself?"

"You bet."

"It's good."

"You want the recipe?"

The kitchen was quiet except for the scrape of his fork on the plate and the thud of the dog's tail on the floor. Bammy stared at him.

At last, to fill in the silence, Jude said, "Marybeth calls you Bammy. Why's that?"

"Short for my first name," Bammy said. "Alabama. M.B.'s called me that since she was wetting her didies."

A dry mouthful of cold chicken lodged partway down Jude's windpipe. He coughed and thumped his chest and blinked at watering eyes. His ears burned.

"Really," he said, when his throat was clear. "This may be out of left field, but you ever go to one of my shows? Like, did you maybe see me on a twin bill with AC/DC in 1979?"

"Not likely. I didn't care for that kind of music even when I was young. Buncha gorillas stompin' around the stage, shoutin' swear words and screamin' their throats out. I might've caught you if you were openin' for the Bay City Rollers. Why?"

Jude wiped at the fresh sweat on his forehead, his insides all queer with relief. "I knew an Alabama once. Don't worry about it."

"How'd the two of you both get so beat up? You got scrapes on your scrapes."

"We were in Virginia, and we walked to Denny's from our motel. On the way back, we were nearly run down."

"You sure about the 'nearly' part?"

"Going under a train trestle. Fella ran his Jeep right into the stone wall. Bashed his face a good one on his windshield, too."

"How'd he make out?"

"All right, I guess."

"Was he drunk?"

"I don't know. I don't think so."

"What happened when the cops got there?"

"We didn't stay to talk to them."

"You didn't stay—" she started, then stopped and threw the rest of her lemonade into the sink, wiped the back of her mouth with her forearm. Her lips were puckered, as if her last swallow of lemonade had been more sour than she liked.

"You are in some hurry," she said.

"A mite."

"Son," she said, "just how much trouble are the two of you in?"

Georgia called to him from the top of the stairs.

"Come lie down, Jude. Come upstairs. We'll lie down in my room. You wake us up, Bammy, in an hour? We still got some drivin' to do."

"You don't need to go tonight. You know you can stay over."

"Better not," Jude said.

"I don't see the sense. It's almost five already. Wherever you're going, you won't get there till late."

"It's all right. We're night people." He put his plate in the sink.

Bammy studied him. "You won't leave without dinner?"

"No, ma'am. Wouldn't think of it. Thank you, ma'am."

She nodded. "I'll fix it while you nap. What part of the South are you from, anyway?"

"Louisiana. Place called Moore's Corner. You wouldn't have heard of it. There's nothing there."

"I know it. My sister married a man who took her to Slidell. Moore's Corner is right next to it. There's good people around there."

"Not my people," Jude said, and he went upstairs, Angus bounding up the steps after him.

Georgia was waiting at the top, in the cool darkness of the upstairs hallway. Her hair was wrapped in a towel, and she had on a faded Duke University T-shirt and a pair of loose blue shorts. Her arms were crossed under her breasts, and in her left hand was a flat white box, split at the corners and repaired with peeling brown tape.

Her eyes were the brightest thing in the shadows of the hall, greenish sparks of unnatural light, and in her wan, depleted face was a kind of eagerness.

"What's that?" he asked, and she turned it so he could read what was written on the side.

OUIJA ⇌ PARKER BROS. ⇌ TALKING BOARD

29

She led him into her bedroom, where she removed the towel from her head and slung it over a chair.

It was a small room, under the eaves, with hardly enough space in it for them and the dogs. Bon was already curled up on the twin bed tucked against one wall. Georgia made a clicking sound with her tongue and patted the pillow, and Angus leaped up beside his sister. He settled.

Jude stood just inside the closed door—he had the Ouija board now—and turned in a slow circle, looking over the place where Georgia had spent most of her childhood. He had not been prepared for anything quite so wholesome as what he found. The bedspread was a hand-stitched quilt, patterned after an American flag. A herd of dusty-looking stuffed unicorns, in various sherbet colors, were corralled in a wicker basket in one corner.

She had an antique walnut dresser, with a mirror attached to it, one that could be tilted back and forth. Photos had been stuck into the mirror frame. They were sun-faded and curled with age and showed a toothy, black-haired girl in her teens, with a skinny, boyish build. In this picture she wore a Little League uniform a size too big for her, her ears jutting out under the cap. In that picture she stood between girlfriends, all of them sunburned, flat-chested, and self-conscious in their bikini tops, on a beach somewhere, a pier in the background.

The only hint of the person she was to become was in a final still, a graduation picture, Georgia in the mortarboard and black gown. In the photo she stood with her parents: a shriveled woman in a flower-print dress, straight off the rack in Wal-Mart, a potato-shaped man with a bad comb-over and a cheap checked sport coat. Georgia posed between them, smiling, but her eyes sullen and sly and resentful. And while she held her graduation certificate in one hand, the other was raised in the death-metal salute, pinkie and index finger sticking up in devil horns, her fingernails painted black. So it went.

Georgia found what she was looking for in the desk, a box of kitchen matches. She leaned over the windowsill to light some dark candles. Printed on the rear of her shorts was the word VARSITY. The backs of her thighs were taut and strong from five years of dancing.

"Varsity what?" Jude asked.

She glanced back at him, brow furrowed, then saw where he was looking, took a peek at her own backside, and grinned.

"Gymnastics. Hence most of my act."

"Is that where you learned to chuck a knife?"

It had been a stage knife when she performed, but she could handle a real one, too. Showing off for him once, she'd thrown a bowie into a log from a distance of twenty feet, and it had hit with a solid thunk, followed by a metallic, wobbling sound, the low, musical harmonic of trembling steel.

She shot him a shy look and said, "Naw. Bammy taught me that. Bammy has some kind of throwing arm. Bowling balls. Softballs. She has a mean curve. She was pitching for her softball team when she was fifty. Couldn't no one hit her. Her daddy taught her how to chuck a knife, and she taught me."

After she lit the candles, she opened both windows a few inches, without raising the plain white shades. When the breeze blew, the shades moved and pale sunshine surged into the room, then abated, soothing waves of subdued brightness. The candles didn't add much light, but the smell of them was pleasant, mixed with the cool, fresh, grassy scent of the outdoors.

Georgia turned and crossed her legs and sat on the floor. Jude lowered himself to his knees across from her. Joints popped.

He set the box between them, opened it, and took out the gameboard—was a Ouija board a gameboard, exactly? Across the sepia-colored board were all the letters of the alphabet, the words **YES** and **NO**, a sun with a maniacally grinning face, and a glowering moon. Jude set upon the board a black plastic pointer shaped like a spade in a deck of cards.

Georgia said, "I wasn't sure I could turn it up. I haven't looked at the damn thing in probably eight years. You remember that story I told you, 'bout how once I saw a ghost in Bammy's backyard?"

"Her twin."

"It scared hell out of me, but it made me curious, too. It's funny how people are. Because when I saw the little girl in the backyard, the ghost, I just wanted her to go away. But when she vanished, pretty soon I got to wishin' I'd see her again. I started wantin' to have another experience like it sometime, to come across another ghost."

"And here you are now with one hot on your tail. Who says dreams don't come true?"

She laughed. "Anyway. A while after I saw Bammy's sister in the backyard, I picked this up at the five-and-dime. Me and one of my girlfriends used to play around with it. We'd and quiz the spirits about boys at school. And a lot of times I'd be movin' the pointer in secret, makin' it say things. My girlfriend, Sheryll Jane, she knew I was makin' it say things, but she'd always pretend like she really believed we were talkin' to a ghost, and her eyes would get all big and round and stick out of her head. I'd slide the pointer around, and the Ouija board would tell her some boy at school had a pair of her underwear in his locker, and she'd let out a screech and say, 'I always knew he was weird about me!' She was sweet to hang around with me and be so silly and play my games." Georgia rubbed the back of her neck. Almost as an afterthought, she added, "One time, though, we were playin' Ouija and it started workin' for real. I wasn't movin' the pointer or anything."

"Maybe Sheryll Jane was moving it."

"No. It was movin' on its own, and we both knew it. I could tell it was movin' on its own because Sheryll wasn't puttin' on her act with them big eyes of hers. Sheryll wanted it to stop. When the ghost told us who it was, she said I wasn't being funny. And I said I wasn't doin' nothin', and she said stop it. But she didn't take her hand off the pointer."

"Who was the ghost?"

"Her cousin Freddy. He had hung himself in the summer. He was fifteen. They were real close . . . Freddy and Sheryll."

"What'd he want?"

"He said there was pictures in his family's barn of guys in their underwear. He told us right where to find them, hidden under a floorboard. He said he didn't want his parents to know he was gay and be any more upset than they were. He said that's why he killed himself, because he didn't want to be gay anymore. Then he said souls aren't boys and aren't girls. They're only souls. He said there is no gay, and he'd made his momma sorrowful for nothin'. I remember that exactly. That he used the word 'sorrowful.'"

"Did you go look for the pictures?"

"We snuck into the barn, next afternoon, and we found the loose floorboard, but there was nothin' hidden under it. Then Freddy's father came up behind us and gave us a good shoutin' at. He said we had no business snoopin' around his place and sent us runnin'. Sheryll said not finding any pictures proved it was all a lie and that I had faked the whole thing. You wouldn't believe how mad she was. But I think Freddy's father came across the pictures before us and got rid of them, so no one would know his kid was a fairy. The way he shouted at us was like he was scared about what we might know. About what we might be lookin' for." She paused, then added, "Me and Sheryll never really made it up. We pretended like we put it behind us, but after that we didn't spend as much time together. Which suited me fine. By then I was sleepin' with my daddy's pal George Ruger, and I didn't want a whole bunch of friends hangin' around askin' me questions about how come I had so much money in my pockets all of a sudden."

The shades lifted and fell. The room brightened and dimmed. Angus yawned.

"So what do we do?" Jude said.

"Haven't you ever played with one of these?"

Jude shook his head.

"Well, we each put a hand on the pointer," she said, and started to reach forward with her right hand, then changed her mind and tried to draw it back.

It was too late. He reached out and caught her wrist. She winced—as if even the wrist were tender.

She had removed her bandages before showering and not yet put on fresh. The sight of her naked hand drove the air out of him. It looked as if it had been soaking in bathwater for hours, the skin wrinkly, white, and soft. The thumb was worse. For an instant, in the gloom, it looked almost skinless. The flesh was inflamed a startling crimson, and where the thumbprint belonged was a wide circle of infection, a sunken disk, yellow with pus, darkening to black at the center.

"Christ," Jude said.

Georgia's too-pale, too-thin face was surprisingly calm, staring back at him through the wavering shadows. She yanked her hand away.

"You want to lose that hand?" Jude asked. "You want to see if you can die from blood poisoning?"

"I am not as scared to die as I was a couple days ago. Isn't that funny?"

Jude opened his mouth for a reply and found he had none to make. His insides were knotted up. What was wrong with her hand would kill her if nothing was done, and they both knew it, and she wasn't afraid.

Georgia said, "Death isn't the end. I know that now. We both do."

"That isn't any reason to just *decide* to die. To not take care of yourself."

"I haven't just decided to die. I've decided there isn't goin' to be any hospital. We've already talked that idea in circles. You know we can't bring the dogs into no emergency room with us."

"I'm rich. I can make a doctor come to us."

"I told you already, I don't believe that what's wrong with me can be helped by any doctor." She leaned forward, rapped the knuckles of her left hand on the Ouija board. "This is more important than the hospital. Sooner or later Craddock is going to get by the dogs. I think sooner. He'll find a way. They can't protect us forever. We are livin' minute to minute, and you know it. I don't mind dyin' as long as he isn't waitin' for me on the other side."

"You're sick. That's the fever thinking. You don't need this voodoo. You need antibiotics."

"I need you," she said, her bright, vivid eyes steady on his face, "to shut the fuck up and put your hand on the pointer."

Georgia said she would do the talking, and she put the fingers of her left hand next to his on the pointer—it was called the planchette, Jude remembered now. He looked up when he heard her draw a steadying breath. She shut her eyes, not as if she were about to go into a mystic trance but more as if she were about to leap from a high diving board and was trying to get over the churning in her stomach.

"Okay," she said. "My name is Marybeth Stacy Kimball. I called myself Morphine for a few bad years, and the guy I love calls me Georgia, even though it drives me nuts, but Marybeth is who I am, my true name." She opened her eyes to a squint, peeped at Jude from between her eyelashes. "Introduce yourself."

He was about to speak when she held up a hand to stop him.

"Your real name, now. The name that belongs to your true self. True names are very important. The right words have a charge in them. Enough charge to bring the dead back to the living."

He felt stupid—felt that what they were doing couldn't work, was a waste of time, and they were acting like children. His career had afforded him a variety of occasions to make a fool out of himself, however. Once, for a music video, he and his band—Dizzy, Jerome, and Kenny—had run in mock horror through a field of clover, chased by a dwarf dressed in a dirty leprechaun suit and carrying a chain saw. In time Jude had developed something like an immunity to the condition of feeling stupid. So when he paused, it wasn't out of a reluctance to speak but because he honestly didn't know what to say.

Finally, looking at Georgia, he said, "My name is . . . Justin. Justin Cowzynski. I guess. Although I haven't answered to that since I was nineteen."

Georgia closed her eyes, withdrawing into herself. A dimple appeared between her slender eyebrows, a little thought line. Slowly, softly, she spoke. "Well. There you go. That's us. We want to talk to Anna McDermott. Justin and Marybeth need your help. Is Anna there? Anna, will you speak to us today?"

They waited. The shade moved. Children shouted in the street.

"Is there anyone who would like to speak to Justin and Marybeth? Will Anna McDermott say somethin' to us? Please. We're in trouble, Anna. Please hear us. Please help us." Then, in a voice that approached a whisper, she said, "Come on. Do somethin'." Speaking to the planchette.

Bon farted in her sleep, a squeaking sound, like a foot skidding across wet rubber.

"She didn't know me," Georgia said. "You ask for her."

"Anna McDermott? Is there an Anna McDermott in the house? Could you please report to the Ouija information center?" he asked, in a big, hollow, public-announcer's voice.

Georgia smiled, a wide, humorless grin. "Ah, yes. I knew it was only a matter of time before the fuckin'-around would commence."

"Sorry."

"Ask for her. Ask for real."

"It's not workin'."

"You haven't tried."

"Yes I have."

"No you haven't."

"Well, it just isn't workin'."

He expected hostility or impatience. Instead her smile broadened even more, and she regarded him with a quiet sweetness that he instantly mistrusted. "She was waitin' for you to call, right up to the day she died. Like there was any chance of that. What, did you wait a whole week, before moving on in your state-by-state tour of America's easiest snatch?"

He flushed. Not even a week. "You might not want to get too hot under the collar," he said, "considering you're the easy snatch in question."

"I know, and it disgusts me. Put! Your! Hand! Back on the mother-fuckin' pointer. We are *not* done here."

Jude had been withdrawing his hand from the planchette, but at Georgia's outburst he set his fingers back upon it.

"I'm disgusted with the both of us. You for bein' who you are and me for lettin' you stay that way. Now, you call for her. She won't come for me, but she might for you. She was waitin' for you to call right to the end, and if you ever had, she would've come running. Maybe she still will."

Jude glared down at the board, the old-timey alphabet letters, the sun, the moon.

"Anna, you around? Will Anna McDermott come on and talk to us?" Jude said.

The planchette was dead, unmoving plastic. He had not felt so grounded in the world of the real and the ordinary in days. It wasn't going to work. It wasn't right. It was hard to keep his hand on the pointer. He was impatient to get up, to be done.

"Jude," Georgia said, then corrected herself. "Justin. Don't quit on this. Try again."

Jude. Justin.

He stared at his fingers on the planchette, the board beneath, and tried to think what wasn't right, and in another moment it came to him. Georgia had said that true names had a charge in them, that the right words had the power to return the dead to the living. And he thought then that Justin wasn't his true name, that he had left Justin Cowzynski in Louisiana when he was nineteen, and the man who got off the bus in New York City forty hours later was someone different entirely, capable of doing and saying things that had been beyond Justin Cowzynski. And what they were doing wrong now was calling for Anna McDermott. He had never called her that. She had not been Anna McDermott when they were together.

"Florida," Jude said, almost sighed. When he spoke again, his voice was surprising to him, calm and self-assured. "Come on and talk to me, Florida. It's Jude, darlin'. I'm sorry I didn't call you. I'm calling now. Are you there? Are you listening? Are you still waiting for me? I'm here now. I'm right here."

The planchette jumped under their fingers, as if the board had been struck from beneath. Georgia jumped with it and cried out weakly. Her bad hand fluttered to her throat. The breeze shifted direction and sucked at the shades, snapping them against the windows and darkening the room. Angus lifted his head, eyes flashing a bright, unnatural green in the weak light from the candles.

Georgia's good hand had remained on the pointer, and no sooner had it rattled back to rest on the board than it began to move. The sensation was unnatural and made Jude's heart race. It felt as if there were another pair of fingers on the planchette, a third hand, reaching into the space between his hand and Georgia's and sliding the pointer around, turning it without warning. It slipped across the board, touched a letter, stayed there for a moment, then *spun* under their fingers, forcing Jude to twist his wrist to keep his hand on it.

"W," Georgia said. She was audibly short of breath. "H. A. T."

"What," Jude said. The pointer went on finding letters, and Georgia continued calling them out: a **K**, an **E**. Jude listened, concentrating on what was being spelled.

Jude: "Kept. You."

The planchette made a half turn—and stopped, its little casters squeaking faintly.

"What kept you," Jude repeated.

"What if it isn't her? What if it's him? How do we know who we're talking to?"

The planchette surged, before Georgia had even finished speaking. It was like having a finger on a record that has suddenly begun to turn.

Georgia: "W. H. Y. I. . . ."

Jude: "Why. Is. The. Sky. Blue." The pointer went still. "It's her. She always said she'd rather ask questions than answer them. Got to be kind of a joke between us."

It was her. Pictures skipped in his head, a series of vivid stills. She was in the backseat of the Mustang, naked on the white leather except for her cowboy boots and a feathered ten-gallon hat, peeking out at him from under the brim, eyes bright with mischief. She was yanking his beard backstage at the Trent Reznor show, and he was biting the inside of his cheek to keep from shrieking. She was dead in the bathtub, a thing he hadn't ever seen except in his mind, and the water was ink, and her stepfather, in his black undertaker's suit, was on his knees beside the tub, as if to pray.

"Go on, Jude," Georgia said. "Talk to her."

Her voice was strained, pitched to just above a whisper. When Jude glanced up at Georgia, she was shivering, although her face was aglow with sweat. Her eyes glittered from deep in their dark and bony hollows . . . fever eyes.

"Are you all right?"

Georgia shook her head—*Leave me alone*—and shuddered furiously. Her left hand remained on the pointer. "Talk to her."

He looked back at the board. The black moon stamped on one corner was laughing. Hadn't it been glowering a moment before? A black dog at the bottom of the board was howling up at it. He didn't think it had been there when they first opened the board.

He said, "I didn't know how to help you. I'm sorry, kiddo. I wish you fell in love with anyone but me. I wish you fell in love with one of the good guys. Someone who wouldn't have just sent you away when things got hard."

"A. R. E. Y. O. . . ." Georgia read, in that same effortful, short-of-breath voice. He could hear, in that voice, the work it took to suppress her shivering.

"Are. You. Angry."

The pointer went still.

Jude felt a boil of emotions, so many things, all at once, he wasn't sure he could put them into words. But he could, and it turned out to be easy.

"Yes," he said.

The pointer flew to the word "**NO**."

"You shouldn't have done that to yourself."

"D. O. N. . . ."

"Done. What." Jude read. "Done what? You know what. Killed your—"

The pointer skidded back to the word **NO**.

"What do you mean, no?"

Georgia spoke the letters aloud, a **W**, an **H**, an **A**.

"What. If. I. Can't. Answer." The pointer came to rest again. Jude stared for a moment, then understood. "She can't answer questions. She can only ask them."

But Georgia was already spelling again. "I. S. H. E. A. . . ."

A great fit of shivering overcame her, so her teeth clattered, and when Jude glanced at her, he saw the breath steam from her lips, as if she were standing in a cold-storage vault. Only the room didn't feel any warmer or colder to Jude.

The next thing he noticed was that Georgia wasn't looking at her hand on the pointer, or at him, or at anything. Her eyes had gone unfocused, fixed on the middle distance. Georgia went on reciting the letters aloud, as the planchette touched them, but she wasn't looking at the board anymore, couldn't see what it was doing.

"Is." Jude read as Georgia spelled the words in a strained monotone. "He. After. You."

Georgia quit calling the letters, and he realized a question had been asked.

"Yes. Yeah. He thinks it's my fault you killed yourself, and now he's playing get-even."

NO. The planchette pointed at it for a long, emphatic moment before beginning to scurry about again.

"W. H. Y. R. U. . . ." Georgia muttered thickly.

"Why. Are. You. So. Dumb." Jude fell silent, staring.

One of the dogs on the bed whined.

Then Jude understood. He felt overcome for a moment by a sensation of light-headedness and profound disorientation. It was like the head rush that comes from standing up too quickly. It was also a little like feeling rotten ice give way underfoot, the first sickening moment of plunge. It staggered him, that it had taken him so long to understand.

"Fucker," Jude said, his voice strangled with anger. "That fucker."

He noticed that Bon was awake, staring apprehensively at the Ouija board. Angus was watching, too, his tail thumping against the mattress.

"What can we do?" Jude said. "He's coming after us, and we don't know how to get rid of him. Can you help us?"

The pointer swung toward the word **YES**.

"The golden door," Georgia whispered.

Jude looked at her—and recoiled. Her eyes had rolled up in her head, to show only the whites, and her whole body was steadily, furiously trembling. Her face, which had already been so pale it was like wax, had lost even more color, taking on an unpleasant translucence. Her breath steamed. He heard the planchette beginning to scrape and slide wildly across the board, looked back down. Georgia wasn't spelling for him anymore, wasn't speaking. He strung together the words himself.

"Who. Will. Be. The. Door. Who will be the door?"

"I will be the door," Georgia said.

"Georgia?" Jude said. "What are you talking about?"

The pointer began to move again. Jude didn't speak now, just watched it finding letters, hesitating on each for only an instant before whirring on.

Will. U. Bring. Me. Thru.

"Yes," Georgia said. "If I can. I'll make the door, and I'll bring you through, and then you'll stop him."

Do. You. Swear.

"I swear," she said. Her voice was thin and compressed and strained with her fear. "I swear I swear oh God I swear. Whatever I have to do, I just don't know what to do. I'm ready to do whatever I have to do, just tell me what it is."

Do. You. Have. A. Mirror. Marybeth.

"Why?" Georgia said, blinking, her eyes rolling back down to look blearily about. She turned her head toward her dresser. "There's one—"

She screamed. Her fingers sprang up off the pointer, and she pressed her hands to her mouth to stifle the cry. In the same instant, Angus came to his feet and began to bark from where he stood on the bed. He was staring at what she was staring at. By then Jude was twisting to see for himself, his own fingers leaving the planchette—which began to spin around and around on its own, a kid doing doughnuts on his dirt bike.

The mirror on the dresser was tilted forward to show Georgia, sitting across from Jude, with the Ouija board between them. Only in the mirror her eyes were covered by a blindfold of black gauze and her throat was slashed. A red mouth gaped obscenely across it, and her shirt was soaked in blood.

Angus and Bon bounded from the bed in the same moment. Bon hit the floor and launched herself at the planchette, snarling. She closed her jaws on the pointer, the way she might have attacked a mouse scampering for its hole, and it burst into pieces in her teeth.

Angus hurled himself against the dresser and put his front paws on the top of it, barking furiously at the face in the mirror. The force of his weight rocked the dresser onto its rear legs. The mirror could be rotated forward and back, and now it swung back, tilting to show its face to the ceiling. Angus dropped to all fours, and an instant later the dresser did the same, coming down onto its wooden legs with a ringing crash. The mirror swung forward, pivoting to show Georgia her own reflection once more. It was only her reflection. The blood—and the black blindfold— were gone.

31

In the late-afternoon cool of the room, Jude and Georgia stretched out together on the twin bed. It was too small for the both of them, and Georgia had to turn on her side and throw a leg over him to fit beside him. Her face nestled into his neck, the tip of her nose cold against his skin.

He was numb. Jude knew he needed to think about what had just happened to them, but he could not seem to turn his thoughts back to what he'd seen in the mirror, back to what Anna had been trying to tell them. His mind wouldn't go there. His mind wanted away from death for a few moments. He felt crowded by death, felt the promise of death all around, felt death on his chest, each death a stone heaped on top of him, driving the air out of him: Anna's death, Danny's, Dizzy's, Jerome's, the possibility of his own death and Georgia's waiting just down the road from them. He could not move for the weight of all those deaths pressing down on him.

Jude had an idea that as long as he was very still and said nothing, he and Georgia could stay in this quiet moment together indefinitely, with the shades flapping and the dim light wavering around them. Whatever bad thing that was waiting for them next would never arrive. As long as he remained in the little bed, with Georgia's cool thigh over him and her body clasped to his side, the unimaginable future wouldn't come for them.

It came anyway. Bammy thumped softly on the door and when she spoke, her voice was hushed and uncertain.

"You all right in there?"

Georgia pushed herself up on one elbow. She swiped the back of a hand across her eyes. Jude had not known until now that she'd been crying. She blinked and smiled crookedly, and it was *real,* not a smile for show, although for the life of him he couldn't imagine what she had to smile about.

Her face had been scrubbed clean by her tears, and that smile was heartbreaking in its easy, girlish sincerity. It seemed to say, *Oh, well. Sometimes you get a bad deal.* He understood then that she believed that what they'd both seen in the mirror was a kind of vision, something that was going to happen, that maybe they could not avert. Jude quailed at the idea. No. No, better Craddock should get him and be done with it than Georgia should die gasping in her own blood, and why would Anna show them that, what could she want?

"Honey?" Bammy asked.

"We're fine," Georgia called back.

Silence.

Then: "You aren't fightin' in there, are you? I heard bangin' around."

"*No,*" Georgia said, sounding affronted by the very suggestion. "Swear to God, Bammy. Sorry about the racket."

"Well," Bammy said. "Do you need anything?"

"Fresh sheets," Georgia said.

Another silence. Jude felt Georgia trembling against his chest, a sweet shivering. She bit down on her lower lip to keep from laughing. Then he was fighting it, too, was overcome with a sudden, convulsive hilarity. He jammed a hand into his mouth, while his insides hitched with trapped, strangled laughter.

"Jesus," said Bammy, who sounded like she wanted to spit. "Jesus Christ." Her tread moving away from the door as she said it.

Georgia fell against Jude, her cool, damp face pressed hard to his neck. He put his arms around her, and they clutched each other while they gasped with laughter.

32

After dinner Jude said he had some phone calls to make and left Georgia and Bammy in Bammy's living room. He didn't really have anyone to call but knew that Georgia wanted some time with her grandmother and that they would be more themselves without him there.

But once he was in the kitchen, a fresh glass of lemonade before him and nothing to occupy himself with, he found the phone in his hand anyway. He dialed the office line to pick up his messages. It felt queer, to be busy with something so entirely grounded in the ordinary after all that had happened in the day, from their run-in with Craddock at Denny's to the encounter with Anna in Georgia's bedroom. Jude felt disconnected from who he'd been before he first saw the dead man. His career, his living, both the business and the art that had preoccupied him for more than thirty years, seemed matters of no particular importance. He dialed the phone, watching his hand as if it belonged to someone else, feeling he was a passive spectator to the actions of a man in a play, an actor performing the part of himself.

He had five messages waiting for him. The first was from Herb Gross, his accountant and business manager. Herb's voice, which was usually oily and self-satisfied, was, in the recording, grainy with emotion.

"I just heard from Nan Shreve that Danny Wooten was found dead in his apartment this morning. Apparently he hanged himself. We're all dismayed here, as I'm sure you can imagine. Will you call me when you get this message? I don't know where you are. No one does. Thank you."

There was a message from an Officer Beam, who said that the Piecliff police were trying to reach Jude about an important matter, and would he call back. There was a message from Nan Shreve, his lawyer, who said she was handling everything, that the police wanted to collect a statement from him about Danny, and he should call as soon as he could.

The next message was from Jerome Presley, who had died four years ago, after he drove his Porsche into a weeping willow at just under a hundred miles an hour. "Hey, Jude, I guess we're getting the band back together soon, huh? John Bonham on drums. Joey Ramone on backup vocals." He laughed, then went on in his familiar, weary drawl. Jerome's croak of a voice had always reminded Jude of the comic Steven Wright. "I hear you're driving a souped-up Mustang now. That's one thing we always had, Jude—we could talk cars. Suspensions, engines, spoilers, sound systems, Mustangs, Thunderbirds, Chargers, Porsches. You know what I was thinking about, night I drove my Porsche off the road? I was thinking about all the shit I *never* said to you. All the shit we didn't talk about. Like how you got me hooked on your coke, and then you went and got straight and had the balls to tell me if I didn't do the same, you'd throw me out of the band. Like how you gave Christine money to set herself up with her own place after she left me, when she ran off with the kids without a word. How you gave her money for a lawyer. There's loyalty for you. Or how you wouldn't make a simple fucking loan when I was losing everything—the house, the cars. And here I let you sleep on the bed in my basement when you were fresh off the bus from Louisiana and you didn't have thirty dollars in your pocket." Jerome laughed again—his harsh, corrosive, smoker's laugh. "Well, we'll get a chance to finally talk about all that stuff soon. I guess I'll be seeing you any day.

I hear you're on the nightroad now. I know where that road goes. Straight into a fucking tree. They picked me out of the branches, you know. Except for the parts I left on the windshield. I miss you, Jude. I'm looking forward to putting my arms around you. We're going to sing just like the old days. Everyone sings here. After a while it kind of sounds like screaming. Just listen. Listen and you can hear them screaming."

There was a clattering sound as Jerome took the phone from his ear and held it out so Jude could hear. What came through the line was a noise like no other Jude had ever heard before, alien and dreadful, a noise like the hum of flies, amplified a hundred times, and the punch and squeal of machinery, a steam press that banged and seethed. When listened to carefully, it was possible to hear words in all that fly hum, inhuman voices calling for Mother, calling for it to stop.

Jude was primed to delete the next message, expecting another dead person, but instead it was a call from his father's housekeeper, Arlene Wade. She was so far from his thoughts that it was several moments before he was able to identify her old, warbly, curiously toneless voice, and by then her brief message was almost done.

"Hello, Justin, it's me. I wanted to update you on your father. Hasn't been conscious in thirty-six hours. Heartbeat is all fits and starts. Thought you'd want to know. He isn't in pain. Call if you like."

After Jude hung up, he leaned over the kitchen counter, looking out into the night. He had his sleeves rolled to his elbows, and the window was open, and the breeze that drifted in was cool on his skin and perfumed with the smell of the flower garden. Frogs peeped.

Jude could see his father in his head: the old man stretched out on his narrow cot, gaunt, wasted, his chin covered in a mangy white bristle, his temples sunken and gray. Jude even half believed he could smell him, the rank bad sweat, the stink of the house, an odor that included but was not limited to chicken shit, pig, and the ashtray smell of nicotine absorbed into everything—curtains, blankets, wallpaper. When Jude had finally lit out of Louisiana, he'd been fleeing that smell as much as escaping his father.

He had run and run and run, made music, made millions, spent a lifetime trying to put as much distance between himself and the old man as he could. Now, with a little luck, he and his father might die on the same day. They could walk the nightroad together. Or maybe they would ride, share the passenger seat of Craddock McDermott's smoke-colored pickup. The two of them sitting so close to one another that Martin Cowzynski could rest one of his gaunt claws on the back of Jude's neck. The smell of him filling the car. The smell of home.

Hell would smell like that, and they would drive there together, father and son, accompanied by their hideous chauffeur, with his silver crew cut and Johnny Cash suit and the radio turned to Rush Limbaugh. If hell was anything, it was talk radio—and family.

In the living room, Bammy said something in a low, gossipy murmur. Georgia laughed. Jude tilted his head at the sound and a moment later was surprised to find himself smiling in automatic response. How it was she could be in stitches again, with everything that was up against them and everything they'd seen, he couldn't imagine.

Her laughter was a quality he prized in her above all others—the deep, chaotic music of it and the way she gave herself over to it completely. It stirred him, drew him out of himself. It was just after seven by the clock on the microwave. He would step back into the living room and join the two of them for a few minutes of easy, pointless talk, and then he would get Georgia's attention and shoot a meaningful look at the door. The road was waiting.

He had made up his mind and was turning from the kitchen counter when a sound caught his attention, a lilting, off-key voice, singing: *bye-bye, bay-bee*. He turned on his heel, glanced back into the yard behind the house.

The rear corner of the yard was lit by a streetlamp in the alley. It cast a bluish light across the picket fence and the big leafy oak with the rope hanging from one branch. A little girl crouched in the grass beneath the tree, a child of perhaps six or seven, in a simple red-and-white checkered dress and with her dark hair tied in a ponytail. She sang to herself, that old one by Dean Martin about how it was time to hit the road to dreamland, digya in the land of nod. She picked a dandelion, caught her breath, and blew. The seed parachutes came apart, a hundred drifting white umbrellas that soared out into the gloom. It should've been impossible to see them, except that they were faintly luminescent, drifting about like improbable white sparks. Her head was raised, so she seemed almost to be staring directly at Jude through the window. It was hard to be sure, though. Her eyes were obscured by the black marks that jittered before them.

It was Ruth. Her name was Ruth. She was Bammy's twin sister, the one who had disappeared in the 1950s. Their parents had called them in for lunch. Bammy had come running, but Ruth lingered behind, and that was the last anyone ever saw of her . . . alive.

Jude opened his mouth—to say what, he didn't know—but found himself unable to speak. The breath caught in his chest and stayed there.

Ruth stopped singing, and the night went still, no sound even of frogs or insects now. The little girl turned her head, to glance into the alley behind the house. She smiled, and a hand flapped up in a small wave, as if she'd just noticed someone standing there, someone she knew, a friendly neighborhood acquaintance. Only there wasn't anyone in the alley. There were old pages from a newspaper stuck to the ground, some broken glass, weeds growing between the bricks. Ruth rose from her crouch and walked slowly to the fence, her lips moving—talking soundlessly to a person who wasn't there. When had Jude become unable to hear her voice? When she gave up singing.

As Ruth approached the fence, Jude felt a rising alarm, as if he were watching a child about to stray onto a busy highway. He wanted to call to her but could not, couldn't even inhale.

He remembered then what Georgia had told him about her. That people who saw little Ruth always wanted to call to her, to warn her that she was in danger, to tell her to run, but that no one could manage it. They were too stricken by the sight of her to speak. A thought formed, the sudden, nonsensical thought that this was every girl Jude had ever known who he hadn't been able to help; it was Anna and Georgia both. If he could just speak her name, get her attention, signal to her that she was in trouble, anything was possible. He and Georgia might beat the dead man yet, survive the impossible fix they had got themselves in.

And still Jude could not find his voice. It was maddening to stand there and watch and not be able to speak. He slammed his bandaged, injured hand against the counter, felt a shock of pain travel through the wound in his palm—and still could not force any sound up through the tight passage of his throat.

Angus was at his side, and he jumped when Jude pounded the counter. He lifted his head and lapped nervously at Jude's wrist. The rough, hot stroke of Angus's tongue on his bare skin startled him. It was immediate and real and it yanked him out of his paralysis as swiftly and abruptly as Georgia's laughter had pulled him out of his feeling of despair only a few moments before. His lungs grabbed some air, and he called through the window.

"Ruth!" he shouted—and she turned her head. She heard him. She *heard* him. "Get away, Ruth! Run for the house! Right now!"

Ruth glanced again at the darkened, empty alley, and then she took an off-balance, lunging step back toward the house. Before she could go any farther, her slender white arm came up, as if there were an invisible line around her left wrist and someone was pulling on it.

Only it wasn't an invisible line. It was an invisible hand. And in the next instant, she came right off the ground, hauled into the air by some-one who wasn't there. Her long, skinny legs kicked helplessly, and one of her sandals flew off and disappeared into the dark. She wrestled and fought, suspended two feet in the air, and was pulled steadily backward. Her face turned toward his, helpless and beseeching, the marks over her eyes blotting out her desperate stare, as she was carried by unseen forces over the picket fence.

"Ruth!" he called again, his voice as commanding as it had ever been onstage, when he was shouting to his legions.

She began to fade away as she was hauled off down the alley. Now her dress was gray-and-white checks. Now her hair was the color of moonsilver. The other sandal fell off, splashed in a puddle, and disappeared, although ripples continued to move across the shallow muddy water—as if it had fallen, impossibly, right out of the past and into the present. Ruth's mouth was open, but she couldn't scream, and Jude didn't know why. Maybe the unseen thing that was tugging her away had a hand over her mouth. She passed under the bright blue glare of the streetlamp and was gone. The breeze caught a newspaper, and it flapped down the empty alley with a dry, rattling sound.

Angus whined again and gave him another lick. Jude stared. A bad taste in his mouth. A feeling of pressure in his eardrums.

"Jude," Georgia whispered from behind him.

He looked at her reflection in the window over the sink. Black squiggles danced in front of her eyes. They were over his eyes, too. They were both dead. They just hadn't stopped moving yet.

"What happened, Jude?"

"I couldn't save her," he said. "The girl. Ruth. I saw her taken away." He could not tell Georgia that somehow his hope that they could save themselves had gone with her. "I called her name. I called her name, but I couldn't change what happened."

"Course you couldn't, dear," said Bammy.

33

Jude pivoted toward **Georgia and Bammy.** Georgia stood across the kitchen from him, in the doorway. Her eyes were just her eyes, no death marks over them. Bammy touched her granddaughter on the hip to nudge her aside, then eased into the kitchen around her and approached Jude.

"You know Ruth's story? Did M.B. tell you?"

"She told me your sister got taken when you were little. She said sometimes people see her out in the yard, getting grabbed all over again. It isn't the same as seeing it yourself. I heard her sing. I saw her taken away."

Bammy put her hand on his wrist. "Do you want to set?"

He shook his head.

"You know why she keeps coming back? Why people see her? The worst moments of Ruth's life happened out in that yard, while we all sat in here eating our lunch. She was alone and scared, and no one saw when she was taken away. No one heard when she stopped singing. It must've been the most awful thing. I've always thought that when something really bad happens to a person, other people just have to know about it. You can't be a tree falling in the woods with no one to hear you crash. Can I at least get you something else to drink?"

He only noticed in that moment that his mouth was unpleasantly tacky. He nodded. She got the pitcher of lemonade, almost drained now, and sloshed the last of it into his glass.

While she poured, she said, "I always thought if someone could speak to her, it might take a weight off her. I always thought if someone could make her feel not so alone in those last minutes, it might set her free." Bammy tipped her head to the side—a curious, interrogatory gesture Jude had seen Georgia perform a million times. "You might've done her some good and not even know it. Just by saying her name."

"What did I do? She still got taken." Downing the glass in a swallow and then setting it in the sink.

Bammy was close beside him, and her tone was both gentle and forgiving. "I never thought for a moment anyone could change what happened to her. That's done. The past is gone. Stay the night, Jude."

Her last statement was so completely unrelated to the one that had preceded it, Jude needed a moment to understand she had just made a request of him.

"Can't," Jude said.

"Why?"

Because anyone who offered them aid would be infected with the death on them, and who knew how much they had risked Bammy's life just by stopping a few hours? Because he and Georgia were dead already, and the dead drag the living down. "Because it isn't safe," he said at last. That was honest, at least.

Bammy's brow knotted, screwing up in thought. He saw her struggling for the right words to crack him open, to force him to talk about the situation they were in.

While she was still thinking, Georgia crept into the room, almost tiptoeing, as if afraid to make any sound. Bon was at her heels, gazing up with a look of idiot anxiety.

Georgia said. "Not every ghost is like your sister, Bammy. There's some that are real bad. We're having all kinds of trouble with dead people. Don't ask either one of us to explain. It would just sound crazy."

"Try me anyway. Let me help."

"Mrs. Fordham," Jude said, "you were good to have us. Thank you for dinner."

Georgia reached Bammy's side and tugged on her shirtsleeve, and when her grandmother turned toward her, Georgia put her pale and skinny arms around her and clasped her tight. "You are a good woman, and I love you."

Bammy still had her head turned to look at Jude. "If I can do something . . ."

"But you can't," Jude said. "It's like with your sister there in the backyard. You can shout all you want, but it won't change how things play out."

"I don't believe that. My sister is dead. No one paid any attention when she quit singing, and someone took her away and killed her. But you are not dead. You and my granddaughter are alive and here with me in my house. Don't give up on yourself. The dead win when you quit singing and let them take you on down the road with them."

Something about this last gave Jude a nervous jolt, as if he'd touched metal and caught a sudden stinging zap of static electricity. Something about giving up on yourself, something about singing. There was an idea there, but not one he could make sense of yet. The knowledge that he and Georgia had about played out their string—the feeling that they were both as dead as the girl he'd just seen in the backyard—was an obstacle no other thought could get around.

Georgia kissed Bammy's face, once, and again: kissing tears. And at last Bammy turned to look at her. She put her hands on her granddaughter's cheeks.

"Stay," Bammy said. "Make him stay. And if he won't, then let him go on without you."

"I can't do that," Georgia said. "And he's right. We can't bring you into this any more than we already have. One man who was a friend to us is dead because he didn't get clear of us fast enough."

Bammy pressed her forehead to Georgia's breast. Her breath hitched and caught. Her hands rose and went into Georgia's hair, and for a moment both women swayed together, as if they were dancing very slowly.

When her composure returned—it wasn't long—Bammy looked up into Georgia's face again. Bammy was red and damp-cheeked, and her chin was trembling, but she seemed to be done with her crying.

"I will pray, Marybeth. I will pray for you."

"Thank you," Georgia said.

"I am countin' on you coming back. I am countin' on seeing you again, when you've figured out how to make things right. And I know you will. Because you're clever and you're good and you're my girl." Bammy inhaled sharply, gave Jude a watery, sidelong look. "I hope he's worth it."

Georgia laughed, a soft, convulsive sound almost like a sob, and squeezed Bammy once more.

"Go, then," Bammy said. "Go if you got to."

"We're already gone," Georgia said.

34

He drove. His palms were hot and slick on the wheel, his stomach churning. He wanted to slam his fist into something. He wanted to drive too fast, and he did, shooting yellow lights just as they turned red. And when he didn't make a light in time and had to sit in traffic, he pumped the pedal, revving the engine impatiently. What he had felt in the house, watching the little dead girl get dragged away, that sensation of helplessness, had thickened and curdled into rage and a sour-milk taste in his mouth.

Georgia watched him for a few miles, then put a hand on his forearm. He twitched, startled by the clammy, chilled feel of her skin on his. He wanted to take a deep breath and recover his composure, not so much for himself as for her. If one of them was going to be this way, it seemed to him it ought to be Georgia, that she had more right to rage than he did, after what Anna had shown her in the mirror. After she had seen herself dead. He did not understand her quiet, her steadiness, her concern for him, and he could not find it in him to take deep breaths. When a truck in front of him was slow to get moving after the light turned green, he laid on the horn.

"Head out of your ass!" Jude yelled through the open window as he tore by, crossing the double yellow line to go past.

Georgia removed her hand from his arm, set it in her lap. She turned her head to stare out the passenger-side window. They drove a block, stopped at another intersection.

When she spoke again, it was in a low, amused mumble. She didn't mean for him to hear, was talking to herself, and maybe not even completely aware she'd spoken aloud.

"Oh, look. My least favorite used-car lot in the whole wide world. Where's a hand grenade when you need one?"

"What?" he asked, but as he said it, he already knew and was yanking at the steering wheel, pulling the car to the curb, and jamming on the brake.

To the right of the Mustang was the vast sprawl of a car lot, brightly illuminated by sodium-vapor lights on thirty-foot-tall steel posts. They towered over the asphalt, like ranks of alien tripods, a silent invading army from another world. Lines had been strung between them, and a thousand blue and red pennants snapped in the wind, adding a carnival touch to the place. It was after 8 P.M., but they were still doing business. Couples moved among the cars, leaning toward windows to peer at price stickers pasted against the glass.

Georgia's brow furrowed, and her mouth opened in a way that suggested she was about to ask him what in the hell he thought he was doing.

"Is this his place?" Jude asked.

"What place?"

"Don't act stupid. The guy who molested you and treated you like a hooker."

"He didn't . . . It wasn't . . . I wouldn't exactly say he—"

"I would. Is this it?"

She looked at his hands clenched on the wheel, his white knuckles.

"He's probably not even here," she said.

Jude flung open the car door and heaved himself out. Cars blasted past, and the hot, exhaust-smelling slipstream snatched at his clothes. Georgia scrambled out on the other side and stared across the Mustang at him.

"Where are you goin'?"

"To look for the guy. What's his name again?"

"Get in the car."

"Who am I looking for? Don't make me go around slugging used-car salesmen at random."

"You're not goin' in there alone to beat the shit out of some guy you don't even know."

"No. I wouldn't go alone. I'd take Angus." He glanced into the Mustang. Angus's head was already sticking into the gap between the two front seats, and he was staring out at Jude expectantly. "C'mon, Angus."

The giant black dog leaped onto the driver's seat and then into the road. Jude slammed the door, started around the front of the car, the dense, sleek weight of Angus's torso pressed against his side.

"I'm not gonna tell you who," she said.

"All right. I'll ask around."

She grabbed his arm. "What do you mean, you'll ask around? What are you going to do? Start askin' salesmen if they used to fuck thirteen-year-olds?"

Then it came back to him, popped into his head without any forewarning. He was thinking he'd like to stick a gun in the son of a bitch's face, and he remembered. "Ruger. His name was Ruger. Like the gun."

"You're going to get arrested. You're not goin' in there."

"This is why guys like him get away with it. Because people like you go on protecting them, even when they ought to know better."

"I'm not protectin' *him*, you asshole. I'm protectin' *you*."

He yanked his arm out of her grip and started to turn back, ready to give up and already seething about it—and that was when he noticed Angus was gone.

He cast a swift look around and spotted him an instant later, deep in the used-car lot, trotting between a row of pickups and then turning and disappearing behind one of them.

"Angus!" he shouted, but an eighteen-wheeler boomed past, and Jude's voice was lost in the diesel roar.

Jude went after him. He glanced back and saw Georgia right behind him, her own face white, eyes wide with alarm. They were on a major highway, in a busy lot, and it would be a bad place to lose one of the dogs.

He reached the row of pickups where he'd last seen Angus and turned, and there he was—ten feet away, sitting on his haunches, allowing a skinny, bald man in a blue blazer to scratch him behind the ears. The bald man was one of the dealers. The tag on his breast pocket said RUGER. Ruger stood with a rotund family in promotional T-shirts, their ample bellies doing double duty as billboards. The father's gut was selling Coors Silver Bullet; the mother's breast made an unpersuasive pitch for Curves fitness; the son, about ten, had on a HOOTERS shirt, and probably could've fit into a C-cup himself. Standing next to them, Ruger seemed almost elflike, an impression enhanced by his delicate, arched eyebrows and pointy ears with their fuzzy earlobes. His loafers had tassels on them. Jude despised loafers with tassels.

"There's a good boy," Ruger said. "Look at this good boy."

Jude slowed, allowing Georgia to catch up. She was about to go past Jude but then saw Ruger and shrank back.

Ruger looked up, beaming politely. "Your dog, ma'am?" His eyes narrowed. Then a puzzled recognition passed across his face. "It's little Marybeth Kimball, all grown up. Look at you! Are you down visiting? I heard you were in New York City these days."

Georgia didn't speak. She glanced sidelong at Jude, her blue eyes bright and stricken. Angus had led them right to him, as if he'd known just who they were looking for. Maybe Angus *did* know somehow. Maybe the dog of black smoke who lived inside Angus had known. Georgia began shaking her head at Jude—*No, don't*—but he paid her no mind, stepped around her, closing in on Angus and Ruger.

Ruger shifted his gaze to Jude. His face came alive with amazement and pleasure. "Oh, my God! You're Judas Coyne, the famous rock-and-roll fellow. My teenage son has every single one of your albums. I can't say I quite care for the volume he plays them at"—digging a finger in one ear, as if his eardrums were still ringing from just such a recent encounter with Jude's music—"but I'll tell you what, you've made quite a mark on him."

"I'm about to make quite a mark on you, asshole," Jude said, and drove his right fist into Ruger's face, heard his nose snap.

Ruger staggered, half doubled over, one hand cupping his nose. The roly-poly couple behind him parted to let him stumble past. Their son grinned and stood on his toes to watch the fight from around his father's shoulder.

Jude sank a left into Ruger's breadbasket, ignoring the burst of pain that shot through the gouge in his palm. He grabbed the car dealer as he started to drop to his knees, and threw him onto the hood of a Pontiac with a sign stuck inside the windshield: **IT'S YOURS IF YOU WANT IT!!! CHEAP!!!**

Ruger tried to sit up, and Jude grabbed him by the crotch, found his scrotum, and squeezed, felt the stiff jelly of Ruger's balls crunch in his fist. Ruger sat bolt upright and shrieked, dark arterial blood gouting from his nostrils. His trousers were hiked up, and Angus jumped, snarling, and clamped his jaws on Ruger's foot, then yanked, tearing off one of his loafers.

The fat woman covered her eyes but kept two fingers apart to peek between them.

Jude only had time to get a couple more licks in before Georgia had him by the elbow and was hauling him off. Halfway to the car she began to laugh, and as soon as they were packed back into the Mustang, she was all over him, chewing his earlobe, kissing him above his beard, shivering against his side.

Angus still had Ruger's loafer, and once they were on the interstate, Georgia traded him a Slim Jim for it, then tied it from the rearview mirror by the tassels.

"Like it?" she asked.

"Better than fuzzy dice," Jude said.

HURT

35

Jessica McDermott Price's house was in a new development, an assortment of handsome Colonials and Capes with vinyl siding in various ice-cream-shop colors—vanilla, pistachio—laid out along streets that twisted and looped in the way of intestines. They drove by it twice before Georgia spotted the number on the mailbox. Home was a Day-Glo yellow, like mango sherbet, like the caution light, and it wasn't in any particular architectural style, unless big, bland, American suburban was a style. Jude glided past it and continued down the block about a hundred yards. He turned in to an unpaved driveway and rolled across dried yellow mud to an unfinished house.

The garage had only just been framed, beams of new pine sticking up from the cement foundation and more beams crisscrossing overhead, the roof covered in plastic sheeting. The house attached to it was only a little further along, plywood panels nailed up between the beams, with gaping rectangles to show where windows and doors belonged.

Jude turned the Mustang so the front end was facing the street and backed into the empty, doorless bay of the garage. From where they parked, they had a good view of the Price house. He switched off the engine. They sat for a while, listening to the engine tick as it cooled.

They had made good time coming south from Bammy's. It was just going on one in the morning.

"Do we have a plan?" Georgia asked.

Jude pointed across the street, at a couple large trash cans on the curb. Then he gestured down the road, toward more green plastic barrels.

"Looks like tomorrow is garbage day," Jude said. He nodded toward Jessica Price's house. "She hasn't brought her cans out yet."

Georgia stared at him. A streetlight down the road cast a wan beam of light across her eyes, which glittered, like water at the bottom of a well. She didn't say anything.

"We'll wait until she carries out the trash, and then we'll make her get in the car with us."

"Make her."

"We'll drive around awhile. We'll talk some—the three of us."

"What if her husband brings out the trash?"

"He isn't going to. He was in the reserves, and he got wiped out in Iraq. It's one of the few things Anna told me about her sister."

"Maybe she has a boyfriend now."

"If she's got a boyfriend, and he's a lot bigger than me, we wait and look for another shot. But Anna never said anything about a boyfriend. The way I heard it, Jessica was just living here with their stepdad, Craddock, and her daughter."

"Daughter?"

Jude looked meaningfully at a pink two-wheeler leaned against Price's garage. Georgia followed his gaze.

Jude said, "That's why we're not going in tonight. But tomorrow is a school day. Sooner or later Jessica is going to be alone."

"And then?"

"Then we can do what we need to do, and we don't have to worry about her kid seeing."

For a while they were both quiet. Insect song rose from the palms and the brush behind the unfinished house, a rhythmic, inhuman pulsing. Otherwise the street was quiet.

Georgia said, "What are we gonna do to her?"

"Whatever we have to."

Georgia lowered the seat all the way back and stared into the dark at the ceiling. Bon leaned into the front and whined urgently in her ear. Georgia rubbed her head.

"These dogs are hungry, Jude."

"They'll have to wait," he said, staring at Jessica Price's house.

He was headachy and his knuckles were sore. He was overtired, too, and his exhaustion made it difficult to follow any one line of reasoning for long. His thoughts, instead, were black dogs that chased their own tails, going around and around in maddening circles without ever getting anywhere.

He had done some bad things in his life—putting Anna on that train, for starters, sending her back to her kin to die—but nothing like what he thought might be ahead of him. He wasn't sure what he would have to do, if it would end in killing—it might end in killing—and he had Johnny Cash in his head singing "Folsom Prison Blues," momma told me be a good boy, don't play with guns. He considered the gun he had left at home, his big John Wayne .44. It would be easier to get answers out of Jessica Price if he had the gun with him. Only, if he had the gun with him, Craddock would've persuaded him to shoot Georgia and himself by now, and the dogs, too, and Jude thought about guns he'd owned, and dogs he'd owned, and running barefoot with the dogs in the hillocky acres behind his father's farm, the thrill of running with the dogs in the dawn light, and the clap of his father's shotgun as he fired at ducks, and how his mother and Jude had run away from him together when Jude was nine, only at the Greyhound his mother lost her nerve and called her parents, and wept to them, and they told her to take the boy back to his father and try to make peace, make peace with her husband and with God, and his father was waiting with the shotgun on the porch when they returned, and he smashed her in the face with the gunstock and then put the barrel on her left breast and said he'd kill her if she ever tried to run away again, and so she never ran away again. When Jude—only he was Justin then—tried to walk inside the house, his father said, "I'm not mad at you, boy, this ain't your fault," and caught him in one arm and hugged him to his leg. He bent for a kiss and said he loved him, and Justin automatically said he loved him back, a memory he still flinched from, a morally repugnant act, an act so shameful he could not bear to be the person who had done it, so he had eventually needed to become someone else. Was that the worst thing he'd ever done, planted that Judas kiss on his father's cheek while his mother bled, taken the worthless coin of his father's affection? No worse than sending Anna away, and now he was back where he'd started, wondering about tomorrow morning, wondering if he could, when he had to, force Anna's sister into the back of his car and take her away from her home and then do what needed to be done to make her talk.

Although it was not hot in the Mustang, he wiped at the sweat on his brow with the back of one arm, before it could drip into his eyes. He watched the house and the road. A police car went by once, but the Mustang was tucked well out of sight, in the shadows of the half-built garage, and the cruiser didn't slow.

Georgia dozed beside him, her face turned away. A little after two in the morning, she began fighting something in her sleep. Her right hand came up, as if she were raising it to get the attention of teacher. She had not rebandaged it, and it was white and wrinkled, as if it had been soaking in water for hours. White and wrinkled and terrible. She began to lash at the air, and she moaned, a cringing sound of terror. She tossed her head.

He leaned over her, saying her name, and firmly but gently took one shoulder to jostle her awake. She slapped at him with her bad hand. Then her eyes sprang open, and she stared at him without recognition, gazed up with complete, blind horror, and he knew in those first few moments she was seeing not his face but the dead man's.

"Marybeth," he said again. "It's a dream. *Shh.* You're all right. You're all right now."

The fog cleared from her eyes. Her body, which was clenched up and rigid, sagged, the tension going out of it. She gasped. He brushed back some hair that was stuck to the sweat on her cheek and was appalled at the heat coming off her.

"Thirsty," she said.

He reached into the back, dug through a plastic bag of groceries they'd picked up at a gas station, found her a bottled water. Georgia unscrewed the top, drank a third of it in four big swallows.

"What if Anna's sister can't help us?" Georgia asked. "What if she can't make him go away? Are we gonna kill her if she can't make Craddock go away?"

"Why don't you just rest? We're going to be waiting awhile."

"I don't want to kill anyone, Jude. I don't want to use my last hours on earth to murder anyone."

"These aren't your last hours on earth," he said. He was careful not to include himself in that statement.

"I don't want you to kill anyone either. I don't want you to be that person. Besides, if we kill her, then we'll have two ghosts hauntin' us. I don't think I can take any more ghosts after me."

"You want some radio?"

"Promise me you won't kill her, Jude. No matter what."

He turned on the radio. Low on the FM dial, he found the Foo Fighters. David Grohl sang that he was hanging on, just hanging on. Jude turned the volume low, to the faintest of murmurs.

"Marybeth," he began.

She shivered.

"You okay?"

"I like when you call me by my real name. Don't call me Georgia anymore, okay?"

"Okay."

"I wish you didn't first see me takin' my clothes off for drunks. I wish we didn't meet in a strip club. I wish you could've known me before I started with that kind of thing. Before I got like I am. Before I did all the things I wish I could take back."

"You know how people pay more money to buy furniture that's been roughed up a little? What do they call it? Things that have been distressed? That's because something that's seen a little wear is just more interesting than something brand-new that hasn't ever had a scuff on it."

"That's me," she said. "Attractively distressed." She was shivering again, steadily now.

"How you holding up?"

"Okay," she said, voice trembling along with the rest of her.

They listened to the radio through the faint hiss of static. Jude felt himself settling, his head clearing, felt muscles he hadn't known were knotted up beginning to loosen and relax. For the moment it didn't matter what was ahead of them or what they would have to do come morning. It didn't matter what was behind them either—the days of driving, the ghost of Craddock McDermott with his old truck and his scribbled-over eyes. Jude was somewhere in the South, in the Mustang, with the seat cranked back and Aerosmith on the radio.

Then Marybeth had to ruin it.

"If I die, Jude, and you're still alive," she said. "I'm gonna try to stop him. From the other side."

"What are you talking about? You aren't going to die."

"I know. I'm just sayin'. If things don't break our way, I'll find Anna, and us girls will try and make him stop."

"You aren't going to die. I don't care what the Ouija board said or what Anna showed you in the mirror either." He had decided this very thing a few hours back down the road.

Marybeth frowned thoughtfully. "Once she started talking to us, it got cold in my room. I couldn't stop shakin'. I couldn't even feel my hand on the pointer. And then you'd ask Anna somethin', and I'd just know how she was gonna answer. What she was tryin' to say. I wasn't hearin' voices or anything. I just knew. It all made sense then, but it doesn't now. I can't remember what she wanted me to do or what she meant by bein' a door. Except . . . I think she was saying that if Craddock can come back, so can she. With a little help. And somehow I can help. It's just—and I got this loud and clear—I might have to die to do it."

"You aren't going to die. Not if I have any say in it."

She smiled. It was a tired smile. "You don't have any say in it."

He didn't know how to reply, not at first. It had crossed his mind already that there was *one* way he could assure her safety, but he wasn't about to put it into words. It had occurred to him that if *he* died, Craddock would go away and Marybeth would live. That Craddock only wanted him, maybe only had a claim on this world as long as Jude was alive. After all, Jude had bought him, paid to own him and his dead man's suit. Craddock had spent most of a week now trying to make Jude kill himself. Jude had been so busy resisting he hadn't stopped to wonder if the price of surviving would be worse than giving the dead man what he wanted. That he was sure to lose, and that the longer he held out, the more likely he would drag Marybeth with him. Because the dead pull the living down.

Marybeth stared at him, her eyes a wet, lovely ink in the dark. He stroked the hair away from her forehead. She was very young and very beautiful, her brow damp with her fever sweat. The idea that her death should precede his was worse than intolerable, it was obscene.

He slid toward her, reached and took her hands in his. If her forehead was damp and too warm, her hands were damp and too cold. He turned them over in the gloom. What he saw was a nasty sort of shock. Both of her hands were pruned up, white and shriveled, not just the right one—although the right was more terrible, the entire pad of her thumb a glistening, rotted sore and the thumbnail itself gone, dropped off. On the surface of both palms, red lines of infection followed the delicate branches of her veins, down into her forearms, where they spread out, to etch diseased-looking crimson slashes across her wrists.

"What's happening to you?" he asked, as if he didn't already know. It was the story of Anna's death, written on Marybeth's skin.

"She's a part of me somehow: Anna. I'm carryin' her around inside me. I have been for a while, I think." A statement that should've surprised but didn't. He had sensed it, on some level, that Marybeth and Anna were coming together, merging somehow. He'd heard it in the way Marybeth's accent had resurfaced, becoming so like Anna's laconic, country-girl drawl. He had seen it in the way Marybeth played with her hair now, like Anna used to. Marybeth went on, "She wants me to help her back into our world, so she can stop him. I am the doorway—she told me that."

"Marybeth," he began, then couldn't find anything else to say.

She closed her eyes and smiled. "That's my name. Don't wear it out. Actually. On second thought. Go ahead and wear it out. I like when you say it. The way you say all of it. Not just the Mary part."

"Marybeth," he said, and let go of her hands and kissed her just above the left eyebrow. "Marybeth." He kissed her left cheekbone. She shivered—pleasantly this time. "Marybeth." He kissed her mouth.

"That's me. That's who I am. That's who I want to be. Mary. Beth. Like you're gettin' two girls for the price of one. Hey—maybe you really are gettin' two girls now. If Anna's inside of me." She opened her eyes and found his gaze. "When you're lovin' me, maybe you're lovin' her, too. Isn't that a good deal, Jude? Aren't I one hell of a bargain? How can you resist?"

"Best deal I've ever had," he said.

"Don't you forget it," she said, kissing him back.

He opened the door and told the dogs to get, and for a while Jude and Marybeth were alone in the Mustang, while the shepherds lay about on the cement floor of the garage.

36

He started awake, heart beating too fast, to the sound of the dogs barking, and his first thought was, *It's the ghost. The ghost is coming.*

The dogs were back in the car, had slept in the rear. Angus and Bon stood on the backseat together, the both of them peering out the windows at an ugly yellow Labrador. The Lab stood with her back rigid and her tail up, yapping repetitively at the Mustang. Angus and Bon watched her with avid, anticipatory expressions and barked occasionally themselves, booming, harsh woofs that hurt Jude's ears in the close confines of the Mustang. Marybeth twisted in the passenger seat, grimacing, not asleep anymore, but wishing she were.

Jude told them all to shut the fuck up. They didn't listen.

He looked out the windshield and straight into the sun, a copper hole punched through the sky, a bright and merciless spotlight pointed into his face. He made a complaining sound at the glare, but before he could lift a hand to shade his eyes, a man stepped in front of the car, and his head blocked the sun.

Jude squinted at a young man wearing a leather tool belt. He was a literal redneck, skin cooked to a fine, deep shade of carmine. He frowned at

Jude. Jude waved and nodded to him and started the Mustang. When the clock on the radio face lit up, he saw it was seven in the morning.

The carpenter stepped aside, and Jude rolled out of the garage and around the carpenter's parked pickup. The yellow Lab chased them down the driveway, still yapping, then stopped at the edge of the yard. Bon woofed back at her one last time as they pulled away. Jude eased past the Price house. No one had put the garbage out yet.

He decided there was still time and drove out of Jessica Price's little corner of suburbia. He walked first Angus, then Bon, in the town square, and got tea and doughnuts at a Honey Dew Drive-Thru. Marybeth rebandaged her right hand with some gauze from the dwindling supplies in the first-aid kit. She left her other hand, which at least had no visible sores, as it was. He gassed up the car at a Mobil, and then they parked at one edge of the concrete apron and snacked. He tossed plain crullers to the dogs.

Jude steered them back to Jessica Price's. He parked on the corner, half a block from her house, on the opposite side of the street and a long walk down the road from the construction site. He didn't want to take a chance on being seen by the laborer who'd been hovering over the car when they woke up.

It was after seven-thirty, and he hoped Jessica would bring the garbage out soon. The longer they sat, the more likely they were to draw attention, the two of them in their black Mustang, dressed in their black leather and black jeans, with their visible wounds and their tattoos. They looked like what they were: two dangerous lowlifes staking out a place where they planned to commit a crime. A NEIGHBORHOOD WATCH sign on a nearby lamppost stared them in the face.

By then his blood was flowing and his head was clear. He was ready, but there was nothing to do except wait. He wondered if the carpenter had recognized him, what he would say to the other men when they arrived on site. *I still can't believe it. This guy who looks just like Judas Coyne, sleepin' it off in the garage. Him and some amazingly hot chick. He looked so much like the real guy, I almost asked him if he was takin' requests.*

And then Jude thought that the carpenter was also one more person who could positively identify them, after they were done doing whatever it was they were about to do. It was hard to live the outlaw life when you were famous.

He wondered idly who among rock stars had spent the most time in jail. Rick James, maybe. He did—what?—five years? Three? Ike Turner had done a haul. Five years at least. Others must've done more than that. Leadbelly had been in for murder, broke rocks for ten years, then was pardoned after putting on a good show for the governor and his family. Well. Jude thought if he played his cards right, he could do more time than all three of them put together.

Prison didn't frighten him especially. He had a lot of fans in there.

The garage door at the end of Jessica McDermott Price's concrete driveway rumbled open. A weedy girl, about eleven or twelve years old, her golden hair clipped into a short, flouncy bob, hauled a garbage can down to the side of the road. The sight of her gave him a tingle of surprise, the resemblance to Anna was so close. With her strong, pointy chin, towhead, and wide-spaced blue eyes, it was as if Anna had stepped out of her childhood in the eighties and straight into the bright, full morning of today.

She left the trash can, crossed the yard to the front door, and let herself in. Her mother met her just inside. The girl left the door open, allowing Jude and Marybeth to watch mother and daughter together.

Jessica McDermott Price was taller than Anna had been, her hair a shade darker, and her mouth bracketed by frown lines. She wore a peasant blouse, with loose, frilly cuffs, and a crinkly flower-print skirt, an outfit that Jude surmised was meant to make her look like a free spirit, an earthy and empathic Gypsy. But her face had been too carefully and professionally made up, and what he could see of the house was all dark, oiled, expensive-looking furniture and seasoned wood paneling. It was the home and the face of a forty-year-old investment banker, not a seer.

Jessica handed her little girl a backpack—a shiny purple-and-pink thing that matched her windbreaker and sneakers as well as the bike outdoors—and air-kissed her daughter's forehead. The girl tripped out, slammed the door, and hurried over the yard, pulling the pack onto her shoulders. She was across the street from Jude and Marybeth, and on her way by she shot them a look, measuring them up. She wrinkled her nose, as if they were some litter she'd spotted in someone's yard, and then she was around the corner and gone.

The moment she was out of sight, Jude's sides began to prickle, under his arms, and he became aware of the tacky sweat gluing his shirt to his back.

"Here we go," he said.

He knew it would be dangerous to hesitate, to give himself time to think. He climbed out of the car. Angus bounded after him. Marybeth got out on the other side.

"Wait here," Jude said.

"Hell no."

Jude walked around to the trunk.

"How we goin' in?" Marybeth asked. "Were we just gonna knock on the front door? Hi, we've come to kill you?"

He opened the trunk and pulled out the tire iron. He pointed it at the garage, which had been left open. Then he slammed the trunk and started across the street. Angus dashed ahead, came back, raced ahead again, lifted a leg, and pissed on someone's mailbox.

It was still early, the sun hot on the back of Jude's neck. He held one end of the tire iron in his fist, the socket-wrench end, and clasped the rest of it against the inner part of his forearm, trying to hide it alongside his body. Behind him a car door slammed. Bon lunged past him. Then Marybeth was at his side, short of breath and trotting to keep up.

"Jude. Jude. What if we just . . . just try and talk to her? Maybe we can . . . persuade her to help us willingly. Tell her you never . . . never wanted to hurt Anna. Never wanted her to kill herself."

"Anna didn't kill herself, and her sister knows it. That's not what this is about. Never has been." Jude glanced at Marybeth and saw she had fallen a few steps behind him, was regarding him with a look of unhappy shock. "There's always been more to this than we figured at first. I'm not so sure we're the bad guys in this story."

He walked up the driveway, the dogs loping along, one on either side of him, like an honor guard. He took a passing glance at the front of the house, at windows with white lace curtains in them and shadows behind. If she was watching them, he couldn't tell. Then they were in the gloom of the garage, where a cherry two-door convertible with a vanity plate that read HYPNOIT was parked on the clean-swept concrete floor.

He found the inside door, put his hand on the knob, tilted his head toward the house, and listened. The radio was on. The most boring voice in the world said blue chips were down, tech stocks were down, futures all across the spectrum were looking down. Then he heard heels clicking across tile, just on the other side of the door, and he instinctively leaped back, but it was too late, the door was opening and Jessica McDermott Price was coming through.

She almost walked right into him. She wasn't looking. She had her car keys in one hand and a garishly colored purse of some kind in the other. As she glanced up, Jude grabbed the front of her blouse, gathering a bunch of silky fabric in his fist, and shoved her back through the door.

Jessica reeled backward, tottering in her heels, then twisted an ankle, her foot coming out of one shoe. She let go of her small, unlikely purse. It fell at their feet, and Jude kicked it aside, kept going.

He drove her across the mudroom and into a sun-splashed kitchen in the rear of the house, and that was when her legs gave out. The blouse tore as she went down, buttons popping off and ricocheting around the room. One of them nailed Jude in the left eye—a black spoke of pain. The eye watered over, and he blinked furiously to clear it.

She slammed hard against the island in the center of the kitchen and grabbed the edge to stop her fall. Plates rattled. The counter was at her back—she was still turned to face Jude—and she reached behind her without looking and grabbed one of the plates and broke it over Jude's head as he came at her.

He didn't feel it. It was a dirty plate, and toast crusts and curds of scrambled egg went flying. Jude shot out his right arm, let the tire iron slip down, grabbed the upper end, and, holding it like a club, swatted her across her left kneecap, just below the hem of her skirt.

She dropped, as if both legs had been jerked out from under her. Started to shove herself up, and then Angus flattened her again, climbed on top of her, paws scrabbling against her chest.

"Get off her," Marybeth said, and grabbed Angus by the collar, wrenched him back so hard he was flipped over, rolling in one of those faintly ridiculous doggy somersaults, his legs kicking in the air for an instant before getting up on his paws again.

Angus heaved himself at Jessica once more, but Marybeth held him back. Bon ambled into the room, shot a guilty-nervous look at Jessica Price, then stepped over pieces of shattered plate and began snarfing up a toast crust.

The droning voice on the radio, a small pink boom box on the counter, said, "Book clubs for kids are a hit with parents, who look to the written word as a place to shelter their children from the gratuitous sexual content and explicit violence that saturate video games, television programs, and movies."

Jessica's blouse was torn open to the waist. She wore a lacy peach-colored bra that left the tops of her breasts exposed, and they shuddered and fell with her breath. She bared her teeth—was she grinning?—and they were stained with blood.

She said, "If you came to kill me, you ought to know I'm not afraid of dying. My father will be on the other side to receive me with open arms."

"I bet you're looking forward to that," Jude said. "I get the picture you and him were pretty close. Least until Anna was old enough and he started fucking her instead of you."

37

One of Jessica McDermott Price's eyelids twitched irregularly, a drop of sweat in her lashes, ready to fall. Her lips, which were painted the deep, almost black red of bing cherries, were still stretched wide to show her teeth, but it wasn't a grin anymore. It was a grimace of rage and confusion.

"You aren't fit to speak of my father. He scraped uglier messes than you off the heel of his boot."

"You got that about half right," Jude said. He was also breathing fast, but a little surprised by the evenness of his own voice. "You both stepped in a pile when you screwed with me. Tell me something, did you help him kill her, to keep her from talking about what he did? Did you watch while your own sister bled to death?"

"The girl who came back to this house wasn't my sister. She wasn't anything like her. My sister was already dead by the time you got through with her. You ruined her. The girl who came back to us was poison inside. The things she said. The threats she made. Send our daddy to prison. Send me to prison. And my daddy didn't harm a hair on her goddam disloyal head. Daddy loved her. He was the best, the best man."

"Your daddy liked to fuck little girls. First you, then Anna. It was right in front of me the whole time."

He was bending over her now. He felt a little dizzy. Sunlight slashed through the windows above the sink, and the air was warm and close, smelled overpoweringly of her perfume, a jasmine-flavored scent. Just beyond the kitchen, a sliding glass door was partly open and looking out onto an enclosed back porch, floored in seasoned redwood and dominated by a table covered in a lace cloth. A gray longhaired cat was out there, watching fearfully from up on the table, fur bristling. The radio voice was droning now about downloadable content. It was like bees humming in a hive. A voice like that could hum you right to sleep.

Jude looked around at the radio, wanting to give it a whack with the tire iron, shut it off. Then he saw the photograph next to it and forgot about taking out the radio. It was an eight-by-ten picture in a silver frame, and Craddock grinned out from it. He wore his black suit, the silver-dollar-size buttons gleaming down the front, and one hand was on his fedora, as if he were about to lift it in greeting. His other hand was on the shoulder of the little girl, Jessica's daughter, who so resembled Anna, with her broad forehead and wide-set blue eyes. Her sunburned face, in the picture, was an unsmiling, unreadable blank, the face of someone waiting to get off a slow elevator, a look that was entirely empty of feeling. That expression caused the girl to resemble Anna more than anything, Anna at the height of one of her depressions. Jude found the similarity disturbing.

Jessica was squirming back over the floor, using his distraction to try to get some distance between them. He grabbed her blouse again as she pulled away, and another button flew. Her shirt was hanging off her shoulders now, open to the waist. With the back of one arm, Jude wiped at the sweat on his forehead. He wasn't done talking yet.

"Anna never came right out and said she'd been molested as a kid, but she worked so hard to avoid being asked it was kind of obvious. Then, in her last letter to me, she wrote that she was tired of keeping secrets, couldn't stand it anymore. On the face of it, sounds like a suicidal statement. It took me a while to figure out what she really meant by it, that she wanted to get the truth off her chest. About how her stepfather used to put her into trances so he could do what he liked with her. He was good—he could make her forget for a while, but he couldn't completely wipe out the memories of what he'd done. It kept resurfacing, whenever she'd have one of her emotional crack-ups. Eventually, in her teens, I guess, she tipped to it, understood what he'd been up to. Anna spent a lot of years running from it. Running from him. Only I put her on a train and sent her back, and she wound up facing him again. And saw how old he was and how close to dying. And maybe decided she didn't need to run from anything anymore.

"So she threatened to tell what Craddock did to her. Is that right? She said she'd tell everyone, get the law after him. That's why he killed her. He put her in one more trance and cut her wrists in the bath. He fucked with her head and put her in the bath and slashed her open and watched her bleed out, sat there and watched—"

"You shut up about him," Jessica said, her voice spiking, high-pitched and harsh. That last night was awful, the things she said and did to him were awful. She spat on him. She tried to kill him, tried to shove him down the stairs, a weak old man. She threatened us, all of us. She said she was going to take Reese away from us. She said she'd use you and your money and your lawyers and send Daddy to jail."

"He was only doing what he had to, huh?" Jude said. "It was practically self-defense."

An expression flickered across Jessica's features, there and gone so quickly Jude half thought he'd imagined it. But for an instant the corners of her mouth seemed to twitch, in a dirty, knowing, appalling sort of smile. She sat up a little straighter. When she spoke again, her tone both lectured and crooned. "My sister was sick. She was confused. She'd been suicidal for a long time. Anna cut her wrists in the bath like everyone always knew she was going to, and there isn't anyone who can say different."

"Anna says different," Jude said, and when he saw the confusion on Jessica's face, he added, "I been hearing from all kinds of dead folks lately. You know, it never did make sense. If you wanted to send a ghost to haunt me, why not her? If her death was my fault, why send Daddy? But your stepfather isn't after me because of what *I* did. It's because of what *he* did."

"Who do you think you are, anyway, calling our daddy a child molester? How many years you got on that whore behind you? Thirty? Forty?"

"Take care," Jude said, hand tightening on the tire iron.

"My father deserved anything he asked of us," Jessica went on, couldn't shut up now. "I always understood that. My daughter understood it, too. But Anna made everything dirty and horrible and treated him like a rapist, when he didn't do anything to Reese she didn't like. She would've spoiled our daddy's last days on this earth, just to win favor with you, to make you care about her again. And now you see where it gets you, turning people against their families. Sticking your nose in."

"Oh, my God," Marybeth said. "If she's sayin' what I think she's sayin', this is about the most wrong fuckin' conversation I ever heard."

Jude put his knee between Jessica's legs and forced her back against the floor with his bad left hand. "That's enough. I hear any more about what your stepdaddy deserved and how much he loved all of you, I'm going to puke. How do I get rid of him? Tell me how to make him go away, and we'll walk out of here, and that'll be the end of it." Saying it without knowing if it was really true.

"What happened to the suit?" Jessica asked.

"What the fuck does it matter?"

"It's gone, isn't it? You bought the dead man's suit, and now it's gone, and there's no getting rid of him. All sales are final. No returns, especially not after the merchandise has been damaged. It's over. You're dead. You and that whore with you. He won't stop until you're both in the ground."

Jude leaned forward, set the tire iron across her neck, and applied some weight. She began to choke. Jude said, "No. I do not accept that. There better be another fucking way, or— Get the fuck off me." Her hands were tugging at his belt buckle. He recoiled from her touch, drawing the tire iron off her throat, and she began to laugh.

"Come on. You already got my shirt pulled off. Haven't you ever wanted to say you fucked sisters?" she asked. "I bet your girlfriend would like to watch."

"Don't touch me."

"Listen to you. Big tough man. Big rock star. You're afraid of me, you're afraid of my father, you're afraid of yourself. Good. You ought to be. You're going to die. By your own hand. I can see the death marks on your eyes." She flicked her glance at Marybeth. "They're on you, too, honey. Your boyfriend is going to kill you before he kills himself, you know. I wish I could be there to see it happen. I'd like to see how he does it. I hope he cuts you, I hope he cuts your little hooker face—"

Then the tire iron was back across Jessica's throat and he was squeezing as hard as he could. Jessica's eyes popped open wide, and her tongue poked out of her mouth. She tried to sit up on her elbows. He slammed her back down, banging her skull on the floor.

"Jude," Marybeth said. "Don't Jude."

He relaxed the pressure on the tire iron, allowed her to take a breath—and Jessica screamed. It was the first time she'd screamed. He pushed down again, cutting off the sound.

"The garage," Jude said.

"Jude."

"Close the door to the garage. The whole fucking street is going to hear her."

Jessica raked at his face. His reach was longer than hers, and he leaned back from her hands, which were bent into claws. He rapped her skull against the floor a second time.

"You scream again, I'll beat you to death right here. I'm going to ease this thing off your throat, and you better start talking, and you better be telling me how to make him go away. What about if you communicate with him directly? With a Ouija board or something? Can you call him off yourself?"

He relaxed the pressure again, and she screamed a second time—a long, piercing note, that dissolved at last into a cackle of laughter. He drove a fist into her solar plexus and knocked the air out of her, shut her up.

"Jude," Marybeth said again, from behind him. She had gone to shut the garage door but was back now.

"Later."

"Jude."

"What?" he said, twisting at the waist to glare at her.

In one hand Marybeth held Jessica Price's shiny, squarish, brightly colored purse, holding it up for him to look at. Only it wasn't a purse at all. It was a lunch box, with a glossy photo of Hillary Duff on the side.

He was still staring at Marybeth and the lunch box in confusion—didn't understand why she wanted him to see it, why it mattered—when Bon began to bark, a full, booming bark that came from the deepest part of her chest. As Jude turned his head to see what she was barking at, he heard another noise, a sharp, steely click, the unmistakable sound of someone snapping back the hammer of a pistol.

The girl, Jessica Price's daughter, had entered through the sliding glass door of the porch. Where the revolver had come from, Jude didn't know. It was an enormous Colt .45, with ivory inlays and a long barrel, so heavy she could barely hold it up. She peered intently out from beneath her bangs. A dew of sweat brightened her upper lip. When she spoke, it was in Anna's voice, although the really shocking thing was how calm she sounded.

"Get away from my mother," she said.

38

The man on the radio said, "What's Florida's number-one export? You might say oranges—but if you did, you'd be mistaken."

For a moment his was the only voice in the room. Marybeth had Angus by the collar again and was holding him back, no easy task. He strained forward with all his considerable will and muscle, and Marybeth had to keep both heels planted to prevent him going anywhere. Angus began to growl, a low, choked rumble, a wordless yet perfectly articulate message of threat. The sound of him got Bon barking again, one explosive yawp after another.

Marybeth was the first to speak. "You don't need to use that. We'll go. Come on, Jude. Let's get out of here. Let's get the dogs and go."

"Watch 'em, Reese!" Jessica cried. "They came here to kill us!"

Jude met Marybeth's gaze, tossed his head in the direction of the garage door. "Get out of here." He rose, one knee popping—old joints—put a hand on the counter to steady himself. Then he looked at the girl, making good eye contact, staring right over the .45 pointed into his face.

"I just want to get my dog," he said. "And we won't trouble you anymore. Bon, come here."

Bon barked, on and on, in the space between Jude and Reese. Jude took a step toward her to grab for Bon's collar.

"Don't let him get too close to you!" Jessica screamed. "He'll try and take the gun!"

"Stay back," the little girl said.

"Reese," he said, using her name to soothe and to create trust. Jude was a man who knew a thing or two about psychological persuasion himself. "I'm putting this down." He held up the tire iron so she could see it, then set it on the counter. "There. Now you have a gun and I'm unarmed. I just want my dog."

"Let's go, Jude," Marybeth said. "Bonnie will follow us. Let's just get out of here."

Marybeth was in the garage now, staring back through the doorway. Angus barked for the first time. The sound of it rang off the concrete floor and high ceiling.

"Come to me, Bon," Jude said, but Bon ignored him, actually made a nervous half jump at Reese instead.

Reese's shoulders twitched in a startled shrug. She swung the gun toward the dog for a moment, then back to Jude.

Jude took another shuffling step toward Bon, was almost close enough to reach her collar.

"Get away from her!" Jessica screamed, and Jude saw a flash of movement at the edge of his vision.

Jessica was crawling across the floor, and when Jude turned, she shoved herself to her feet and fell upon him. He saw a gleam of something smooth and white in one hand, didn't know what it was until it was in his face—a dagger of china, a wide shard of broken plate. She drove it at his eye, but he turned his head and she stabbed it into his cheek instead.

He brought his left arm up and clipped her across the jaw with one elbow. He pulled the spike of broken plate out of his face and threw it away. His other hand found the tire iron on the counter, and he swung it into the side of Jessica's neck, felt it connect with a solid, meaty thud, saw her eyes straining from their sockets.

"No, Jude, no!" Marybeth screamed.

He pivoted and ducked as she shouted. He had a glimpse of the girl, her face startled and her eyes wide and stricken, and then the cannon in her hands went off. The sound of it was deafening. A vase, filled with white pebbles and with a few waxy fake orchids sticking out of it, exploded on the kitchen counter. Splinters of glass and pieces of rock flailed through the air around him.

The little girl stumbled backward. Her heel caught on the edge of a carpet, and she almost fell. Bon jumped at her, but Reese righted herself, and as the dog hit her—crashing into her hard enough to sweep her off her feet—the gun went off again.

The bullet struck Bon low, in the abdomen, and flipped her rear end into the air, so she did a twisting, head-over-heels somersault. She rolled and slammed into the cabinet doors beneath the sink. Her eyes were turned up to show the whites, and her mouth lolled open, and then the black dog of smoke that was inside her leaped out from between her jaws, like a genie spilling from the spout of an Arabian lamp, and rushed across the room, past the little girl, out onto the porch.

The cat that was crouched on the table saw it coming and screeched, her gray hair spiking up along her spine. She dived to the right as the dog of black smoke bounded lightly onto the table. The shadow Bon took a playful snap at the cat's tail, then leaped after her. As Bon's spirit dropped toward the floor, she passed through a beam of intense, early-morning sunshine and winked out of being.

Jude stared at the place where the impossible dog of black shadow had vanished, too stunned for a moment to act, to do anything but feel. And what he felt was a thrill of wonder, so intense it was a kind of galvanic shock. He felt he had been honored with a glimpse of something beautiful and eternal.

And then he looked over at Bon's dead, empty body. The wound in her stomach was a horror show, a bloody maw, a blue knot of intestines spilling out of it. The long pink strip of her tongue hung obscenely from her mouth. It didn't seem possible that she could be blown so completely open, so it seemed she had not been shot but eviscerated. The blood was everywhere, on the walls, the cabinets, on him, spreading out across the floor in a dark pool. Bon had been dead when she hit the ground. The sight of her was another kind of galvanic shock, a jolt to his nerve endings.

Jude returned his disbelieving gaze to the little girl. He wondered if she had seen the dog of black smoke when it ran past her. He almost wanted to ask, but he couldn't speak, was momentarily at a loss for words. Reese sat up on her elbows, pointing the Colt. 45 at him with one hand.

No one spoke or moved, and into the stillness came the droning voice on the radio: "Wild stallions in Yosemite Park are starving after months of drought, and experts fear many will die if there isn't swift action. Your mother will die if you don't shoot him. You will die."

Reese gave no sign that she heard what the man on the radio was saying. Maybe she didn't, not consciously. Jude glanced toward the radio. In the photograph next to the boom box, Craddock still stood with his hand on Reese's shoulder, but now his eyes had been blotched out with death marks.

"Don't let him get any closer. He's here to kill you both," said the radio voice. "Shoot him, Reese. Shoot him."

He needed to silence the radio, should've followed his impulse to smash it earlier. He turned toward the counter, moving a little too quickly, and his heel shot out from under him, slipping in the blood underfoot with a high-pitched squeak. He tottered and took a lunging, off-balance step back in Reese's direction. Her eyes widened in alarm as he lurched toward her. He raised his right hand, in a gesture he meant to calm, to reassure, then realized at the last instant that he was holding the tire iron and that it would look to her as if he were lifting it to swing.

She pulled the trigger, and the bullet struck the tire iron with a ringing *bong*, corkscrewed up, and took off his index finger. A hot spray of blood hit him in the face. He turned his head and gaped at his own hand, as stunned by the wonder of his vanishing finger as he'd been by the miracle of the vanishing black dog. The hand that made the chords. Almost the whole finger was gone. He was still gripping the tire iron with his remaining fingers. He let it go. It clanged to the floor.

Marybeth screamed his name, but her voice was so far away she might've been out on the street. He could barely hear it through the whine in his ears. He felt dangerously light in the head, needed to sit down. He did not sit down. He put his left hand on the kitchen counter and began backpedaling, retreating slowly in the direction of Marybeth and the garage.

The kitchen stank of burnt cordite, hot metal. He held his right hand up, pointing at the ceiling. The stump of his index finger wasn't bleeding too badly. Blood wetted his palm, dribbled down the inside of his arm, but it was a slow dribble, and that surprised him. Nor was the pain so bad. What he felt was more an uncomfortable sensation of weight, of pressure concentrated in the stump. He could not feel his slashed face at all. He glanced at the floor and saw he was leaving a trail of fat drops of blood and red boot prints.

His vision seemed both magnified and distorted, as if he wore a fishbowl on his head. Jessica Price was on her knees, clutching her throat. Her face was crimson and swollen, as if she were suffering a severe, allergic reaction. He almost laughed. Who wasn't allergic to a pipe across the neck? Then he thought he'd managed to mutilate both hands in the space of barely three days and fought an almost convulsive need to giggle. He'd have to learn to play guitar with his feet.

Reese stared at him through the pall of filthy gunsmoke, her eyes wide and shocked—and somehow apologetic—the revolver on the floor next to her. He flapped his bandaged left hand at her, although what this gesture meant, even he wasn't sure. He had an idea he was trying to reassure her he was okay. He was worried about how pale she looked.

The kid was never going to be right after this, and none of it was her fault.

Then Marybeth had him by the arm. They were in the garage. No, they were out of the garage and into the white blaze of the sun. Angus put his front paws on his chest, and Jude was almost knocked flat.

"Get off him!" Marybeth screamed, but she still sounded a long distance away.

Jude really did want to sit down—right here in the driveway, where he could have the sun on his face.

"Don't," Marybeth said as he began to sink to the concrete. "No. The car. Come on." She hauled on his arm with both hands to keep him on his heels.

He swayed forward, staggered into her, got an arm over her shoulder, and the two of them reeled down the incline of the driveway, a pair of stoned teenagers at the prom, trying to dance to "Stairway." He did laugh this time. Marybeth looked at him with fright.

"Jude. You have to help. I can't carry you. We won't make it if you fall."

The need in her voice concerned him, made him want to do better. He drew a deep, steadying breath and stared at his Doc Martens. He concentrated on shuffling them forward. The blacktop underfoot was tricky stuff. He felt a little as if he were trying to walk across a trampoline while drunk. The ground seemed to flex and wobble beneath him, and the sky tilted dangerously.

"Hospital," she said.

"No. You know why."

"Got to—"

"Don't have to. I'll stop the bleeding." Who was replying to her? It sounded like his own, surprisingly reasonable voice.

He looked up, saw the Mustang. The world wheeled around him, a kaleidoscope of too-bright green yards, flower gardens, Marybeth's chalky, horrified face. She was so close that his nose was practically stuck into the dark, floating swirl of her hair. He inhaled deeply, to breathe in her sweet, reassuring scent, then flinched at the stink of cordite and dead dog.

They went around the car, and she dumped him in on the passenger side. Then she hurried around the front of the Mustang, caught Angus by the collar, and began to haul him toward the driver's-side door.

She was fumbling it open when Craddock's pickup screamed out of the garage, tires spinning on concrete, greasy smoke roiling, and Craddock behind the wheel. The truck jumped the side of the driveway and thudded across the lawn. It hit the picket fence with a crack, swatted it flat, slammed over sidewalk, banged into the road.

Marybeth let go of Angus and threw herself across the hood of the car, sliding on her belly, just before Craddock's truck nailed the side of the Mustang. The force of the impact threw Jude into the passenger-side door. The collision spun the Mustang, so the rear end swung into the road and the front was shoved up over the curb, with such suddenness that Marybeth was catapulted off the hood and thrown to earth. The pickup struck their car with a strangely plastic crunch, mixed with a piercing yelp.

Broken glass fell tinkling into the road. Jude looked and saw Jessica McDermott Price's cherry convertible in the street next to the Mustang. The truck was gone. It had never been there in the first place. The white egg of the airbag had exploded from the steering wheel, and Jessica sat holding her head in both hands.

Jude knew he should be feeling something—some urgency, some alarm—but was instead dreamy and dull-witted. His ears were plugged up, and he swallowed a few times to clear them, make them pop.

He peeled himself off the passenger-side door, looked to see what had happened to Marybeth. She was sitting up on the sidewalk. There was no reason to worry. She was all right. She looked as dazed as Jude felt, blinking in the sunlight, a wide scrape on the point of her chin and her hair in her eyes. He glanced back at the convertible. The driver's-side window was down—or had fallen into the road—and Jessica's hand hung limply out of it. Otherwise she was slumped out of sight.

Somewhere, someone began to scream. It sounded like a little girl. She was screaming for her mother.

Sweat, or maybe blood, dripped into Jude's right eye and stung. He lifted his right hand, without thinking, to wipe at it and brushed the stump of his index finger across his brow. It felt as if he had stuck his hand against a hot grill. The pain shot all the way up his arm and into his chest, where it bloomed into something else, a shortness of breath and an icy tingling behind his breastbone—a sensation both dreadful and somehow fascinating.

Marybeth walked unsteadily around the front of the Mustang and pulled the driver's-side door open with a screech of bent metal. She stood with what looked like a giant black duffel bag in her arms. The bag was dripping. No—not a duffel bag, but Angus. She pulled the driver's seat forward and slung him into the back before getting in.

Jude turned as she started the car, both needing and desperately not wanting to look back at his dog. Angus lifted his head to stare at him with wet, glazed, bloodshot eyes. He whined softly. His rear legs were smashed. A red bone stuck through the fur of one of them, just above the joint.

Judas looked from Angus to Marybeth, her scraped jaw set, her lips a thin, grim line. The wraps around her dreadful, shriveled right hand were soaked through. Them and their hands. They'd be hugging each other with hooks before this was over.

"Look at the three of us," Jude said. "Aren't we a picture?" He coughed. The pins-and-needles feeling in his chest was subsiding . . . but only slowly.

"I'll find a hospital."

"No hospital. Get on the highway."

"You could die without a hospital."

"If we go to a hospital, I'm going to die for sure, and you, too.

Craddock will finish us off easy. As long as Angus is alive, we got a chance."

"What's Angus going to—"

"Craddock's not scared of the dog. He's scared of the dog *inside* the dog."

"What are you talking about, Jude? I don't understand."

"Get going. I can stop my finger bleeding. It's only one finger. Just get on the highway. Go west." He held his right hand up in the air, by the side of his head, to slow the bleeding. He was beginning to think now. Not that he needed to think to know where they were going. The only place they could go.

"What the fuck is west?" Marybeth asked.

"Louisiana," he said. "Home."

39

The first-aid kit that had accompanied them from New York was on the floor of the backseat. There was one small roll of gauze left, and pins, and Motrin in shiny, difficult-to-open pouches. He took the Motrin first, tearing the packets open with his teeth and dry-swallowing them, six in all, 1,200 milligrams. It wasn't enough. His hand still felt as if it were a lump of hot iron resting on an anvil, where it was slowly but methodically being pounded flat.

At the same time, the pain kept the mental cloudiness at bay, was an anchor for his consciousness, a tether holding him to the world of the real: the highway, the green mile-marker signs zipping past, the rattling air conditioner.

Jude wasn't sure how long he would remain clear in the head, and he wanted to use whatever time he had to explain things. He spoke haltingly, through clenched teeth, as he rolled the bandage around and around the ruined hand.

"My father's farm is just across the Louisiana line, in Moore's Corner. We can be there in less than three hours. I'm not going to bleed out in three hours. He's sick, rarely conscious. There's an old woman there, an aunt by marriage, a registered nurse. She looks after him. She's on the payroll. There's morphine. For his pain. And he'll have dogs. I think he's got— Oh, motherfucker. Oh, Mother. Fucker. Two dogs. Shepherds, like mine. Savage fuckin' animals."

When the gauze was gone, he pinned it tight with alligator clips. He used his toes to force off his boots. He pulled a sock over his right hand. He wound the other sock around his wrist and knotted it tight enough to slow, but not cut off, the circulation. He stared at the sock puppet of his hand and tried to think if he could learn to make chords without the index finger. He could always play slide. Or he could switch back to his left hand, like he'd done when he was a kid. At the thought he began to laugh again.

"Quit that," Marybeth said.

He clenched his back teeth together, forced himself to stop, had to admit he sounded hysterical, even to himself.

"You don't think she'll call the cops on us? This old auntie of yours? You don't think she'd want to get a doctor for you?"

"She's not going to do that."

"Why not?"

"We aren't going to let her."

Marybeth didn't say anything for a while after that. She drove smoothly, automatically, slipping by people in the passing lane, then sliding back into the cruising lane, keeping at a steady seventy. She held the steering wheel gingerly with her white, wrinkled, sick left hand, and she didn't touch it with the infected right hand at all.

At last Georgia said, "How do you see all this endin'?"

Jude didn't have an answer for that. Angus replied instead—a soft, miserable whine.

40

He tried to keep an eye on the road behind them, watching for police, or the dead man's truck, but in the early afternoon Jude laid his head against the side window and closed his eyes for a moment. The tires made a hypnotic sound on the road, a monotonous *thum-thum-thum*. The air conditioner, which had never rattled before, rattled in sudden bursts. That had something of a hypnotic effect as well, the cyclical way the fans vibrated furiously and fell silent, vibrated and fell silent.

He had spent months rebuilding the Mustang, and Jessica McDermott Price had made it junk again in a single instant. She'd done things to him he thought only happened to characters in country-western songs, laying waste to his car, his dogs, driving him from his home, and making an outlaw of him. It was almost funny. And who knew that getting a finger blown off and losing half a pint of blood could be so good for your sense of humor?

No. It wasn't funny. It was important not to laugh again. He didn't want to frighten Marybeth, didn't want her thinking he was drifting out of his head.

"You're out of your head," Jessica Price said. "You aren't going anywhere. You need to calm down. Let me get something to relax you, and we'll talk."

At the sound of her voice, Jude opened his eyes.

He sat in a wicker chair, against the wall, in the dim upstairs hallway of Jessica Price's house. He'd never seen the upstairs, had not got that far into her home, but knew immediately where he was all the same. He could tell from the photographs, the large framed portraits that hung from the walls of dark-paneled hardwood. One was a soft-focus school picture of Reese, about age eight, posing in front of a blue curtain and grinning to show braces. Her ears stuck out: goofy-cute.

The other portrait was older, the colors slightly faded. It showed a ramrod-straight, square-shouldered captain who, with his long, narrow face, cerulean eyes, and wide, thin-lipped mouth, bore more than a passing resemblance to Charlton Heston. Craddock's stare in this picture was faraway and arrogant at the same time. Drop and give me twenty.

Down the corridor to Jude's left was the wide central staircase, leading up from the foyer. Anna was halfway up the steps, with Jessica close behind her. Anna was flushed, too thin, the knobs of her wrists and elbows protruding under her skin and her clothes hanging loose on her. She wasn't a Goth anymore. No makeup, no black fingernail polish, no earrings or nose rings. She wore a white tunic, faded pink gym shorts, and untied tennis sneakers. It was possible her hair hadn't been brushed or combed in weeks. She should've looked terrible, bedraggled and starved, but she wasn't. She was as beautiful now as she ever had been the summer they spent out in the barn working on the Mustang with the dogs underfoot.

At the sight of her, Jude felt an almost overwhelming throb of emotion: shock and loss and adoration all together. He could hardly bear to feel so much at once. Maybe it was more feeling than the reality around him could bear as well—the world bent at the edges of his vision, became blurred and distorted. The hall turned into a corridor out of *Alice in Wonderland,* too small at one end, with little doors only a house cat could fit through, and too big at the other, the portrait of Craddock stretching until he was life-size. The voices of the women on the stairs deepened and dragged to the point of incoherence. It was like listening to a record slow down after the record player has been abruptly unplugged.

Jude had been about to cry out to Anna, wanted more than anything to go to her—but when the world warped all out of shape, he pressed himself back into the chair, his heartbeat racing. In another moment his vision cleared, the hallway straightened out, and he could hear Anna and Jessica clearly again. He grasped, then, that the vision surrounding him was fragile and that he could not put much strain on it. It was important to be still, to take no rash action. To do and feel as little as possible; to simply watch.

Anna's hands were closed into small, bony fists, and she went up the steps in an aggressive rush, so her sister stumbled trying to keep up, catching the banister to avoid a pratfall down the staircase.

"Wait—Anna—*stop!*" Jessica said, steadying herself, then lunging up the stairs to catch at her sister's shirtsleeve. "You're hysterical—"

"No I'm not don't touch me," Anna said, all one sentence, no punctuation. She yanked her arm away.

Anna reached the landing and turned toward her older sister, who stood rigid two steps below her, in a pale silk skirt and a silk blouse the color of black coffee. Jessica's calves were bunched up, and the tendons showed in her neck. She was grimacing, and in that moment she looked old—not a woman of about forty but one well past fifty—and afraid. Her pallor, especially at her temples, was gray, and the corners of her mouth were pinched, webbed with crow's-feet.

"You *are.* You're imagining things, having one of your terrible fantasies. You don't know what's real and what isn't. You can't go anywhere like you are."

Anna said, "Are these imaginary?" Holding up the envelope in her hand. "These pictures?" Taking out Polaroids, fanning them in one hand to show Jessica, then throwing them at her. "Jesus! It's your daughter. She's eleven."

Jessica Price flinched from the flying snapshots. They fell on the steps, around her feet. Jude noticed that Anna still held one of them, which she shoved back into the envelope.

"I know what's real," Anna said. "First time ever, maybe."

"Daddy," Jessica said, her voice weak, small.

Anna went on, "I'm going. Next time you see me, I'll be back with his lawyers. To get Reese."

"You think *he'll* help you?" Jessica said, her voice a tremulous whisper. *He? His?* It took Jude a moment to process that they were talking about him. His right hand was beginning to itch. It felt puffy and hot and insect-bitten.

"Sure he will."

"Daddy," Jessica said again, her voice louder now, wavering.

A door popped open, down the dark hallway to Jude's right. He glanced toward it, expecting to see Craddock, but it was Reese instead. She peeked around the edge of the doorframe, a kid with Anna's pale golden hair, a long strand of it hanging across one of her eyes. Jude was sorry to see her, felt a twinge of pain at the sight of her large, stricken eyes. The things some children had to see. Still—it was not as bad as some of what had been done to her, he supposed.

"It's going to come out, Jessie. All of it," Anna said. "I'm glad. I want to talk about it. I hope he goes to jail."

"Daddy!" Jessica screamed.

And then the door directly across from Reese's room opened, and a tall, gaunt, angular figure stepped into the hallway. Craddock was a black cutout in the shadows, featureless except for his horn-rimmed spectacles, the ones he seemed to put on only every now and then. The lenses of his glasses caught and focused the available light, so they glowed, a faint, livid rose in the gloom. Behind him, back in his room, an air conditioner was rattling, a steady, cyclical buzzing sound, curiously familiar.

"What's the racket?" Craddock asked, his voice a honeyed rasp.

"Daddy," Jessica said. "Anna's leaving. She says she's going back to New York, back to Judas Coyne, and she's going to get his lawyers—"

Anna looked down the hall, toward her father. She didn't see Jude. Of course she didn't. Her cheeks were a dark, angry red, with two spots of no color at all showing high on her cheekbones. She was shaking.

"—get lawyers, and police, and tell everyone that you and Reese—"

"Reese is right here, Jessie," Craddock said. "Calm yourself. Calm down."

"—and she . . . she found some pictures," Jessica finished lamely, glancing at her daughter for the first time.

"Did she?" Craddock said, sounding perfectly at ease. "Anna baby. I'm sorry you're worked up. But this is no time of the day to run off upset like you are. It's late, girl. It's almost nightfall. Why don't you sit down with me, and we'll talk about what's bothering you. I'd like to see if I can't put your mind at ease. You give me half a chance, I bet I can."

Anna seemed to be having trouble finding her voice all of a sudden. Her eyes were flat and bright and frightened. She looked from Craddock to Reese and finally back to her sister.

"Keep him away from me," Anna said. "Or so help me I'll kill him."

"She can't go," Jessica said to Craddock. "Not yet."

Not yet? Jude wondered what that could mean. Did Jessica think there was more to talk about? It looked to him as if the conversation was already over.

Craddock glanced sidelong at Reese.

"Go on in your room, Reese." He reached out toward her as he spoke, to put a reassuring hand on her small head.

"*Don't touch her!*" Anna screamed.

Craddock's hand stopped moving, hung in the air, just above Reese's head—then fell back to his side.

Something changed then. In the dark of the hall, Jude could not see Craddock's features well, but he thought he detected some subtle shift in body language, in the set of his shoulders or the tilt of his head or the way his feet were planted. Jude thought of a man readying himself to grab a snake out of the weeds.

At last Craddock spoke to Reese again, without turning his gaze away from Anna. "Go on, sweetheart. You let the grown-ups talk now. It's night-fall, and it's time for the grown-ups to talk without little girls underfoot."

Reese glanced down the hall at Anna and her mother. Anna met her gaze, moved her head in the slightest of nods.

"Go ahead, Reese," Anna said. "Just grown-ups talkin'."

The little girl ducked her head back into her room and pulled her door shut. A moment later the sound of her music came in a muffled blast through the door, a barrage of drums and a screech of train-coming-off-the-tracks guitar, followed by children jubilantly shrieking in rough harmony. It was the Kidz Bop version of Jude's last Top 40 hit, "Put You in Yer Place."

Craddock jerked at the sound of it, and his hands closed into fists.

"That man," he whispered.

As he came toward Anna and Jessica, a curious thing happened. The landing at the top of the staircase was illuminated by the failing sunshine that shone through the big bay window at the front of the house, so that as Craddock approached his stepdaughters, the light rose into his face, etching fine details, the tilt of cheekbone, the deep-set brackets around his mouth. But the lenses of his spectacles darkened, hiding his eyes behind circles of blackness.

The old man said, "You haven't been the same since you came home to us from living with that man. I can't tell what's got into you, Anna darling. You've had some bad times—no one knows that better than me—but it's like that Coyne fella took your unhappiness and cranked up the volume on it. Cranked it up so loud you can't hear my voice anymore when I try and talk to you. I hate to see you so miserable and mixed up."

"I ain't mixed up, and I ain't your darlin'. And I am tellin' you, if you come within four feet of me, you'll be sorry."

"Ten minutes, Daddy," Jessica said.

Craddock whisked his fingers at her, an impatient, silencing gesture.

Anna darted a look at her sister, then back to Craddock. "You are both wrong if you think you can keep me here by force."

"No one is going to make you do anything you don't want," Craddock said, stepping past Jude.

His face was seamed and his color bad, his freckles standing out on his waxy-white flesh. He didn't walk so much as shuffle, bent over with what Jude guessed was some permanent curvature of the spine. He looked better dead.

"You think Coyne is going to do you any favors?" Craddock went on. "I seem to recall he threw your ass out. I don't think he even answers your letters anymore. He didn't help you before—I don't see why he will now."

"He didn't know how. I didn't know myself. I do now. I'm gonna tell him what you did. I'm gonna tell him you belong in jail. And you know what? He'll line up the lawyers to put you there." She flicked a look at Jessica. "Her, too—if they don't put her in the fuckin' nut farm. Doesn't make a difference to me, as long as they stick her a long way off from Reese."

"Daddy!" Jessica cried, but Craddock gave his head a quick shake: *Shut up.*

"You think he'll even see you? Open the door when you come knocking? I imagine he's shacked up with someone else by now. There's all sorts of pretty girls happy to lift their skirts for a rock star. It's not like you have anything to offer him he can't get elsewhere, minus the emotional headaches."

At this a look of pain flickered across Anna's features, and she sagged a little: A runner winded and sore from the race.

"It doesn't matter whether he's with someone else. He's my friend," she said in a small voice.

"He won't believe you. No one will believe you, because it just isn't true, dear. Not a word of it," Craddock said, taking a step toward her. "You're getting confused again, Anna."

"That's right," Jessica said fervently.

"Even the pictures aren't what you think. I can clear this up for you if you'll let me. I can help you if—"

But he had gone too close. Anna leaped toward him. She put one hand on his face, snatching off his round, horn-rimmed spectacles and crushing them. She placed the other hand, which still clutched the envelope, in the center of his chest and shoved. He tottered, cried out. His left ankle folded, and he went down. He fell away from the steps, not toward them—Anna had come nowhere near throwing him down the staircase, no matter what Jessica had said about it.

Craddock landed on his scrawny rear with a thud that shook the whole corridor and jarred the portrait of him on the wall out of true. He started to sit up, and Anna put her heel on his shoulder and shoved, driving him down onto his back. She was shaking furiously.

Jessica squealed and dashed up the last few steps, swerving around Anna and dropping to one knee, to be by her stepfather's side.

Jude found himself climbing to his feet. He couldn't sit still any longer. He expected the world to get bent again, and it did, distending absurdly, like an image reflected in the side of an expanding soap bubble. His ears popped. His head felt a long way off from his feet—miles. And as he took his first step forward, he felt curiously buoyant, almost weightless, a scuba diver crossing the floor of the ocean. As he made his way down the hall, though, he *willed* the space around him to recover its proper shape and dimensions, and it did. His will meant something, then. It was possible to move through the soap-bubble world around him without popping it, if he took care.

His hands hurt, both of them, not only the right. It felt as if they were swollen to the size of boxing gloves. The pain came in steady, rhythmic waves, beating in time with his pulse, *thum-thum-thum,* like tires on blacktop. It mingled with the rattle and buzz of the air conditioner in Craddock's room, to create an oddly soothing chorus of background nonsense sound.

He wanted desperately to tell Anna to get out, to get downstairs and out of the house. He had a strong sense, though, that he could not shove himself into the scene before him without tearing through the soft tissue of the dream. And anyway, past was past. He couldn't change what was going to happen now any more than he'd been able to save Bammy's sister, Ruth, by calling her name. You couldn't change, but you could bear witness.

Jude wondered why Anna had even come upstairs, then thought that probably she wanted to throw some clothes in a bag before she left. She wasn't afraid of her father and Jessica, didn't think they had any power over her anymore—a beautiful, heartbreaking, fatal confidence in herself.

"I told you to stay away," Anna said.

"You doin' this for him?" Craddock asked. Until this moment, he had spoken with courtly southern inflections. There was nothing courtly about his voice now, though, his accent all harsh twang, a good ol' boy with nothing good about him. "This all part of some crazy idea you have to win him back? You think you're going to get his sympathy, you go crawlin' off to him, with your sob story about how your pop made you do terrible things and it ruined you for life? I bet you can't wait to boast to him 'bout how you told me off and shoved me down, an old man who cared for you in times of sickness and protected you from yourself when you were out of your mind. You think he'd be proud of you if he was standin' here right now and saw you attack me?"

"No," Anna said. "I think he'd be proud of me if he saw this." She stepped forward and spat into his face.

Craddock flinched, then let out a strangled bellow, as if he'd caught an eyeful of some corrosive agent. Jessica started to haul herself to her feet, fingers hooked into claws, but Anna caught her by the shoulder and shoved her back down next to their stepfather.

Anna stood over them, trembling, but not as furiously as she had been a moment before. Jude reached tentatively for her shoulder, put his bandaged left hand on it, and squeezed lightly. Daring finally to touch her. Anna didn't seem to notice. Reality warped itself out of shape for an instant when his hand settled upon her, but he thought everything back to normality by focusing on the background sounds, the music of the moment: *thum-thum-thum*, rattle and hum.

"Good for you, Florida," he said. It was out before he could catch himself. The world didn't end.

Anna wagged her head back and forth, a dismissive little shake. When she spoke, her tone was weary. "And I was scared of you."

She turned, slipping out of Jude's grasp, and went down the hall, to a room at the end. She closed the door behind her.

Jude heard something go *plink,* looked down. His right hand was in the sock, soaked through with blood and dripping on the floor. The silver buttons on the front of his Johnny Cash coat flashed in the very last of the salmon-colored light of day. He hadn't noticed he was wearing the dead man's suit until just now. It really was a hell of a good fit. Jude had not wondered for one second how it was possible he could be seeing the scene before him, but now an answer to that unasked question occurred. He had bought the dead man's suit and the dead man, too—owned the ghost and the ghost's past. These moments belonged to him, too, now.

Jessica crouched beside her stepfather, the both of them panting harshly, staring at the closed door to Anna's room. Jude heard drawers opening and closing in there, a closet door thudding.

"Nightfall," Jessica whispered. "Nightfall at last."

Craddock nodded. He had a scratch on his face, directly below his left eye, where Anna had caught him with a fingernail as she tore off his glasses. A teardrop of blood trickled along his nose. He swiped at it with the back of his hand and made a red smear along his cheek.

Jude glanced toward the great bay window into the foyer. The sky was a deep, still blue, darkening toward night. Along the horizon, beyond the trees and rooftops on the other side of the street, was a line of deepest red, where the sun had only just disappeared.

"What'd you do?" Craddock asked. He spoke quietly, voice pitched just above a whisper, still tremulous with rage.

"She let me hypnotize her a couple times," Jessica told him, speaking in the same hush. "To help her sleep at night. I made a suggestion."

In Anna's room there was a brief silence. Then Jude distinctly heard a glassy *tink,* a bottle tapping against glass, followed by a soft gurgling.

"What suggestion?" Craddock asked.

"I told her nightfall is a nice time for a drink. I said it's her reward for getting through the day. She keeps a bottle in the top drawer."

In Anna's bedroom a lingering, dreadful quiet.

"What's that going to do?"

"There's phenobarbital in her gin," Jessica said. "I got her sleeping like a champ these days."

Something made a clunking sound on the hardwood floor in Anna's room. A tumbler falling.

"Good girl," Craddock breathed. "I knew you had something."

"Daddy," Jessica said, "you need to make her forget—the photos, what she found, *everything.* Everything that just happened. You have to make it all go away."

"I can't do that," Craddock said. "I haven't been able to do that in a long while. When she was younger . . . when she trusted me more. Maybe you . . ."

Jessica was shaking her head. "I can't take her deep like that. She won't let me—I've tried. The last time I hypnotized her, to help with her insomnia, I tried to ask her questions about Judas Coyne, what she wrote in her letters to him, and if she ever said anything to him about . . . about you. But whenever I got too personal, whenever I'd ask her something she didn't want to tell me, she'd start singing one of his songs. Holdin' me back, like. I never seen anything like it."

"Coyne did this," Craddock said again, his upper lip curling. "He ruined her. *Ruined her.* Turned her against us. He used her for what he wanted, wrecked her whole world, and then sent her back to us to wreck ours. He might as well have sent us a bomb in the mail."

"What are we going to do? There's got to be a way to stop her. She can't leave this house like she is. You heard her. She'll take Reese away from me. She'll take you, too. They'll arrest you, and me, and we'll never see each other again, except in courtrooms."

Craddock was breathing slowly now, and all the feeling had drained from his face, leaving behind only a look of dull, saturnine hostility. "You're right on one thing, girl. She can't leave this house."

It was a moment before this statement seemed to register with Jessica. She turned a startled, confused glance upon her stepfather. "Dad? Daddy?"

"Everyone knows about Anna," he went on. "How unhappy she's always been. Everyone's always known how she was going to wind up. That she was going to slit her wrists one of these days in the bath."

Jessica began to shake her head. She made to rise to her feet, but Craddock caught her wrists, pulled her back to her knees.

"The gin and the drugs make sense. Lots of 'em knock back a couple drinks and some pills before they do it. Before they kill themselves. It's how they quiet their fears and deaden the pain," he said.

Jessica was still shaking her head, a little frantically, her eyes bright and terrified and blind, not seeing her stepfather anymore. Her breath came in short bursts—she was close to hyperventilating.

When Craddock spoke again, his voice was steady, calm. "You stop it, now. You want Anna to take Reese away? You want to spend ten years in a county home?" He tightened his hold on her wrists and drew her closer, so he was speaking directly into her face. And at last her eyes refocused on his and her head stopped wagging back and forth. Craddock said, "This isn't our fault. It's Coyne's. He's the one backed us into this corner, you hear? He's the one sent us this stranger who wants to tear us down. I don't know what happened to our Anna. I haven't seen the real Anna since I can't remember when. The Anna you grew up with is dead. Coyne saw to that. Far as I'm concerned, he finished her off. He might as well have cut her wrists himself. And he's going to answer for it. Believe it. I'll teach him to meddle with a man's family. Shh, now. Catch your breath. Listen to my voice. We'll get through this. I'm going to get you through this, same as I've got you through every other bad thing in your life. You trust in me now. Take one deep breath. Now take another. Better?"

Her blue-gray eyes were wide and avid: entranced. Her breath whistled, one long, slow exhalation, then another.

"You can do this," Craddock said. "I know you can. For Reese, you can do whatever has to be done."

Jessica said, "I'll try. But you have to tell me. You have to say what to do. I can't think."

"That's all right. I'll think for both of us," Craddock said. "And you don't need to do anything except pick yourself up and go draw a warm bath."

"Yes. Okay."

Jessica started to rise again, but Craddock tugged at her wrists, held her beside him a moment longer.

"And when you're done," Craddock said, "Run downstairs and get my old pendulum. I'll need something for Anna's wrists."

At that he let her go. Jessica rose to her feet so quickly she stumbled and put a hand against the wall to steady herself. She stared at him with dazed and astounded eyes for a moment, then turned in a kind of trance and opened a door just to her left, let herself into a white-tiled bathroom.

Craddock remained on the floor until there came the sound of water rushing into the tub. Then he helped himself to his feet and stood shoulder to shoulder with Jude.

"You old cocksucker," Jude said. The soap-bubble world flexed and wobbled. Jude clenched his teeth together, pulled it back into shape.

Craddock's lips were thin and pale, stretched back across his teeth in a bitter, ugly grimace. The old flesh on the backs of his arms wobbled. He made his slow way down to Anna's room, reeling a little—getting shoved down had taken something out of him. He pushed the door in. Jude followed at his heels.

There were two windows in Anna's room, but they both faced the back of the house, away from where the sun had gone down. It was already night in there, the room sunk into blue shadows. Anna sat at the very end of the bed, an empty tumbler on the floor between her sneakers. Her duffel bag was on the mattress behind her, some laundry hastily thrown into it, the sleeve of a red sweater hanging out. Anna's face was a pleasant blank, her forearms resting on her knees, her eyes glassy and fixed on a point in the impossible distance. The cream-colored envelope with the Polaroid of Reese in it—her evidence—was in one hand, forgotten. The sight of her that way made Jude ill.

Judas sank onto the bed beside her. The mattress creaked beneath him, but no one—not Anna, not Craddock—seemed to notice. He put his left hand over Anna's right. His left hand was bleeding again from the puncture wound, the bandages stained and loose. When had that started? He couldn't even lift the right hand, which was too heavy now and too painful. The thought of moving it made him dizzy.

Craddock paused before his stepdaughter, bent to peer speculatively into her face.

"Anna? Can you hear me? Can you hear my voice?"

She went on smiling, did not reply at first. Then she blinked and said, "What? Did you say something, Daddy? I was listening to Jude. On the radio. This is my favorite song."

His lips tightened until there was no color in them. "That man," he said again, almost spitting it. He took one corner of the envelope and jerked it out of her hands.

Craddock straightened up, turned toward one of the windows to pull down the shade.

"I love you, Florida," Jude said. The bedroom around him bulged when he spoke, the soap bubble swelling so that it threatened to explode, then shrank again.

"Love you, Jude," Anna said softly.

At this, Craddock's shoulders jumped in a startled shrug. He looked back, wondering. Then the old man said, "You and him are going to be back together soon. That's what you wanted, and that's what you'll get.

Daddy's going to see to it. Daddy's going to put you two together just as soon as he can."

"Goddamn you," Jude said, and this time when the room bloated and stretched itself out of shape, he couldn't, no matter how hard he concentrated on *thum-thum-thum,* make it go back the way it was supposed to be. The walls swelled and then sank inward, like bed linens hanging on a line and moving in a breeze.

The air in the room was warm and close and smelled of exhaust and dog. Jude heard a soft whining sound behind him and looked back at Angus, who lay on the bed where Anna's duffel bag had been only a moment before. His breathing was labored, and his eyes were gummy and yellow. A sharp-tipped red bone stuck through one bent leg.

Jude looked back toward Anna, only to find that it was Marybeth sitting next to him on the bed now, face dirty, expression hard.

Craddock pulled down one of the shades, and the room darkened some more. Jude glanced out the other window and saw the greenery at the side of the interstate, palms, rubbish in the weeds, and then a green sign that said EXIT 9. His hands went *thum-thum-thum.* The air conditioner hummed, buzzed, hummed. Jude wondered for the first time how he could still be hearing Craddock's air conditioner. The old man's room was all the way down the hall. Something began to click, a sound as repetitive as a metronome: the turn signal.

Craddock moved to the other window, blocking Jude's view of the highway, and he ran down that shade as well, plunging Anna's room into darkness. Nightfall at last.

Jude looked back at Marybeth, her jaw set, one hand on the wheel. The blinker signal flashed repetitively on the dash, and he opened his mouth, to say something, he didn't know what, something like . . .

41

"**What are you doin'?**" His voice an unfamiliar croak. Marybeth was aiming the Mustang at an exit ramp, had almost reached it. "This ain't it."

"I was shakin' you for about five minutes, and you wouldn't wake up. I thought you were in a coma or somethin'. There's a hospital here."

"Keep going. I'm awake now."

She swerved back onto the highway at the last moment, and a horn blared behind her.

"How you doin', Angus?" Jude asked, and peeked back at him.

Jude reached between the seats and touched a paw, and for an instant Angus's gaze sharpened a little. His jaws moved. His tongue found the back of Jude's left hand and lapped at his fingers.

"Good boy," Jude whispered. "Good boy."

At last he turned away, settled back into his seat. The sock puppet on his right hand wore a red face. He was in dire need of a shot of something to dull the pain, thought he might find it on the radio: Skynyrd or, failing that, the Black Crows. He touched the power button and flipped rapidly from a burst of static to the Doppler pulse of a coded military transmission to Hank Williams III, or maybe just Hank Williams, Jude couldn't tell because the signal was so faint, and then—

Then the tuner landed on a perfectly clear broadcast: Craddock.

"I never would've thought you had so much in the tank, boy." His voice was genial and close, coming out of the speakers set in the doors. "You don't have any quit in you. That usually counts for something with me. This ain't usually, of course. You understand that." He laughed. "Now, I do like an afternoon drive with the window down. Get on the road, just go. Doesn't matter where. Anyplace will do. You know, most people like to think they don't know the meaning of the word 'quit,' but it isn't true. Most people, you put them under, put them under deep, maybe help 'em along with some good dope, sink them into a full trance state, and then tell them they're burnin' alive? They'll scream for water till they got no voice left. They'll do anything to make it stop. Anything you like. That's just human nature. But some people—children and crazy folks, mostly—you can't reason with, even when they're in a trance. Anna was both, God love her. I tried to make her forget about all the things that made her feel so bad. She was a good girl. I hated the way she tore herself up over things—even over you. But I couldn't ever really make her go all the way blank, even though it would've saved her pain. Some people would just rather suffer. No wonder she liked you. You're the same way. I wanted to deal with you quick. But you had to go and drag this out. And now you got to wonder why. You got to ask yourself. You know, when that dog in the backseat stops breathing, so do you. And it ain't going to be easy, like it could've been. You spent three days livin' like a dog, and now you have to die like one, and so does that two-dollar bitch next to you—"

Marybeth thumbed the radio off. It came right back on again.

"—you think you could turn my own little girl against me and not have to answer for it—"

Jude lifted his foot and slammed the heel of his Doc Marten into the dash. It hit with a crunch of splintering plastic. Craddock's voice was instantly lost in a sudden, deafening blast of bass. Jude kicked the radio again, shattering the face. It went silent.

"Remember when I said the dead man didn't come for talk?" Jude told her. "I take it back. Lately I been thinking that's all he came for."

Marybeth didn't reply. Thirty minutes later Jude spoke again, to tell her to get off at the next exit.

They drove on a two-lane state highway, with southern, semitropical forest growing right up to the sides of the road, leaning over it. They passed a drive-in that had been closed since Jude was a child. The giant movie screen towered over the road, holes torn in it, offering a view of the sky. This evening's feature was a drifting pall of dirty smoke. They rolled by the New South Motel, long since shut up and being reclaimed by the jungle, windows boarded over. They glided past a filling station, the first place they'd seen that was open. Two deeply sunburned fat men sat out front and watched them go by. They did not smile or wave or acknowledge the passing car in any way, except that one leaned forward and spat in the dirt.

Jude directed her to take a left off the highway, and they followed a road up into the low hills. The afternoon light was strange, a dim, poisonous red, a stormy twilight color. It was the same color Jude saw when he shut his eyes, the color of his headache. It was not close to nightfall but looked it. The bellies of the clouds to the west were dark and threatening. The wind lashed the tops of the palms and shook the Spanish moss that straggled down from low-hanging oak branches.

"We're here," he said.

As Marybeth turned into the driveway, the long run-up to the house, the wind gusted with more force than usual and threw a burst of plump, hard raindrops across the windshield. They hit in a sudden, furious rattle, and Jude waited for more, but there was no more.

The house stood at the top of a low rise. Jude had not been here in more than three decades and had not realized until this moment how closely his home in New York resembled the home of his childhood. It was as if he had leaped ten years into the future and returned to New

York to find his own farm neglected and disused, fallen to ruin. The great rambling place before him was the gray color of mouse, with a roof of black shingles, many of them crooked or missing, and as they drew closer, Jude actually saw the wind snag one, strip it loose, and propel the black square away into the sky.

The abandoned chicken coop was visible to one side of the house, and its screen door swung open, then banged shut with a crack like a gunshot. The glass was missing from a window on the first floor, and the wind rattled a sheet of semitransparent plastic stapled into the frame.

The dirt lane that led to the house ended in a loop. Marybeth followed it around, turning the Mustang to point back the way they'd come, before putting it into park. They were both staring down the road when the floodlights of Craddock's truck appeared at the bottom of the drive.

"Oh, God," Marybeth said, and then she was out of the Mustang, going around the front to Jude's side.

The pale truck at the foot of the drive seemed to pause for a moment, then began rolling up the hill toward them.

Marybeth jerked his door open. Jude almost fell out. She pulled on his arm.

"Get on your feet. Get in the house."

"Angus . . ." he said, glancing into the back at his dog.

Angus's head rested on his front paws. He stared wearily back at Jude, his eyes red-rimmed and wet.

"He's dead."

"No," Jude said, sure she was mistaken. "How you doin', boy?"

Angus regarded him mournfully, didn't move. The wind got into the car, and an empty paper cup scooted around on the floor, rattling softly. The breeze stirred Angus's fur, brushing it in the wrong direction. Angus paid it no mind.

It didn't seem possible that Angus could just have died like that, with no fanfare. He'd been alive only a few minutes ago, Jude was convinced of it. Jude stood in the dirt next to the Mustang, sure if he just waited another moment, Angus would move, stretch his front paws, and lift his head. Then Marybeth was hauling on his arm again, and he didn't have the strength to resist her, had to stagger along after or risk being toppled.

He fell to his knees a few feet from the front steps. He didn't know why. He had an arm over Marybeth's shoulders, and she had one looped around his waist, and she moaned through her clenched lips, dragging him back onto his heels. Behind him he heard the dead man's pickup rolling to a stop in the turnaround. Gravel crunched under the tires.

Hey, boy, Craddock called from the open driver's-side window, and at the door Jude and Marybeth stopped to look back.

The truck idled beside the Mustang. Craddock sat behind the wheel, in his stiff, formal black suit with the silver buttons. His left arm hung out the window. His face was hard to make out through the blue curve of glass.

This your place, son? Craddock said. He laughed. *How could you ever stand to leave?* He laughed again.

The razor shaped like a crescent moon fell from the hand hanging out the window, and swung from its gleaming chain.

You're gonna cut her throat. And she's goin' to be glad when you do. Just to have it over with. You should've stayed away from my little girls, Jude.

Jude turned the doorknob, and Marybeth shouldered it inward, and they crashed through into the dark of the front hall. Marybeth kicked the door shut behind them. Jude threw a last glance out the window beside the door—and the truck was gone. The Mustang stood alone in the drive. Marybeth turned him and shoved him into motion again.

They started down the corridor, side by side, each holding the other up. Her hip caught a side table and overturned it, and it smashed to the floor. A phone that had been sitting on it toppled to the boards, and the receiver flew off the cradle.

At the end of the hall was a doorway, leading into the kitchen, where the lights were on. It was the only source of light they'd seen so far in the entire house. From the outside the windows had been dark, and once they were in, it was shadows in the front hall and a cavernous gloom waiting at the top of the stairs.

An old woman, in a pastel flower-print blouse, appeared in the kitchen doorway. Her hair was a white frizz, and her spectacles magnified her blue, amazed eyes to appear almost comically large. Jude knew Arlene Wade at a glance, although he could not have said how long it had been since he'd last seen her. Whenever it had been, she'd always been just as she was now—scrawny, perpetually startled-looking, old.

"What is this business?" she called out. Her right hand reached up to curl around the cross that hung at her throat. She stepped back as they reached the doorway to let them by. "My God, Justin. What in the name of Mary and Joseph happened to you?"

The kitchen was yellow. Yellow linoleum, yellow tile countertops, yellow-and-white check curtains, daisy-patterned plates drying in the basket next to the sink, and as Jude took it all in, he heard that song in his head, the one that had been such a smash for Coldplay a few years before, the one about how everything was all yellow.

He was surprised, given the way the house looked from the outside, to find the kitchen so full of lively color, so well kept up. It had never been this cozy when he'd been a child. The kitchen was where his mother had spent most of her time, watching daytime TV in a stupor while she peeled potatoes or washed beans. Her mood of numb, emotional exhaustion had drained the color from the room and made it a place where it seemed important to speak in quiet voices, if at all, a private and unhappy space that you could no more run through than you could make a ruckus in a funeral parlor.

But his mother was thirty years dead, and the kitchen was Arlene Wade's now. She had lived in the house for more than a year and very likely passed most of her waking hours in this room, which she'd warmed with the everyday business of being herself, an old woman with friends to talk to on the phone, pies to bake for relatives, a dying man to care for. In fact, it was a little *too* cozy. Jude felt dizzy at the warmth of it, at the suddenly close air. Marybeth turned him toward the kitchen table. He felt a bony claw sink into his right arm, Arlene grabbing his biceps, and was surprised at the rigid strength in her fingers.

"You got a sock on your hand," she said.

"He got one of his fingers taken off," Marybeth said.

"What are you doing here, then?" Arlene asked. "Shoulda drove him to the hospital."

Jude fell into a chair. Curiously, even sitting still, he felt as if he were still moving, the walls of the room sliding slowly past him, the chair gliding forward like a car in a theme-park amusement: *Mr. Jude's Wild Ride*. Marybeth sank into a chair next to him, her knees bumping his. She was shivering. Her face was oiled in sweat, and her hair had gone crazy, was snarled and twisted. Strands stuck to her temples, to the sweat on the sides of her face, to the back of her neck.

"Where are your dogs?" Marybeth asked.

Arlene began to untie the sock wound around Jude's wrist, peering down her nose at it through the magnifying lenses of her glasses. If she found this question bizarre or startling, she showed no sign of it. She was intent on the work of her hands.

"My dog is over there," she said, nodding at one corner of the room. "And as you can see, he's quite protective of me. He's a fierce old boy. Don't want to cross him."

Jude and Marybeth looked to the corner. A fat old rottweiler sat on a dog pillow in a wicker basket. He was too big for it, and his pink, hairless ass hung over the side. He weakly lifted his head, regarded them through rheumy, bloodshot eyes, then lowered his head again and sighed softly.

"Is that what happened to this hand?" Arlene asked. "Were you bit by a dog, Justin?"

"What happened to my father's shepherds?" Jude asked.

"He hasn't been up to takin' care of a dog for a while now. I sent Clinton and Rather off to live with the Jeffery family." Then she had the sock off his hand and drew a sharp breath when she saw the bandage beneath.

It was soaked—saturated—with blood. "Are you in some kinda stupid race with your daddy to see who can die first?" She set his hand on the table without unwrapping the bandages to see more. Then she glanced at Jude's bandaged left hand. "You missin' any parts off that one?"

"No. That one I just gouged real good."

"I'll get you the ambulance," Arlene said. She had lived in the South her whole life and she pronounced the word *amble-lance*.

She picked up the phone on the kitchen wall. It made a noisy, repetitive blatting at her, and she jerked her ear away from the receiver, then hung up.

"You crashed my phone off the hook in the hall," she said, and disappeared into the front of the house to right it.

Marybeth stared at Jude's hand. He lifted it—discovered he had left a wet red handprint on the table—and put it weakly back down.

"We shouldn't have come here," she said.

"Nowhere else to go."

She turned her head, looked at Arlene's fat Rottie. "Tell me he's gonna help us."

"Okay. He's going to help us."

"You mean it?"

"No."

Marybeth questioned him with a glance.

"Sorry," Jude said. "I might've misled you a bit 'bout the dogs. Not just any dogs will do. They have to be mine. You know how every witch has a black cat? Bon and Angus were like that for me. They can't be replaced."

"When did you figure that out?"

"Four days ago."

"Why didn't you tell me?"

"I was hoping to bleed to death before Angus went and croaked on us. Then you'd be okay. Then the ghost would have to leave you alone. His business with us would be done. If my head was clearer, I wouldn't have bandaged myself up so well."

"You think it'll make it okay if you let yourself die? You think it'll make it okay to give him what he wants? Goddamn you. You think I came all this way to watch you kill yourself? *Goddamn* you."

Arlene stepped back through the kitchen doorway, frowning, eyebrows knitted together in a look of annoyance or deep thought or both.

"There's somethin' wrong with that phone. I can't get dial tone. All I do get, when I pick up, is some local AM station. Some farm program. Guy chatterin' about how to cut open animals. Maybe the wind yanked down a line."

"I have a cell phone—" Marybeth began.

"Me, too," Arlene said. "But we don't get no reception up in these parts. Let's get Justin laid down, and I'll see what I can do for his hand right now. Then I'll drive down the road to the McGees and call from there."

Without any forewarning she reached between them and snatched at Marybeth's wrist, lifting her own bandaged hand for a moment. The wraps were stiff and brown with the dried bloodstains on them.

"What the hell have you two been doin'?" she asked.

"It's my thumb," Marybeth said.

"Did you try to trade it to him for his finger?"

"It's just got an infection."

Arlene set the bandaged hand down and looked at the unbandaged hand, terribly white, the skin wrinkled. "I never seen any infection like this. It's in both hands—is it anywhere else?"

"No."

She felt Marybeth's brow. "You're burnin' up. My God. The both of you. You can rest in my room, honey. I'll put Justin in with his father. I shoved an extra bed in there two weeks ago, so I could nap in there and keep a closer eye on him. Come on, big boy. More walkin' to do. Get yourself up."

"If you want me to move, you better get the wheelbarrow and roll me," Jude said.

"I got morphine in your daddy's room."

"Okay," Jude said, and he put his left hand on the table and struggled to get to his feet.

Marybeth jumped up and took his elbow.

"You stay where you are," Arlene said. She nodded in the direction of her rottweiler and the door beyond, which opened into what had once been a sewing room but was now a small bedroom. "Go on and rest in there. I can handle this one."

"It's all right," Jude said to Marybeth. "Arlene's got me."

"What are we gonna do about Craddock?" Marybeth asked.

She was standing almost against him, and Jude leaned forward and put his face in her hair and kissed the crown of her head.

"I don't know," Jude said. "I wish like hell you weren't in this with me. Why didn't you go? Why didn't you get away from me when you still had the chance? Why you got to be such a stubborn pain in the ass about things?"

"I been hangin' around you for nine months," she said, and stood on her tiptoes and put her arms around his neck, her mouth searching for his. "I guess it just rubbed off on me."

And then for a while they stood rocking back and forth in each other's arms.

42

When Jude stepped away from Marybeth, Arlene turned him around and started him walking. He expected her to march him back down the front hall, so they could go upstairs to the master bedroom, where he assumed his father lay. Instead, though, they continued along the length of the kitchen to the back hall, the one that led to Jude's old bedroom.

Of course his father was there, on the first floor. Jude vaguely recalled that Arlene had told him, in one of their few phone conversations, that she was moving Martin downstairs and into Jude's old bedroom, because it was easier than going up and down the stairs to tend to him.

Jude cast one last look back at Marybeth. She was watching him go, from where she stood in the doorway of Arlene's bedroom, her eyes fever-bright and exhausted—and then Jude and Arlene were moving away, leaving her behind. He didn't like the idea of being so far from Marybeth in the dark and decayed maze of his father's house. It did not seem too unreasonable to think that they might never find their way back to each other.

The hall to his room was narrow and crooked, the walls visibly warped. They passed a screen door, the frame nailed shut, the screens rusty and bellied outward. It looked into a muddy hog pen, three medium-size pigs in it. The pigs peered at Jude and Arlene as they went by, their squashed-in faces benevolent and wise.

"There's still pigs?" Jude said. "Who's carin' for them?"

"Who do you think?"

"Why didn't you sell them?"

She shrugged, then said, "Your father took care of pigs all his life. He can hear them in where he's layin'. I guess I thought it would help him know where he was. Who he was." She looked up in Jude's face. "You think I'm foolish?"

"No," Jude said.

Arlene eased the door to Jude's old bedroom inward, and they stepped into a suffocating warmth that smelled so strongly of menthol it made Jude's eyes water.

"Hang on," Arlene said. "Lemme move my sewin'."

She left him leaning against the doorway and hastened to the little bed against the wall, to the left. Jude looked across the room to an identical cot. His father was in it.

Martin Cowzynski's eyes were narrow slits, showing only glazed slivers of eyeball. His mouth yawned open. His hands were gaunt claws, curled against his chest, the nails crooked, yellow, sharp. He had always been lean and wiry. But he had lost, Jude guessed, maybe a third of his weight, and there was barely a hundred pounds of him left. His cheeks were sunken caves. He looked like he was already dead, although breath yet whined in his throat. There were streaks of white foam on his chin. Arlene had been shaving him. The bowl of hand-whipped foam was on the nighttable, a wood-handled brush sitting in it.

Jude had not seen his father in thirty-four years, and the sight of him—starved, hideous, lost in his own private dream of death—brought on a fresh wave of dizziness. Somehow it was more horrible that Martin was breathing. It would've been easier to look upon him, as he was now, if he were dead. Jude had hated him for so long that he was unprepared for any other emotion. For pity. For horror. Horror was rooted in sympathy, after all, in understanding what it would be like to suffer the worst. Jude had not imagined he could feel either sympathy or understanding for the man in the bed across the room.

"Can he see me standing here?" Jude asked.

Arlene looked over her shoulder at Jude's father.

"Doubt it. He hasn't responded to the sight of anything in days. Course it's been months since he could talk, but until just a little while ago he did sometimes make faces or give a sign when he wanted something. He enjoyed when I shaved him, so I still do that ever' day. He liked the hot water on his face. Maybe some part of him still likes it. I don't know." She paused, considering the gaunt, rasping figure in the far bed. "It's sorry to see him die this way, but it's worse to keep a man going after a certain point. I believe that. There comes a time, the dead have a right to claim their own."

Jude nodded. "The dead claim their own. They do."

He looked at what Arlene held in her hands, the sewing kit she was moving off the other cot. It was his mother's old kit, a collection of thimbles, needles, and thread, jumbled in one of the big yellow heart-shaped candy boxes his father used to get for her. Arlene squeezed the lid on it, closing it up, and set it on the floor between the cots. Jude eyed it warily, but it didn't make any threatening moves.

Arlene returned and guided him by the elbow to the empty bed. There was a light on a mechanical arm, screwed to the side of the nighttable. She twisted the lamp around—it made a sproingy, creaking sound as the rusted coil stretched itself out—and clicked it on. He shut his eyes against the sudden brightness.

"Let's look at that hand."

She brought a low stool to the side of the bed and began to unwind the sopping gauze, using a pair of forceps. As she peeled the last layer away from his skin, a flush of icy tingling spread through his hand, and then the missing finger began, impossibly, to burn, as if it were crawling with biting fire ants.

She stuck a needle into the wound, injecting him here, and here, while he cursed. Then came a rush of intense and blessed cold, spreading through the hand and into his wrist, pumping along the veins, turning him into an iceman.

The room darkened, then brightened. The sweat on his body cooled rapidly. He was on his back. He didn't remember lying down. He distantly felt a tugging on his right hand. When he realized that this tugging was Arlene doing something to the stump of his finger—clamping it, or putting hooks through it, or stitching it—he said, "Gonna puke." He fought the urge to gag until she could place a rubber trough next to his cheek, then turned his head and vomited into it.

When Arlene was finished, she laid his right hand on his chest. Wrapped in layer upon layer of muffling bandage, it was three times the size it had been, a small pillow. He was groggy. His temples thudded. She turned the harsh, bright light into his eyes again and leaned over for a look at the slash in his cheek. She found a wide, flesh-colored bandage and carefully applied it to his face.

She said, "You been leakin' pretty good. Do you know what type of motor oil you run on? I'll make sure the amble-lance brings the right stuff."

"Check on Marybeth. Please."

"I was going to."

She clicked off the light before she went. It was a relief to be joined to darkness once more.

He closed his eyes, and when they sprang open again, he did not know whether one minute had passed or sixty. His father's house was a place of restful silence and stillness, no sound but for the sudden whoosh of the wind, lumber creaking, a burst of rain on the windows. He wondered if Arlene had gone for the amble-lance. He wondered if Marybeth was sleeping. He wondered if Craddock was in the house, sitting outside the door. Jude turned his head and found his father staring at him.

His father's mouth hung agape, the few teeth that were left stained brown from nicotine exposure, the gums diseased. Martin stared, pale gray eyes confused. Four feet of bare floor separated the two men.

"You aren't here," Martin Cowzynski said, his voice a wheeze.

"Thought you couldn't talk," Jude said.

His father blinked slowly. Gave no sign he'd heard. "You'll be gone when I wake up." His tone was almost wishful. He began to cough weakly. Spit flew, and his chest seemed to go hollow, sinking inward, as if with each painful hack he were coughing up his insides, beginning to deflate.

"You got that wrong, old man," Jude told him. "You're my bad dream, not the other way around."

Martin continued staring at him with that look of stupid wonder for a few moments longer, then turned his gaze to the ceiling once more. Jude watched him warily, the old man in his army cot, breath screaming from his throat, dried streaks of shaving cream on his face.

His father's eyes gradually sank shut. In a while Jude's eyes did the same.

43

He wasn't sure what woke him, but later on Jude looked up, coming out of sleep in an instant, and found Arlene at the foot of the bed. He didn't know how long she'd been standing there. She'd wearing a bright red rain slicker with the hood pulled up. Droplets of rain glittered on the plastic. Her old, bony face was set in a blank, almost robotic expression that Jude did not at first recognize and which he needed several moments to interpret as fear. He wondered if she'd gone and come back or not yet left.

"We lost the power," she said.

"Did we?"

"I went outside, and when I came back in, we lost the power."

"Uh-huh."

"There's a truck in the driveway. Just settin' there. Sort of no particular color. I can't see who is settin' in it. I started to walk out to it, to see if it was someone who could maybe drive somewhere and call emergency for us—but then I got scared. I got scared of who was in it, and I came back."

"You want to stay away from him."

She went on as if Jude had said nothing. "When I got back inside, we didn't have power, and it's still just some crazy talk radio on the telephone. Bunch of religious stuff about ridin' the glory road. The TV was turned on in the front room. It was just runnin'. I know it couldn't be, because there isn't any power, but it was turned on anyway. There was a story on it. On the news. It was about you. It was about all of us. About how we was all dead. It showed a picture of the farmhouse and everythin'. They were coverin' my body with a sheet. They didn't identify me, but I saw my hand stickin' out and my bracelet. And policemen standin' ever'where. And that yellow tape blockin' the driveway. And Dennis Woltering said how you killed us all."

"It's a lie. None of that is really going to happen."

"Finally I couldn't stand it. I shut it off. The TV came right back on, but I shut it off again and jerked the plug out of the wall, and that fixed it." She paused, then added, "I have to go, Justin. I'll call for the amblelance from the neighbors. I have to go. . . . Only I'm scared to try and drive around that truck. Who drives the pale truck?"

"No one you want to meet. Take my Mustang. The keys are in it."

"No thank you. I seen what was in the back."

"Oh."

"I got my car."

"Just don't mess with that truck. Drive right over the lawn and through the fence if you have to. Do what you need to do to stay away from it. Did you look in on Marybeth?"

Arlene nodded.

"How is she?"

"Sleepin'. Poor child."

"You said it."

"Good-bye, Justin."

"Take care."

"I'm bringin' my dog with me."

"All right."

She took a sliding half step toward the door.

Then Arlene said, "Your uncle Pete and I took you to Disney World when you were seven. Do you remember?"

"I'm afraid I don't."

"In your whole life, I never once saw you smile until you were up in them elephants, goin' 'round and 'round. That made me feel good. When I saw you smile, it made me feel like you had a chance to be happy. I was sorry about how you turned out. So miserable. Wearin' black clothes and sayin' all them terrible things in your songs. I was sick to death for you. Wherever did that boy go, the one who smiled on the elephant ride?"

"He starved to death. I'm his ghost."

She nodded and backed away. Arlene raised one hand in a gesture of farewell, then turned and was gone.

Afterward Jude listened intently to the house, to the faint straining sounds it made in the wind and the splatter of the rain falling against it. A screen door banged sharply somewhere. It might have been Arlene leaving. It might have been the door swinging on the chicken coop outside.

Beyond a feeling of gritty heat in the side of his face, where Jessica Price had cut him, he was not in great pain. His breathing was slow and regular. He stared at the door, waiting for Craddock to appear. He didn't look away from the door until he heard a soft tapping sound off to his right.

He peered over. The big yellow heart-shaped box sat on the floor. Something thumped inside. Then the box moved, as if jolted from beneath. Titched a few inches across the floor and jumped again. The lid was struck from within once more, and one corner was knocked up and loose.

Four gaunt fingers slipped out from inside the box. Another thump and the lid came free and then began to rise. Craddock pulled himself up from inside the box, as if it were a heart-shaped hole set in the floor. The lid rode on top of his head, a gay and foolish hat. He removed it, cast it aside, then hitched himself out of the box to the waist in a single, surprisingly athletic move for a man who was not only elderly but dead. He got a knee on the floor, climbed the rest of the way out, and stood up. The creases in the legs of his black trousers were perfect.

In the pen outside, the pigs began to shriek. Craddock reached a long arm back into the bottomless box, felt around, found his fedora, and set it on his head. The scribbles danced before his eyes. Craddock turned and smiled.

"What kept you?" Jude asked.

44

Here we are, you and me. All out of road, the dead man said. His lips were moving but making no sound, his voice existing only in Jude's head. The silver buttons on his black suit coat glinted in the darkness.

"Yeah," Jude said. "The fun had to stop sometime."

Still full of fight. Isn't that somethin'? Craddock placed one gaunt hand on Martin's ankle and ran it over the sheet and up his leg. Martin's eyes were closed, but his mouth hung open and breath still came and went in thin, pneumatic whistles. *A thousand miles later, and you're still singin' the same song.*

Craddock's hand glided over Martin's chest. It was something he seemed to be doing almost absentmindedly, did not once look at the old man fighting for his last breaths in the bed beside him.

I never did like your music. Anna used to play it so loud it'd make a normal person's ears bleed. You know there's a road between here and hell? I've driven it myself. Many times now. And I'll tell you what, out on that road there's only one station, and all they play is your music. I guess that's the devil's way of gettin' straight to punishin' the sinners. He laughed.

"Leave the girl."

Oh, no. She's going to sit right between us while we ride the nightroad. She's come so far with you already. We can't leave her behind now.

"I'm telling you Marybeth doesn't have any part in this."

But you don't tell me, son. I tell you. You're going to choke her to death, and I'm going to watch. Say it. Tell me how it's going to be.

Jude thought, *I won't,* but while he was thinking it, he said, "I'm going to choke her. You're going to watch."

Now you're singin' my kind of music.

Jude thought of the song he'd made up the other day, at the motel in Virginia, how his fingers had known where the right chords were and the feeling of stillness and calm that had come over him as he played them. A sensation of order and control, of the rest of the world being far away, kept back by his own invisible wall of sound. What had Bammy said to him? The dead win when you quit singing. And in his vision Jessica Price had said Anna would sing when she was in a trance, to keep from being made to do things she didn't want to do, to block out voices she didn't want to hear.

Get up, the dead man said. *Stop lazin' around, now. You have business in the other room. The girl is waitin'.*

Jude wasn't listening to him, though. He was focused intently on the music in his head, hearing it as it would sound when it had been recorded with a band, the soft clash of cymbal and snare, the deep, slow pulse of the bass. The old man was talking at him, but Jude found that when he fixed his mind on his new song, he could ignore him almost completely.

He thought of the radio in the Mustang, the old radio, the one he'd pulled out of the dash and replaced with XM and a DVD-Audio disc player. The original radio had been an AM receiver with a glass face that glowed an unearthly shade of green and lit up the cockpit of the car like the inside of an aquarium. In his imagination Jude could hear his own song playing from it, could hear his own voice crying out the lyrics over the shivery, echo-chamber sound of the guitar. That was on one station.

The old man's voice was on another, buried beneath it, a faraway, south-ern, late-night, let's-hear-it-for-Jesus, talk-all-the-time station, the recep-tion no good, so all that came through was a word or two at a time, the rest lost in waves of static.

Craddock had told him to sit up. It was a moment before Jude real-ized he hadn't done it.

Get on your feet, I said.

Jude started to move—then stopped himself. In his mind he had the driver's seat cranked back and his feet out the window and it was his song on the radio and the crickets hummed in the warm summer darkness. He was humming himself, and in the next moment he realized it. It was a soft, off-key humming, but recognizable, nonetheless, as the new song.

Do you hear me talkin' to you, son? the dead man asked. Jude could tell that was what he said, because he saw his lips moving, his mouth shaping the words very clearly. But in fact Jude could not really hear him at all.

"No," Jude said.

Craddock's upper lip drew back in a sneer. He still had one hand on Jude's father—it had moved up over Martin's chest and now rested on his neck. The wind roared against the house, and raindrops rapped at the windowpanes. Then the gust abated, and in the hush that followed, Martin Cowyznski whimpered.

Jude had briefly forgotten his father—Jude's thoughts pinned on the echoing loops of his own imagined song—but the sound drew his gaze. Martin's eyes were open, wide and staring and horrified. He was gazing up at Craddock. Craddock turned his head toward him, the sneer fading, his gaunt and craggy face composing itself into an expression of quiet thought.

At last Jude's father spoke, his voice a toneless wheeze. "It's a mes-senger. It's a messenger of death."

The dead man seemed to look back at Jude, the black marks boiling in front of his eyes. Craddock's lips moved, and for a moment his voice wavered and came clear, muted but audible beneath the sound of Jude's private, inner song.

Maybe you can tune me out, Craddock said. *But he can't.*

Craddock bent over Jude's father and put his hands on Martin's face, one on each cheek. Martin's breath began to hitch and catch, each inhalation short, quick, and panicked. His eyelids fluttered. The dead man leaned forward and placed his mouth over Martin's.

Jude's father pressed himself back into his pillow, shoved his heels down into the bed, and pushed, as if he could force himself deeper into the mattress and away from Craddock. He drew a last, desperate breath—and sucked the dead man into him. It happened in an instant and was like watching a magician pull a scarf through his fist to make it disappear. Craddock *crumpled,* a wad of Saran Wrap sucked up into the tube of a vacuum cleaner. His polished black loafers were the last thing to go down Martin's throat. Martin's neck seemed, for a moment, to distend and swell—bulging the way a snake will bulge after swallowing a gerbil—but then he gulped Craddock down, and his throat shrank back to its normal, scrawny, loose-fleshed shape.

Jude's father gagged, coughed, gagged again. His hips came up off the bed, his back arching. Jude could not help it, thought immediately of orgasm. Martin's eyes strained from their sockets. The tip of his tongue flickered between his teeth.

"Spit it up, Dad," Jude said.

His father didn't seem to hear. He sank back into the bed, then bucked again, almost as if someone were sitting on top of him and Martin was trying to throw him off. He made wet, strangled sounds down in his throat. A blue artery stood out in the center of his forehead. His lips stretched back from his teeth in a doglike grimace.

Then he eased gently down onto the mattress once more. His hands, which had been clutching fistfuls of the sheets, slowly opened. His eyes were a vivid, hideous crimson—the blood vessels had erupted, staining the whites red. They stared blankly at the ceiling. Blood stained his teeth.

Jude watched him for movement, straining for some sound of breath. He heard the house settling in the wind. He heard rain spitting against the wall.

With great effort Jude sat up, then turned himself to set his feet on the floor. He had no doubt his father was dead, he who had smashed Jude's hand in the cellar door and put a single-barreled shotgun to his mother's breast, who had ruled this farmhouse with his knuckles and belt strap and laughing rages, and whom Jude had often daydreamed of killing himself. It had cost him something, though, to watch Martin die. Jude's abdomen was sore, as if he had only just vomited again, as if something had been forced out of him, ejected from his body, something he didn't want to give up. Rage, maybe.

"Dad?" Jude said, knowing no one would answer.

Jude rose to his feet, swaying, light-headed. He took a shuffling, old man's step forward, put his bandaged left hand on the edge of the night-table to support himself. It felt as if his legs might fold beneath him at any moment.

"Dad?" Jude said again.

His father jerked his head toward him and fixed his red, awful, fascinated eyes on Jude.

"Justin," he said, his voice a strained whisper. He smiled, a horrifying thing to see upon his gaunt, harrowed face. *"My boy. I'm all right. I'm fine. Come close. C'mon and put your arms around me."*

Jude did not step forward but took a staggering, unsteady step back. For a moment he had no air.

Then his breath returned, and he said, "You aren't my father."

Martin's lips widened to show his poisoned gums and crooked yellow teeth, what were left of them. A teardrop of blood spilled from his left eye, ran in a jagged red line down the crag of his cheekbone. Craddock's eye had seemed to drip red tears in almost just the same way, in Jude's vision of Anna's final night.

Jude's father sat up and reached past the bowl of shaving lather.

Martin closed his hand on his old straight razor, the one with the hickory handle. Jude hadn't known it was there, hadn't seen it lying behind the white china bowl. Jude took another step away. The backs of his legs struck the edge of his cot, and he sat down on the mattress.

Then his father was up, the sheet slithering off him. He moved more quickly than Jude expected, like a lizard, frozen in place one moment, then lurching forward, almost too quick for the eye to follow. He was naked, except for a pair of stained white boxers. His breasts were little trembling sacks of flab, furred with curling, snow-white hairs. Martin stepped forward, planted his heel on the heart-shaped box, crushed it flat.

"Come here, son," his father said, in Craddock's voice. *"Daddy's going to show you how to shave."*

And he snapped his wrist, and the razor flipped out of the handle, a mirror in which Jude was briefly able to see his own astonished face.

Martin lunged at Jude, slashing at him with the straight razor, but Jude stuck out his foot, jammed it between the old man's ankles. At the same time, he pitched himself to the side with an energy he didn't know he had in him. Martin fell forward, and Jude felt the razor whicker through his shirt and the biceps beneath, with what seemed no resistance at all. Jude rolled over the rusted steel bar at the foot of his cot and crashed to the floor.

The room was almost silent except for their harsh gasps for breath and the shrieking of the wind under the eaves. His father scrambled to the end of the bed and leaped over the side—spry for a man who had suffered multiple strokes and not left his bed in three months. By then Jude was crawling backward, out the door.

He made it halfway down the hall, as far as the screen door that looked into the pigpen. The hogs crowded against it, jostling for the best view of the action. Their squeals of excitement drew his attention for a moment, and when he looked back, Martin was standing over him.

His father dropped onto him. He cocked his arm back to slash the razor across Jude's face. Jude forgot himself and drove his bandaged right hand up into his father's chin, hard enough to snap the old man's head back. Jude screamed. A white-hot charge of pain stabbed through his ruined hand and raced up into his forearm, a sensation like an electrical pulse traveling right through the bone, withering in its intensity.

He caught his father flush and drove him into the screen door. Martin hit it with a splintering crunch and the tinny sound of springs snapping free. The lower screen tore clean out, and Martin fell through it. The pigs scattered. There were no steps below the door, and Martin dropped two feet, out of sight, hitting the ground with a dry thud.

The world wavered, darkened, almost disappeared. *No,* Jude thought, *no no no.* He struggled back toward consciousness, like a man pulled deep underwater, churning toward the surface before he ran out of breath.

The world brightened again, a drop of light that widened and spread, blurred gray ghost shapes appearing before him, then coming gradually into focus. The hall was still. Pigs grunted outside. An ill sweat cooled on Jude's face.

He rested awhile, ears ringing. His hand ringing, too. When he was ready, he used his heels to push himself across the floor to the wall, then used the wall to work his way up into a sitting position. He rested again.

At last he shoved his way to his feet, sliding his back up the wall. He peered out the wreck of the screen door but still could not see his father. He had to be lying against the side of the house.

Jude swayed away from the wall, sagging toward the screen door. He grabbed the frame to keep from falling into the pigpen himself. His legs trembled furiously. He leaned forward to see if Martin was on the ground with a broken neck, and at that moment his father stood up and reached through the screen and grabbed for his leg.

Jude cried out, kicking at Martin's hand and recoiling instinctively. Then he was a man losing his balance on a sheet of black ice, pinwheeling his arms foolishly, sailing back down the hall and into the kitchen, where he fell yet again.

Martin pulled himself up through the torn screen. He crawled toward Jude, made his way to him on all fours, until he was right on top of him. Martin's hand rose, then fell, a glittering silver spark falling with it. Jude brought up his left arm, and the straight razor struck his forearm, scraping bone. Blood leaped into the air. More blood.

The palm of Jude's left hand was bandaged, but the fingers were free, sticking out of the gauze as if it were a glove with the fingers snipped off. His father lifted the razor in the air to strike again, but before he could bring it down, Jude stuck his fingers in Martin's glimmering red eyes. The old man cried out, twisting his head back, trying to get free of his son's hand. The razor blade waved in front of Jude's face without touching skin. Jude forced his father's head back, and back, baring his scrawny throat, wondering if he could push hard enough to break the cocksucker's spine.

He had Martin's head back as far as it would go when the kitchen knife slammed into the side of his father's neck.

Marybeth was ten feet away, standing at the kitchen counter, beside a magnetized strip on the wall with knives stuck to it. Her breath came in sobs. Jude's father turned his head to stare at her. Air bubbles foamed in the blood that leaked from around the hilt of the knife. Martin reached for it with one hand, closed his fingers feebly about it, then made a sound, a rattling inhalation, like a child shaking a stone in a paper bag, and sagged to his side.

Marybeth snapped another wide-bladed knife off the magnetic rack, then another. She took the first by the tip of the blade and chucked it into Martin's back as he slumped forward. It hit with a deep, hollow *thunk,* as if she'd driven the blade into a melon. Martin made no sound at this second blow, aside from a sharp huff of breath. Marybeth started to walk toward him, holding the last knife in front of her.

"Keep away," Jude said to her. "He won't lie down and die." But she didn't hear him.

In another moment she stood over Martin. Jude's father looked up, and Marybeth whacked the knife across his face. It went in close to one corner of his lips and came out a little past the other corner, widening his mouth into a garish red slash.

As she struck at him, he struck at her, lashing out with his right hand, the hand that held the razor. The blade drew a red line across her thigh, above the right knee, and the leg buckled.

Martin pitched himself up off the floor as Marybeth started to go down, roaring as he rose to his feet. He caught her in the stomach in an almost perfect flying tackle, smashed Marybeth into the kitchen counter. She slammed her last knife into Martin's shoulder, burying it to the hilt. She might've pounded it into a tree trunk for all the good it did.

She slipped toward the floor, Jude's father on top of her, blood still foaming from the knife planted in his neck. He slashed his straight razor toward her again.

Marybeth grabbed her neck, clutching it weakly with her bad hand. Blood pumped through her fingers. There was a crude black grin dug into the white flesh of her throat.

She slid onto her side. Her head banged the floor. She was staring past Martin at Jude. The side of her face lay in blood, a thick, scarlet puddle of it.

Jude's father dropped to all fours. His free hand was still wrapped around the base of the knife in his own throat, fingers exploring it blindly, taking its measure, but doing nothing to pull it out. He was a pincushion, knife in the shoulder, knife in the back, but he was interested only in the one through his neck, didn't seem to have noticed the other pieces of steel sticking into him.

Martin crawled unsteadily away from Marybeth, away from Jude. His arms gave out first, and his head dropped to the floor, his chin striking with enough force to make his teeth audibly click together. He tried to push himself up and almost made it, but then his right arm gave out, and he rolled onto his side instead. Away from Jude, a small relief. Jude wouldn't have to look into his face while he died. Again.

Marybeth was trying to speak. Her tongue came out of her mouth, moved over her lips. Her eyes pleaded for Jude to come closer. Her pupils had shrunk to black dots.

He pulled himself across the floor, elbow over elbow, dragging himself to her. She was already whispering. It was hard to hear her over his father, who was making the cough-choking sounds again and kicking his heels loudly against the floor, in the throes of some kind of convulsion.

"He's not . . . done," Marybeth said. "He's comin' . . . again. He'll never . . . be done."

Jude glanced around for something he could stick against the slash across her throat. He was close enough now so his hands were in the puddle of blood surrounding her, splashing in it. He spotted a dishrag hanging from the handle of the oven, pulled it down.

Marybeth was staring into his face, but Jude had an impression of not being seen—the sense that she was staring right through him and into some unknowable distance.

"I hear . . . Anna. I hear her . . . calling. We have . . . to make . . . a door. We have to . . . let her in. Make us a door. Make a door . . . and I'll open it."

"Stop talking." He lifted her hand and pressed the rolled-up dish towel against her neck.

Marybeth caught at his wrist.

"Can't open it . . . once I'm on . . . the other . . . side. It has to be now. I'm gone already. Anna is gone. You can't . . . save . . . us," she said. So much blood. "Let. Us. Save. You."

Across the room Jude heard a fit of coughing, then his father gagging. He was choking something up. Jude knew what.

He stared at Marybeth with a disbelief more intense than grief. He found his hand cupping her face, which was cool to the touch. He had promised. He had promised himself, if not her, that he would take care of her, and here she was, with her throat cut, saying how she was going to take care of him. She was fighting for each breath, shivering helplessly.

"Do it, Jude," she said. "Just do it."

He lifted her hands and put them against the dish towel, to keep it pressed to her open throat. Then he turned and crawled through her blood, to the edge of the puddle. He heard himself humming again, his song, his new song, a melody like a southern hymn, a country dirge. How did you make a door for the dead? Would it be enough just to draw one? He was trying to think what to draw with, when he saw the red handprints he was leaving on the linoleum. He dipped a finger in her blood and began to draw a line along the floor.

When he judged he had made it long enough, he started a new line, at a right angle to the first. The blood on his fingertip thinned and ran dry. He shuffled slowly around, turning back to Marybeth and the wide, trembling pool of blood in which she lay.

He looked past her and saw Craddock, pulling himself out of his father's gaping mouth. Craddock's face was contorted with strain, his arms reaching down, one hand on Martin's forehead, the other on Martin's shoulder. At the point of his waist, his body was crushed into a thick rope—Jude thought again of a great mass of cellophane, wadded up and twisted into a cord—which filled Martin's mouth and seemed to extend all the way down into his engorged throat. Craddock had gone in like a soldier leaping into a foxhole but was hauling himself out like a man sunk to his waist in sucking mud.

You will die, the dead man said. *The bitch will die you will die we will all ride the nightroad together you want to sing la la la I'll teach you to sing I'll teach you.*

Jude dipped his hand in Marybeth's blood, wetting it entirely, turned away again. There was no thought in him. He was a machine that crawled stupidly forward as he began to draw once more. He finished the top of the door, shuffled around, and started a third line, working his way back to Marybeth. It was a crude, meandering line, thick in some places, barely a smear in others.

The bottom of the door was the puddle. As he reached it, he glanced into Marybeth's face. The front of her T-shirt was soaked through. Her face was a pallid blank, and for a moment he thought it was too late, she was dead, but then her eyes moved, just slightly, watching him approach, through a dull glaze.

Craddock began to scream in frustration. He had pulled all of himself out except for one leg, was already trying to stand up, but his foot was stuck somewhere in Martin's gullet, and it was unbalancing him. In Craddock's hand was the blade shaped like a crescent moon, the chain hanging from it in a bright, swinging loop.

Jude turned his back on him once more and looked down at his uneven blood doorway. He stared stupidly at the long, crooked red frame, an empty box containing only a few scarlet handprints. It wasn't right yet, and he tried to think what else it needed. Then it came to him that it wasn't a door if there was no way to open it, and he crawled forward and painted a circle for a doorknob.

Craddock's shadow fell over him. Ghosts could cast shadows? Jude wondered at it. He was tired. It was hard to think. He knelt on the door and felt something slam against the other side of it. It was as if the wind, which was still driving against the house in furious, steady gusts, were trying to come up through the linoleum.

A line of brightness appeared along the right-hand edge of the door, a vivid streak of radiant white. Something hit the other side again, a mountain lion trapped under the floor. It struck a third time, each impact producing a thunderous boom that shook the house, caused the plates to rattle in the plastic tray by the sink. Jude felt his elbows give a little, and decided there was no reason to stay on all fours anymore, and besides, it was too much effort. He fell to his side, let himself roll right off the door and onto his back.

Craddock stood over Marybeth in his black dead man's suit, one side of his collar askew, hat gone. He wasn't coming forward, though, had stopped in his tracks. He stared mistrustfully down at the hand-drawn door at his feet, as if it were a secret hatch and he had come close to stepping on it and falling through.

What is that? What did you do?

When Jude spoke, his voice seemed to come from a long distance off, as by some trick of ventriloquism. "The dead claim their own, Craddock. Sooner or later they claim their own."

The misshapen door bulged, then receded into the floor. Swelled again. It seemed almost to be breathing. The line of light raced across the top of it, a beam of brightness so intense it couldn't be looked at directly. It cornered and continued on down the other side of the door.

The wind keened, louder than ever, a high, piercing shriek. After a moment Jude realized it wasn't the wind outside the house but a gale wailing around the edges of the door drawn in blood. It wasn't blowing out but being sucked *in,* through those blinding white lines. Jude's ears popped, and he thought of an airplane descending too rapidly. Papers ruffled, then lifted off the kitchen table and began to swirl above it, chasing one another. Delicate little wavelets raced across the wide pool of blood around Marybeth's blank, staring face.

Marybeth's left arm was stretched out, across the lake of blood, into the doorway. When Jude wasn't looking, she had pulled herself over onto her side, reaching out with one arm. Her hand rested over the red circle he had drawn for a doorknob.

Somewhere a dog began to bark.

In the next instant, the door painted on the linoleum fell open. Marybeth should've dropped through it—half her body was stretched across it—but she didn't. Instead she floated, as if sprawled on a sheet of polished glass. An uneven parallelogram filled the center of the floor, an open trap, flooded with an astonishing light, a blinding brilliance that rose all around her.

In the intensity of that light pouring from below, the room became a photographic negative, all stark whites and flat, impossible shadows. Marybeth was a black, featureless figure, suspended upon the sheet of light. Craddock, standing over her, arms flung up to protect his face, looked like one of the victims of the atom bomb at Hiroshima, an abstract life-size sketch of a man, drawn in ash on a black wall. Papers still whirled and spun above the kitchen table, only they had gone black and looked like a flock of crows.

Marybeth rolled over onto her side and lifted her head, only it wasn't Marybeth anymore, it was Anna, and spokes of light filled her eyes, and her face was as stern as God's own judgment.

Why? she asked.

Craddock hissed. *Get away. Get back.* He swung the gold chain of his pendulum in circles, the crescent blade whining in the air, tracing a ring of silver fire.

Then Anna was on her feet, at the base of the glowing door. Jude had not seen her rise. One moment she was prone, and in the next she was standing. Time had skipped, maybe. Time didn't matter anymore. Jude held up a hand to shield his eyes from the worst of the glare, but the light was everywhere, and there was no blocking it out. He could see the bones in his hand, the skin over them the color and clarity of honey. His wounds, the slash in his face, the stump of his index finger, throbbed with a pain that was both profound and exhilarating, and he thought he might cry out, in fear, in joy, in shock, in all those things, in what was more than those things. In rapture.

Why? Anna said again as she approached Craddock. He whipped the chain at her, and the curved razor at the end drew a wide slash across her face, from the corner of her right eye, across her nose, and down to her mouth—but it only opened a fresh ray of brilliance, and where the light struck him, Craddock began to smoke. Anna reached for him. *Why?*

Craddock shrieked as she gathered him into her arms, shrieked and cut her again, across her breasts, and opened another seam in the eternal, and into his face poured the bountiful light, a light that burned away his features, that erased everything it touched. His wail was so loud Jude thought his eardrums would explode.

Why? Anna said, before she put her mouth on his, and from the door behind her leaped the black dogs, Jude's dogs, giant dogs of smoke, of shadow, with fangs of ink.

Craddock McDermott struggled, trying to push her away, but she was falling backward with him, falling toward the door, and the dogs raced around his feet, and as they ran, they were stretched and pulled out of shape, unraveling like balls of yarn, becoming long scarves of darkness that wound around him, climbing his legs, lashing him about the waist, and binding the dead man to the dead girl. As he was pulled down, into the brightness of the other side, Jude saw the back of Craddock's head come off, and a shaft of white light, so intense it was blue at the edges, slammed through and struck the ceiling, where it burnt the plaster, causing it to bubble and seethe.

They dropped through the open door and were gone.

45

The papers that had been swirling above the kitchen table settled with a faint rustle, collecting into a pile, in almost the exact same spot from which they'd risen. In the hush that followed, Jude became aware of a gentle humming sound, a deep, melodic pulse, which was not heard so much as felt in his bones. It rose and fell and rose again, a sort of inhuman music—inhuman, but not unpleasant. Jude had never heard any instrument produce sounds like it. It was more like the accidental music of tires droning on blacktop. That low, powerful music could be felt on the skin as well. The air throbbed with it. It seemed almost to be a property of the light, flooding in through the crooked rectangle on the floor. Jude blinked into the light and wondered where Marybeth had gone. *The dead claim their own,* he thought, and shivered. It took several moments to get control of himself.

No. She hadn't been dead a moment ago when she opened the door. He did not accept that she could just be gone, no trace of her left on the earth. He crawled. He was the only thing moving in the room now. The stillness of the place, after what had just happened, seemed more jarring and incredible than a hole between worlds. He hurt, his hands hurt, his face hurt, and his chest tingled, a deadly icy-hot prickling, although he was fairly certain, if he was meant to have a heart attack this afternoon, it would've happened by now. Aside from the continuous humming that was all around him, there was no sound at all, except his sobs for breath, his hands scratching at the floor. Once he heard himself say Marybeth's name.

The closer he came to the light, the harder it was to stare into it. He shut his eyes—and found himself still able to see the room before him, as if through a pale curtain of silver silk, the light penetrating his closed lids. The nerves behind his eyeballs throbbed in steady time with that ceaseless pulsing sound.

He couldn't bear all the light, turned his head aside, kept crawling forward, and in that way Jude did not realize he had reached the edge of the open door until he put his hands down and there was nothing there to support him. Marybeth—or had it been Anna?—had hung suspended over the open door, as if on a sheet of glass, but Jude dropped like a condemned man through the hangman's trap, did not even have time to cry out before plummeting into the light.

♥ 46

The sensation of falling—a weightless-sick feeling in the pit of his stomach and the roots of his hair—*has hardly passed before he realizes that the light is not so intense now. He lifts a hand to shield his eyes and blinks into it, dusty yellow sunshine. He makes it midafternoon and can tell somehow, from the angle of the sun, that he's in the South. Jude is in the Mustang again, sitting in the passenger seat. Anna has the wheel, is humming to herself as she drives. The engine is a low, controlled roar—the Mustang has made itself well. It might've just rolled off the showroom floor in 1965.*

They travel a mile or so, neither of them speaking, before he finally identifies the road they're on as State Highway 22.

"Where we goin'?" *he asks at last.*

Anna arches her back, stretching her spine. She keeps both hands on the wheel. "I don't know. I thought we were just drivin'. Where do you wanna go?"

"Doesn't matter. How about Chinchuba Landing?"

"What's down there?"

"Nothing. Just a place to set and listen to the radio and look at the view. How's that sound?"

"Sounds like heaven. We must be in heaven."

When she says this, his left temple begins to ache. He wishes she hadn't said that. They aren't in heaven. He doesn't want to hear talk like that.

For a time they roll on cracked, faded, two-lane blacktop. Then he sees the turnoff coming up on the right and points it out, and Marybeth turns the Mustang onto it without a word. The road is dirt, and trees grow close on either side and bend over it, making a tunnel of rich green light. Shadows and fluttering sunlight shift across Marybeth's scrubbed, delicate features. She looks serene, at ease behind the wheel of the big muscle car, happy to have the afternoon ahead of her, and nothing particular to do in it except park someplace with Jude and listen to music. When did she become Marybeth?

It is as if he has spoken the question aloud, because she turns and gives him an embarrassed grin. "I tried to warn you, didn't I? Two girls for the price of one."

"You warned me."

"I know what road we're on," *Marybeth says, without any trace of the southern accent that has muddled up her own voice in the last few days.*

"I told you. One that goes to Chinchuba Landing."

She turns a knowing, amused, slightly pitying glance upon him. Then, as if he hadn't said anything, Marybeth continues: "Hell. After all the stuff I've heard about this road, I expected worse. This isn't bad. Kinda nice, actually. With a name like the nightroad you at least expect it to be night. Maybe it's only night here for some people."

He winces—another sharp stabbing pain in the head. He wants to think she's mixed up, wrong about where they are. She could be wrong. Not only isn't it night, it's hardly a road.

In another minute they're bumping along through two ruts in the dirt, narrow troughs with a wide bed of grass and wildflowers growing between them, swatting the fender and dragging against the undercarriage. They pass the wreck of a pale truck, parked under a willow, the hood open and weeds growing right up through it. Jude doesn't give it more than a sidelong look.

The palms and the brush open up just around the next bend, but

Marybeth slows, so the Mustang is barely rolling along, and for the moment anyway they're still back in the cool shade of the trees bending overhead. Gravel crunches pleasantly under the tires, a sound Jude has always loved, a sound everyone loves. Out beyond the grassy clearing is the muddy brown sea of Lake Pontchartrain, the water ruffled up in the wind and the edges of the waves glinting like polished, new-minted steel. Jude is a little taken aback by the sky, which is bleached a uniform and blinding white. It is a sky so awash in light it's impossible to look directly into it, to even know where the sun is. Jude turns his head away from the view, squinting and raising a hand to shield his eyes. The ache in his left temple intensifies, beating with his pulse.

"Damn," *he says.* "That sky."

"Isn't it somethin'?" *Anna says from inside Marybeth's body.* "You can see a long way. You can see into forever."

"I can't see shit."

"No," *Anna says, but it's still Marybeth behind the wheel, Marybeth's mouth moving.* "You need to protect your eyes from the sight. You can't really look out there. Not yet. We have trouble lookin' back into your world, for whatever it's worth. You maybe noticed the black lines over our eyes. Think of them as the sunglasses of the livin' dead." *A statement that starts her laughing, Marybeth's husky, rude laughter.*

She stops the car at the very edge of the clearing, puts it into park. The windows are down. The air that soughs in over him smells sweetly of the sun-baked brush and the unruly grass. Beneath that he can detect the subtle perfume of Lake Pontchartrain, a cool, marshy odor.

Marybeth leans toward him, puts her head on his shoulder, puts an arm across his waist, and when she speaks again, it is in her own voice. "I wish I was driving back with you, Jude."

He breaks out in a sudden chill. "What's that mean?"

She looks fondly up into his face. "Hey. We almost got it right. Didn't we almost get it right, Jude?"

"Stop it," *Jude says.* "You're not going anywhere. You're staying with me."

"I don't know," *Marybeth says.* "I'm tired. It's a long haul back, and I don't think I could make it. I swear this car is using some part of me for gas, and I'm about all out."

"Stop talking that way."

"Were we going to have some music?"

He opens the glove compartment, fumbles for a tape. It's a collection of demos, a private collection. His new songs. He wants Marybeth to hear them. He wants her to know he didn't give up on himself. The first track begins to play. It is "Drink to the Dead." The guitar chimes and rises in a country hymn, a sweet and lonely acoustic gospel, a song for grieving. Goddamn, his head hurts, both temples now, a steady throbbing behind his eyes. Goddamn that sky with its overpowering light.

Marybeth sits up, only it isn't Marybeth anymore, it's Anna. Her eyes are filled with light, are filled with sky. "All the world is made of music. We are all strings on a lyre. We resonate. We sing together. This was nice. With that wind on my face. When you sing, I'm singin' with you, honey. You know that don't you?"

"Stop it," *he says. Anna settles behind the wheel again and puts the car into drive.* "What are you doing?"

Marybeth leans forward from the backseat and reaches for his hand. They're separate now—they are two distinct individuals maybe for the first time in days. "I have to go, Jude." *She bends over the seat to put her mouth on his. Her lips are cold and trembling.* "This is where you get out."

"We," *he says, and when she tries to withdraw her hand, he doesn't let go, squeezes harder, until he can feel the bones flexing under the skin. He kisses her again, says into her mouth,* "Where we get out. We. We."

Gravel under the tires again. The Mustang rolls forward, out under the open sky. The front seat is filled with a blast of light, an incandescence that erases all the world beyond the car, leaving nothing but the interior, and even that Jude can hardly see, peering out through slitted eyes. The pain that flares behind his eyeballs is staggering, wonderful. He still has Marybeth by the hand. She can't go if he doesn't let her, and the light—oh, God, there is so much light. There's something wrong with the car stereo, his song wavering in and out, drowning beneath a deep, low, pulsing harmonic, the same alien music he heard when he fell through the door between worlds. He wants to tell Marybeth something, he wants to tell her he is sorry he couldn't keep his promises, the ones he made her and the ones he made himself, he wants to say how he loves her, loves her so, but cannot find his voice and cannot think with the light in his eyes and that humming in his head. Her hand. He still has her hand. He squeezes her hand again, and again, trying to tell her what he needs to tell her by touch, and she squeezes back.

*And out in the light, he sees Anna, sees her shimmering, glowing like a firefly, watches her turn from the wheel, and smile, and reach toward him, putting her hand over his and Marybeth's, and that's when she says, "God-*damn, I think this hairy son of a bitch is trying to sit up."

47

Jude blinked into the clear, painful white light of an ophthalmoscope pointed into his left eye. He was struggling to rise, but
someone had a hand on his chest, holding him pinned to the floor. He
gasped at the air, like a trout just hauled out of Lake Pontchartrain
and thrown onto the shore. He had told Anna they might go fishing
there, the two of them. Or had that been Marybeth? He didn't know
anymore.

The ophthalmoscope was removed, and he stared blankly up at the -
mold-spotted ceiling of the kitchen. The mad sometimes drilled holes in
their own heads, to let the demons out, to relieve the pressure of
thoughts they could no longer bear. Jude understood the impulse. Each
beat of his heart was a fresh and staggering blow, felt in the nerves behind his eyes and in his temples, punishing evidence of life.

A hog with a squashy pink face leaned over him, smiled obscenely
down, and said, "Holy shit. You know who this is? It's Judas Coyne."

Someone else said, "Can we clear the fucking pigs out of the
room?"

The pig was booted aside, with a shriek of indignation. A man with a neatly groomed, pale brown goatee and kind, watchful eyes, leaned into Jude's field of view.

"Mr. Coyne? Just lie still. You've lost a lot of blood. We're going to lift you onto a gurney."

"Anna," Jude said, his voice unsteady and wheezing.

A brief look of pain and something like an apology flickered in the young man's light blue eyes. "Was that her name?"

No. No, Jude had said the wrong thing. That wasn't her name, but Jude couldn't find the breath to correct himself. Then it registered that the man leaning over him had referred to her in the past tense.

Arlene Wade spoke for him. "He told me her name was Marybeth."

Arlene leaned in from the other side, peering down at him, her eyes comically huge behind her glasses. She was talking about Marybeth in the past tense, too. He tried to sit up again, but the goateed EMT firmly held him down.

"Don't try and get up, dear," Arlene said.

Something made a steely clatter nearby, and he looked down the length of his body and past his feet and saw a crowd of men rolling a gurney past him and into the hall. An IV bag, pregnant with blood, swung back and forth from a metal support rod attached to the cot. From his angle on the floor, Jude could not see anything of the person on the gurney, except for a hand hanging over the side. The infection that had made Marybeth's palm shriveled and white was gone, no trace of it left. Her small, slender hand swung limply, jostled by the motion of the cart, and Jude thought of the girl in his obscene snuff movie, the way she had seemed to go boneless when the life went out of her. One of the EMTs pushing the gurney glanced down and saw Jude staring. He reached for Marybeth's hand and tucked it back up against her side. The other men pushed the gurney on out of sight, all of them talking to each other in low, feverish voices.

"Marybeth?" Jude managed, his voice the faintest of whispers, carried on a pained exhalation of breath.

"She's got to go now," Arlene said. "There's another amble-lance comin' for you, Justin,"

"Go?" Jude asked. He really didn't understand.

"They can't do any more for her in this place, that's all. It's just time to take her on." Arlene patted his hand. "Her ride is here."

ALIVE

48

Jude was in and out for twenty-four hours.

He woke once and saw his lawyer, Nan Shreve, standing in the door of his private room, talking with Jackson Browne. Jude had met him, years before, at the Grammys. Jude had slipped out midceremony to visit the men's, and as he was taking a leak, he happened to look over to find Jackson Browne pissing in the urinal next to him. They had only nodded to each other, never even said hello, and so Jude couldn't imagine what he was doing now in Louisiana. Maybe he had a gig in New Orleans, had heard about Jude nearly being killed, and had come to express his sympathies. Maybe Jude would now be visited by a procession of rock-and-roll luminaries, swinging through to tell him to keep on keepin' on. Jackson Browne was dressed conservatively—blue blazer, tie—and he had a gold shield clipped to his belt, next to a holstered revolver. Jude allowed his eyelids to sink shut.

He had a dark, muffled sense of time passing. When he woke again, another rock star was sitting beside him: Dizzy, his eyes all black scribbles, his face still wasted with AIDS. He offered his hand, and Jude took it.

Had to come, man. You were there for me, Dizzy said.

"I'm glad to see you," Jude told him. "I been missing you."

"Excuse me?" said the nurse, standing on the other side of the bed. Jude glanced over at her, hadn't known she was there. When he looked back for Dizzy, Jude discovered his hand hanging empty.

"Who you talkin' to?" the nurse asked.

"Old friend. I haven't seen him since he died."

She sniffed. "We got to scale back your morphine, hon."

Later Angus wandered through the room and disappeared under the bed. Jude called to him, but Angus never came out, just stayed under the cot, thumping his tail on the floor, a steady beat that kept time with Jude's heart.

Jude wasn't sure which dead or famous person to expect next and was surprised when he opened his eyes to find he had his room to himself. He was on the fourth or fifth floor of a hospital outside of Slidell. Beyond the window was Lake Pontchartrain, blue and wintry in the late-afternoon light, the shoreline crowded with cranes, a rusty oil tanker struggling into the east. For the first time, he realized he could smell it, the faint briny tang of the water. Jude wept.

When he'd managed to get control of himself, he paged the nurse. A doctor came instead, a cadaverous black man with sad, bloodshot eyes and a shaved head. In a soft, gravelly voice, he began to fill Jude in on his condition.

"Has anyone called Bammy?" Jude interrupted.

"Who's that?"

"Marybeth's grandma," Jude said. "If no one's called her, I want to be the one to tell her. Bammy ought to know what happened."

"If you can provide us with her last name and a phone number or an address, I can have one of the nurses call her."

"It ought to be me."

"You've been through a lot. I think, in the emotional state you're in, a call from you might alarm her."

Jude stared at him. "Her granddaughter died. Person she loves most in the world. Do you think it will alarm her less getting the news from a stranger?"

"Exactly why we'd rather make the call," the doctor said. "That's the kind of thing we don't want her family to hear. In a first phone call with relatives, we prefer to focus on the positive."

It came to Jude that he was still sick. The conversation had an unreal tinge to it that he associated with a fever. He shook his head and began to laugh. Then he noticed he was crying again. He wiped at his face with trembling hands.

"Focus on what positive?" he asked.

"The news could be worse," the doctor said. "At least she's stable now. And her heart was only stopped for a few minutes. People have been dead for longer. There should be only minimal—"

But Jude didn't hear the rest.

49

T hen he was in the halls, a six-foot-tall, 240-pound man, fifty-four years of age, the great bush of his black beard in ratty tangles and his hospital johnny flapping open in the back to show the scrawny, hairless cheeks of his ass. The doctor jogged beside him, and nurses gathered about, trying to redirect him back to his room, but he strode on, his IV drip still in his arm and the bag rattling along beside him on its wheeled frame. He was clearheaded, all the way awake, his hands not bothering him, his breathing fine. As he made his way along, he began calling her name. He was in surprisingly good voice.

"Mr. Coyne," said the doctor. "Mr. Coyne, she isn't well enough—you aren't well enough—"

Bon raced past Jude, down the hall, and hung a right at the next corner. He quickened his step. He reached the turn and looked down another corridor in time to see Bon slip through a pair of double doors, twenty feet away. They gasped shut behind her, closing on their pneumatic hinges. The glowing sign above the doors said ICU.

A short, dumpy security officer was in Jude's way, but Jude went around him, and then the rent-a-cop had to jog and huff to keep up. He shoved through the doors and into the ICU. Bon was just disappearing into a darkened room on the left.

Jude went in right after her. Bon was nowhere in sight, but Marybeth was in the only bed, with black stitches across her throat, an air tube poked into her nostrils, and machines bleeping contentedly in the dark around her. Her eyes opened to puffy slits as Jude entered saying her name. Her face was battered, her complexion greasy and pale, and she seemed emaciated, and at the sight of her his heart contracted with a sweet tightness. Then he was next to her, on the edge of the mattress, and gathering her into his arms, her skin paper, her bones hollow sticks. He put his face against her wounded neck, into her hair, inhaling deeply, needing the smell of her, proof she was there, real, proof of life. One of her hands rose weakly to his side, slid up his back. Her lips, when he kissed them, were cold, and they trembled.

"Thought you were gone," Jude said. "We were in the Mustang again with Anna, and I thought you were gone."

"Aw, shit," Marybeth whispered, in a voice hardly louder than breath. "I climbed out. Sick of being in cars all the time. Jude, you think when we go home we can just fly?"

50

He wasn't asleep, but thinking he ought to be, when the door clicked open. He rolled over, wondering which dead person or rock legend or spirit animal might be visiting now, but it was only Nan Shreve, in a tan business skirt and suit jacket and nude-colored nylons. She carried her high heels in one hand and scuffled quickly along on tiptoes. She eased the door softly shut behind her.

"Snuck in," she said, wrinkling her nose and throwing him a wink. "Not really supposed to be here yet."

Nan was a little, wiry woman, whose head barely came to Jude's chest. She was socially maladroit, didn't know how to smile. Her grin was a rigid, painful fake that projected none of the things a smile was supposed to project: confidence, optimism, warmth, pleasure. She was forty-six and married and had two children and had been his attorney for almost a decade. Jude, though, had been her friend for longer than that, going back to when she was just twenty. She hadn't known how to smile then either, and in those days she didn't even try. Back then she was strung out and mean, and he had not called her Nan.

"Hey, Tennessee," Jude said. "Why aren't you supposed to be here?"

She had started toward the bed but hesitated at this. He hadn't meant to call her Tennessee, it had just slipped out. He was tired. Her eyelashes fluttered, and for a moment her smile looked even more unhappy than usual. Then she found her step again, reached his cot, planted herself in a molded chair next to him.

"I made arrangements to meet Quinn in the lobby," she said, wiggling her feet back into her heels. "He's the detective in charge of nailing down what happened. Except he's late. I passed a *horrible* wreck on the highway, and I thought I saw his car pulled over to the side of the road, so he must've stopped to help out the state troopers."

"What am I charged with?"

"Why would you be charged with anything? Your father—Jude, your father attacked you. He attacked both of you. You're lucky you weren't killed. Quinn just wants a statement. Tell him what happened at your father's house. Tell him the truth." She met his gaze, and then she was speaking very carefully, a mother repeating simple but important instructions to a child. "Your father had a break with reality. It happens. They've even got a name for it: age rage. He attacked you and Marybeth Kimball, and she killed him saving the both of you. That's all Quinn wants to hear. Just like it happened." And in the last few moments, their conversation had ceased to be friendly and social in any way. Her plastered-on grin had disappeared, and he was back with Tennessee again—cold-eyed, sinewy, unbending Tennessee.

He nodded.

She said, "And Quinn might have some questions about the accident that took off your finger. And killed the dog. The dog in your car?"

"I don't understand," Jude said. "He doesn't want to talk to me about what happened in Florida?"

Her eyelashes fluttered rapidly, and for a moment she was staring at him with unmistakable confusion. Then the cold-eyed look reasserted itself and became even colder. "Did something happen in Florida? Something I need to know about, Jude?"

So there was no warrant on him in Florida. That didn't make sense.

He had attacked a woman and her child, been shot, been in a collision—but if he was a wanted man in Florida, Nan would already know about it. She would already be planning his plea.

Nan went on, "You came south to see your father before he passed away. You were in an accident just before you reached his farm. Out walking the dog by the side of the road, and the two of you got hit. An unimaginable chain of events, but that's what happened. Nothing else makes sense."

The door opened, and Jackson Browne peeked into the room. Only he had a red birthmark on his neck that Jude hadn't noticed before, a crimson splotch in the rough shape of a three-fingered hand, and when he spoke, it was in a clownish honk, his inflections soupy and Cajun.

"Mr. Coyne. Still with us?" His gaze darting from Jude to Nan Shreve beside him. "Your record company will be disappointed. I guess they were already planning the tribute album." He laughed then, until he coughed, and blinked watering eyes. "Mrs. Shreve. I missed you in the lobby." He said it jovially enough, but the way he looked at her, his eyes hooded and wondering, it sounded almost like an accusation. He added, "So did the nurse at the reception desk. She said she hadn't seen you."

"I waved on the way by," Nan said.

"Come on in," Jude said. "Nan said you'd like to talk to me."

"I ought to place you under arrest," said Detective Quinn.

Jude's pulse quickened, but his voice, when he spoke, was smooth and untroubled. "For what?"

"Your last three albums," Quinn said. "I got two daughters, and they play 'em and play 'em at top volume, until the walls shake and the dishes rattle and I feel I am close to perpetratin' dough-mestic abuse, you understan'? And this is on my lovely, laughin' daughters, who I wouldn't under normal conditions want hurt for any reason nohow." He sighed, used his tie to wipe his brow, made his way to the foot of the bed. He offered Jude his last stick of Juicy Fruit. When Jude declined, Quinn popped the stick into his mouth and began to chew. "You got to love 'em, somehow, no matter how crazy you feel sometimes."

"That's right," Jude said.

"Just a few questions," Quinn said, pulling a notebook out of an inner pocket of his jacket. "We want to start before you got to your father's house. You were in a hit-and-run, is that it? Some awful kind of day for you and your lady friend, huh? And then attacked by your dad. Course, the way you look, and the condition he was in, he probably thought you were . . . I don't know. A murderer come to loot his farm. An evil spirit. Still, I can't think why you wouldn't have gone to a hospital after the accident that took off your finger."

"Well," Jude said. "We weren't far from my daddy's place, and I knew my aunt was there. She's a registered nurse."

"That so? Tell me about the car that hit you."

"A truck," Jude said. "A pickup." He glanced at Nan, who nodded, just slightly, eyes watchful and certain. Jude drew a deep breath and began to lie.

51

Before Nan left his room, she hesitated in the doorway and looked back at Jude. That grin was on her face again, the stretched, forced one that made Jude sad.

"She really is beautiful, Jude," Nan said. "And she loves you. You can tell the way she talks about you. I spoke to her. Only for a moment, but . . . but you can tell. Georgia, is she?" Nan's eyes were shy, and pained, and affectionate, all at once. She asked the question like she wasn't sure if she really wanted to know.

"Marybeth," Jude said firmly. "Her name is Marybeth."

52

They were back in New York two weeks later for Danny's memorial service. Marybeth wore a black scarf around her neck that matched her black lace gloves. The afternoon was windy and cold, but the gathering was well attended nonetheless. It seemed everyone Danny had ever chatted up, gossiped with, or blabbed to on the phone was there, and that was a lot, and none of them left early, not even when the rain began to fall.

53

In the spring Jude recorded an album, stripped down, mostly acoustic. He sang about the dead. He sang about roads at night. Other men played the guitar parts. He could handle rhythm, but that was all, had needed to switch back to making chords with the left, as he had in his childhood, and he wasn't as good at it.

The new CD sold well. He did not tour. He had a triple bypass instead.

Marybeth taught dance at a tony gym in High Plains. Her classes were crowded.

54

Marybeth found a derelict Dodge Charger in a local auto grave-
yard, brought it home for three hundred dollars. Jude spent the next summer sweating in the yard with his shirt off, restoring it. He came in late
each night, all of him tanned, except for the shiny silver scar down the
center of his chest. Marybeth was always waiting just inside the door,
with a glass of homemade lemonade. Sometimes they would trade a kiss
that tasted of cold juice and motor oil. They were his favorite kisses.

55

One afternoon, close to the end of August, Jude wandered inside, sweating and sunburned, and found a message on the machine from Nan. She said she had some information for him and he could call her back anytime. Anytime was now, and he rang her in her office. He sat on the edge of Danny's old desk while Nan's receptionist patched him through.

"I'm afraid I don't have a lot to tell you about this George Ruger person," Nan said without any preamble. "You wanted to know if he's been mentioned in any criminal proceedings in the last year, and the answer to that appears to be no. Maybe if I had more information from you, as to exactly what your interest in him is . . ."

"No. Don't worry about it," Jude said.

So Ruger hadn't brought any kind of complaint to the authorities; no surprise. If he was going to bring a suit, or try to have Jude arrested, Jude would've known about it by now anyway. He hadn't really expected Nan to come up with anything. Ruger couldn't talk about what Jude had done to him without risking that it would come out about Marybeth, how he'd slept with her when she was still in junior high. He was, Jude remembered, an important figure in local politics. It was hard to run a really effective fund-raiser after you'd been accused of statutory rape.

"I had a little more luck concerning Jessica Price."

"You did," Jude said. Just hearing her name made his stomach knot up.

When Nan spoke again, it was in a falsely casual tone, a little too cool to be persuasive. "This Price is under investigation for child endangerment and sexual abuse. Her own daughter, if you can imagine. Apparently the police came to her home after someone called in an accident report. Price drove her car into someone else's vehicle, right in front of her house, forty miles an hour. When the police got there, they found her unconscious behind the wheel. And her daughter was in the house with a gun and a dead dog on the floor."

Nan paused to allow Jude a chance to comment, but Jude didn't have anything to say.

Nan went on, "Whoever Price drove her car into took off. Never found."

"Didn't Price tell them? What's her story?"

"No story. See, after the police calmed the little girl down, they took the gun away. When they went to put it back where it belonged, they found an envelope with photos in it, hidden in the velvet lining of the pistol's case. Polaroids of the girl. Criminal stuff. Horrible. Apparently they can establish that the mother took them. Jessica Price could be looking at up to ten years. And I understand her girl is only just thirteen. Isn't that the most terrible thing?"

"It is," Jude said. "Just about."

"Would you believe all of this happened—Jessica Price's car accident, dead dog, photos—on the same day your daddy died in Louisiana?"

Again Jude did not reply—silence felt safer.

Nan went on, "Following her lawyer's advice, Jessica Price has been exercising her legal right to remain silent ever since her arrest. Which makes sense for her. And is also a lucky break for whoever else was there. You know—with the dog."

Jude held the receiver to his ear. Nan was silent for so long he began to wonder if they'd been cut off.

At last, just to find out if she was still on the line, he said, "That all?"

"One other thing," Nan said. Her tone was perfectly bland. "A carpenter doing work down the street said he saw a suspicious pair in a black car lurking around earlier in the day. He said the driver was the spitting image of the lead singer of Metallica."

Jude had to laugh.

56

On the second weekend of November, the Dodge Charger pulled out of a churchyard on a red clay dirt road in Georgia, cans rattling from the back. Bammy stuck her fingers in her mouth and blew rude whistles.

57

One fall they went to Fiji. The fall after, they visited Greece. Next October they went to Hawaii, spent ten hours a day on a beach of crushed black sand. Naples, the year following, was even better. They went for a week and stayed for a month.

In the autumn of their fifth anniversary, they didn't go anywhere. Jude had bought puppies and didn't want to leave them. One day, when it was chilly and wet, Jude walked with the new dogs down the driveway to collect the mail. As he was tugging the envelopes out of the box, just beyond the front gate, a pale pickup blasted by on the highway, throwing cold spray at his back, and when he turned to watch it go, he saw Anna staring at him from across the road. He felt a sharp twinge in the chest, which quickly abated, leaving him panting.

She pushed a yellow strand of hair back from her eyes, and he saw then that she was shorter, more athletically built than Anna, just a girl, eighteen at best. She lifted one hand in a tentative wave. He gestured for her to cross the road.

"Hi, Mr. Coyne," she said.

"Reese, isn't it?" he said.

She nodded. She didn't have a hat, and her hair was wet. Her denim jacket was soaked through. The puppies leaped at her, and she twisted away from them, laughing.

"Jimmy," Jude said. "Robert. Get down. Sorry. They're an uncouth bunch, and I haven't taught them their manners yet. Will you come in?" She was shivering just slightly. "You're getting drenched. You'll catch your death."

"Is that catching?" Reese asked.

"Yeah," Jude said. "There's a wicked case going around. Sooner or later everyone gets it."

He led her back to the house and into the darkened kitchen. He was just asking her how she'd made her way out to his place when Marybeth called down from the staircase and asked who was there.

"Reese Price," Jude said back. "From Testament. In Florida. Jessica Price's girl?"

For a moment there was no sound from the top of the stairs. Then Marybeth padded down the steps, stopped close to the bottom. Jude found the lights by the door, flipped them on.

In the sudden snap of brightness that followed, Marybeth and Reese regarded one another without speaking. Marybeth's face was composed, hard to read. Her eyes searched. Reese looked from Marybeth's face, to her neck, to the silvery white crescent of scar tissue around her throat. Reese pulled her arms out of the sleeves of her coat and hugged herself beneath it. Water dripped off her and puddled around her feet.

"Jesus Christ, Jude," Marybeth said. "Go and get her a towel."

Jude fetched a towel from the downstairs bathroom. When he returned to the kitchen with it, the kettle was on the stove and Reese was sitting at the center island, telling Marybeth about the Russian exchange students who had given her a ride from New York City and who kept talking about their visit to the Entire Steak Buildink.

Marybeth made her hot cocoa and a grilled cheese and tomato sandwich while Jude sat with Reese at the counter. Marybeth was relaxed and sisterly and laughed easily at Reese's stories, as if it were the most natural thing in the world to play host to a girl who had shot off a piece of her husband's hand.

The women did most of the talking. Reese was on her way to Buffalo, where she was going to meet up with friends and see 50 Cent and Eminem. Afterward they were traveling on to Niagara. One of the friends had put money down on an old houseboat. They were going to live in it, half a dozen of them. The boat needed work. They were planning to fix it up and sell it. Reese was in charge of painting it. She had a really cool idea for a mural she wanted to paint on the side. She had already done sketches. She took a sketchbook from her backpack and showed them some of her work. Her illustrations were unpracticed but eye-catching, pictures of nude ladies and eyeless old men and guitars, arranged in complicated interlocking patterns. If they couldn't sell the boat, they were going to start a business in it, either pizza or tattoos. Reese knew a lot about tattoos and had practiced on herself. She lifted her shirt to show them a tattoo of a pale, slender snake making a circle around her bellybutton, eating its own tail.

Jude interrupted to ask her how she was getting to Buffalo. She said she ran out of bus money back at Penn Station and figured she'd hitch the rest of the way.

"Do you know it's three hundred miles?" he asked.

Reese stared at him, wide-eyed, then shook her head. "You look at a map and this state doesn't seem so gosh-darn big. Are you sure it's three hundred miles?"

Marybeth took her empty plate and set it in the sink. "Is there anyone you want to call? Anyone in your family? You can use our phone."

"No, ma'am."

Marybeth smiled a little at this, and Jude wondered if anyone had ever called her "ma'am" before.

"What about your mother?" Marybeth asked.

"She's in jail. I hope she doesn't ever get out," Reese said, and she looked into her cocoa. She began to play with a long yellow strand of her hair, curling it around and around her finger, a thing Jude had seen Anna do a thousand times. She said, "I don't even like to think about her. I'd rather pretend she was dead or something. I wouldn't wish her on anyone. She's a curse, is what she is. If I thought someday I was going to be a mother like her, I'd have myself sterilized right now."

When she finished her cocoa, Jude put on a rain slicker and told Reese to come on, he would take her to the bus station.

For a while they rode without speaking, the radio off, no sound but the rain tapping on the glass and the Charger's wipers beating back and forth. He looked over at her once and saw she had the seat cranked back and her eyes closed. She had taken off her denim jacket and spread it over herself like a blanket. He believed she was sleeping.

But in a while she opened one eye and squinted at him. "You really cared about Aunt Anna, didn't you?"

He nodded. The wipers went *whip-thud, whip-thud*.

Reese said, "There's things my momma did she shouldn't have done. Some things I'd give my left arm to forget. Sometimes I think my Aunt Anna found out about some of what my momma was doing—my momma and my granddaddy—and that's why she killed herself. Because she couldn't live anymore with what she knew, but she couldn't talk about it either. I know she was already real unhappy. I think maybe some bad stuff happened to her, too, when she was little. Some of the same stuff happened to me." She was looking at him directly now.

So. Reese at least did not know everything her mother had done, which Jude could only take to mean that there really was some mercy to be found in the world.

"I am sorry about what I did to your hand," she said. "I mean that. I have dreams sometimes, about my Aunt Anna. We go for rides together. She has a cool old car like this one, only black. She isn't sad anymore, not in my dreams. We go for rides in the country. She listens to your music on the radio. She told me you weren't at our house to hurt me. She said you came to end it. To bring my mother to account for what she let happen to me. I just wanted to say I'm sorry and I hope you're happy."

He nodded but did not reply, did not, in truth, trust his own voice.

They went into the station together. Jude left her on a scarred wooden bench, went to the counter and bought a ticket to Buffalo. He had the station agent put it inside an envelope. He slipped two hundred dollars in with it, folded into a sheet of paper with his phone number on it and a note that she should call if she ran into trouble on the road. When he returned to her, he stuck the envelope into the pouch on the side of her backpack instead of handing it to her, so she wouldn't look into it right away and try to give the money back.

She went with him out onto the street, where the rain was falling more heavily now and the last of the day's light had fled, leaving things blue and twilighty and cold. He turned to say good-bye, and she stood on her tiptoes and kissed the chilled, wet side of his face. He had, until then, been thinking of her as a young woman, but her kiss was the thoughtless kiss of a child. The idea of her traveling hundreds of miles north, with no one to look out for her, seemed suddenly all the more daunting.

"Take care," they both said, at exactly the same time, in perfect unison, and then they laughed. Jude squeezed her hand and nodded but had nothing else to say except good-bye.

It was dark when he came back into the house. Marybeth pulled two bottles of Sam Adams out of the fridge, then started rummaging in the drawers for a bottle opener.

"I wish I could've done something for her," Jude said.

"She's a little young," Marybeth said. "Even for you. Keep it in your pants, why don't you?"

"Jesus. That's not what I meant."

Marybeth laughed, found a dishrag, and chucked it in his face.

"Dry off. You look even more like a pathetic derelict when you're all wet."

He rubbed the rag through his hair. Marybeth popped him a beer and set it in front of him. Then she saw he was still pouting and laughed again.

"Come on, now, Jude. If you didn't have me to rake you over the coals now and then, there wouldn't be any fire left in your life at all," she said. She stood on the other side of the kitchen counter, watching him with a certain wry, tender regard. "Anyway, you gave her a bus ticket to Buffalo, and . . . what? How much money?"

"Two hundred dollars."

"Come on, now. You did something for her. You did plenty. What else were you supposed to do?"

Jude sat at the center island, holding the beer Marybeth had set in front of him but not drinking it. He was tired, still damp and chilly from the outside. A big truck, or a Greyhound maybe, roared down the highway, fled into the cold tunnel of the night, was gone. He could hear the puppies out in their pen, yipping at it, excited by its noise.

"I hope she makes it," Jude said.

"To Buffalo? I don't see why she wouldn't," Marybeth said.

"Yeah," Jude said, although he wasn't sure that was what he'd really meant at all.

HEART-SHAPED ACKNOWLEDGMENTS

Raise your lighters for one last schmaltzy power ballad and allow me to sing the praises of those folks who gave so much to help bring *Heart-Shaped Box* into existence. My thanks to my agent, Michael Choate, who steers my professional ship with care, discretion, and uncommon good sense. I owe much to Jennifer Brehl, for all the hard work she put into editing my novel, for guiding me through the final draft, and especially for taking a chance on *Heart-Shaped Box* in the first place. Maureen Sugden did an extraordinary job of copyediting my novel. Thanks are also due to Lisa Gallagher, Juliette Shapland, Kate Nintzel, Anna Maria Allessi, Lynn Grady, Rich Aquan, Lorie Young, Kim Lewis, Seale Ballenger, and everyone else at William Morrow who went to bat for the book.

My deepest appreciation to Andy and Kerri, for their enthusiasm and friendship, and to Shane, who is not only my compadre but who also keeps my web site, joehillfiction.com, flying with spit and imagination. And I can't say how grateful I am to my parents and siblings for their time, thoughts, support, and love.

Most of all, my love and thanks to Leanora and the boys. Leanora spent I don't know how many hours reading and rereading this manuscript, in all its various forms, and talking with me about Jude, Marybeth, and the ghosts. To put it another way: she read a million pages, and she rocked them all. Thanks, Leanora. I am so glad and so lucky to have you as my best friend.

That's all and thanks for coming to my show everyone. Good night, Shreveport!